The Song of
PETERLOO

Carolyn O'Brien

Legend Press Ltd, 107-111 Fleet Street, London, EC4A 2AB
info@legend-paperbooks.co.uk | www.legendpress.co.uk

Contents © Carolyn O'Brien 2019
The right of the above author to be identified as the author of this work has been asserted in accordance with the Copyright, Designs and Patents Act 1988. British Library Cataloguing in Publication Data available.

Print ISBN 978-1-78955-075-7
Ebook ISBN 9-781-78955-076-4
Set in Times. Printing managed by Jellyfish Solutions Ltd
Cover design by Simon Levy | www.simonlevyassociates.co.uk

Carolyn O'Brien was born in Manchester and lives in the nearby market town of Altrincham with her husband and two children. Carolyn studied English at the University of Cambridge before qualifying as a solicitor, and now works part-time as a consultant lawyer, as well as writing.

Follow Carolyn
@CarolynManc

For Annie and Carmel

CONTENTS

PRELUDE

7th June 1832
Royal Assent granted to *The Representation of the People Act 1832 (2 & 3 Wm. IV, c. 45): An Act to amend the representation of the people in England and Wales*

After years of agitation for Parliamentary reform, the Great Reform Act of 1832 at last granted seats in the House of Commons to many of the large towns which had sprung up during the Industrial Revolution. It also extended the franchise to men of property of qualifying value: about one in five.
The working class remained excluded from the vote.
(Not to mention women.)

WALTER

A lot of folk are talking about it again, though talking's never really been for me. Mary says this new Act's roused memories but mine need no stirring. I'm not sure a body can even call it memory when, after all these years, it's still so present. For just the thought of it can take so fierce a grip on me, like a bridle to a frightened horse, that to shake it off, I'm forced to make myself think on something else. To picture a time before it all began. But even then, it's always the one same night my thoughts steer towards, as though my mind were somehow fixed, as the North Star, burning bright, in the midsummer of 1819.

It was stifling, the yard like a furnace, with all the day's heat trapped between the blackened walls of the houses, and the sinking sun lost behind low, gathering clouds. Me, short for my age, still no more than waist-high to the older boys wrestling in the centre, I didn't venture further than a small patch beyond the open door. I could never tolerate the sound of boots on cobbles; I always felt it as a scratch to my skin. Then there were the hollers and hooting I couldn't understand. Often, I'd break off my solitary play to listen for comforting noises within, my grandmother sweeping the hearth or laying a late supper for Mam.

I always played alone. That day, I remember, I'd fashioned myself a stick. There weren't many trees down our way, but I'd picked up this one in the graveyard that afternoon. I'd gone over there especially, and I wasn't disappointed. Under the shadow of the yews, the winding path was strewn with twigs and branches still aleaf, brought down in one of those thunderstorms that kept blowing up late in the sultry nights.

I'd found myself a shady spot to sit, leaning against one of those grand, stone coffins that lie aside of the church. Resting my head on the cool moss, I happily set about stripping my branch of its shoots with a sharp piece of slate I'd found, as good as any knife-blade. By the time I got up and scattered the shavings from my legs, I'd smoothed it to its simple, naked line. It was so white and clean and beautiful, I daresay a passer-by might think I'd plucked one of the bones from the grave beneath.

Later, as I paced my small section of yard, drawing the stick up above my head and bringing it down to slice the air, over and over, one of our neighbours, Mrs Wilson, a sturdy housewife who lived above us, stepped into the yard with an empty basket to collect her washing. She stopped and watched me for a moment with that air of amusement most people reserve for me and observed, not unkindly, "My my, if it's not the Iron Duke himself!"

No doubt some other boy thrashing about in this fashion would indeed fancy himself charging into battle, but her words were lost on me. I was too immersed in the feel of the stick in my hand and my satisfaction in its strange music as it traced an arc through the air. I didn't reply, which won't have surprised her, and she moved over to the washing line and set her basket on the ground.

It must have been getting late as Grandma shuffled from the door. She was slowing down by then, and her face, red and wet from the heat of the day and all her exertion, was screwed in a grimace of pain. She and Mrs Wilson nodded to one another.

"Come on now, lad, come on inside."

But I didn't want to go. I raised the stick high above my head and swung it down in a temper this time.

"It's no use waiting on her," she said to me roughly. "Shift finished half-hour ago."

I leant on the stick then and looked up. The sun had sunk completely, and the sky's colours were draining into a dreary yellow-grey, the same colour as the bruises Mam got from working the mule.

"She's wi' him again." This, spoken under her breath, was not meant for me, but I knew who she was talking about. Mam had told me about him; a bricklayer, she'd said, a steeplejack no less, and "right clever". She'd met him at Knott Mill, and afterwards he'd turned up one day at the factory gates with a whole group of them, men who were working on the new mill next door, all of them young and strong and eager and alive with talk of change.

I drew a figure in the dry dirt with my stick: a line down and from the bottom of the first line, another across like a horizon. I couldn't read much then, we were only just learning, but I knew this shape began the word they were all talking about. '*Liberty*'.

Grandma was going back in and looked round at me, more sad than stern this time. "Come on now. They won't be done 'til gone ten."

Inside, the room was already dark enough for a candle which flickered on the mantel. I eyed the plate Grandma had laid and, with a single finger, tentatively lifted the cloth to reveal the last of the bread and a slice of sweating cheese. The smell of it prodded my hunger, and I thought about twisting a morsel from the crust.

Grandma must've noticed. "She'll be famished when she gets in."

I sat back.

"Pour tha'sel a drop of water, lad. Not too much, mind. And then away to bed."

Watching her, huddled in the chair, guarding the single candle, I must've drifted off, because the next thing I recall was Mam's breath warm upon me. I opened my eyes sleepily enough, but then sat up with a start. In the moonlight from the window, her smile had exposed a row of bloodied teeth. But when she saw my stare, she only laughed and opened her mouth the wider to show off her blackened tongue. Confused, I drew forward as she bent to the floor and, with both hands, lifted up a bowl, proffering it to me with a flourish.

"Raspberries!" I exclaimed.

"By, Nancy, tha's never giving him them now!" scolded Grandma's voice from behind.

"Away, Mam, tha couldn't stop me!"

In the half-light, the plump fruits' soft fur seemed to glow from within, and the empty ache in my belly awoke with a pang that was painful.

"Go on!" Mam said, grinning, though when she saw I was too astonished to move, she picked one herself and leant forward to drop it in my mouth with a light laugh. I'd been salivating so much by then that on my first bite, the crushed juice dribbled down my chin and we both laughed again. But then the fruit's sweetness washed down my throat, like a taste from another life, feeding and stoking my hunger all at once, so that before I knew it, my bony fingers were scrambling for another and then another, as, all the while, my mother kept the bowl aloft.

"There now, aren't they grand? Even better than when I were a lass."

We both heard Grandma sniff at this and Mam winked.

When they were all gone, she placed the bowl back on the floor and, with a cool waft, raised the single sheet to climb in and join me. Even now I can still recall the scent of her as we curled together: a long day's sweat, freshened by the open air of the grassy banks where she'd spent the evening. It wasn't long though before we were overcome by the heat and drew apart again, settling on our sides instead, to face one another.

She talked then of the reformers on the moor, good men and women, she said, who'd spoken of the future she wanted for me. Her words, whispered low and quick so as not to agitate Grandma, nonetheless tumbled and coursed, fresh and clear, and I think I must have mirrored some of her excitement because the last thing I remember, she cried, "Ah, Walter! My bonny babe!" and drew me to her again, nestling me against her body, bestowing tiny kisses across my damp head with a gentle popping sound.

That night.

Yes, that night's what my thoughts fix on, when the other memory threatens to take hold. On those wild raspberries, brought to my bed as though in a dream. A dream so perfect you're afeared to wake from it. And I begin to wonder, if there'd not been that night, if we'd not eaten those fruits, would all that happened afterwards never have been, like a dream itself? So that even these things from the time before, the raspberries like jewels, her breath sweet with them, even her love for me, all these things are still always about what happened next.

THE TURN OF THE YEAR

ONE

MARY

Aye, there's them that's bitter. Them that say this Act's a betrayal. Thirteen long years and Walter nearly of age, but still no vote to look forward to. Not yet, any road. Aye, we'd do better to say, not yet. For as Nancy always told me, "If tha can manage to change summat the once, Mary, then there's nowt to stop thee changing it again." Ee, I can't tell thee how much all this talk's got me thinking on her, and everything that happened to us, and wondering just how *she'd* tell the tale.

My best guess is she'd start with that morning when Johnny Clegg met with his accident. I mean, Lord alone knows, there's calamities enough in that place, but there was something particular about what happened to poor Johnny that really worked on Nancy. I knew she was determined, but even I'd never seen her quite so fierce.

It was still black as pitch outside at the start of the shift. January '19, and one of them frozen Manchester mornings when, for once, you're glad of the heat off the machines. Already, lads were unloading cargo from the barges waiting in the canal basin, their breath curling up into the wintry air, fluffs of cloud, like raw cotton in the sacks they were lugging. As we passed by, me and Nancy, stragglers bringing up the rear of the morning shift, shawls gathered close over our shoulders, treading carefully so as not to slip on the slutch, a few of 'em stopped and looked over, and sent up piercing whistles into the cold air, faster swirls of mist which twisted and turned above the dark pool of the basin and eventually slowed to drift out beyond the mill. I was not so daft to think such attention was for *my* benefit, but Nancy didn't ever seem to notice such things. Or if she did, she never let on.

We never spoke much that time in the morning, not as we joined the clatter of clogs upstairs to the mule room. Any road, the roll of our eyes at one another at the sight of the overlooker, Dick Yates, was communication enough. A short fella he was, not many years on me, maybe twenty-nine I'd say, but he had a right old way on him, and more of a waddle than a walk. His job, you understand, was to pace the length of the floor, overseeing all us workers: the men, steering back and forth of the spinning mules, us lasses piecing, our fingers flying to tie together any broken threads and the little 'uns scavenging for waste on the oily floor.

Sometimes, when he disappeared during the short break we'd get at nine, I'd make 'em all giggle, taking him off, like. Nancy of course, and the other lasses. Even them sullen Kennedy sisters, Molly and Peg, who were always leaning against the wall with their arms folded, waiting to be impressed, couldn't help themselves. I'd puff out my chest – though it's already more ample than most – and widen my legs in an ungainly squat. Then, holding my arms behind my back in a pretend grip on his leather strap, I'd trot off down the floor, grunting and grumbling, and, with the occasional cock o' me leg, blow a pretend fart.

Well, Nancy always had a ready laugh, and loud too. I loved to make her! Ee, we did have some good times. But you know, she was always first with a wary eye on the door and all, whispering, "Mary, take care, it's nearly time." Not out of timidity, mind. Never out of timidity. Nay, you could never say that about Nancy Kay. Certainly not after what happened that day. As I say, we'd had the measure of Dick Yates a long while. A right nasty piece of work he was, and so he proved.

By the time we were stationed at the mules, the steam was up and so was the noise. Yates had lined up the children, a ragged bunch, beside the long wall of windows and was delivering his daily instruction. After a short night of head to toe in cold, damp beds, the warmth of the mule room could prove too much for the young 'uns. Despite the racket of the machines, you'd oft see a pair of heavy eyes droop closed, whilst stick legs wobbled underneath, until just at the brink o' sleep, the child'd jerk awake with a wide-eyed startle. Yates was as aware of this as any and kept his hand poised to swipe.

Johnny Clegg. What can I say about him? Poor friendless soul, he was. Never wore nowt but a blank expression. Folk say his da was one of General Ludd's lads that were transported for burning the Jennys. Left his mam deranged it did. Well, I don't know owt about that, but back then, he stayed with his uncle, a right rough sort, who worked in the furnace room.

Any road, he can't have been much older than eight, with a knotted mop of straw-coloured hair sitting atop his hollow-cheeked face as though planted in jest, and an upper lip glistening with the contents of his runny nose, which he'd absently lick from time to time. A good two inches shorter than most his age, he should've been the most useful, as it's them little 'uns who can more easily dart 'neath the machines. But Johnny was always a clumsy clot. The one who'd likely break a thread than mend it. And the one most familiar with the back of Yates's hand, or worse.

That morning, Yates put Johnny and the others to work as usual, collecting tufts of raw that gather all along the edges of the mule and in the carriageway underneath. "Not that one!" he'd barked, belting Johnny over the head for setting off in the wrong direction, and I watched the lad, stunned from the clout, stagger towards the machine he was properly assigned. Of course, it was the one Nancy was working.

Well, at first, the room settled into its usual measure, same old screech, clang, whirr, screech, clang, whirr, and we lasses with our backs bent over, bodies stretched, began to acquaint with yesterday's aches. The pull in your calves, the drag of weight in your arms and that gap between your shoulder blades where I always felt it worst; a branding of pain, searing hot from the base of my neck down to a burning spot right in the centre, as though the Devil himself was poking me in the back with his pointed tail.

I remember I'd just needed to straighten mi'sel, standing tall, then leaning back to snatch a few seconds of relief, when I heard an almighty clatter, followed by such a scream as to waken the dead. Well, course I strained past my own machine to try and get a look, but all I could make out was Nancy's was deserted. The spinner, Nancy, Johnny – all nowhere to be seen. Then, above the noise of the blasted mules which kept on running, I heard a terrible, low moaning, such as I imagine you might hear from the bodies of dying soldiers on an abandoned field. Well, at that, I left my station, even though I knew there'd be hell to pay, shouting over the din, "Nancy! Nancy! Is tha hurt?"

Some of the others joined me too, making towards her machine, which I could see now one of the spinners was desperately trying to slow down. Meanwhile, little 'uns had stopped their racing and gathered, confused and scared, in a gaping group in the middle of the aisle. Yates then came charging up from t' other end of the room and, though his face was thunderous, I followed him round to the far side.

I'll never forget the sight of it. Sent a hot rush of sick right up into my throat it did. Nancy, half-crouched, was cradling Johnny Clegg, who lay prone across her. Put me in mind of that painting I've so often looked on; the one down at St Mary's in the centre of town, the small Roman one, where my Mick's sort go. I've slipped in with him on occasion, them times when he's felt the need. The hour after we were wed at chapel, and the evening we got word of his old fella passing. Them quiet times of disappointment too, after my mishaps.

Aye, well.

A strange smoky smell it has in there I don't much care for, like burning leaves, and everything all gold and silver and over-showy to look at and not at all where I'd imagine the good Lord to abide. But then over to the side, there's this picture, drew me in the very first time I laid eyes on it, like nothing I'd seen afore or since. Ee, I can't tell thee the times I've thought on it. Christ crucified, his wounds still bleeding, stretched over his grieving mother's lap, and she with a face o' sorrow that would break your heart.

Well, it was clear Johnny'd had an almighty wallop to the head. There was a gash of purplish gore above his temple, and the rest of his face was marble-pale and shiny with clamminess. He was turned inward towards her like a great big babby and wailing just as good as 'un.

Nancy looked up at us, her face pinpricked red and her clothes so spotted you'd think she was wearing a crimson-sprigged muslin. Then, as she shifted slightly, I saw another bigger patch on the pocket of her apron. It was bright at first, like an apple in size and colour, but even as I watched, it grew larger and darker. She caught my look and placed her hand over the spot.

"It's his finger," she mouthed to me, and I realised Johnny mustn't have cleared the mule in time. He howled again, and an answering cry broke out amongst the children.

"Enough!" shouted Yates, who was red in the face with fury and pacing round the machine.

"Sir," Nancy addressed him, "if we're quick to th' Infirmary, I've heard say they can maybe do summat wi' it." She gestured to her apron and whispered, "Tha knows, the *finger*."

He looked down at her a second, taking her meaning, and then laughed harshly, "What a load of shite! Not at Manchester Infirmary they can't!"

"But we have to try! We have to do summat!"

Yates ignored her this time, his eyes shifting round the

room, which was strangely quiet as most of the machines had slowed to a halt. All that echoed round its vast, brick walls were the wails of distress from the casualty and his unfortunate workmates. One of 'em, a little lass, and a kindly soul, was sobbing like a young widow, repeating again and again, "Poor Johnny, poor, poor Johnny," which only served to make the lad himself that more fretful.

Nancy whispered in his ear then, gentle like, trying to soothe him, and when he'd quietened a touch, she looked over her shoulder and started to slide herself across the floor, easing him along with her, making towards a girder, where she struggled to free herself from behind and set to propping him up. Glancing at me a second, she widened her eyes, and I realised she wanted us to swap places, so I rushed over to sit with the lad. In the speed of the moment, there was no time for reserve, and before I knew it, the lad's head was lay on my breast like a babe just done with feeding, and Nancy on her feet squaring up to Yates.

"Please let me take him!"

"Enough!" he roared back. "We have to get these mules back to work," and looking down at me and Johnny, he added, "These things happen. They'll see to him downstairs. Now get back to it."

"Nay!" she cried. "Nay!"

Ee, she was proper agitated now, and Yates was all for raising his hand to her, but just as he'd shouted, "Insolent bitch!" another voice broke in, booming, "Yates!"

All heads turned.

"Desist this minute, man!" This last was from Mr Henshaw, the mill's senior manager, normally a stiff, sober sort of fella.

Well, all had been astir, with the workers whispering, or else trying to comfort the little 'uns, and, of course, I was still on the floor, so I can't say for sure exactly when these gentlemen – for, of course, there were two of 'em – had arrived, or how much of the previous exchange they'd witnessed, but they'd already advanced up the aisle, and now stepped forward into the crowd still gathered around me and Johnny.

"Clearly this is not the most auspicious moment," continued Henshaw, fixing a stern eye on Yates, who looked as though he might burst with the effort of self-restraint. "But I should introduce our new proprietor, Samson Wright, Mr Wright senior's nephew."

We didn't know much about this change at the top, only that Mr Wright, the older one, Silas, who'd had the mill put up over twenty year ago, had passed away just afore Christmas. Ee, how we'd all had high hopes of a day off for the funeral! A right grand affair it was too, by all accounts, down at the Collegiate Church. But his widow, Adelaide Wright, a fine Miss Hoity-Toity if ever there was one, put paid to any idea of a holiday, good and proper. An hour we got; that was all. A paltry hour, can you believe it? Aye, but you'd best not get me started on her, least not yet, any road.

Truth is, their only son – Silas and Adelaide's – he'd been a wrong 'un. A taste for ale and laudanum, that's what did for him. That and too much brass in his pocket to indulge himself. Not that we were meant to know, mind, but it was a poorly kept secret since there weren't many of us who'd not seen him for ourselves, lurching round town with a glazed eye. And so, with young 'un dead and buried, Silas had gone and passed himself, without an heir any of us lot in the mule room knew owt about.

Except now here he was, this man in front of us: Samson, the new master.

Well, I'll tell thee, I've had enough instruction in the Bible to know this fella didn't look anything like his namesake. Granted, he was tall and of broad bearing, but there was something about him. I don't know how you'd put it. A careworn air, you might say, as though he'd already had enough of this world. Certainly, he didn't seem a man of strength to me. And as for any Delilah? Well, I'd have said, he'll be lucky!

We all watched him ignore Yates, who was bent in an awkward sort of a bow. Instead, he was looking down at the sorry sight of Johnny, still making a dreadful sound, more like the whimper of a wounded animal than a little lad.

"What's to be done with the boy?" he said in a deep voice, though it wasn't clear who he was asking, and Yates, who was readjusting his kecks and unsure of the new master's tone, hesitated.

Ee, but Nancy didn't! Right there and then, she stepped forward, her face aglow with urgent appeal, and cried, "Sir, if we make haste, I do believe summat could be done for him. For his finger, I mean. He must get to th' Infirmary straightaway."

In the astonished hush that followed, I held my breath. I knew nowt about what she was suggesting, of course; she always did know more than most. Nay, nay, all *I* could do was wonder at her boldness, fearful for her and admiring all at the same time.

TWO

He must be well-read, Nancy thought. A man of his station, highly educated and surely with an inkling of what she meant. Three years or more, it must be now, since the clerk in the yard had looked up from his newspaper in amazement and there'd been all that talk of surgeons and fingers. He *must* know about it.

"Sir, please…" she tried again, raising her chin, so that her voice, which was naturally low, came out in a new, high note of indignance she couldn't contain. "Please…!"

She wasn't sure now why she'd been so certain of his help, only that he'd seemed so different to the usual sort at first. Not grand and full of pomp like Henshaw, nor vicious like Yates. There was something singular about him, something calm and gentle, despite the great height of him – she'd felt it straightaway. There was compassion, she was certain of it, in the way he looked at Johnny – those eyes, so tired and sad.

So why then didn't he speak? Or do something? For heaven's sake, couldn't he see the urgency? What was it she had to do? At the least, he might agree she should stay with the lad, wherever he was to be taken. But, instead, he was biding time, keeping quiet. Brooding like a philosopher, he was, and doing nothing.

Nothing! Silent and remote and useless.

He moved a step backwards. Oh Lord, was he really going

to leave? Nay, nay, for Johnny's sake, she couldn't let him! She wouldn't! What was to be done?

Her eyes blazed at him, a ferocious mix of entreaty and fury she could no longer quell, until, almost without thinking, a notion came to her, and in a single movement, she delved into the sodden depth of her pocket, snatched at its contents and stretched out her arm, opening her palm.

"Look!" she cried savagely, thrusting it nearer. "It's still warm, for pity's sake!" And there it was, like a tiny scrap of skinned meat coated in blood, its chewed, blackened nail still recognisably that of Johnny Clegg.

From behind, she was half-aware of a woman's shriek and of the older lads' ghoulish laughter ringing the length of the room, echoing so horribly it set the children crying again, whilst just beside her, Yates took a step closer, on the brink of seizing her. Yet, throughout it all, Nancy remained intent on nothing and no one but Wright.

For a second his hooded eyes had flashed back at her, before he'd mastered himself again, but she'd snared his gaze all right, and Lord, would she hold his stare! The moment lengthened, as the room seemed to sink into a new, dark silence, the charge in the air deepening like a mystery, and all the while her palm outspread between them in lurid challenge.

"Henshaw!" he pronounced, suddenly decisive. "I shall leave it to you."

Her mouth fell open, incredulous, though he didn't see. He was no longer looking at her at all. Instead, he'd set off already, adding over his shoulder, "I'll find my own way back."

She blew out her held breath. The coward! The man was a feeble coward, and what she'd taken for concern was, in truth, no more than the alarm of a body out of his depth. Nay, it was fear! Just look at him, loping the length of the aisle, as fast as his daddy-long-legs could carry him. No better than a deserter from the field he was, slipping through the door. She shook her head bitterly and closed her hand around the finger, flinching at the flesh gone cold, swiftly returning it to her pocket.

"Mad bitch!"

She turned quickly. It was Yates, in her ear, sniggering, his eyes filching a greedy look the length of her body, as he brushed up so close, she thought he might be smeared by the still-wet blood on the front of her apron. Lord, to think she'd even pitied him before now, those times the others liked to joke he was the sort who'd only ever find love in a whorehouse.

"What did you ever think *you* could do?" he leered, closer still, and with a morning-breath so sour she stepped back, unable to disguise her disgust. But instantly his eyes narrowed at her, so stone-cold and mean that fear flickered for a second, like a snatched candle, before Henshaw called him away again and he was gone.

God, that such a man could make her feel afraid.

Or stupid, for that matter, though she knew she wasn't that. And nor had she dreamt the piece in the newspaper about the surgeon in Scotland who'd saved his son's fingers. A story, like so many others, she'd eavesdropped over the years as she lingered close to the clerks' bench at lunchtime when they spread the papers Silas had delivered to the mill; she, hungry for any crumbs of information they might let drop. Fixing her cap, arranging her shawl, pretending a dozen ways at nonchalance, so as not to risk their attention, but all the while intent on the stories and reports they read aloud to one another, listening out for any scrap of news she could gather of the wide world beyond Manchester, which she'd no hope of discovering any other way.

"By, that sounds too grisly for me," one of them had said, pulling a face.

"Aye, but amazing an' all," said another, "'Appen we should let owd Silas know, it might save him losing a trained worker or two!"

The conversation had digressed then, to the fate of the last poor girl who'd been forced from the factory, and Nancy had been obliged to curb her curiosity. But like most things she learned, she'd never forgotten it, and it was the first thing she'd thought of the instant she'd set eyes on Johnny's hand, and its terrible, red gap, gushing like an unstoppered plug.

It was knowledge without understanding though, wasn't it, she realised now, judging from Yates's reaction. That surgery in Scotland they'd all talked of as though it would become commonplace had, in fact, been something extraordinary, something freakish, a miracle never to be repeated. All of which she might have known, if she could but read and find out things for herself. Instead, here she was again, feeling one moment stupid, and the next, furious at being made to look the fool.

She closed her eyes, hoping to steady herself, but instead the darkness triggered a memory, the same one which always surfaced whenever she felt like this: a vision of her mam, shiny cheeks flared red and all puffed up with outrage. "Get tha hands off that!" she'd yelled so loudly Nancy had startled.

They'd been in the low-ceilinged kitchen of the farm; another of those deathly quiet afternoons, when the warmth of the sun slanted in only a brief while before it was blocked out by the fells behind them, and the long evening came on. Nancy must've been about seven and not yet accustomed to the terrible hush which had descended like cloud when the last of the younger siblings, baby Fred, had not long since become another angel.

Her mam, sleeves rolled above her elbows, had been kneading dough for the bread, and Nancy at the other end of the long table, tracing the curve of the figures on the first page of the book with her finger.

"I'm just looking…"

But her mam was already flying at her, wiping her floury hands down her apron, "Nay, nay, that's not for thee," and she swooped to pluck the book from her grasp. "It's Edward needs learning. Not thee."

"But Mam!" she cried, "It's not fair! Besides, he said I could…"

"Whist, Nancy! It's tha brother'll be in charge one day. It's him who needs to know his letters. Lasses have other chores to do. Look, see them carrots, they'll not peel themsel'," and she'd cocked her head towards the mound of roots lying in a pool of mud in the sink.

Nancy's lips had set into a firm, flat line then, her small hands balling into sticky fists as she considered keeping up the protest. But her mother had clicked her tongue as she wiped a dab of flour from the cover, "Now look what tha's made me do!" She was so often in a temper then, or else red-eyed and silent beside the fire, and as for when Nancy got on the wrong side of her like this, no longer above doling out a clout round the head. And so, with her tiny chest still heaving at the injustice, Nancy had slid from the bench and slunk with drooping shoulders towards the vegetables.

From the mule room floor, Johnny suddenly gave out a single, wretched sob and she looked across at him, desperate with pity. Above anything, she was most mortified she might have given him false hope, the poor lad. He quietened again now, just as quickly as he'd roused, and was lolling half-asleep across Mary. With a start, Nancy saw that from this angle, and with that crop of fair hair, he had a look of Walter.

She placed her hand protectively over her pocket, like a woman with child before she's told a soul, and at once became conscious of a new warmth spread across her belly. Looking down, she understood straightaway; the wet spot had seeped through every layer of her clothes and was now coating her skin. The realisation made her head swim, forcing her to inhale deeply, an overpowering smell of iron, like the butcher's shop, and too many of the dry, cotton wisps which floated on the air. It sent her, half-choked, into a coughing fit.

Lord, she was sick of this place, she thought as she banged at her chest, and of her own ignorance. Heartily sick of scavenging around for half-stories and still never knowing enough to be of use to herself or to anyone.

THREE

The Rectory
St Cuthbert's
Cheshire
18th January 1819

My dear Samson,
My letter of 16th inst. was dispatched too soon to afford the
opportunity of enclosing this most interesting parcel which
arrived for you at the cottage only yesterday morning. The
new tenant, (the retired verger from Chester of whom I
spoke) was good enough to walk up with it straightaway,
notwithstanding his personal indisposition. (The poor man
is crippled with rheumatism.)

As the sender of the parcel is Booseys, I fancy the occasion
of its arrival will be a very happy one for you! Imagine your
man's surprise when you inform him of your new situation!

On no account must you concern yourself with an early
response to this, or indeed my first letter. Catherine and I fully
understand you will be greatly occupied with the demands of
your new position and do not wish to add to your numerous
obligations the burden of prompt reply. We are content to wait
until such time as you are at liberty to let us know your first
impressions of the manufacturing life.

Once again, we send our best wishes to poor Aunt Adelaide.

We are sure your solicitous presence must be of great comfort to her.

We all continue as well as on 16th inst. Little Lydia is greatly excited about the new puppies, but Jonathan continues to lament the curtailment of his pianoforte lessons.

We pray God you remain in good health.

Yours truly, Daniel

Samson set aside the letter, carefully unsealed the inner package and extracted another note.

T.&T. BOOSEY & CO.
4 Old Bond Street, London

9th January 1819

Dear Captain Wright,
I take up my pen with sincere apologies for the delay in sending to you the pieces you requested in your letter of 7th October last. As I endeavoured to explain in my letter of 17th November last, we have, most lamentably, been at the mercy of the continent's inclement weather and, since that time, have experienced yet more delays of the most severe and vexing kind to all our shipments.

Happily, I am at last able to enclose herewith the selection of lieder which you required. A most interesting collection. Less happily, I am sorry to inform you, despite extensive enquiries, it was not possible to obtain the Schubert sonata you'd learned about. Indeed, we have discovered that it is not yet published.

I am taking the liberty, however, to put up an edition of Beethoven's 'Sonata quasi una Fantasia Op.27 No.2', being a token of my personal esteem and gratitude for your continued patience. It is possible you may already know the piece, or indeed have a copy, but this is the finest imprint I have come across. The sonata's first movement has, in my opinion, a sublime and haunting melody and is most deserving of its growing popularity. I hope that it will, in some measure, compensate for the missing Schubert.

I beg to remain, Sir, your must humble and obedient servant,
Thomas Boosey

He picked out the ribboned bundle of sheets, held it up to his face and inhaled deeply, closing his eyes, savouring the dry, foreign tang of the paper, allowing himself to yield for a moment to an easeful darkness, listening for the memory of music even over the din of the mill, so that when he finally opened his eyes again and looked once more upon the dreary room that had been Silas's office, it was with an audible sigh.

The room was on the ground floor of one of the large mill buildings – which themselves formed a giant quadrant round a vast, open yard – and the furthest in a long corridor of offices of varying size, all of which gave on to one another, in a similar manner to the servant quarters in Elton Hall, or some such other grand house. It only had one small, high window and even this was blackened with smoke from the adjacent chimney, so that there was a mere trickle of weak, northern light to illumine the dark wood of his uncle's desk and the red paint on the walls.

It was cold as the grave too; a fire had not yet been set, and the grate was swept clean. Samson surmised it had likely not been lit since Silas last left, clammy and feverish, to take to his sickbed. A portrait of him, the old manufacturer, hung over the fireplace and dominated the cramped room. Emerging from its smudge of dark oils, the dome of the old man's bald head glowed, and his shrewd eyes shone out knowingly as though in the making of a private bargain with the viewer.

When Samson had returned here from the factory floor, shivering violently at the contrast from the heat within the mule room and the freezing blast of the court, brushing off one of the clerks who'd jostled for his attention, he'd shut the door firmly behind him and reached immediately for the travelling cloak he'd unwittingly discarded earlier. Now, hunched in a chair that was too small for him, the folds of his cape wedged tight within its armrests, he lay down the newly arrived papers he'd momentarily seized and shook his head.

Dear God, what manner of enterprise had he embarked upon? He could scarcely believe... That woman... No, no... Not to mention the poor child. How young had that little fellow been? Samson pictured him again. Short, bone-thin, barely more than an infant. Younger than his nephew, certainly, and not much older than another boy... He shook his head again to dismiss the thought.

This manner of risk was well-documented, of course. From all the evidence he'd studied, such accidents were frequent, if not inevitable. He'd read all about them during those final, industrious weeks in the cottage – long days spent perusing Silas's memoranda and the mill's records, even papers put before Parliament on the question of safety – and he'd understood very well it could be a dangerous business. In any event, it wasn't the gore itself which had shocked him. He was a soldier, wasn't he? Inured by battle to blood and injury, witness to countless horrors more gruesome than a severed finger. Yet, nevertheless, the thought had struck him, and most forcibly too, that the mill was, or at least should be, different. For even suppose those workers – women and children most of them – even suppose they comprised a perverse army of sorts, as his uncle had so often liked to suggest, even supposing that, wasn't the boy simply too young? After all, even the freshest of his striplings to fall on the field had sported at least the first wisp of whisker on his chin.

He sighed once more. This time he watched his breath disperse in a slow, ghostly cloud towards the ceiling.

When this absurd scheme of taking on the mill had been suggested by his brother on his uncle's behalf, Samson's first response had been astonished disbelief. Daniel, about to set out on his parish round, had called at the cottage to find him in the sitting room, not long up, still unshaven and abashed to be discovered in his nightshirt.

"Me!" he'd cried, uncharacteristically exuberant, as much to disguise his discomfort at his déshabillé as at the suggestion. "What do I know of trade? Not to mention cotton mills!" and he'd laughed heartily at first, waiting for the joke to be revealed, followed by creeping caution when his brother failed to join in.

"Samson, I am not in jest, I assure you." Daniel's tone was grieved. "Silas is anxious to secure the future of the business with cousin Robert gone and, given your own circumstances…" At this, he swept his hand round the room and its litter of books and papers and sheet music, the wine glass on the mantelpiece stained dark with dregs. "I'd say it makes perfect sense."

Samson's mouth had dropped and his eyes grown large and doubtful. Without thinking, he snatched up an open newspaper from the sofa and, glad of the distraction, set to folding it neatly.

Meanwhile Daniel, still with his solemn Sunday face, persisted, "Besides, it will do you good. We are anxious for you, Samson. You know that. You can't possibly wish to spend the rest of your life hiding away here?"

His voice had taken on its habitual sermon-like quality and Samson, discerning him strain to keep the judgment from it, all at once felt a spasm of fraternal anger. What business was it of Daniel's to preach to him about life anyway? Whatever could a country clergyman comprehend of its miseries, never mind its horrors? All Daniel had ever known was an untroubled existence, curled up here in the safety of his sleepy parish, like a dormouse in a hedgerow, and yet, even after everything Samson had endured, he'd now deny him a share of the nest. It wasn't as though Samson had Daniel's other consolations to sustain him either: the support of an intelligent wife and the affection of lively children. The blessing of theological certainty.

Ah, there was a pang, as the thought of his own mutilated spirit summoned, in turn, the memory of their devout mother; a memory he too often shrank from these days, though the idea of her goodness rose no less frequently, unbidden as a trace of fragrance in a garden. At least Daniel hadn't yet spoken of her, for which he was grateful, though they both knew well enough how she would've grieved his retreat from the world. Nay, worse: his faith shrivelled to naught, and his soul – whatever a soul might be – as washed-up and useless as that pale piece of driftwood he'd mistaken, in wide-eyed horror, for a man-overboard, during his last, delirious seasickness on the long voyage home.

"Please, Sam," Daniel entreated, but his voice was gentle this time, and when Samson looked across, he saw kindness in his brother's smile. It served, momentarily, to ease his agitation. His brother was a good man, Samson knew, and only trying to do what he thought was right.

He returned a sad smile, dropped heavily into an armchair and looked round the room; ashamed of its disarray, he resolved to tidy it as soon as his brother was gone. Daniel had been under no obligation to take him in here all those months ago, and nor could Samson claim any entitlement to remain. Indeed, a new thought occurred to him: with this pressing concern for Silas, and the business in Manchester, how long before his brother's patience was stretched too far? His goodwill exhausted?

Samson knitted his hands together, forming a steeple of his fingers which he set over his lips, though he flinched a second at the prickle of his stubble, conscious all over again of his own dishevelment.

"Sam, will you not at least consider it?"

Daniel stepped closer, smiling fondly so that Samson knew he'd sensed he was about to yield. The presumption rubbed up a fresh irritation, even as he relented.

"Very well," he had barely recognised his own voice snap, "Very well, I'll talk to him."

Uncle Silas, already frail and housebound, had indeed been in the same earnest. A few days after his conversation with Daniel, Samson had taken a bitterly cold chaise to Manchester and met with him in the front study of his town house in Charlotte Street; an early November hoar frost coating the trees outside the large window, and Silas blanketed in a wingback chair up close to the fire.

Ever the negotiator, the old man had known exactly what he wanted. Samson, as a Wright, should involve himself in the running of the mill and, subject to two stipulations, namely this agreement to personally oversee the business, and a trust for life in favour of his aunt, he would inherit everything.

Samson, notwithstanding his instinctive scepticism, had been astonished to find himself persuaded, though less by any pragmatic argument than by straightforward compassion. For looking into Silas's watery eyes, he'd understood the old man's unspoken disappointment and been touched by it and grieved for him. After all, he knew well enough the painful prospect of bequeathing to a nephew what should have gone to a son. Of course, he hadn't wished to remove to Manchester. Indeed, he'd had no more desire to disturb his voluntary exile in the country than any interest in the attendant financial improvement. Nevertheless, aside from Daniel's feelings on the matter – which were pressing enough – he'd felt honour-bound to meet the generosity of Silas's gesture and thus, effectively ambushed by the twin armies of embarrassed gratitude and obliged duty, he had conceded.

From the outset, he'd realised his new role would require serious study. There was much to learn: the principles of the market, a grasp of commerce, not to mention an understanding of engineering. Yet once he'd begun, he found to his surprise these were not, in themselves, matters that daunted him. On the contrary, once he'd got used to the idea, he even discovered some appeal to this new aspect of enquiry. Yes, in truth, his interest was piqued. Perhaps Daniel had been right after all. He remembered now how he'd pictured himself, sitting in this very office, poring over profit and loss accounts and bills of trade, studying models of steam engines and elevation plans for the proposed extension.

He rubbed his hands together for warmth and smiled weakly at the extent of his ingenuousness.

Seven? Eight at the most, surely?

To think he'd considered his role here an intellectual exercise. Ha! How could he ever have been so green? No, indeed, this was no genteel pursuit. Today, he'd seen things clearly at last and known just how it would be. Here, amongst the smoking ambition of Manchester, he would be thrust every day into turmoil, into a combat he didn't fully understand, a maelstrom of managers and millhands, all of them at odds with one another, and every last one of them demanding more from him, just as though he were being sallied back into battle, every hour and on every front.

From the yard, the smoke, sharp and acrid, intensified and caught in his throat. It conjured a familiar vision of a battle plain, obscured by the grey murk of cannon fire. He felt a wave of weariness. By God, he'd had his fill of war for one lifetime. And after today, he felt as old as Methuselah. His first instinct had been right; he should never have come. This was too complex a business, and too rough. Not one for a man already seven and thirty to master. Silas's wishes aside, wouldn't it be best left to those who knew it? This Henshaw, he thought, seemed a steady sort of fellow. The workers seemed to respect him, and no doubt the man would be happier left to manage as he pleased. If Silas were still here, Samson was sure he would be persuaded eventually.

He shot a shamefaced frown of apology at the portrait on the wall and scraped back the chair. Yes, he would speak to Henshaw in the morning. For now, though, he'd had enough for one day. He retrieved the sheet music and tucked it inside his cloak.

Outside, the wind was strong and knifing cold. It almost knocked his hat off, and he had to struggle to pull the door to the offices shut. As he descended the stone steps, drawing his cloak around him, he noticed with relief the yard was quieter than before. Evidently, all the morning's deliveries had been unloaded, and it was not yet time to pack the cargo leaving the factory.

He set off determinedly towards the iron gates, picking his way over the cobbles, head-first against the weather, when, out of the corner of his eye, he spotted a figure, so slight he might have walked past without noticing. There was, however, something so peculiarly arresting about its grey solitariness in the empty yard that even in his haste to get away, he stopped to look. The person was turned from him, standing at the edge of the choppy water of the basin.

It was a woman, he saw, dressed like all the others in the same plain cloth uniform of sorts, but with no shawl to protect her from the bite of the wind, and her cap half-off, trails of curls blowing. He could tell she was trembling, quivering like the last leaf on a tree in winter. A strange shame crept over him, like the warmth of the heavy wool on his back.

Then she turned around, and he saw it was her again, that girl. At the same moment, he realised her tremble was no mere shiver, but the rack of tears as she wiped at her face with the back of her hand.

A gust picked up, he heard his breath catch.

Then she snatched at her hair, tucking it back into place, and hastened to the door of the factory. She did not see him, or if she did, she gave no sign.

FOUR

MARY

It was a long time 'til we found out what happened to the poor beggar after the accident, and where he did eventually turn up was quite a surprise. One of many, of course, but that was much later, and I mustn't get ahead of mi'sel.

I was speaking of that winter's morning, and me and the lad stiffening up with cold together on the mule room floor. There was such a strangeness to it, I still recall, the quiet that had befallen the room, the lightness of his body slumped against mine, and the warmth of his breath spread upon my chest so that if I closed my eyes, I could almost have imagined him an infant ready for bed, were it not for the reek of blood and the terrible wonder that such a little mite could have lost so much.

Meanwhile, Nancy was silent. Her colour, which had been high when she was pleading, had drained away now, and she was as white as salt. I could tell she was still shaken up though, from the heaving of her chest. Put me in mind of a bird that's been soaring on the wing and suddenly hits a closed window. Stunned, she was, and needing to bide a while, just like a little sparrow, wobbling on the sill.

Well, next thing, Henshaw ordered one of t' other piecers to fetch some water and rags to clean up the blood that was splattered all over the floor and still spreading from a dark, shining heart next to the mule, so that I'd had to shift my legs to save my dress from it. Then he fixed his eye on me, and cocked his head at the other machines, meaning I had to get up and leave Johnny. The lad had drifted into a kind of sickened half-sleep by then, and though I tried my best not to disturb him, he could not but feel me move and roused with a groan, clutching desperately at me to stay, so that it was worse than horrible to have to wrench mi'sel away.

"Whist, lad," I whispered, "tha'll be all right." Though, course, I knew nowt of the sort.

Henshaw had moved on, speaking low to one of the older children, a lank and spotty sort, one of them as always does as they're told. The lad now crossed over and bent down, placing Johnny's arm – the good one – around his own feeble shoulder and, with a great deal of effort, hoisted him up to standing. All us workers, still gathered round, stood and watched them then, as they made their slow and sorry way to the stairs, all the while, poor Johnny still crying like a babby.

It was only after they'd gone that Henshaw seemed to notice Nancy for the first time, looking her up and down, taking in the state of her clothes, and said to her, "You'd better get to the pump and tidy yourself up."

She blinked at him, a little dazed, and her hand touched her pocket.

"Off you go," he repeated, "and be quick about it."

I didn't see her leave, as we were herded back to the mules, and once again started on the bend and stretch. It was only then I realised how shaken up *I* was, and I had to have proper words with mi'sel to keep concentrating to avoid an accident of my own. Even so, I still kept half an eye out for Nancy. Ee, she was gone such a long while, and I remember wishing she'd get a shift on, 'cos whenever I looked over, I saw Yates, who was back in control after a stern word from Henshaw, watching the clock.

Eventually, she emerged at the door from the stairwell and

stepped out of her clogs. Her soiled apron was gone, but there was a large, damp patch on her dress, traced with pink. Soon as Yates spotted her, he stomped over. His face was flushed, and his small piggy eyes were shining. Well, you don't work in a place like a mule room 'midst the noise of machinery and not learn a little of how to read folks' lips, so I could make him out asking, "What's taken thee so long?"

Problem was, I couldn't see Nancy's face, though I saw by the tilt of her head, she'd raised her chin and was answering back with some spirit, so that Yates moved in closer, bearing down upon her, until I could make out no more than that they were having an argument.

I realised more of what had passed between 'em when it came to lunchtime. As I approached Nancy to take our leave, she shook her head, tight-lipped, at me and stole a glance at Yates, who smirked back. She wasn't to get a break, it seemed, and all I could do was send a look of sympathy as I left the room. I was glad to be of more use on my return though, slipping her a crust as I passed her machine.

Well, it was dark again by the time we were leaving the factory. I know my belly's always aching with emptiness by then, so I can't imagine how famished Nancy must've felt. She was worn out and quiet with it as we curled our way downstairs and came out into a storm of sleet, driving horizontal across the blackness of the basin. All us lasses, faces screwed up at the whipping from the wind, clutched at our shawls and crowded together so closely for warmth that when I think on it, from back up on the fourth floor, we must've looked like a single creature, crawling from under a stone in our escape from the mill.

Then, just as we came up aside of the water, Nancy stopped, all abrupt like. Although we'd none of us bothered with lanterns on account of the rain, I could see by the light from the factory a look of terror pass over her face. Behind, the other lasses tutted as they came hard upon us, though Nancy paid them no mind, so that they had to shift past us, grumbling as they rearranged themselves back into their scurrying huddle.

"What is it?" I asked, unnerved by her look.

She turned to me then, the whites of her eyes flashing in the dark, shining with pooling tears. "Oh, Mary. I threw it in there." And she nodded to the waters of the canal. "What were I meant to do?"

"Oh, tha poor lass," I said and took her to me.

"Not me, not me," she cried, even though I still can't be sure what she meant by it.

I let her weep awhile, her body trembling with a mix of anguish and the biting cold, and me patting her back, the way I've watched plenty a young mam pacing the court with a colicky babby. But it wasn't like her, all this skriking, and I began to wonder if I knew everything, so that after a few moments, I took a step back and asked, "What went on wi' Yates? I can't believe he kept tha back like that."

"That's not all!" she cried with a short, harsh laugh, wiping first her eyes and then her nose with the back of her hand. "If only it were."

"What's tha mean?"

"He's docking me wages too. Says I took too long, doing this..." and her eyes were once more drawn to the water.

"Oh, the bastard!" I cried out, and at such volume Nancy put a finger to her lips.

"Whist, Mary! Unless tha wants some of t' same."

Straightaway I looked over my shoulder to check we'd not been heard, but the yard was already deserted. All of them on our shift were gone, though inside the factory another set of workers were still labouring under the lamps which blazed from the windows.

"But I'm not going to let him away wi' it."

"Eh?"

"He might've been able to stop me helping Johnny, but he's not going to punish me mam and Walter too."

"But what can tha do?" I asked, half-fearful, half-admiring again.

"I'm going to speak to t' new Mr Wright. He'll overrule Yates."

Well, I couldn't credit she'd believe this, and I told her so. "Nancy, he won't."

"Why not?"

"Well, he didn't seem in any hurry to help thee today, did he?"

Nancy shrugged, and her face wore an expression I didn't understand.

I pressed on, "Tha saw what he did, he just left us all to it."

"I know." She was looking over at the office. "But don't tha see? It's not a case of *my* word against Yates. Wright were there. He saw Johnny. He saw what happened. He saw none of it were my fault."

"Aye, but it still don't mean he won't take Yates's side. Tha wants to be careful tha doesn't go making things wuss for tha'sel."

"I've no choice though, Mary, have I? I *have* to try. Nowt ever changes if tha doesn't try."

The sleet was getting heavier now. In the dim light, I could see it blowing straight at us, or else plopping at our feet in enormous white rings on the shining cobbles.

"Come on, I'm starved," I said and nudged her elbow to turn her away from the water. We linked arms, and I gently moved her along towards the gates. Save for the wind, it was already graveyard quiet, and as we reached the shelter of the arch, there were only a few bodies left lingering.

"There ye are!" A voice floated from the darkness, unmistakably Irish, and with a flavour of merriment. I knew it was him before I could even make him out. My Mick.

"What ye been doing?" he chastised in a pretence at irritation. He must've been leaning against the far end of the wall for he suddenly appeared now, out of the shadows, hands deep in his pockets, hat low over his eyes.

"Nowt to concern thee!" I said as I gave Nancy's arm one last squeeze. "Sounds like someone's after his dinner." I laughed, forcing a bit of jollity as I fell in with him. "Though Lord knows we've nowt to eat!"

Nancy hung back, reluctant to join our banter.

"Get tha'sel home, lass," I said, "and think no more on it tonight."

"Aye, thanks, Mary," she smiled wearily.

"Si'thee Monday then," I called over my shoulder as Mick had picked up pace and was almost dragging me away.

"Aye, goodnight."

I looked back one more time. She was just an outline now, a slender figure cut out from the sleet that was lit up white from behind. What a forlorn sight! To think all she could do was walk home alone to that cantankerous old mam of hers, and to little Walter, who was still such an awkward babby of a boy. It fair made me want to weep. Aye, I know Mick and me, we've had our fair share of heartache, like most folk round here, but we're not short on laughs neither, and I have to say, at that hour, on that cold night, in the dead time of the year, I was right glad of him, that I was.

FIVE

"This won't do, girls, it just won't do." Adelaide set down the five-branch candelabra. "Can't you see? It's still tarnished. All of these need more polishing." Her ringed fingers fluttered over the silverware collected on the dining table: a further two candelabra, three pairs of additional candlesticks, a large platter, a sauce boat and the glorious epergne with its elaborate twisted arms which she'd suggested Silas purchase on the occasion of their first wedding anniversary, and which had served as the centrepiece for every dinner party she had presided over ever since.

Ellen, the senior of the two maids, bobbed a curtsey, "Yes, ma'am," and whispered instructions to the younger girl. They were both wearing the same dresses and caps they'd worn since December, each item boiled black for the deceased master. Now, with their heads bent in concentration, as though in prayer for his soul, they looked a picture of solemnity.

Adelaide frowned. Was it too soon to have guests to dinner? Her mourning observances had been exemplary of course. She continued to dress in the black bombazine gowns she'd ordered even as Silas had lingered on, admitting herself too stout these days to reuse the ones she'd had made on Robert's death. Her jewels and pearls were put away, her colourful silks hung up, their softnesses all untouched, closeted from the world in the coolness of her chamber, whilst the only adornment on her heavy dress was a brooch displaying a lock of Robert's hair – Silas having had none – a flash of gold within a setting of shining jet.

She hadn't made any calls either, not since the beginning of December, and here in Charlotte Street, she'd only received a handful of visitors, come to sit out the short, draughty afternoons of midwinter to offer their condolences. Tonight would necessarily remain in keeping with this regimen, although her frown had momentarily betrayed a flicker of doubt. However, considering the party was to be so small in number and comprised of company of the closest acquaintance – nay, friends indeed – her qualm of conscience was soon dispelled.

Besides, she reasoned, she really had no choice. Unless she exerted her influence and seized this singular opportunity to steer Samson in the right direction, she might very well be too late. There were far too many in town with modern opinions these days, even amongst some of the mill-owners. Heaven knows who might seek to sway his judgement. After all, had not his own mother been too susceptible to new ideas; a clergyman's wife, she'd nevertheless liked to dabble in dissent. Whenever she'd visited in Manchester, she'd gone to listen to that unholy lot in Cross Street, much to Silas's chagrin, and afterwards added to the injury by only ever speaking with admiration of their charitable works. Even as a widow in her son's country parish, she'd not left off. Hadn't she embarrassed Daniel by taking an entire Quaker family under her wing, offering them lodgings in that cottage in the grounds of the rectory where Samson had lived this past year?

Now, though, it wasn't just the Church that was challenged. Talk of reform was everywhere, and though she'd not attended the Theatre Royal since before Silas had fallen ill, only this morning she'd read all about that Jacobin-in-chief, Henry Hunt, and his disgraceful disruption of the evening's play. The blaggard seemed intent on stirring up the people to hatred. To give the workers a vote? Why, these were dangerous times.

For in such a world, a world with authority tipped on its head and a jealous mob clamouring to take charge, whatever would become of all that she and Silas had achieved? Indeed, what would become of her?

Dear me, she breathed in deeply, what a moment Silas had chosen to die, and she clicked her tongue in consternation, so that Ellen's head darted up from the silver, expecting further instruction. But Adelaide merely wafted her hand, batting away the girl's attention. She must quell these fears, she told herself. She must be firm. All would be well if she could but be secure in Samson, and she set to the task in hand.

Downstairs in the kitchen, preparations were already well-advanced. The butcher's boy had delivered the chuck this morning, and Mrs Halliwell had browned the meat and set it on to braise. The larder, which was still well-stocked after Adelaide's abstemious winter, had been plundered for a wealth of root vegetables. Potatoes, parsnips, carrots and beets, together with a variety of different berries, had been hauled from the cold and colourfully heaped on the kitchen worktop. Ellen had been ordered down to the market early as well, long before the sun was up, to purchase lemons and oranges, newly arrived on the barges loaded from the ships docked in Liverpool, which in turn had sailed from Spain.

Adelaide paced the length of the dining room, brushing past the girls as they leaned over their work, silently assigning a seat to each of the evening's guests. She'd just stopped at the head of the table to visualise the party, absently fingering the carving of one of the rosewood chairs, when she heard a door shut somewhere down the empty hallway. Turning her head towards the sound, she said aloud, "Who was that?"

"Must be t' master back," replied Ellen, matter-of-factly.

Adelaide, her eyes flicking over the girl's bowed head, bristled at the word, even as she acknowledged Silas was gone and everything was changed. She frowned again. How strange it was, his absence could still take her by surprise like this, in sudden swells of affection for the shrewd old man she'd not felt these last years since Robert's death.

"Already?" she exclaimed with brittle lightness, shaking her head a little to dispel her reverie.

In truth, she hadn't anticipated Samson's return for hours. She'd understood Henshaw was to spend the day with him, discussing the business and conducting a tour of the factory. The man was reliable and had always been faithful to Silas. There was no doubt he could be trusted to instruct Samson capably. What then might such an early departure mean? Taking a last look down the table, she hastened towards the door. "Carry on. Carry on," she wafted her hand at Ellen again, "and when you're done, don't forget to attend to the table linen. It will need pressing."

In the corridor, an intense chill confirmed the front door had indeed been recently opened, and she folded her arms against a shiver as she clipped across the tiled floor, sweeping round the foot of the staircase, where she spotted what she'd expected to see on the console outside the study: a gentleman's top hat. She hesitated only a moment to approve her reflection in the looking glass, patting her hair, which despite her fifty years was still dark and full, before briskly knocking on the door, barely waiting for a murmur of consent, and bursting into the room.

"Aunt Adelaide?" Samson turned quickly from the window, where he appeared to be arranging some papers. She didn't fail to notice his face drop before his features swiftly rearranged themselves into an expression of polite surprise.

Until the day of Silas's funeral, Adelaide had not set eyes on her nephew since she'd been a young wife of five and twenty and he a reserved, bookish child of twelve. (Indeed, she'd made a point of being out of town when he'd visited last November to meet with Silas to discuss the new arrangements.) In the intervening years, she'd been astonished by the reports of his success in the army, conjuring, as they did, a vigorous man, deserving of his name, wholly at odds with her memory of the quiet child. Nevertheless, on first observation, he had certainly appeared to have the bearing of a commanding soldier. It was only as he'd drawn closer, she'd noticed, with grim satisfaction, he looked tired and much older than she'd expected.

His brown hair was starting to recede from a face that was both craggy and thin. The sunken skin beneath his cheekbones was pitted and pale, and there was none of the ruddiness she imagined he might have enjoyed during his campaigns in the South. Indeed, in every aspect of his appearance, he was unrecognisable, save for one. As a studious child, some years older than her own boisterous boy, Adelaide had seldom seen him, but on the infrequent occasions they had met, it was always his searching blue eyes she'd noticed. Deep-set and soulful, they'd never failed to unnerve her. Now, aged with heavy lids, she saw they were just the same, if only grown a little more melancholy.

"Samson, I hardly know you!" she'd exclaimed on that occasion, drawing herself up handsomely in her black velvet cape and extending a gloved hand.

"It's been too many years, Aunt," he smiled sadly, taking the proffered hand with a courteous bow. "And I'm especially sorry I couldn't be here when Robert—"

"Yes. A long time." She dropped his hand and nodded firmly, the black plume from her bonnet almost poking him in the eye. She could scarcely conceive he, of all people, should expect her to speak of such a time, though from the stricken look on his face, she was satisfied he understood now well enough, it was a matter never to be discussed.

Notwithstanding this awkward beginning, Adelaide had been encouraged by his behaviour at the funeral. Throughout the solemnities, there was no air of presumption about him. He conducted himself with grace and tact, displaying respect for her late husband and affording her a proper degree of deference. In particular, the quietness of his manner, almost to the point of self-effacement, had offered some reassurance he had no intention of disrupting her life, nor any desire to make any radical alterations to the Charlotte Street house in which he was invited to join her. Indeed, the only stipulation he made in that regard was to be afforded some suitable space in which to position his pianoforte.

"How charming!" she'd exclaimed with genuine surprise, making sure she didn't betray how womanly she regarded the request. "You can offer us a recital!" Then, remembering herself and the occasion, she'd added in more sombre tones, "In due course."

Samson had responded with a modest smile, and she'd known very well he'd no intention of ever performing. In fact, when the time had come for his small number of effects to be distributed throughout the house, he directed a rearrangement of the furniture in Silas's private study to accommodate the pianoforte in the far corner by the window.

"Ah yes, how novel!" Adelaide had allowed herself some sport. "You'd prefer a select audience, then?"

Glancing at the instrument now, she realised the papers he'd been sorting when she'd arrived were sheet music. She raised her eyebrows. What was this man about?

"Back so soon?" She spoke almost teasingly, registering his discomfort, then added with a short laugh, "Surely they've not frightened you off already?" She hardly dared hope this might be the truth.

Samson didn't answer and instead murmured something about his papers, which he'd taken to riffling again. Good heavens, the man was infuriating!

An uncomfortable silence opened up, broken only by the sound of the clock beyond the door. Evidently, she was to learn nothing about his visit to the mill. Her brow furrowed, and she reached for the brooch at her breast.

"Not to worry, Samson!" she tried. "Not to worry! I shall leave you in peace." Wary of his reserve, she'd spoken lightly this time, almost with affection, and the change in tone produced its desired effect, for he met her eye again and offered a pained smile. She nodded back, satisfied. It would do for now.

Yet, at the door, something made her hesitate. She found she couldn't stop herself from turning around once more.

"You know, Samson," her voice was smooth again, "there's really no need to worry. I've friends who can show you the way. Tonight, I shall introduce you to the *'Wright'* circle!" and she laughed throatily at her own witticism, even as she watched him force another smile.

SIX

By the time Nancy had struggled the short distance from the mill and turned into the shadowy passage that gave on to their yard, she was already soaked. All her clothes, cap and shawl were heavy with water and the hem of her dress was mottled various shades of grey and brown from the wretched puddles she'd failed to avoid in the dark. The sleet itself, which had kept up all the way, was needle-sharp, so that even though she was ice-cold and shivering, her face burned with a fiery prickle.

"Ee, lass, where've tha been?" cried her mother from across the room as she heaved herself up from her seat by the hearth.

Aside from the glow of the fire, the room was dimly lit by two tallow candles, one set on a square table in the middle and another on the mantelpiece above the fire in the far wall; they both guttered at the draught she brought in, sending smoke and shadows skittering upwards. Then, from the darkest corner to her right, Nancy heard a high-pitched cry, and Walter leapt from the gloom, crashing towards her.

"Slow down, lad!" Her mother thrust an arm out sideways, stopping him in his tracks. "We don't want thee as cowd as tha mother."

Walter, blinking his long lashes, slunk back to the bed.

"Nancy, stay by t' door. We'll take tha clothes off there, so's tha's not dripping all over t' place."

Too exhausted to argue, Nancy obeyed without a word, though it still wasn't easy. Her arms were so leaden, she could barely keep them raised, and her clothes so drenched, they stuck to every curve of her body, so that her mother had to peel away each layer in an awkward tussle, careful not to get herself wet, placing each of the sodden items in a bucket left by the door for the purpose. When she eventually removed Nancy's last shift, she lay it down separately over the back of a chair, it being less wet than the rest.

"Now quick, over by t' fire."

Nancy, naked, skin pale to near translucence, darted over the room in two leaps, shaking all the while even as she moved up close to the hearth and grabbed at the sheet her mother had warming in anticipation. She wrapped it round herself tightly, savouring its brief, blissful heat, before patting her goose-bumps dry with short, vigorous rubs. At the same time, her mother brought her nightdress and held it aloft in front of the fire.

"Hurry up, Mam, I'm starved!"

"Aye, well turn tha'sel this way then."

Her mother reached up to lift it over Nancy's head, then went to fetch a blanket from the bed, which she proceeded to spread over Nancy's shoulders, steering her to sit on a low stool by the fire, where a pair of thick bedsocks awaited. In her haste to pull them on, Nancy's still-damp feet snagged on the wool, but once she'd wriggled her toes to the end, she straightened up and held her hands to the flames. At last, she breathed an enormous sigh at the first suggestion of warmth.

Next, her mother wrung out the shift she'd set aside, into the bucket, and when she was done, recrossed the room to set about drying Nancy's hair with it in a fast and forceful scrub. This way and that, her mother jerked her head, and from side to side, so that by the time she was finished, her curls were a mass of frizz and her mother's hands raw pink from the water.

Meanwhile Walter, having silently watched this ritual from

the dark, approached cautiously. His eyes wide and wary, fearful he might be sent away again.

"'S'all right, Walt, tha can come over now," and Nancy opened out the blanket to swoop him up. "Let's get warm!"

He giggled, revealing the gummy gap where one of his front baby teeth had only yesterday evening fallen out. The shock of it was like a fresh blow; it made her heart ache, and she buried her head into the soft curve of his neck, inhaling its sweet milkiness.

"Thank Lord it's Sunday tomorrow and tha doesn't have to go to that place," her mother observed. She was fetching a small covered pan over to the stove at the fire. "And that I can feed thee." She lifted the lid to look inside, adding gruffly, "There's not much, mind."

Nancy shrugged and pulled Walter into an even tighter squeeze as a warm and fusty steam curled into the room, and the smell of turnip soup mingled with the rising stink of her own soggy feet. When it was hot enough, her mother served up a meagre portion in one of the small glazed bowls they'd brought with them from the farm so many years ago.

"Stay by t' fire," she said, handing it over. Thus, balancing it on her lap, Nancy set to eating hungrily in the firelight, with a clinking spoon.

Released from the blanket, Walter remained close, hovering at her elbow, yet strangely quiet. She was soon nearly done, and looked up to check on him, only to discover his hollow eyes were fixed, not on her, but on the bowl. Lord, he looked clem! On the brink of another mouthful, she stayed the spoon.

"Oh, Walt!" she cried with a yelping sound she knew he liked. "Does tha want to be a doggy again?"

Walter's eyes instantly brightened, and he yapped happily in return.

Smiling, she handed him the bowl, keeping back the spoon. "Wipe it clean now, there's a good doggy!" and she patted him on the head as he set to licking up the last of the soup with an enthusiastic slobber.

"Good dog! Good dog!" she clapped her hands together as he excitedly discarded the cleaned-out bowl on the floor, and started spinning and barking round the room, just as her mother had finished tidying.

"Now, now, lad. Calm tha'sel." Her mother's tone was stern as she bent stiffly to retrieve the bowl. "What's tha playing at, Nancy, getting him so agitated? Just before bed an' all!"

Nancy sighed in response but found she'd no energy to raise the usual objection. It never failed to nettle her, this sort of thing. This sort of put-down, this way her mam had of taking over, undermining her own mothering. It wasn't right. Walter was her lad, wasn't he? It was she who understood him better than anyone. Yet tonight, she knew, was not the night to go spoiling for that particular fight all over again.

"Now then, Walt. Listen to tha grandma," she said, beckoning him to her. "Come on, be a good doggy, and give tha mam a kiss!"

Nancy knew her mother understood from this she'd gained the victory, and she watched her give a short nod of satisfaction and take up the candle to draw Walter away, retreating to the bed in the corner where Nancy would join him later. Behind them, she chewed at her lip.

Still perched on the stool, she wrapped the blanket more tightly and bent closer to the fire. It was labouring feebly now against the gust which rushed without pause down the chimney, the flames only occasionally flaring to spit back at large gobbets of sleet.

What a terrible day, she shuddered, and, as though summoned by the thought, the black, churning waters of the canal at once flooded her mind, filling her with rising dread and an image she couldn't help but dwell on, bobbing up in the corner of her mind's eye: a tiny finger floating this way and that, making its slow descent towards the bottom of the water.

Behind her in the shadows, Walter was already settling under the blankets, and her mother had begun to sing.

"A North Country maid up to London had strayed
Although with her nature it did not agree,
Which made her repent, and so bitterly lament,
Oh, I wish again for the North Country.
Oh, the oak and the ash and the bonnie ivy tree,
They flourish at home in my own country."

It was an old song which straightaway took Nancy back to
the timbered upper room of their Westmoreland farmhouse.
She, beneath the cotton sheets, her younger brothers already
slumbering in the bed beside her, an open casement to a sky
streaked with pink, and the scent of honeysuckle borne in on
a gentle breeze. Her mother's voice was still as lovely as it
had been then, low but tuneful, and Nancy smiled to think of
Walter lulled to sleep by it.

"O fain would I be in the North Country,
Where the lads and lasses are making of hay..."

With each verse, her mother's voice softened, singing
the words with ever more gentleness, until even now Nancy
herself began to feel heavy, as though she too would once
again sink drowsily to sleep to the song. But then, out of the
darkness surrounding her like a vast lake on a moonless night,
there drifted a heart-breaking question: Who'd ever sing a
lullaby to poor Johnny?

Instantly, tears stung her eyes, quick as if she'd chopped
an onion, though she tutted at herself just as swiftly with
frustration. Lord, she mustn't cry! She was determined. Aye,
once she'd bidden Mary goodnight, hadn't she solemnly
promised herself her skriking was done? Her mother mustn't
find out. Not a thing about the whole sorry mess. Not a word
about Johnny, or the accident, or the money.

It was to keep her from worry, Nancy had tried to persuade
herself. Her mam was getting old, she reasoned, and not so
spry; she mustn't be made to fret. Heaven knows it was

terrible enough to think of Walter having less to eat next week without her mam's anxiety over him too. Nay, there was no question but that she'd have to find a way of sorting it without troubling her.

All of which was right and true and proper, of course, but closer to the nub – she'd admit if pushed – was another, altogether less worthy reason. For wasn't there her mam's temperament to think of too? Aye, and after the day she'd had, Nancy simply couldn't face the scolding her news was bound to provoke. She didn't know which was worse, bitter words or sour silence, just that her mother was practised in serving up both, and if she got so much as a whiff of what had gone on at the mill, she'd no doubt give her a double helping.

"... Oh, the oak and the ash and the bonnie ivy tree,
They flourish at home in my own country."

The song was over, and her mother was taking whispered leave of Walter. Hurriedly, Nancy dried her eyes on the sleeve of her nightdress, sniffed hard and, with a deep breath, steeled herself to betray nothing.

"I'll not be long away mi'sel." Her mother slumped into the upright chair beside her, wincing with pain as she shuffled to get comfortable.

"What is it, Mam?"

Still straining to find the right spot, her mother took in a breath with a strange whistling sound. From his bed, Walter giggled.

"Nothing to go frettin' about. I'm just getting owd."

Nancy was unconvinced but too tired to press the point. Instead, she said, "We had a visit from the new master today."

"Oh! And what's he like then?"

"Lily-livered as it happens."

"What makes tha say that?"

"Oh, I don't know," she lied, at once cross with herself for bringing him up at all. "Aren't they always? Them masters in their grand houses playing at high and mighty. What do they know about owt?"

Her mother smiled wearily, "Aye, tha's not wrong there, lass!"

"Mind, he's not quite so puny as t' other one."

"Eh? Tha means owd Silas? God bless him. He won't be warm in t' grave no more, not after a night like tonight!"

They both laughed, and from his bed Walter whooped, not listening to their words but responding to the sound of happiness.

"Whist, Walt!" said Nancy, fondly. "Get tha'sel to sleep now like a good lad."

"He may be cowd, owd Silas, but at least he's free of tha-knows-who!"

"Ee, Mam, I'm shocked! Does tha dare speak ill of mi'lady, the grand Duchess Adelaide?" Nancy flounced her head back, pointing her nose in the air as though at a bad smell.

"Aye. That's her. Ada Froggatt!"

More spluttering laughter ensued, and their efforts to stifle it for Walter's sake only made the joke seem funnier.

Nancy's mother hadn't been long at the mill after their arrival in Manchester before she'd heard the story of the master's wife, and how she was not so finely bred as she'd have folk believe. Ada Froggatt was, in truth, the daughter of an innkeeper, an astute businessman who'd lost his wife early in life and subsequently overindulged their only child. She'd been lucky in her looks, Miss Froggatt, as even the most resentful millworker had to concede, and the apple of her father's eye. A fine-skinned brunette with an elegant figure, and a dash of her father's acumen, she'd managed to catch the eye of one of Manchester's men on the make. A slight man in the flesh, Silas Wright, the son of a Cheshire landowner, was nonetheless financially substantial, with ambition to match. No one was quite sure when Ada gave way to the altogether more decorative Adelaide, but most surmised it was one candlelit night over the bar of the Red Lion, with a flutter of dark eyelashes at the defenceless Silas.

Just then, a loud rasping noise came from the corner of the room and both women broke off their laughter, "Walt, is th' all right?"

"Croak!"

"What…?"

Walter was advancing in the gloom, his eyes shining with merriment. "Croak!"

"Walter! Bed!" Nancy shook off her blanket and took up a pretend broom, miming a sweeping action back across the room. "Shoo, shoo!"

"Croak!" he continued, giggling, even as he climbed back under the covers. "Croooak!"

"What is tha…? Oh! Tha's a frog! *Frog*gatt. Did tha hear us? Is tha being a frog, Walter?"

"Aye! Croaaak!"

"Oh, Walt, tha clever lad! Mam, he's being a frog!"

Her mother was shaking her head, "Very good, very good, but it's time for bed, young man."

"Croak!"

Nancy widened her eyes and put a finger to her lips, all the while grinning to show she appreciated his joke. She bent down and smoothed the hair from his forehead and kissed him. "We can have more frogs in t' morning."

She rejoined her mother back by the fire. They smiled quietly at one another. Outside, the wind was getting up again. The windows rattled in their frames and a whistling draught swept in under the door.

"By, it's rough."

"Aye," agreed Nancy, but she was keen to maintain the good mood and didn't want to dwell on the weather. Persevering with the joke, she observed, "Mary can't half take her off. Ada, I mean. Got her right down to a T!" She laughed, thinking of her friend, expecting her mother to join in, but to her surprise, she now turned to her with a serious look.

"You lasses need to watch tha'sel. It's all very well wi' tha sniggering and tha snorting, but *you*, Nancy Smith, have responsibilities."

Nancy's mouth fell open, astonished at this sudden change in her mother's humour. After all, it had been her mam, and not she, who'd started the jest over Ada Froggatt in the first place. Beneath the itchy layers of blanket and nightdress, she felt herself getting hot. She opened her mouth again, this time to protest, but before she could put her defence, her mother added firmly, "Tha just can't afford to be getting into trouble."

At once, Nancy swallowed her response, shooting with the speed of a shuttle, from indignance to shame. Mouth dry, face ablaze, heart pumping fast, it was as though her mother had somehow managed to discover everything about Yates and Johnny and the docked wages, and whilst it stung that she should question her sense of responsibility, there was no denying she'd hit the mark.

The room fell silent, save for the howl of the wind, until her mother eventually cleared her throat to announce, "I'm away to bed."

Still brooding, Nancy could only summon a wordless nod, though she watched her from the corner of her eye, as she struggled to a half-bend and waited the long moment before her old bones were ready to shuffle over to the bed and into her nightclothes.

Nancy turned back to the dying flames. They were sinking even lower now from the relentless sleet, just like her mood, it seemed, and its plummeting descent into gloomy self-reproach. Lord, how was she ever to fix such a dreadful mess?

That night in bed she spent fretfully, half-awake, curled against the cold, turning over desolate thought after desolate thought, trying to block out the noises of the room: Walter's rattling chest beside her and her mother's irregular snores. One minute wishing herself, or every last one of them, dead and free from all this misery, and the next, contorted with the guilt which attended such notions, like the chief mourner at a funeral.

Or else, with arms clutched round herself, she felt the jutted ridge of her ribs and thought of Mary and Mick. Poor childless Mary who didn't know her luck! With no one to please but a decent man who brought home money every week, and the consolation of a grown body to lie warm against at night.

When sleep did eventually come, it was as a falling into watery visions of the canal, lurid and horrible. One moment, she was watching a solitary figure standing at the edge of the water. As she drew closer, the dark body bent forward to peer into the depths, which she could see now were not clear or grey or even black, but a mingling of scarlet and crimson, and in which, as she reached the edge, she finally recognised the figure as her own, her features reflected, swimming in a course of blood.

The next moment, the canal was itself again, and so was she, lost amongst a large gathering of people on the bank by the towpath. There were cries and shouts and a general commotion, which she didn't understand at first. Then she noticed everyone's gaze was directed towards a small boat and the two men sitting in it. They were clutching a rope and earnestly leaning over the side to get a glimpse beneath the surface of the water.

"They've spotted a body!" A rheumy-eyed old woman suddenly appeared and nosed her wrinkled face into Nancy's. "Did tha hear? There's a body a-mouldering in there."

"Nay!" Nancy cried and ran away further along the bank, an ill-defined dread rising.

Once she was at a safe distance from the crowd, she turned back, and it became apparent, in the way of dreams, that the body the men were trying to fish out was that of her estranged husband, Richard Smith, or Smithy as he liked to go by. Smithy, whose golden smile had brightened her first months in this dismal place; Smithy, who'd coaxed her into an empty warehouse after the late shift, and a bed of packed sacking; Smithy, Walter's father, whom they'd not laid eyes on these last five years.

She watched, gripped in sickening suspense, half-wanting to look away, yet strangely compelled, straining to see if the corpse would indeed be recognisably him. There was a loud plop as the men dropped the hooked rope. Then, after an exploratory plunge, came an even greater splash as the men began to heave, and a dark, drenched form slowly started to emerge from the surface, dripping sludge.

Body tensed, eyes fixed dead ahead, suddenly she started at a clumsy tap on her shoulder... Who?... She turned quickly, then shrieked.

It was Smithy! His once handsome face ruddy with drink and smirking. "'Ow do? 'Ow do? Long time, no see!"

But before she could reply, he was gone already. Vanished, even as her heart was still racing at the sight of him. It had always been the same, she thought; he never did stay around for long.

Turning back towards the boat again, she saw the men were sitting upright now and shaking their heads in bewilderment. It was clear there'd never been a corpse. Yet amongst the crowd still assembled on the towpath, the earlier commotion was getting louder, the clamour, raucous and screeching, as ghastly laughter rose, like smoke, into the filthy air. "It were nowt but a finger! All that fuss for nowt but a finger!"

SEVEN

Samson stood dutifully by the drawing room fire in readiness for the guests, though in truth he could think of nothing less appealing than his aunt's dinner party. After his abortive trip to the mill, he'd hoped simply to retreat to the study in Charlotte Street, to play some music to himself and quietly digest his thoughts. Back in Silas's office, he'd been so certain he should relinquish his new authority to Henshaw, but now he was not so sure. Something about that torrid scene in the mule room, the injured boy and that demonic girl had seized his imagination. The child, abject and groaning on the floor. The girl, so unruly and audacious. The way she'd lurched at him, eyes blazing, plunging her hand into all that blood. It was extraordinary. His uncle had been wrong; life in the mill was not a bit like the army, where such indiscipline would never be tolerated. A grotesque scene from Bedlam was more like. Yet, despite the Gothic horror of it, had she not been right? The boy should have been taken to a doctor and the girl permitted to comfort him. And then there'd been that moment later in the yard, the same girl, vulnerable and weeping, crying tears he might have been able to prevent.

If he could but spend some time alone, he thought, he might be able to make sense of these shifting impressions and decide upon his course. Instead, Adelaide's grand plan was not to be avoided. The wretched party was proceeding, despite the rudeness of the weather, the guests put to considerable inconvenience to join them. As the evening was professedly in his honour, there was no question but that he must attend and express his gratitude for such courtesy.

The preparations now complete, Adelaide was circling the room with an air of satisfaction, treading the sea of Persian carpet and running her fingers along the swags of crimson damask at the windows, her considerable figure reflected in a myriad of curlicued mirrors, as she admired the blazing effect of a surfeit of candles across the tall mantel, and ostentatiously breathed in the scent of an arrangement of early hyacinths.

Eventually, Samson sensed her gaze fall upon him and noticed her mouth tighten. She regarded him openly a moment, a peculiar glint in her eye, until she said without smiling, "Goodness, Samson, you could almost pass for handsome!" To which he bowed modestly, and she launched into another deep-throated laugh.

The party, once assembled – every one of them shaking off dripping capes and exclaiming at the storm – comprised Hugh Osborne, a widowed landowner who lived next door, James Slater, an unmarried physician of advanced years who occupied rooms around the corner, and two couples, the Chadwicks and the Baldwins, who arrived together from across town in the same carriage.

Eli Chadwick, Adelaide had explained before he arrived, was a leading merchant in the town and owned a significant number of warehouses, some of them built on land he'd acquired many years ago from Samson's grandfather. From his wide smile and eager laugh, it was clear he was ready to enjoy himself, unlike his homely-looking wife, whose name Samson didn't catch. She looked ten years her husband's senior and, Samson noticed with sympathy, disgruntled to be dragged out on such a night.

The Chadwicks had brought with them Harry Baldwin and his wife. Baldwin, a weighty, square-faced cotton manufacturer, was a rival who'd sparred with Silas for decades. His younger wife, Esther, whom Harry had married not three months after the death of his first wife, had smiles enough to match Chadwick, though her good humour seemed largely borne out of satisfaction with her own appearance.

From the moment Baldwin shook his hand with a degree of firmness bordering on aggression, Samson was in no doubt of the older man's distrust. After a cursory enquiry as to how he liked Manchester, the manufacturer had immediately launched into talk of trade with a series of questions, as rapid as a volley of bullets. What were Wright's views on pricing for raw? Where, in his opinion, were the best new markets? Why, in God's name, was the Government listening to that Jacobin, Owen? What business was it of those fellows in London anyway, to interfere with his practices? And so forth, all delivered with a smattering of industry slang so incomprehensible, Samson found himself reminded of a comic encounter during the war, when he'd sought directions from a surly old Portuguese in a cobbled-together patois. After several misunderstandings, he thought he'd secured the route, though, in the event, he still got hopelessly lost. He stifled a smile at the memory.

Baldwin's tirade, he understood, was designed to test him, and confident though he was in his abilities as a student of the trade, he was more acutely aware of his limitations. To every question, therefore, he offered only the sparest of responses, choosing his words with care, though before long it became clear this very guardedness only served to feed the mill-owner's suspicions and provoke him all the more.

"Discipline, that's the thing!" Baldwin was speaking of the workers at the mill. He was clearly enjoying the sound of his own voice and his volume was now so great, the entire party was forced to listen to him. Samson, for his part, found himself frowning, discomfited by the echo of his own thoughts from the mouth of such a man.

"In running any enterprise such as Wrights," Baldwin carried on, "the thing is to steer a steady ship."

"But, Harry, dear," Adelaide interposed from across the room, "he's not a *naval* man!" Her guests obliged with polite laughter.

"Army, navy, it's all the same. Discipline. It's essential. Keep them under control, else where will we be?"

Baldwin's conversational sallies continued in this vein until it was time for dinner, when Samson hoped he might at last escape the intensity of the man's scrutiny.

In the dining room, Adelaide's meticulous preparations had ensured the table was decorated to dazzling effect. The white tablecloth shone brilliantly in the flickering light of the candelabra, which themselves gleamed from the maids' extra polishing. The porcelain glistened, and the crystal sparkled, whilst in the centre an elaborate arrangement of oranges and berries was displayed in the shallow bowls of the epergne, complete with trailing ivy. Another intense fire roared in the hearth, and the air was heavy with the scent of braised beef.

"My goodness, Adelaide, what a spectacle!" the old doctor offered pleasantly.

Adelaide bestowed a magnanimous smile. She was at the top of the table, shoulders back, striking in her velvet gown, soft as fur, shining here and there, the colour of pewter in the candlelight. Her dark hair, shot through with silver at the temples, was swept up elegantly, revealing two eardrops of jet to match the triple strand of twinkling beads displayed upon her exposed neck. From the opposite end of the table, Samson watched her lap up the appreciative chatter.

"Silas's place," Baldwin observed gruffly, nodding towards him and drawing back his attention. The manufacturer unfurled his napkin violently and sat down heavily between Chadwick's wife and the doctor, who, from the beatific smile on his face, was evidently delighted to be placed beside Adelaide, whilst it was equally clear, from the tilt of her head, her own interest lay with her wealthy neighbour, Hugh Osborne.

The other ladies of the party were directed either side of Samson, and, over the soup course, he ventured some polite observations on life in Manchester, whereupon the three of them settled into gentle conversation. Stretching his legs under the table, he drained his glass of wine. The room was low-lit and stuffy, and he began to feel sleepy and hopeful the dinner might yet pass off easily enough in this manner, with harmless pleasantries and a few flutters of Esther's eyelashes.

It was, however, Mrs Chadwick who proved the more voluble of the two, and after Esther had been drawn into an exchange at the other end of the table, the older woman leaned in closer. Her round face, pinkened by the heat from the fire, was softer now, and she spoke with a warm, Lancashire burr, which suggested she came from further north of town.

"I met your mother once," she declared, beaming at Samson's surprise as though she'd expected it and was pleased with herself for the effect.

"Really?"

"Aye, and your father too, of course. Many years ago, when they came to visit Silas."

"I had no idea."

"An intelligent woman, your mother."

"Yes, indeed," said Samson, raising his brows in fresh surprise; not that he disagreed with her estimation – on the contrary, he was deeply gratified – it was simply that her intelligence wasn't the quality for which his mother was ordinarily recognised.

"And tender-hearted." That was more like it, he thought to himself with a smile, only to discover, when he chanced to look down the table, that they were being watched. Adelaide met his eye warily and cracked a tight smile. He raised his glass jovially to her, even as he wondered what she was thinking. She nodded graciously in return.

Something of the moment conjured a fleeting vision of his mother. A slight woman, of simple taste, he could see her clearly, sitting at a similarly candle-lit table, the flame glimmering tremulously, as she guilelessly entreated both him and Daniel to "be kind to Aunt Adelaide". He couldn't for the life of him remember what had prompted such an instruction, only that her phrase "never known a mother's love" was associated with the memory.

"As I recall," Mrs Chadwick continued, "your mother was ever anxious to discover new ways in which to help the poor. Indeed, she showed a lively interest in the work of the Unitarians here in Manchester."

"Yes," Samson replied cautiously, remembering with a small frown the embarrassed nervousness with which his less enquiring father, a sanguine country rector like Daniel, had viewed his wife's broad-ranging interests: her wide theological reading, her frequent visits to the Wesleyan chapel and her befriending of the village's Quaker families.

"Aye, there are a great many inclined to that way of thinking in Manchester these days," smiled Mrs Chadwick. Her eyes were shining, candid as a robin, as Samson registered her meaning, though before she carried on, she cast a short glance at Adelaide to establish she was no longer observing them. "And, if I may say, the Cross Street Chapel which your mother visited – you might have noticed it, just down the road – has become a great example of Christian service to the less fortunate in town."

Samson bent his head towards her with genuine interest as she carried on, though, in the warm glow of candlelight, her homely voice had the strange effect of combining with his own conflicting impressions to stir up new ideas, so that before he knew it, his attention had become distracted, his thoughts returning to the scene in the mule room: those wretched women, the half-starved children and the girl who'd acted so boldly in speaking up.

"You've applied for a subscription, I suppose?" Mrs Chadwick enquired with another smile, but Samson had quite lost the thread of her conversation.

"A subscription?"

"Aye, for the newsroom," she looked puzzled, "at the Portico, the library I was just speaking of."

"Ah, yes that grand temple round the corner?" Samson said good-humouredly, hoping she'd forgive his inattention.

"Aye, it's a fine building, is it not?"

"Indeed, indeed."

"As I say, you'll not get a better flavour of opinions in Manchester anywhere else."

Interested to find out more and determined to demonstrate his renewed attentiveness, Samson sat forward, only for the conversation to be interrupted by the removal of the soup bowls, when Baldwin, evidently feeling neglected by the rest of the party, caught his eye. Straightaway, the man resumed his baiting. Addressing Chadwick, who was sat across from him, he boomed for the benefit of the table, "I hope you're not thinking of bending to any of this pressure on wages, Eli?"

At this, a number of the guests exclaimed, so that Baldwin was encouraged and carried on, decrying the current climate and the workers' effrontery in the face of slow trade. Meanwhile, above the animated chatter, Adelaide swept her head back magnificently. It was evident she wished to be heard. The party turned towards her.

"Hannah More!" she declared authoritatively, tapping the table emphatically with her finger. "They should all heed Hannah More, that's what they should do."

It took Samson a moment to summon the memory of a series of pamphlets, popular during his childhood. As far as he could recall, the old woman More, a sanctimonious crone, had espoused to the lower orders the virtues of piety, hard work and, above all, deference. It didn't surprise him in the least that Adelaide should approve. He studied her again, down the length of the disordered table, now soiled with crumbs, discarded napkins and blood-red wine stains. She was nodding, self-satisfied, buoyed by her guests' murmurs of support, and her eyes twinkling with a new affectation of mischief as she added, deliberately *sotto voce,* "Except half of them haven't the wit to read!"

This last was to the great hilarity of the party, save for Mrs Chadwick, who met Samson's eye and mirrored his frown.

"Our new fella's very quiet," Baldwin observed, his face already florid with too much wine. "What say you? If one mill relents on pay, that's us all sunk."

"I'm afraid my being so newly in Manchester, I don't know enough of the pressure of which you speak."

"By man! Don't they have newspapers in Cheshire? They're always looking for more, even when trade's down, which is precisely when they should be grateful for any work at all."

"Perhaps you've heard of the Blanketeers, Captain Wright?" piped up Osborne, from the other end of the table, who in his former position as one of the town's magistrates had been involved in the suppression of the weavers' march to London a couple of years previously.

"Aye, hand-weavers started it," Baldwin interrupted. "And that sort's not gone away! All of them are at it these days, spinners, weavers, the lot of them, not to mention some of the damned tradesfolk too. Agitating round town, with meetings and turn-outs. And now they say they want the vote! Ha! Mark my words, it's money they're after, it's always more money."

"I imagine they'd argue the one might lead to the other," Samson observed mildly enough.

"They'll have neither if I've got anything to do with it!" Baldwin exploded in response. "Revolution and damnation, that's where it'll lead."

Most of the party was stirred now, though Samson remained conscious of Mrs Chadwick's quiet presence beside him. To his other side, Esther was tutting furiously, though whether at her husband's ill-mannered outburst or the threat of a workers' revolt was not entirely clear. Meanwhile, Adelaide placed a hand to her breast in a show of alarm, prompting the old doctor to lean in with a look of concern, tapping at her elbow as though to say, "there, there". Samson noticed her frown line deepen in irritation.

"He's right," Osborne resumed. He was a slight, wiry man with a neat head of white hair. Not given to the kind of bluster to which Baldwin had descended, his cool demeanour was nevertheless rattled. "There's hundreds of them. Thousands. Organising. Assembling. Call it what you will. Why, what of that dreadful fellow, Hunt? You know, the 'Orator'? He was in Manchester only last week."

"The rogue at the theatre?" This was from Chadwick, half-laughing.

"Yes. That's him," Osborne replied, unamused and throwing Chadwick a disdainful look. He addressed Samson again. "You must've heard of the disturbance he caused at the Theatre Royal? Calling for the vote, I ask you, in the middle of a play! Disgraceful business."

"Well said," Adelaide nodded vigorously.

"Yes indeed, Hugh, I do hear what you say," chipped in Chadwick, who'd remained altogether better-humoured than the other guests and, from his tone, was clearly set on a more reasoned approach. Samson looked up with interest. "And whilst I'm not for universal suffrage, not like Hunt's lot—"

"Glad to hear it, man!" Baldwin exclaimed.

"Far from it, far from it," smiled Chadwick affably. "Nevertheless, Harry, surely you agree it's high time men like you and me were able to send a Manchester man to Parliament?"

"Pah!" cried Baldwin.

Chadwick's eyes widened in surprise. "Well, I know *I'd* certainly welcome a representative of our interests. After all, aren't we the ones refilling the coffers? They've had enough off us in Manchester since the war, and that's a fact."

"You're not wrong on that last point, Eli, I grant you," Baldwin began. "But listen here, we'd manage very nicely, thank you, if them in London, who know nothing, would just leave us to our business and stop with their meddling. Telling us what to do with their rules and their Acts and their legislation. What do they know? No, we've no need of *more* of them, thank you very much, not with the present danger in town. If you ask me, any talk of the vote is the last thing we need. Not what we need at all."

For a moment, Samson hoped Chadwick might press his point, and sensed Mrs Chadwick was stirred to join in. But instead, the man shrugged and sat back, and when his wife clicked her tongue in disapproval, he shot her a quieting look so that her lips flattened to a straight line, though her face showed as disgruntled as when she'd first arrived. Unmoved by her expression, Chadwick sank further into his chair and reached for his glass, so that Samson couldn't be sure whether the man had conceded out of politeness, understanding his views to be too modern for the party's taste, or simply out of boredom with Baldwin's stupidity. Either way, after a long draught of wine, he appeared as sanguine as before.

There were more expressions of dismay around the table however, as Osborne picked up the theme. "You know the authorities are hard-pressed trying to keep up with them, these self-styled 'reformers'. Our agents tell us there's a new tone – sedition's on their mind, and that's a fact. It stands to reason; why else do they meet so often in secret?"

Samson raised his eyebrows but didn't make the mistake of a second interjection, especially since he'd noticed Adelaide turn suddenly pale, her fingers working the mourning brooch pinned over her heart. All at once, he was struck by how tired she appeared and quite alone at the top of the table. He felt a pang of remorse. Perhaps he should better try to appreciate the alteration in her circumstances these last months, no less dramatic than his own, and undoubtedly more painful. It didn't take any great leap of imagination to understand her fears, that instinct for the old certainties. Had he not himself shown some of the same aversion to change when Daniel had come to him with his proposal, or indeed this very day, plotting his own ignoble escape? Yes, for his uncle's sake, he had come here to protect her, and in the spirit of his mother's admonishment, he must resolve to make a greater effort. Yet even as he did so, the woman went and irritated him all over again, his jaw tightening involuntarily, as she shook off her reverie and offered a new and simpering smile to Osborne, "Thank heavens for the Yeomanry!"

"Yes, indeed!" Osborne noticeably puffed out his chest. "The Manchester and Salford Yeomanry, Captain Wright. Formed in '17, you know, after we'd stopped the marchers. All volunteers, of course, modelled on the Cheshire regiment. No doubt you're familiar? They may not be highly trained, but with all this agitation on suffrage and whatnot, we need them more than ever."

From the chimney, a sudden flurry of sleet splashed with a vicious hiss upon the fire, causing Esther to cry out and creating a momentary pause.

Then Osborne thumped the table with his fist, and the party turned towards him once more. His eyes had grown large, and it was clear an idea had occurred to him. "Why, Captain Wright," he declared. "Of course! *You* should volunteer!"

Esther gave another little shriek and clapped her hands, and there were warm cries of agreement from around the table, though Mrs Chadwick remained silent. Adelaide, delighted, arched a brow in enquiry, whilst Baldwin, sensing a victory of sorts, looked directly at Samson and smiled coldly, "Of course! A man of your experience would be indispensable."

* * *

Later, when they were all gone, Samson took up a candle, the wax already half-dripped into the holder, and a replenished glass of wine to the study. It was past eleven, and the maids, having assumed he'd no further requirement of the room, had allowed the fire to die to its embers. He squatted down to prod at the ashes, but the room remained as cold as a tomb. Yet still he didn't want to go to bed. He found he needed to retrieve a fragment of the evening for himself. Shuddering into the leather chill of the wingback, he once again stretched out his legs. Closing his eyes, he tried to dismiss some of the evening's images: Baldwin's red face ranting, and Adelaide, basking in her realm, tittering.

At the same time, he was aware of something specific nagging at him, pulling at the edge of his consciousness. For a moment, he thought it might be the question of his volunteering for the Yeomanry. Eyes still shut, he winced at the objection he'd raised: No, no, he'd be far too busy at the mill to offer his services. Ha! Yet even this argument had not deterred their enthusiasm. He tried to recall whether his remonstrance had remained unequivocal, afraid he may have demurred too feebly and given a false impression of consent.

The question of the Yeomanry aside, there was something else too, something more important, something that had been touched upon, which had bothered him enormously. He wasn't sure it was anything he'd spoken of precisely, though he sensed it had to do with Mrs Chadwick and their conversation. What the devil was it? At this late hour, tired and straining to recall his thoughts, he felt an uncomfortable knot tighten in his stomach.

He drained the last of the wine and, tonguing its grit from his teeth, set down the glass next to a discarded book on the table beside him. Ah yes, of course! That was it! He remembered at last, and with the same rush of relief a man feels on discovering a precious item already given up for lost. Yes, it was something Adelaide had said. It had got him thinking. He would look into it straightaway.

EIGHT

There was a hard pull on the blanket and Nancy blinked open her eyes. The room was still dim but half-lit with a curious, silver-whiteness. She turned slowly, stiff with cold, to discover Walter, already clambered out, was standing beside her, his fingers still tugging at the blanket. He was fully dressed, just as he'd gone to bed to fend off the chill. His big eyes were shining with excitement, and he was grinning a gummy smile, like a little old man, she thought.

"Look!" he breathed and tottered over to the window, which gave onto the yard. Propping herself up, Nancy saw from the pillow that, overnight, the pane had been woven from one side to the other with a delicate lace of ice. He beckoned her again – this time, more pressing and eager. For a moment, she sank back and blew out a sigh. It was cold and Sunday and still so early, but he was getting louder, and they mustn't disturb her mother. Shivering, she got out of bed, dragging the blanket along with her.

At the window, she understood his excitement. A good two feet of snow had fallen, and no one was about yet, so the effect was unspoilt. The familiar, brown bumps of the cobbles were gone, transformed into a giant, smooth eiderdown, whilst the roofs and chimneys were laden with vast, fluffy pillows. Above, the sky seemed immense, turning from grey to white, like a blank new beginning.

"Mammy?"

Nancy cast a quick glance at her mother's bed. She wasn't sure whether they'd woken her, but beneath the hunched blanket, her back was turned to the room.

"All right, Walt," she whispered, "but not wi'out tha jacket." She walked to the hook by the door and took it down, feeling for the woollen cap, which had long ago been her brother's, stuffed inside the pocket. She helped him into the coat, buttoning it all the way, and fitted the hat firmly on his head. "Now tha can go!"

With the blanket still wrapped round her, Nancy gently closed their door to watch from the threshold of the shared entrance as Walter dashed into the snow, blinking back at her in wonder. Her darling boy. For once venturing the full length of the yard, racing in circles, occasionally turning to look behind, each time surprised and delighted by the shape of his own tracks.

She breathed in deeply. This crisp, chill air felt good and clean, as though all Manchester's coal-black grime had been wiped away by a fresh, new world of white. It dispelled the phantoms of the night, this brilliance, and gave her a renewed clarity. She knew what she must do. There was no use in being afraid. She'd tried to do the right thing by Johnny and, although she wasn't sure how, now she'd do what she'd spoken of to Mary, and seek justice for herself.

It was a problem though, this need to find a way of speaking directly to Samson Wright, and one that she found herself pondering the rest of the day. Of course, it was out of the question for her to simply request an interview. Neither Yates nor Henshaw would ever allow it, even if she was so daft as to ask. So how exactly was it to be done?

The answer, when it came late that evening as they finished supper, was wholly unexpected, in a chance remark made by her mother about a conversation she'd had after chapel that morning. She'd fallen in with a widow from New Cross as they were leaving, an elderly woman with whom she was on nodding terms. It transpired, however, the woman was a neighbour of their old friend, Charlie Bell.

"He's better! Thank Lord!" Her mother broke into a rare smile. "Ee, I'm that relieved. It seems it were only a head cold, after all. And I were so sure he were in for summat wuss last time I were over there. I hope he's keeping himsel' warm, mind."

Nancy was pleased to hear the news and had just expressed her own relief when a thought struck her. She'd been running a damp cloth over the table and stopped a second. Then, careful to keep her tone light, she carried on cleaning, as she wondered aloud, "He'll be back in wuk tomorrow, will he?"

"Aye, old lass seemed to think so."

Nancy nodded and smiled widely, for more reason than her mother could know.

It was getting late and time to settle by the fire. She folded the cloth and stowed it away and came to join her mother, scooping up Walter to sit with them awhile before bed. As he wriggled to get comfortable on her knee, she leaned her chin on top of his curls and looked at a small framed sketch propped on the mantelpiece. It was a picture of the Westmoreland farm where she'd been born, penned in ink by her brother Edward not long before she and her mam had been obliged to come to Manchester.

Charlie Bell was a friend from this old country. A mild man, not given to idle talk, he'd grown up with her father back in Westmoreland, firm friends since their schooldays in the village hall where they'd been taught by the local minister. Nancy, herself, had no childhood memories of the "Uncle Charlie" her family had so often spoken of, Charlie having left when she was no more than a baby. Gone to find his fortune in Manchester, so the story went, though the truth Nancy now imagined to be more prosaic. Escaping the north – and, she'd heard rumoured, a romantic disappointment – Charlie had had to toil hard at first as a millhand; long, gruelling hours on the factory floor, broken only by nights of profound loneliness in rude lodgings shared with shifting strangers. Nevertheless, he had endured, and his quiet good sense and ability to read had eventually earned him promotion to a junior clerk's position. After that, life had become a little easier, as he progressed through the office ranks at Wrights' mill. Even so, whether because of the solitariness established during those early years, or as a consequence of natural inclination, he remained a loner.

It was when Edward, always foolhardy, had followed her father into an early grave – dying on a lark, trying to reach the ridge of Whitbarrow by moonlight – that her mother had first appealed to Charlie. With no man left in the family to take on the farm, they'd been forced to give it up, and Charlie had found them both work at Wrights, where he'd become a trusted favourite of the master.

Nancy remembered how they'd arrived on the edge of town in a borrowed cart. Themselves and their bundles drenched in dismal October rain, which poured in lines, hard and straight as pokers. Brought low with grief and bewildered by Manchester, Charlie had been a steadfast friend. He'd secured them rooms and showed them round, introducing them to other workers from Wrights, and advising on those parts of town safe for decent folk and those to avoid.

Then, not three years later and hadn't they needed him again? When Smithy had abandoned them, her mother already ailing and Walter barely a year old, it was Charlie who'd tramped the terraced streets of Ancoats once more, looking for a vacant room, and bartering with the landlord to agree a rent cheap enough for them to afford.

Charlie had never married, which, given his solitary temperament, was no surprise, but Nancy often wondered if he didn't harbour feelings of a tender persuasion for her mother. Certainly, she'd spied him more than once, in the candlelight after a shared meal, raptly watching her mam sing one of the old songs, a dry, gnarled hand dabbing at his watery eyes. As a young girl, the idea of this attraction had made her nothing short of queasy, not to mention resentful on her father's behalf. But these days, it only struck her how much happier life might have been if Charlie had been able to overcome his reserve and persuade her mother to choose a different path.

Still, of one thing she was certain, as she risked her mother's frown and jigged Walter, giggling, up and down on her knee, if she framed her request as being of service to her mother, Charlie Bell would be unlikely to turn her down.

The following morning, with another snowfall freshly deep, the top layer not yet compacted hard, Nancy wrapped herself in a blanket for a shawl, and in the drear light before dawn, set out to crunch the towpath beside the iced-up canal. She was determined to arrive at the factory ahead of the shift and walked as quickly as the snow would allow, her breath streaming behind her. On reaching the arch, she stopped just inside the gates, stomping her feet on the frosted cobbles to shed the clumps of powdered snow which had clung to her clogs as she waited to waylay Charlie on his way to the office.

"'Ow do!" she smiled brightly on spotting him, though the movement set her teeth chattering. He'd turned into the arch, head down against the wind, and looked up in surprise, which swiftly gave way to the slightly nervous air he always had around her. "Glad to see thee up and about. Mam tells me tha's had a bad do."

"Aye. But I'm in fine fettle now, thank you." He nodded in a manner designed to end the exchange and ploughed on over the yard. Nancy, undaunted, lunged after him, her feet sinking through the fresh snow, reaching out her hand to touch his arm. They both stopped.

"Charlie, I need a word."

He smiled at her wearily then, and their breath clouded between them. She saw, with a clutch of pity, his latest illness had left its mark. His eyes were red-rimmed and his gaunt face, even thinner than before, was white-pale in the cold. She gave a small, apologetic shrug, to which he gave another wordless nod and pointed towards the office building. She followed him to the bottom of the steps, where he stopped to hear her out.

"Tha must tell Ann," he said when she was finished explaining.

"I can't do, Charlie. Don't tha see? She doesn't seem so well, not at the moment. So why go upsetting her if I can avoid it?"

Charlie wasn't convinced, and his eyes remained grave with concern. He had reasons to be wary on his own account too. Although he'd been advanced by Silas Wright, he didn't yet know whether he'd receive the same treatment from the nephew. From all he'd heard, the new master was a bit of a "cowd fish", and, of course, there were always plenty of younger lads who might be preferred over him if there were any jobs to be lost. His being absent from work this last week wouldn't help his case either. He was sorry, but he wasn't keen to distinguish himself by association with trouble.

"But he doesn't need to know tha helped me," Nancy assured him. "Really he doesn't. All tha needs do is give me a sign. I'll look out of t' window when we're on t' morning break and tha can wave to me if he's in his office."

Charlie laughed at this, shaking his head in wonder at the forethought in her scheme, but his good humour made her more certain of him. Surely he'd do it.

"Go on, Charlie. If not for me, think on me mam and Walter?"

At this, Charlie held up his hands, an acquiescent smile deepening the lines on his face, "Aye, all right, go on. Tha's a bold lass, Nancy Kay, and that's a fact!"

She laughed then, and thanked him, and he headed off, making towards the warmth of the office when a thought seemed to occur to him halfway up the stairs and he stopped.

"Nancy," he leaned out over the snow-capped rail towards her. His brief smile was gone, and he spoke with renewed gravity, "I've said it afore, lass, tha wants to be careful."

* * *

Nancy spent the following week in a state of nervous suspense. Her conversation with Charlie had been on Monday, and by Thursday she was beginning to worry he might have thought better of their arrangement. Every morning break, she'd taken up position at the window which gave the best view of the office door, and, each time, the brief minutes had come and gone without any sign from him. If she weren't able to speak to Samson Wright before Friday afternoon, she'd be too late to prevent the docking of her week's wages. Not only would they be deprived of sufficient food and coal, she'd have to confess the whole sorry story to her mother and admit to its deliberate concealment too.

Nevertheless, she was sure the only reason Charlie hadn't emerged yet was because the snow had remained thick on the ground. If she was right about the new master, he was as nesh as he was cowardly and had chosen to sit out the cold weather, warm and cosseted, in his fine house in town. However, late yesterday, the sun had struggled for a few, brief hours through a layer of cloud, and this morning it had broken free again, so that here, at the window, she was dazzled by its reflection on the vast puddles forming in the yard. Now, with a fresh surge of hope, she saw a large clump of snow break and plunge from the ledge, as long drips of water coursed down the pane from yet more snowmelt above.

"What's tha doing there again?" It was Molly Kennedy, one of the other young piecers, whose talent for sniffing out trouble was better than a prize hound after a scent. Nancy merely glanced at her, but Mary, who was also on the lookout, fended her off.

"Nowt wrong in taking in t' view."

"The *view*! A fine *view*!" Molly pulled a face and began to laugh at Mary, who folded her arms over her bosom and stared back, her head tilted to one side, so that a few of the other girls had begun to congregate around them, wondering at the trouble brewing, when Nancy suddenly spun round, her face lit with passion. Molly stopped abruptly, alarmed at her intent, but Nancy simply swept past her, mouthing over her shoulder to Mary, "Cover for me."

Down the empty stairwell, the clatter of her hastily retrieved clogs rang strange and hollow, drowning the sound of her own breathing, which was fast and shallow. This was it. Samson Wright had finally deigned to come back to the mill. Out the door, without her shawl, the cold crashed at her like a wave, knocking her further out of breath. Gasping, she charged on. Hurry up, don't stop!

Nay, nay there was no time to stop, no time to gather herself. Grabbing at her skirts from the brown slop that swam between the cobbles, she made her way as quick as she could over the slippery ground, past the basin where men were taking poles to the last of the creaking ice, straight to the bottom of the steps leading to the office. Now she was here, the building looming above her, the only certain thing was not to hesitate, so she dashed up the stairs, which had been shovelled clear of ice, and, giving a short knock on the door, opened it before she was asked.

There were three men in the first office, who all looked up, Charlie feigning the same surprise as the others. Each of them had been leaning over their work, which was set on shelves angled beneath the windows for the best light. Their quills now suspended, they surveyed her with interest to see what had brought her from the factory.

As she'd promised, Nancy ignored Charlie, whom, being the most senior in the room, she might have been expected to approach, and spoke instead to one of the other clerks, a serious-faced young man with neatly parted hair and spectacles.

"I'd like to see Mr Wright, please."

The man's mouth fell open in surprise at her address, though it was clear his self-importance was also gratified, as he puffed himself up a little and adopted a formal air, "I assume you mean *Captain* Wright."

"The new master?" She'd no notion he was a "captain".

The young man closed his eyes in solemn confirmation. "Yes," she replied.

"May I ask why? Have you been sent by someone?"

Nancy considered this a moment and then answered, "Aye, tha could say that."

"What do you mean? Speak plainly if you please, and I'll see if Captain Wright will receive you."

"Tell him," she paused. "Tell him I've come on account of Mr Yates."

From the corner of her eye, Nancy saw Charlie Bell smile to himself.

Meanwhile, the young man had begun to peer at her closely from over his spectacles, so that she found herself grinning back awkwardly, whereupon his demeanour changed again and he became suddenly, unaccountably, flustered. His eyes dropped and the skin above his collar began to redden. He was, it seemed without question, green around women. "Wait here a minute, please," he mumbled, setting down his quill, and disappeared through an internal door.

In an instant, the room fell quiet, except for the subdued tick of the clock and the muffled noise of the machines, which felt strangely far away. She looked around with interest, breathing in the strong, foreign smells of polished wood and paper and men. In all her years at the factory, this was her first time in the office.

A large sketch-plan of the mill itself hung over the door, and there were half a dozen other framed documents on the walls between the windows, in which she recognised, amongst the lines, the shape of the name "Wright" from the sign over the factory gates. There were numerous inkpots and pads with stampers, as well as an array of quills, whose feathered plumes looked soft to the touch. A globe was set atop a chest of drawers in the corner, next to a pyramid of rolled and ribboned parchments, and there were several reams of smaller dockets piled high on the desk in the middle of the room.

Amongst all this sober paraphernalia, Charlie and the other clerk had returned to work. She watched them diligently consult the top sheet of a stack of papers to their left and then turn to a vast leather-bound ledger in front, poring over its entries, before dipping the quill and carefully raising a hand to write.

There was no alchemy to it, she knew. It was not magic. Yet, standing here, like a supplicant behind a priest conducting a holy rite, this mysterious translation of lines and marks into substance and meaning remained for Nancy an everyday miracle. And as the clerks' pens continued to scratch across the page, a familiar itch began to prickle at the back of her neck. She set her jaw and clenched her fists, but there was no stopping it. Here it was, that familiar rush of memory: her mother's cheeks, the cloud of flour and that snatch of the book, rescued for Edward.

Edward, Nancy's older brother, tutored every week by the local minister, along with all the other sons of the village, whilst she was made to stand by the stove, stirring the soup for his return. Later, he'd read to them after supper, fluently enough, passages from the Bible and translations from Homer, her mother listening enthralled, then clapping her hands in delight like an easily pleased child, and Nancy knowing exactly what she'd say next, "My, my, Eddie, tha's a grand clever lad!" Much good it had done him, or them. The clever lad who capered into a hollow grave and cost them the future his education was supposed to secure. Spiteful, ugly thoughts they were, she knew. Full of an envy she'd tried hard to tame, though she still heard its hiss every week as she watched the line of children snake out from chapel to Sunday school, and now, once again, she'd felt the flick of its venomous tongue.

What on earth was she doing here? Perhaps it would be better to leave? But then how wretched would she be? After all, she hadn't wavered in her purpose until now, not since that first morning of the snows. Nay, despite her fears, she'd not once doubted she should assert herself. Yet not five minutes spent cloistered in this scholarly room, and here she was again, that little girl from the farm, feeling small and stupid and furious.

She was still pondering the prospect of escape, when it became clear there was no longer any possibility of retreat. The young man had returned and was beckoning her to follow him. All she could do was take a deep breath, smooth down the patched apron she'd been wearing since Saturday's accident when she'd had to throw away her good one, and enter the door behind him.

He led her on through a long series of rooms, all desks and chairs and ledgers, and more men peering at her as though at a rare curiosity, until eventually they reached a closed door, upon which the young clerk knocked. There was no cry of "Enter", however, only a strange noise from within, and Nancy looked to her guide, assuming he'd hesitate. Yet, to her dismay, he seemed unperturbed, and proceeded to open the door and usher her inside.

Immediately, she was overwhelmed by a fug of warm air and the smell of damp wool, and saw, to her surprise, Captain Wright bent over, his back to the door, putting on the first of his long boots in a hopping manner. Her guide, whose face had blanched at the realisation his knock had not been heard, gave a small cough, "Excuse me, sir."

"What the devil?" Wright looked up and over his shoulder. "I thought I told you to give me a minute, man!"

"Begging your pardon, sir." The man retreated hurriedly, in obvious anxiety, no doubt unsure of what sanction might later be imposed upon him.

Left alone with him, Nancy politely examined her own feet, as Wright struggled with his second boot. Evidently, he'd got them wet during his walk from town and taken them off to dry by the fire, which was crackling with a lively flame in the grate. After a moment, she stole a glance to see if he was ready and happened to catch sight of a portrait of the former master above the fireplace: Silas surveying them with a wily expression. She wondered, with a stifled smile, what he'd make of his nephew's undignified predicament.

At last, Wright straightened up and, without looking at her, moved behind the imposing desk, seemingly searching for a piece of paper. Eventually, he spoke in an absent manner, "I understand you've a message for me from Mr Yates."

Nancy waited for him to look up, unsure whether to begin, as he continued to dither between one document and another. She frowned and took to studying him: the deliberate aversion of his eye, the high colour in his cheeks, the unconvincing riffling through the contents of his desk. It was unexpected behaviour, more strange than rude. Aye, it had an altogether more puzzling quality, she thought, until, with sudden conviction, she realised: He was embarrassed! That was it! He must've thought she'd never seen a man in his stockinged feet before! She suppressed another grin as his awkwardness emboldened her.

"Not exactly, sir."

Finally, he met her eye, though he continued to look uncomfortable. She noticed he needed to swallow before he could speak, "Well then, what is it?"

She paused, then set back her shoulders and raised her chin to show she was determined. "Tha'll 'appen not remember me, sir, but I'm sure tha'll recall the accident that took place in t' mule room last Sat'day?"

"Indeed."

"Poor Johnny who lost his finger."

"Yes. It was most unfortunate."

"Then perhaps tha'll also recall I asked leave to take him to th' Infirmary, or at very least to stay wi' him 'til he were tended to."

Wright nodded. "Yes, since you mention it, I believe I do remember."

"It would've been the decent thing. Any mother'd want to."

Wright frowned, "I'm sorry, I understood the child was an orphan. Are you saying you are, in fact, his mother?"

"Nay! Nay, sir," she breathed, anxious to be understood. "The truth is, I do have a lad at home, not much younger than Johnny." Wright nodded slowly, registering the fact. "And the point I'm trying to make, sir, is no mother could stand to see a child that way and not offer a drop o' mother's love."

At this, he looked at her directly and blinked. The room fell quiet again, save for the snap of the fire, so that she'd just begun to wonder whether she ought to carry on, when, at last, he said, "Forgive me, noble though your sentiments undoubtedly are, I don't see where all this is going?"

"Sir, I'm glad to hear tha thinks me sentiment noble. I'm afraid Mr Henshaw and Mr Yates did not. Tha may have heard they decided it weren't necessary for him to go to th' Infirmary. Or even for me to stay wi' him."

"I'm sure they've dealt with such matters before."

"Aye," she replied flatly, and before she could stop herself, "no doubt that's why tha left them in charge?"

He met her eye again briefly, then dropped her gaze.

"Well, indeed. Look, the boy was tended to and is doing well, I believe. So far as I can see, that's an end to the business."

"Not for me it int!"

Wright's eyes widened in genuine surprise.

"All I did were have noble intentions. Them's tha words, sir. But after Johnny were taken away, Mr Henshaw ordered me to tidy mi'sel up. Tha may not have noticed, but I'd got quite bloody."

Wright gave a short nod.

"Well, sir, it were not the work of a moment, and I had to go and dispose of…" She didn't go further, but he winced, and she knew he'd understood.

"For me pains, Yates complained the time I took were too long. He's intending to impose a fine on me wages this week. I'm here to appeal to thee to stop him. Sir, please think on me little lad and me mother too, who rely on me. We can't do wi'out that money!"

"But what of your husband? Does he not support you?"

Nancy, taken aback by the question, made no reply. This wasn't what she'd come to discuss; it wasn't something she ever liked to talk of, if she could help it. All at once, Saturday's dream came back to her, as sudden as Smithy's tap on her shoulder, and she shuddered.

"Never mind." Wright had noticed her disquiet. "It's not necessary for you to explain."

Oh nay, she bristled. Nay, nay, she wouldn't let him away with that. If it was an explanation would persuade him, then she'd damn well offer one, never mind her pride.

"Truth is, sir," she breathed, "if tha must know, he were a wretched drunk, me husband, and left me wi' me boy not much older than a babe in arms." She watched his face for a reaction and felt her mouth turn dry. "Aye, and I've not laid eyes on him for over five year." There, it was said, and she lifted her chin again, clinging to the shadow of her dignity.

Wright didn't reply, though he'd long ago given up the pretence of searching for something on the desk. He stepped from behind it now, over to the hearth, just as a surge of smoke from the stack seemed to snuff out the sun, so that the only light in the dingy room came from the glow of the fire. He placed a hand on the mantel and a booted foot up on the fender. His head hung low, staring into the flames.

Oh, for the Lord's sake, what was he up to now, she thought, worrying about the time and willing him to look back at her, though, when he did, she was struck by a new expression; one she'd seen, but not understood, on their first meeting. On that occasion, she'd noticed only a fleeting suggestion of pain, but now here was a greater intensity of feeling, and despite her own pressing anxiety, she found herself wondering what kind of story was reflected in eyes so sad.

"Tell me, how old is your boy?"

This was unexpected. She couldn't fathom at all where he

might lead with such a question. She replied hesitantly, "He turns seven in September, sir."

But Wright didn't seem to hear her, or at least made no further comment, and resumed his silent contemplation of the fire. Nancy chewed at her lip. What was the man about?

Beyond the window, a sudden shout carried across the yard, closely followed by an army of footsteps on the cobbles. Oh, Lord! The workers who'd ventured outside for their break were returning to the factory. The minutes were speeding by. It wouldn't be long before Yates was back. Her chance was nearly up! In alarm, she tilted her head to one side, desperate to regain his attention, but still he didn't look up.

"Sir, wilt tha help me then?" Her voice was rising higher, pleading. "Wilt tha see to it I don't get fined?" She needed him to understand her urgency, "I have to go now, sir, else I'll be in trouble again. My name's Nancy Smith. Though most folk know me by Kay. Please tell me tha'll make sure Nancy Kay's wages aren't docked?"

"Yes," he said, turning to her at last. "Yes, yes, I'll see to it."

"Oh!" she gasped in relief. She'd known from the first, he was a good man. "Thank thee, sir, thank thee, tha cannot know—"

Wright shook his head, however, as though to say thanks were not necessary, and when she carried on, determined to express her gratitude, he held up his hand to quieten her, and proceeded to raise his own voice, intent upon introducing another idea altogether, "Tell me, Nancy Kay, tell me."

She stopped talking.

"Tell me, are you able to read?"

Instantly, her face dropped, stung by such an astonishing question. Why would he ask such a thing, and so bluntly? So soon after the tumult of her emotions in the clerks' office too, and just as she'd credited him with a sympathetic soul. Yet here was an insult so precise, it was as though he'd read *her* soul to probe its deepest shame and used it against her. Now it was she who had to look down, unable to meet his eyes, as she tried to master herself.

"Well?"

His voice was lower now, soft and almost kind, seemingly unaware of the humiliation he'd inflicted. Yet even if he was stupid and insensible to her pain, she didn't care. She hated him for it. She wondered if he could see, and hoped he would, as she answered coldly, "Nay, sir, I very much regret I've never had the opportunity to learn."

His face remained impassive, however, and he nodded to himself as he returned to the desk. This time he seemed to be searching for something in genuine earnest so that her dismissal, when he remembered, was almost perfunctory, "Thank you, Miss Kay. Thank you. That's most helpful. You'd better get back to work now."

Bewildered, Nancy shut the door behind her, relieved and enraged in almost equal measure.

NINE

Towards the end of the afternoon, Samson sent a boy to Charlotte Street to advise Mrs Halliwell not to delay dinner but to put by a light supper, which he'd take in the study on his return; he anticipated a late hour. The interval would afford him time to collect his thoughts and settle the detail of his plan, after which he'd summon Henshaw to take instruction.

It was already darkening and the lamps just lit, when the older man knocked on the door of the office. The high window had started up a whistling draught, and Samson was busy adding fresh coals to the fire. He was prodding the flames as he looked over his shoulder in greeting, only to catch the old man frown; evidently, he thought it a waste of fuel so late in the afternoon. Samson wondered if he ought to warn him he expected to take some time and was about to suggest they stay warm by the fire when, with mannered dignity, Henshaw sat down, ramrod straight, on the chair in front of Silas's desk, undoubtedly his customary place. No matter, Samson thought, hanging up the poker, reckoning it best to indulge the man in this small point. Instead, he rounded the corner of the desk and took up Silas's chair, knitted his hands together, placed them on the blotter and leant forward.

There was much to discuss, and he was determined that nothing should deter him. Certainly not the discernible startle with which Henshaw received the news, his whiskery brows shooting upwards, nor, once Samson had made clear there were to be no objections, the pointed manner in which the man repeatedly consulted his fob watch. Never mind the hour, it was imperative that everything was put in place for the next day.

"And the mistress approves?" Henshaw enquired doubtfully when Samson had finished explaining.

Samson looked back at him blankly a moment, before understanding his meaning: Adelaide.

"Of course, of course," he replied with forced jollity, and a lie so blithe he shocked himself; scarcely a week living with his aunt and already adept at dissembling. He pressed his lips together, momentarily wondering how indeed he might best present the plan at Charlotte Street, before his enthusiasm claimed mastery again, and he dismissed the thought; he'd think of something later.

Eventually, when the details of the business were decided, Samson closed up the office, and he and Henshaw made their way towards the yard. It was quieter now, though there was still a knot of men beside the basin, loading the last of the day's cargo. Overhead, the sky was black and cloudless, save for the late shift's spiral of pale chimney-smoke.

"Shall I arrange a cab, sir?" Henshaw offered somewhat wearily.

"No, no," Samson replied, not wishing to put the man to more trouble. "Thank you, that won't be necessary." Indeed, the vigour of a brisk walk would suit his present mood far better, he thought. He reached to pat the fellow on the back and bade him a warm goodnight. Then he set out alone, under the arch, towards the shadows of the street lights.

The slush was all but gone from the pavement now, though the cold was still as clean as a blade to the skin. He sank his chin lower into the collar of his coat. Beside him, what was left of the ice on the canal heaved and creaked, though boats were on the move again, and the breath of a horse further down the towpath carried like more smoke on the air. When he'd picked his way across the snowmelt that morning, the route to the mill had already begun to feel familiar, but tonight, cloaked in darkness, the streets were strange to him again, almost mysterious. Figures like shades slipped here and there from unseen passages, brushing too close, causing him to bury his hands in his pockets, whilst, in the distance, drunkards shouted, and siren voices called, and all about him the factories and chimneys soared.

There was an excitement to it, this chill on the air and the warmth of exercise, this need to keep his wits about him as he picked up pace towards the centre of town. It helped to alleviate the intense impatience with which he'd been gripped all day, like a sudden fever, ever since that girl had departed the room this morning and left him with this pressing new desire to set things right.

He breathed in deeply, savouring this new exhilaration, though the soot in the air caught in his lungs and stopped him in his tracks, coughing in great, hacking gulps. He'd covered some distance now, so that his legs were stiff too, and the shoulder he'd injured at Albuera ached from being hunched over his desk half the day. Yet, he thought, as he recovered himself and walked on, these were gratifying sensations, were they not? Instances of an honest fatigue, of the sort he'd almost forgotten, borne of a day of action, nay, one of purpose.

All his life – Samson observed with the kind of clarity that only rewards exertion – all his life had been in the service of duty. All his actions predicated on other people's plans, even to the subjugation of his own will. It had always been the same: gazetted at the behest of his father, married to please Isabel and now this latest venture, this incongruous displacement to Manchester – to run a cotton mill for pity's sake! – all for his brother and a dead uncle.

Today, however, marked a change. He stopped again in the middle of the street to acknowledge the fact. Yes, indeed this was different he thought, as he set off once more. For this new scheme had the singular appeal of being his own idea, and one which would have made his mother proud to boot. An image of her had floated through his mind all day: her benign face, bathed in a pool of light pouring from the high windows of the church hall, a Bible open in her hands and a row of children cross-legged before her.

He could scarcely credit that only a few wintry days ago, when the snow had first fallen, he'd been on the brink of surrender and ready to run from Manchester and its challenges. Yet something in Adelaide's idle remark at the dinner party had played on his mind. So too had Baldwin's rant, and the very next morning, he'd consulted the latest reports from Parliament over which the manufacturer had been so offended.

Then there'd been Mrs Chadwick's conversation to think of as well, not to mention the poor injured boy and, of course, the girl. The woman whom he now knew to be Miss Kay. Thank goodness for Miss Kay! For even though he'd given many hours of consideration to his idea, it wasn't until this morning, when he'd seen *her* pained reaction to the question of reading, that he'd truly understood how it might feel to be illiterate. Even now, he was shocked at his dearth of imagination, and still more ashamed to think of the woman's distress, which he'd undeniably caused, and to which he'd responded so hopelessly. And yet, it was precisely this, her wounded reaction, which had finally confirmed his belief in setting up a school.

He had recognised her, of course, straightaway. The instant he looked over his shoulder as he was pulling on his boot, like some ridiculous fool. He spotted those unruly curls, trying to escape her cap, and knew at once it was her, the bold girl from the spinning room. When he'd been able to take a closer look, he'd found she had a small, intelligent-looking face, which appeared so freshly awake as to give the impression of having just been washed with a splash of cold water. Her eyes were green and bright too, whilst her skin was fair, though two red spots had formed high on her cheeks, either nipped by the cold or brought on by the steeling of her nerves, and, of course, later, she'd flushed full crimson with anger, and he'd been left to berate his own graceless lack of tact.

At last, he had reached the Charlotte Street house and bounded the salt-spread steps, making directly to the warmth of the study. The walk had stirred a prodigious appetite, one which he feared might not be sated by Mrs Halliwell's cold plate, though straightaway he sent one of the maids to fetch it all the same. He loosened his cravat, opened the top button of his collar and, sinking into the leather wingback, set his feet in front of the fire, his thoughts as shifting and restless as the flames. What a blundering fool he had been! To ask such a question so bluntly. He shook his head in a mix of embarrassment and shame. Still, he assured himself with a nod, so long as Henshaw carried out his directions, then all would be well for her.

Ah, supper! He looked up in expectation at a knock on the door. "Enter!"

The door opened, and Samson stretched expansively, anticipating his glass of wine. There was a pause, however, and a whispered exchange in the hallway and, a moment later, it was Adelaide who appeared, laden with the tray.

"Goodness, Aunt," he shot out of the chair. "This... this is most... kind."

"Nonsense!"

He couldn't see her face as she busied herself at the desk, setting down the tray.

"If you're to work this hard, Samson, the very least I can do is come bid you goodnight." She turned, holding a supper plate of cold pork pie and apple sauce, and gestured him to sit back down. He smiled weakly and obeyed.

Meanwhile, she brought over the plate and a glass of wine and set them within his reach on a low table, before returning to the tray for his cutlery, which she wrapped in a napkin and handed to him. It was so smoothly done, and she so adept at these small gestures of service, that fleetingly he pictured her circling the tables at the tavern where he knew she'd grown up.

Next, she took an upright chair from beside the desk, placed it opposite him in front of the fire and perched on its edge. "Go on, go on, get on with it," she waved her hand at the pie, "don't mind me."

Despite his disconcertment, Samson's hunger was too great, and he didn't hesitate.

"It's really not enough," she nodded at the plate after a moment. "A man of your constitution, you should have taken a hot meal on a night such as this."

Samson swallowed, abashed by her concern. "It's perfectly sufficient, I assure you."

"No, Samson, it is not."

He looked at her in greater surprise.

"I'm quite sure there was no need for you to be so long delayed at the mill. I can't think what Henshaw intended by it. Indeed, I shall come and speak with him myself in the morning."

"No," he said, too quickly, a bite of pork still unchewed in his mouth.

"Why ever not?"

Samson worked at the food as he set down his plate.

"Why should I not speak to him? You surely don't wish to exclude me altogether?" Although she laughed, Samson understood at once this was precisely the reason she was here. He heaved out a long sigh. By God, he didn't want to speak of his plans tonight! It was late, and he was tired, and he'd not yet decided upon a strategem. Nevertheless, she was firmly planted on the chair, and it was evident from the set of her mouth, she wouldn't be satisfied until she'd discovered what was afoot.

"Aunt Adelaide, I'm certain you need no assurance of your welcome at the mill," he began, then stopped and frowned. There really was no way around it. If he didn't tell her this evening, then Henshaw would be sure to do so in the morning, and he'd be discovered in his lie. "It's simply I believe Henshaw will be particularly busy in the morning."

"Indeed?"

"Yes," he paused again. "You should know, Aunt..." he breathed, readying himself. "You should know, I've set in motion an exciting new departure for the business. One which I wholeheartedly believe will benefit everyone, master and hand alike."

Her eyes fixed him with an enquiring stare.

"Yes. I have instructed the institution of an education programme for the children."

Her mouth dropped open, then quickly closed again.

"Henshaw's to put it all in place, appoint a tutor and arrange for the necessary shift changes, and so forth. The idea is to send twenty of them at a time for a lesson at the end of the day." Samson moved forward in his seat, trying to read her reaction. "It will take some time, of course, but I believe we'll be ready by spring."

He risked a smile, but Adelaide remained speechless, her eyes glinting cold. Straightaway, he was struck with the certain conviction he needed her support, or else she'd undoubtedly find a way of preventing him. Yes, indeed, she *must* be persuaded. The plan was too important, too precious to him to fail, and just as he acknowledged the truth of this to himself, all at once he alighted on a new line of argument.

"Yes, Aunt, I think it's a splendid idea, and Silas would, I've no doubt, be very proud of you."

"Of *me*?" she choked in astonishment.

"Why, yes, of course. For it was you who gave me the idea, and I shall be happy to give you full credit for it."

"What do you mean?" she spat at him. "My idea! How can you say such a thing? To reduce shifts? To pay a tutor? To weaken our position even as another mill's being built in our shadow? And for what? To do the work of the chapel and give the ungrateful louts more than we provide already? To hand to them on a platter the written word with which to betray us?"

"No, no!" Samson made sure his face appeared stricken with anguish. "Dear me, no, Aunt!" Then, once he judged he'd achieved his affect, he continued in a careful tone, "That was not my understanding of your meaning at all."

She glared at him, furious, but clearly bewildered.

"Surely you've not forgotten your observation at dinner? On the night it snowed so heavily? Your avowed wish the populace might read so as to gain some instruction of their place in the world?"

At this, her face fell and, with the slow coalescence of memory, gradually rearranged itself, her expression passing as it did so, from anger to doubt until her mouth formed a revelatory "oh".

Samson sensed victory and, standing up to feel the advantage of his height, launched into a final flourish.

"'Inspired' is the word for it, Aunt! Inspired! Don't you see, we shall be at the vanguard of progress? After all, it's only a matter of time before Parliament will oblige us to do such a thing. But we at Wrights, we shall already be ahead of the other mills in Manchester." He was surprisingly good at this. "We shall undertake a noble task. We shall educate our children. We shall promote the value of hard work and gratitude. *Your* values, are they not?"

Adelaide could only stare at him as he opened his arms to deliver his last line, designed especially for her, "And the beauty of it is, in doing so, we shall secure their loyalty."

In the silence that followed, the fire snapped and popped, blasting out an uncomfortable heat. He was at once conscious of a sweat forming, beading on his forehead and damp within his pits. By God, the woman drained him.

Meanwhile, she'd raised her head, though she kept her eyes averted, surveying the room and eventually settling on the piano. Then, in a voice markedly quieter than usual, she slowly enunciated, "I am astounded."

It was clear from her swiftly changing expression, her emotions were in turmoil. Although there remained a grim core of objection, there was also a new, fleeting glimmer of wonder about her eyes, as though she were indeed toying with the notion of allowing his assertion and claiming the idea as her own.

"Samson," she said at last, "I believe I owe you an apology."

He bowed magnanimously, all the while watching her closely, for even as she said sorry, it was done so smoothly, her countenance so inscrutable, he still couldn't be sure if his words had worked their intended flattery or if – and the thought unnerved him – she knew she had been played.

TEN

It had been bitter as a Westmoreland winter since the snow had fallen on Sunday, so that almost a week later, Ann was agonising over the dismal amount of coal, barely a handful left in the bottom of the scuttle. Now a low winter sun was at last trickling through the window, revealing the room to be grimier than ever, she thought perhaps she'd save the coal and allow the fire to die. It was already down to its last embers anyway. She could take the afternoon to do a spot of cleaning.

"Wrap tha'sel up, lad," she called to Walter, who was sitting on his bed, muttering to himself. "We're going to do wi'out t' fire for a bit."

A little later, once she was sure the grate had cooled, she brought the brush and pan and a bucket from the cupboard over to the hearth and lowered herself slowly, one aching joint after the other, to kneel before the fireplace. She was weary from poor sleep and a growing unease at a strange sensation in her belly, as unrelenting as those long-ago pregnancies. Now when she bent forward, wriggling to extend her arms to the back, she found she had to keep shifting her weight to relieve her discomfort, and it was only a short while before the pain became too great; she stopped and sat back on her heels with a loud sigh.

From this spot, the room seemed to loom above her, its layer of dirt overwhelming. Still holding the dustpan aloft in one ash-whitened hand, she dropped her head into the other, as the hard chill from the floor rose through the rag-rug, seeping into her bones, as stiffening as death.

Walter was still on his bed, propped against the wall, swathed in a brown cocoon of blankets. He'd taken to singing to himself as he liked to do, but at his grandmother's sigh, he'd stopped. Now her strange new posture struck him as odd, and he started to titter nervously.

"Grandma! Grandma!"

When she didn't respond, he flung off the blankets in a confusion of amusement and alarm, and jumped across the room, his bony arms flailing.

"Grandma?"

Ann at last looked up, and seeing he was about to clatter into her, swiftly swerved to avoid him, thereby spilling the hard-won contents of the pan in a great white puff over the rug.

"Damnation!" she cried and turned her fury on Walter who was still laughing. "What's so comical?"

Shocked by her vehemence, Walter's glee vanished. His lip trembled and his eyes, suddenly enormous with fear, burst into tears. He raced back to the bed and flung himself under the covers with a yelp.

"Oh, Walter," she snapped. It would be a while until she'd have the patience to deal with him. Instead, she cleared up as much of the ash as she could, but aside from the top pile, which was looser and easier to pick up with the edge of the pan, the brushing only served to embed the rest of the mess into the lumps and bumps of the knotted rags. It would need a firm beating.

She dumped the collected dust in the bucket and rose awkwardly from the floor, standing still a moment and breathing deeply as her legs unstiffened and the white shock of pain that had burst before her eyes dissolved, just like the cloud of ash itself. Then she put on her cap, fixed her winter shawl and picked up the rug, carefully folding it in two so as not to drop any of its content. Taking down the beater from its hook on the wall, she headed towards the door.

From under the bedclothes, Walter was still crying in great gasps, the pile of massed blankets heaving in time with every gulp of air. Ann shook her head. "Hush now, Walter, that's enough." She spoke firmly but added a note more kindness than she was yet able to feel, "I'll just be in t' yard."

Outside, the fresh chill in the air and the brightness of the sky lifted Ann's mood at once. Although the mat, which she'd pegged to the washing line, needed a thorough beating, she found she didn't mind so much. She was glad to be upright again, and once she'd established a rhythm, there was a certain satisfaction, a pleasure almost, in the repetitiveness of the task, and in the great cloud of dirt she released with every wallop.

As she continued to bash at the darkest stain, a bold robin alighted on the still snow-topped coal shed that stood in a shadowed corner of the court. Unafraid of her, and of the noise she was making, it perched on its flimsy twig-legs and watched her with its head cocked in curiosity.

"'Ow do!" she said aloud. "It's good to see thee."

The robin hopped a little, as though to relieve the cold in its feet, but then looked back at her with its black eyes shining.

"Is that Nat? Or is it Eddie? 'Ow do? 'Ow do?" She laughed a little at herself and her foolish superstition. How they would have laughed at her too, her husband and her first-born. But then, in response to the bird's whistle, she started to hum a tune, an old one, from when she was a girl, breaking off now and then to ask, "Does tha remember this one?"

The time went by happily enough in this manner until she was satisfied that most of the ash was gone, and, as though sensing their exchange was coming to an end, the robin took off. She nodded sadly as she watched it fly away, and reached to unpeg the rug from the line, revealing behind it, Walter, cowering at the window; a sorry sight indeed, his face blotched red with tears. Instantly, guilt flared, powerful as a sudden scorching, and she gave him a weak smile, pointing towards the door to indicate she was coming back to him, though his only response was to run from the window in seeming terror.

Sighing, she placed the mat over her arm. Although she wanted to get to him quickly, she'd have to take her time over the slippery cobbles, coated with a deceptive black ice in these gloomy parts of the yard that didn't get the sun. She was just looking down at her clogs, choosing her path carefully, when someone called to her.

"Afternoon, Ann!"

It was their neighbour, David Wilson, Susan's husband, coming into the yard from the ginnel. Ann was surprised to see him at such an hour, when he'd usually be at the factory, though, being a weaver, he still had more freedom that way. He was lugging a bulging sack over his shoulder and looked uncharacteristically cheerful.

"Grand day?" He was closer now, and she could see his weathered face was brimming with merriment. She half-wondered if he might have come from the alehouse, though she knew he wasn't one for that sort of thing.

"Thaw's come, eh?" he persisted. Normally such a quiet soul, she couldn't think when he'd passed more pleasantries.

"Aye, we must be grateful," she said shortly, wary of his levity.

With the rug still in her arms, she indicated he should go ahead, but once he'd opened the door, he remained holding it back for her, welcoming her inside with a low bow and a great sweep of his free arm.

"Eh, what's got into thee?" she tutted, but his good humour was infectious now, and she found herself laughing as he closed the door with another flourish. He laughed in return but said nothing and set off up the stairs at an eager pace, the sack bumping against his back at every step.

Walter was lying in bed again. From what she could see poking out of the covers, his hair was knotted and his eyes swollen, his upper lip shiny with snot brought on by the crying. Her own mood restored, what with the rug-beating and David's joviality, she felt a redoubling of guilt and perched herself on the edge of the bed ready to cajole him, though still a little way off so as not to risk his recoil. Another kind of lad, she thought sadly, would have relished mischief-making and goading his grandmother like that. But there was no sense in wishing for another kind of lad; Walter was what he was.

"Walter, I'm sorry, chuck."

He buried his head into the wet pillow. She winced at the thought of the snot smearing.

"Walter, come on. Really, I am. I didn't mean to shout. But tha shouldn't go dancing about when Grandma's got cleaning to do."

He remained very still, tense like a trapped animal.

"But ne'er mind. It doesn't matter. Really, it doesn't. Let's dry tha tears and give Grandma one of tha best hugs?"

He shifted in the bed, though he still didn't turn to look up at her.

"I know tha's a good lad really," she paused, and he moved again. "Walter?" She placed a hand on his leg through the blankets and patted it. He shuffled some more. "Grandma's best lad."

At this, he finally launched at her, not allowing her to see his face, but throwing his arms wide round her and burying himself in her bosom as she leant her cheek on the top of his head and shushed him.

All the time during this reconciliation, Ann had been conscious of unruly noises from above. Judging from a series of loud cheers, David had evidently returned with some good news. That, or the sack had contained something exciting. Or both. Now there seemed to be a lot of pacing around and rising hilarity. It was all the more noticeable as they sat in their own still quietness, broken only by an occasional sniff from Walter, who nestled closer and closer against the deepening chill.

She was just about to abandon her plan to save the coal and

fetch the tinderbox when there was a boisterous clatter above them, followed by the sound of running steps down the stairs and an energetic rap on their door.

It was Susan Wilson and the daughter, Jemima. "'Ow do?" they grinned.

The Wilsons were already living on the upper floors when Ann and Nancy had moved into the house with Walter as a baby, and they had soon become friends. Even though Susan – now standing on the threshold, beaming excitedly at her – was naturally more outgoing than Ann, the two women had swiftly established a mutual respect, understanding, as they both did, the peculiar cruelty of straitened circumstances. For in the same way as Ann had lost her comfortable home in the country, so Susan had been forced into ever humbler lodgings, as David, a successful handloom weaver when she'd married him, had suffered the fate of so many in that trade faced by the new machines, eventually selling his own loom and taking a role in one of the mixed mills.

Susan had been robust through these trials. Not often given to sentiment, she'd hardened to the changes in their lives, and to keeping in check her three strapping sons, who, by dint of their noise and bulk, won out when it came to a share of their mother's attention. Jemima had always been the quiet one and frequently overlooked. Now she'd reached that awkward stage – her pale face spotted like a currant bun and skinny limbs hanging long and loose. These days, whenever Ann visited upstairs or spoke with Susan in the yard, the girl would studiously ignore them, affecting nonchalance, or otherwise wear an openly surly expression, so that Ann would often come away thinking, *That one needs watching*.

This afternoon, however, both Wilson women were bathed in smiles.

"Is tha going to tell us what all t' bother's about?" Ann said amiably, gesturing them in.

"We're going to do better than that," Susan began mysteriously. "Oh 'ow do, Walter," she added, spotting him sitting on the edge of the bed and speaking in the slow, deliberate fashion she always adopted with him. Jemima, who'd enjoyed petting him as an infant, looked over warily too. Neither she nor Susan seemed to know what to make of him these days.

"Say hello, Walter," Ann said coaxingly.

"Hello, Walter," he said.

"*Walter!*" she chastised, but he was unabashed and looked away.

Embarrassed, Ann shrugged her shoulders, "It's not cheek tha know."

"Aye, don't fuss about that." Susan was too ready to burst with her own news to be concerned with Walter. "Now, let me tell thee. Our Davy's just got back from Greenfield."

"Greenfield! What were he doing away over there?"

"He's got an uncle that way. Or, should I say, he *did* have. Right owd fella he were. His mam's oldest brother. Well, I've not set eyes on him for donkey's. He'd no other family, mind, but he liked to keep himsel' to himsel'. Any road, poor owd sod, the cold spell's done for him."

"Ee, that's sad news. I'm sorry for tha loss."

"Oh, nay! Really, tha needn't be! He were owd and right peevish by all accounts."

Ann smiled but shook her head in half-earnest admonition.

"I know, I know, I shouldn't speak ill of t' dead. 'Specially when they're still warm." Then with a wink, "'Cept he weren't!"

"For shame, Susan Wilson!" Ann couldn't help but laugh.

"Aye, I know. God forgive me, I shouldn't, not when we'll be feastin' tonight!" And she grinned again, clutching her hands together in delight. "Thing is, this uncle had a small plot of land up that way. Grew a right grand lot of roots and herbs. And chickens! Can tha believe it, he kept chickens! Half a dozen of 'em!"

"Goodness."

"Course we couldn't really keep 'em 'ere."

"Nay. Tha's not wrong there."

"So, Davy's already wrung 'em! Dead like their old fella! Well, actually he gave two, still alive, to t' neighbour what looked out for his uncle. It were him that came to let us know. Seemed the right thing to do. Which means he's brought back four. With tatties and parsnips and thyme and rosemary and all sorts. There were eggs too, but Davy couldn't work out how to bring 'em all this way wi'out 'em getting smashed." She paused a moment, her face sagging into a pretend sulk. "It's all right for him! *He's* had a right grand breakfast of 'em! It's such a shame. There's nothing I like better than a boiled egg, wi' a bright yeller yolk melting in t' middle." She sighed, but the smile didn't leave her face for long. "Still, ne'er mind. We've got more than enough to fill our bellies 'til Easter!"

Ann was smiling too, sure that Susan wouldn't come bragging without including them in some way in this good fortune, but as nothing had yet been suggested, she simply offered her congratulations.

"Oh, but, Ann, luv, that's the best bit. We want thee to have one of 'em! Mima, go on." Susan looked meaningfully at the door, and Jemima went back out to the staircase, where they'd evidently left something. When she came back in, the girl was holding a platter bearing a small, badly plucked chicken, its dry, red claws dangling from the plate, together with some carrots, two large, muddy potatoes and, balanced on top of it all, a bright green knot of herbs.

This was far more than Ann had dared hope for. "Oh, Susan! Is tha sure?"

"Aye, of course, lass. Like I said, this is the best part. Tha's always been a good neighbour to us and we want thee to share in it." Then, with a wink, she added, "Any road, it's the smallest one! And Davy loves his parsnips, so tha's not getting any of those!"

Meanwhile, Walter had ventured over, uncertain at first, but increasingly fascinated by the white, pimpled flesh of the chicken and its irregular tufts of feather. He paced round the table, his own eyes wide and fixed on those of the bird which stared, startled, into space, in a look of arrested alarm.

"Ee, lad, int this grand? Aren't our neighbours kind?"

Walter didn't reply, but for once, Ann was glad of his strange intensity, distracting the others, as it did, from her own reaction, and an unsuccessful attempt to blink away a steady flow of tears. Not accustomed to shows of emotion, Ann ordinarily frowned upon crying, and, even now, overcome with her friend's generosity as she was, she roughly batted at the unbidden tears with the back of her hand. But when Susan tactfully made to retreat, wafting her arm as though to say "It was nothing", Ann lurched forward awkwardly, urgently reaching for her hand, as she said with feeling, "Thank thee, Susan, thank thee."

* * *

Later, a small fire was burning with coals also supplied from the Wilsons and the chicken already browned and oozing its fatty juices, when Nancy arrived home from the mill.

"Mam, Walter, tha'll never guess..." She stopped in the doorway, astonished at the mouth-watering aroma, and looked around, speechless, in search of an explanation.

Walter raced up to her, "Mrs Wilson gave us a chicken!"

With a gasp, she scooped him up into her arms and, hoicking him onto her hip, jigged delightedly around the room as Ann, who was tending the meat, explained about the old man in Greenfield and the Wilsons' good fortune.

"Oh, Mam, I didn't think today could get any better!" Nancy grinned. "I've some good news mi'sel an' all."

"Oh aye," said Ann, immediately suspicious. Inured to so many disappointments, she feared for her daughter's excitement.

"Aye! Tha'll never believe it, Mam, I'm going to be taught to read!"

"Eh?"

"Read! I'm going to learn how to read."

"But what about wuk? Tha can't miss that."

"Aye, Mam, let me explain, will thee?" Nancy rolled her eyes. "It were after lunch today, a lad were sent up to speak to Yates. Said *I* were to go and see Mr Henshaw, down in t' office. Well, I had no mind what it were about, and so's off I go, all puzzled like, and when I got there, Henshaw were sat behind his desk, waiting for me, looking right serious and solemn. Gave me a bit of a fright, if I'm honest."

"Why? What's tha mean by that?"

"Oh, nothing. I were just a bit nervous, tha knows what them lot are like."

Ann lifted the chicken, bronzed and shiny, off the heat and, with a long-pronged fork, held it steady over a bowl to collect its juices, which gushed golden at first and then slowed to drip with a satisfying plop.

"Oh, Mam, it smells delicious!"

Walter was circling the table now in a skipping dance of his own. "Is it ready yet, Grandma?"

"Not long, lad, not long."

"Any road," Nancy resumed her story, "turns out new master's keen on improving t' workers. Like some of those mills up north that school 'prentices. So, when spring comes, they're intending on giving the children a couple of hours' daily instruction. Says they don't get enough at Sunday school, them's that go at all."

"I see. Well, I suppose that *is* good news, 'specially for our Walter."

Nancy's smile faded. Ann knew Nancy was troubled by the idea of Walter entering the mill. She'd told her time and again she'd have to get used to it, they mustn't spoil the lad, he would need to work. However, this time she held back. This time she was more concerned to discover exactly why Nancy had been singled out.

"But what's it to do wi' *thee*, Nancy? Why's it *thee* needs to learn?"

"That's the thing, Mam," Nancy began, on the edge of irritation again. "They want someone to assist in t' school. There'll be a schoolmaster, of course, but there's that many children, he'll need help keeping 'em in order at fust and then, later, wi' reading itself. So, they've asked me! I'm to be taught straightaway, so's I'll have an idea what it's all about by time schoolroom's ready. I'll work me shift as usual until the afternoon *and* I'll get an extra sixpence a week into the bargain!"

A smile spilled over her lips, and her eyes sparkled in the candlelight as she settled at the table. Walter, responding to her mood, laughed happily and came over to playfully twist his fingers in the curls of her hair.

"Look, Walt! Look what I've got," Nancy reached into the pocket of her apron and pulled out several rectangular cards, each bearing what Ann knew to be a single letter, together with a slim volume which she recognised as a primer, not unlike the one Edward had learned from.

Nancy sat Walter down beside her and spread the cards out on the table, spacing them with a reverent care.

"But tha still hasn't answered me. Why *thee*?"

"Why not?" Nancy snapped.

Ann turned away, as though to give all her attention to carving the bird, though she made sure Nancy caught her frown. From the corner of her eye, she could see her getting annoyed, ready to protest, in danger of giving way to petulance, just as she'd always done ever since she was a girl, as she repeated with barely disguised indignation, "Why not *me*, Mam?"

Ann looked directly at her again. How beautiful she was, even in a temper. It made her anxious – but then, Nancy always did. She felt it now, that familiar, nervous twist in her belly, the same sense of foreboding. What was it she'd get up to next? She shook herself a little to try and dispel the feeling and at the same time dislodged a stray flake of browned meat from her hand, which she duly popped in her mouth. At once, an almost forgotten flavour, moist and unctuous and completely delicious, slithered down her throat. Instinctively, she closed her eyes to savour the sensation and was straightaway taken back to the heat of her farmhouse kitchen, the same smell of a roast on the spit and Nathaniel – oh, love – back from the fields, breathing cold, clean air and coming up close to her from behind.

When she opened her eyes again, she'd come to a decision. Life was short and cruel, and full of every kind of hardship and worry. But for tonight, just for once, perhaps she should be done with it and put away her fears? Aye, just for this one night, she'd stop her fretting and allow them all to enjoy their good fortune.

"Aye indeed. Why not, Nancy Kay? Tha's a rare spark, and that's no lie."

Nancy's head started up, astonished. Ann nodded, acknowledging her surprise with a small smile, and Nancy beamed back at her, returning to the cards on the table with a contented sigh.

"But shift 'em now," Ann added, picking up the ladle, "dinner's ready!"

ELEVEN

JOSEPH

I know you may hear different, but I swear, you'll not get a dishonest account from me. Some might say I'm not to be trusted, but believe me, I'll tell you exactly how it was.

I wasn't straight with her. That *is* true. But then again, don't forget, she wasn't all that honest with me neither, was she? And it's not as though I don't wish I had been. Perhaps it would've changed things. Or perhaps not.

The thing is, what I never told her – one of so many things – was about the beginning of it all. The *start* of my attraction to Nancy. For me, you see, it actually began long before she knew. Yeah, first time I set eyes on her, Nancy Smith, Nancy Kay, whatever folk called her, it wasn't when she thought it was. Or when I let her believe.

Truth is, it was back in the January of that year. Me and the lads, we'd been waiting for days for the snow to melt, so's we could inspect the new land at Ancoats, and we'd finally got word to go that afternoon, a day or so after the thaw, even though the ground was still that boggy my boots ended all clarted in mud.

It was dusk by the time we were done, and stars already stealing on the sky, which was clear above the reach of the chimney smoke. I was going into town, in the opposite direction to the other lads, so's I was walking on my own, hands in my pockets against the cold. I was just coming alongside the entrance to Wrights' mill when, of a sudden, out of nowhere, I found myself walloped in the chest and all the wind blown out of me. It took me a moment to realise a girl had turned out from the gates in an excited rush and walked straight into my path.

Need I tell you? It was Nancy.

I looked down at her, looking up at me, a sheepish face, like a naughty child, already half-giving way to laughter.

"Oh, Lord, I'm sorry! Did I hurt thee?"

"I'm fine," I said, recovering my breath. "But what about you?"

"Oh, I'm grand! I'm absolutely grand!"

Even though we were in shadow, I could still make out her face, shaped like a sweetheart it was, and alive with happiness. She waved something then, it looked like a slim book, high up in the air, almost in triumph you might say. I was interested, I confess, and hoped she'd linger to explain herself, but before I knew it, she'd already walked past me and was heading off into the gloom.

"Goodnight," I shouted after her, but I didn't hear a reply and some rogues who were loitering by the canal started laughing. Well, if you must know, it got right under my skin. I'm not often poked fun at, any more than I'm ignored by a pretty lass, and I didn't take kindly to either.

"Cut it out, you fuckers," I yelled and took to my heels, away out of Ancoats as fast as I could.

SPRING

ONE

"'Manchester and Liverpool com... com... mer... commer... commercial coaches.' Well, I got that from t' picture! 'From the...'"

"'Angel', that says 'angel'."

"'From the Angel Inn, Dale Street, Liverpool. And Roy... al... Oak?'"

"Aye. 'Oak.'"

"'And Royal Oak, Market Street Lane, Manchester.' Aye well, that one's not hard, seeing's Smithy used to lose half his wages in there every Sat'day."

Charlie shook his head ruefully. Nancy bent over the newspaper again.

"'Nathaniel'." She recognised that, no bother. "Like me dad," she smiled, and Charlie nodded. "'Nathaniel Sher... wood, re... turns his grate... ful thanks to the public for the great en...' eh?" She looked up, baffled.

"'Encouragement.'"

"Ah! 'Encouragement he... has...' Let me see." Her face screwed up in concentration. "'... Ex... perienced?' Yes, 'experienced and re... spect... fully in... forms them that a coach leaves each of the said inns at ten o'clock, in the morning, stops for dinner at the...' What?"

"'Eagle and Child'."

"'Eagle and Child in Bridge Street in...' Now then, oh, is it, 'Warrington'?" This was going well.

"Aye."

"'And arrives at the re... spec... tive places at half-past five.'" Nancy hurried these last words excitedly, "There, I did it!"

"Aye, you did. Very good. Very, very good. I'll hand it to thee, Nancy, you're a right quick learner."

"Aye, well we've got through a fair few candles these past months, I can tell thee!"

Ever since Henshaw had made his surprising offer, through to spring, Nancy had been tutored in the rudiments of reading and writing by none other than Charlie Bell. Henshaw had consulted with the senior clerks as to who might be willing to assist, prior to the engagement of a tutor for the school, and Charlie had been selected as the most patient amongst them. Every other day, he and Nancy had been permitted to take half an hour from their duties, and Nancy would duly make the journey down from the mule room, across the yard and up the steps to the office, just as when she'd made her appeal to Captain Wright.

Charlie would clear the surface of the desk in the middle of the room and bring over another chair for Nancy to sit beside him. At first, she'd been painfully self-conscious, not so much in front of Charlie, who was surprised and pleased by the turn of events, but because the lesson was conducted in that serious room in front of the other clerks. Often, she caught them peering at her over their ledgers, or else the curious stares of any other Tom, Dick or Harry who chanced to come by the office. She was grateful Charlie had the tact to understand this without her having to say. He would keep his own voice soft and low, and never asked her to speak up, even when she read in barely more than a whisper, her head lowered close to the page. Or else he'd pretend not to notice the self-protective arm with which she'd screen the slate upon which she tried to copy the letters she was learning in uncertain, wobbly lines of chalk.

Even so, she progressed rapidly. Her evenings, after Walter was put to bed, were spent in study, as she advanced without difficulty from the primer to word lists, spelling tests and the Lord's Prayer. She was improving all the time and soon became less concerned about being overheard than to ensure she read as much as they could fit into their short half-hour together. It meant that during the rest of the week – the stretches at the mule and her duties at home – there was added a new frustration: being taken away from these studies.

The truth was, she hardly dared believe what was happening in those hours bent over the page. How all those puzzling lines and circles of Edward's books, all the strange loops and small dots, which she'd tried so hard to work out for herself in the snatched moments when her mother's back was turned, were at last being explained to her, their mysteries gradually unfolding like the petals of the scattering of flowers bursting on the canal bank.

Now the days were lengthening, it was only half-dark when her shift finished, and the chill which had lingered into March finally lost its nip, so that the promise of the season, leaves in bud and bluer skies, corresponded with a transformation in her own outlook. Confidence in her new skill thrilled through her, like sap rising, feeding a fresh optimism for the future and especially for Walter. Maybe his path wasn't as inevitable as she feared. Perhaps she might yet be able to earn enough to avoid the necessity of him entering the mill after all. Daring to dream, she'd kiss him goodnight and retreat to the lamp on the table and an open book.

One afternoon, a few weeks before Easter, her spirits were buoyed still further by an altogether unexpected incident. She was grappling with another of Charlie's exercises – an advertisement again, this one from a London paper. It was for a travelling circus, and the words painted such fine pictures, it seemed to Nancy as though the whole show had sprung to magnificent life, right there and then in front of her. It was an extraordinary world of striped Bengal tigers and performing elephants and all manner of wild and exotic beasts prowling: leopards, panthers, and laughing hyenas – though she'd no notion what one of them was – not to mention the terror of Europe's largest, snarling lion, who merited an entire inked portrait of his own, sharp teeth glinting. She smiled to herself, imagining Walter listening to it all. How he'd love it, and how his eyes would grow round with astonishment.

It was just as it occurred to her to ask Charlie if she could take the paper home, when a quiet knock disturbed the hush of the clerk's room. One of the men called, "Enter", and she looked up to see a young boy step inside. Without thinking much of it at first, she noticed he was cleaner and more smartly dressed than the other children who worked in the factory. He had colour in his cheeks too, as though he were outdoors more often. She frowned a second and then returned to the newspaper. After a moment, however, something still niggled. The lad was strangely familiar, and she wanted a closer look.

He was still waiting for the fastidious clerk with spectacles, the one who'd ushered her into Captain Wright's office, and he'd evidently been instructed to bide for a reply to the message he'd delivered. He stood upright, patient and polite, displaying more maturity than his short stature suggested. Then, as he reached to remove his cap, she saw a distinctive crop of straw-coloured hair.

"Johnny!" she cried aloud, and the boy, who'd not yet spotted her, turned and broke into a wide smile of recognition.

The clerk, who was preparing the note for him, glanced briefly over his glasses at her, sniffed shortly and handed Johnny a piece of paper, sternly directing him to hurry along. But just as the lad stepped out, he delighted her by turning again to give her a last cheerful wave. She was still grinning as the door shut behind him.

"Oh my goodness, that were Johnny Clegg!" she whispered to Charlie when he was gone. She could hardly believe it was the same boy; he looked so happy.

"Aye, that's right."

"He were t' one who lost his finger on t' mule that day."

"Aye. Poor beggar. But things have looked up for him since."

"How so?"

"I believe new master's taken an interest in him. Discovered he weren't being treated right by that uncle of his. He's living at Mrs Booth's place now. And working as an errand boy."

Unlike a lot of the older mills beyond Manchester, Wrights had not established an apprentice house and, like many of the factories in town, employed free children who lived with their families at home. Nevertheless, one of the kindlier steps Silas Wright had taken during his time as master was to put in place arrangements for those children who found themselves orphaned whilst working at the factory. With Wrights paying their board and lodging, Mrs Booth, the widow of a former manager, housed and fed them and sent them off to the mill each morning. It wasn't a fine house, nor was Mrs Booth particularly motherly, but she was decent and fair and the children, in many cases, found themselves better off than when they'd lived at home.

This news of Johnny Clegg's change in fortune occupied Nancy's thoughts for the rest of the day. She could hardly believe the lad's transformation from abject misery to such quiet self-assurance. Nor could she ignore the fact that here was another instance of Captain Wright's benevolence.

Ever since she'd begun her studies, Nancy had hoped she might see Wright to thank him, but all these weeks had gone by without so much as laying eyes on him. Disappointed, she'd concluded the time of her lesson didn't coincide with his hours at the mill. Either that, or he'd decided not to take an active role in the business after all.

That evening, she lingered on a stretch of grassy bank along the edge of the canal. It was not yet so foul-smelling as in summer, and the softening light sparkled on the surface of the water. She had not stopped reflecting on Wright's intervention in both her own life and Johnny's. On seeing the lad again, so vastly improved in fortune, she'd felt a renewed stirring of gratitude and the same frustrated impulse to thank him.

At the same time, there were other feelings too, peculiar and indefinable, not of a nature she wished to examine. She chewed at her lip. She'd been wrong. Lord, how poorly she'd misjudged him. How ridiculous her display of disdain and how mean-spirited. To think she'd hoped he could read her feelings, plainly hostile, as she'd flounced, like a fool, out of his office. Oh, it was too awful. Mortified, her hands came up unbidden to hide her face.

TWO

Since the evenings had begun to lighten, Samson had taken to spending more time at the mill; a practice which was no inaccurate measure of his deeper involvement in the enterprise, though it was also, more precisely, borne out of his desire to avoid long, drawn-out evenings in Adelaide's company. It was with this particular object in mind, one spring morning over breakfast, he welcomed her proposal to relax her mourning observances for the evening, having been requested to make up numbers for cribbage at Hugh Osborne's next door. Samson had offered the polite assurances he perceived she required – No, no, it was not too soon. No, no, Silas would wish it – whilst at the same privately determining to seize the opportunity. That afternoon, he swiftly finished up his correspondence, bade farewell to Henshaw and left the factory a good two hours earlier than his custom, with the singular intention of enjoying the freedom of the empty house.

As he emerged from the factory gates, a light breeze was blowing the chimney smoke behind him, so that the sky ahead appeared almost clear. Low-slanting rays streamed from fine cloud, gauzily hitting the surface of the canal, transforming it into liquid gold. How lovely it looked, he observed to himself, though it made him smile to do so; how his former self would have scoffed at the possibility of beauty in such a place.

After that, he noticed signs of spring everywhere: the trees dotted irregularly down the towpath puffed up with blossom, a patch of grass a little further along, dense with sturdy daffodils and, above the relentless sound of the machines, the chirruping music of birdsong. It was novel to him, this sense of well-being, and as he strolled through the bustling streets towards the centre of town, he found himself smiling at strangers, his thoughts wandering cheerfully on what he might be able to achieve in this place.

In the weeks that had followed his idea for the school, he'd often looked out of his window at the hour of Miss Kay's lesson. He had a good view, giving directly onto the yard, and he'd watch for her to emerge from the door in the factory opposite. A slight figure in her cap and shawl, almost indistinguishable at first from the other girls, it was her brisk approach, and the way she looked up at the office with such eagerness that singled her out, that made him quickly step away from the window, not wanting to be seen, conscious of a certain lightness in his chest.

He had resolved not to meet her face to face whilst she studied. In any event, there was really no need for him to speak to her at all. Henshaw had done as he'd instructed and put in place the whole scheme. Even so, he continued to regret how he'd handled their last encounter and regarded it as a kind of unfinished business. Nevertheless, until the school was ready, he knew well enough to keep out of her way.

"What the devil...?" A hoop, trundled inexpertly by a young boy, was rolling straight towards him. Quickly, he stepped out of its way, though it still clipped his ankle, sending the thing clattering to the pavement.

"Begging your pardon, sir," said the boy, who didn't wait to see how his apology was received as he dived at Samson's feet to reclaim his toy.

"Not to worry," Samson laughed good-humouredly, watching after the boy, who was already on his way, the hoop once again wobbling precariously from one side of the pavement to the other.

He looked around now, surprised to find himself already at the corner of Mosley Street and Charlotte Street, the façade of the Portico rising above him. It brought to mind his conversation with Eli Chadwick's amiable wife. Once again, he resolved to enquire about a subscription. From all he'd gathered about the library, its newsroom was frequented by a great many progressive-minded men like Chadwick, quite unlike the rest of the company he'd met at Adelaide's dinner party. Perhaps he would seek Chadwick out, or else acquaint with others with whom he might sensibly discuss his plans for the school.

Encouraged by the prospect, he turned briskly into Charlotte Street, taking the steps up to the house in two great, vigorous strides, and entered the hall only to find Adelaide at the bottom of the staircase, displaying no evident sign of departure.

"Samson! You're back early."

"Aunt Adelaide," he gave an awkward bow designed to mask his dismay, "I thought you'd be out?"

"Ah, no. Alas not." She was standing at the threshold to the drawing room, her face drawn with anxiety, as Samson handed one of the maids his hat and coat.

"Is anything wrong?" he asked. Adelaide opened her mouth to reply but made a show of hesitation and, with a pointed look, indicated she was waiting for the maid to retreat out of earshot.

"Come in, come in, we'd be better in here." She looked down the hallway again and whispered, "There's been trouble in town."

Samson followed her into the drawing room and absently wandered over to the fire that had been lit despite the warmth of the evening, so that the room was oppressively hot.

Adelaide, letting out an exasperated sigh, swept back to the door he'd left open. Shutting it, she turned once again into the room, one hand behind her, staying the handle. "We mustn't unsettle the servants."

"No, indeed," said Samson flatly, less concerned with Adelaide's intrigue than with the scuppering of his hopes for an evening alone. Quite sure she'd volunteer whatever was bothering her, he looked into the fire and considered how he might extricate himself as quickly as possible.

When he didn't speak, Adelaide dropped her hand and, inflating her chest, moved imperiously across the room to take a chair. "Mr Osborne arrived here unexpectedly, not an hour ago."

Samson took out a handkerchief from his pocket.

"I was quite taken aback with what he had to say."

He sneezed.

Adelaide waited for him to recover, but when he still failed to offer a reaction, she continued in hushed tones, "It seems there might've been a riot earlier. At the market. Not a quarter of a mile from here. A group of ruffians, snatching at produce. Acting in concert, you understand, and raising a cry for cheaper prices."

"Well, hunger is a powerful spur." Samson blew his nose.

"Fortunately, the constables arrived before it went to blows, but the magistrates are concerned." She paused. "Very concerned."

Samson took the chair opposite her, but rather than meet her eye, proceeded to neatly refold his handkerchief. He sensed her drawing herself up and knew that the tight smile she reserved for him was coming.

"Naturally, Mr Osborne has been called upon for his wise counsel. These things can get horribly out of hand. They have done before."

"I'm sure the constabulary can manage a skirmish or two."

"Well, yes, that's true enough," Adelaide conceded, and Samson nodded with a weary smile in the hope of bringing an end to the exchange. "Forgive me, Samson, but your sangfroid does rather belie a lack of experience."

He raised his eyebrows.

"You do understand these things will be manipulated by

those blackguard Jacobins? They use hunger for their own ends. They whip up a crowd and then unleash their suffragist nonsense."

"But so long as violence is avoided, I see no reason for alarm."

"Samson!" Her eyes bulged with incredulity. "These people don't know any other way but violence! They're motivated by hate and by jealousy and have no wit but to resort to their fists. Or stones. Or worse. And the pernicious slanders they heap upon us. Those who have the decency to employ them. Those who provide them with food and clothes. Ingrates, they are!"

Her face was lively with anger and the loose skin at the bottom of her neck had blotched red as she leaned towards him, emphasising her words with snatching gesticulation. "You don't know, you weren't here, but during the riots a few years ago, there were smashed windows and pillage all over town. Just imagine, they even occupied the Exchange, for heaven's sake! Oh, you've no idea how I feared for poor Silas's safety every time he left the door." It was her turn now to reach for a handkerchief, deftly dabbing the corners of her mouth where spittle had gathered.

"Aunt Adelaide," Samson began gently, forcing himself to recover from his disappointment for the evening and reminding himself of the woman's tragedies. She hadn't mentioned Robert, but no doubt she had feared for him too, venturing abroad into a violent town on a drunken spree. "You must try to calm yourself. I don't doubt you've known difficult times, turbulent times. I, too, know something of those."

"Precisely, Samson! Revolution! War! Look at France. You better than anyone should know where so-called reform leads. Violence! Looting! Blood on the streets! We can't let it happen here. We mustn't. These people have to be dealt with."

"And so they shall. And so they shall, if there's any violence to be apprehended. But why not be assured by Mr Osborne? The constabulary dealt with the disturbance at the market. No one was hurt, and walking home just now, I was in no danger."

"That's all very well, but these people are meeting and plotting all the time. Their numbers are growing. The magistrates have their informants, and they know trouble is brewing. They have to be stopped, and we must do all that we can to help."

Samson was silent, unsure of what she was proposing.

"We must do what we can to assert ourselves. We must be mindful of talk in the factory and discover any information to the authorities."

He slowly began to shake his head.

"Why, Samson? Why ever not? Why do you not support me?"

She stood up abruptly and began to pace the carpet, her right hand energetically working the ring on her left finger. Eventually, she stopped and stared down at him, calculating whether or not to go on. She was, however, too stirred to restrain herself for long. "Can it be, Samson, that you too are ungrateful? Do you forget what Silas has done for you?"

"Certainly not," he responded with feeling, though he knew at once there was no use in being offended. "You're quite mistaken, I assure you, if you perceive any ingratitude towards my uncle or, indeed, towards your own extraordinary generosity."

"I am very glad to hear it."

Samson bowed his head courteously.

"Well then, you'll instruct Henshaw straightaway that anyone discovered in reform activity, anyone attending a meeting, or circulating material… that any such person shall be punished by summary dismissal."

"Aunt!"

"Well then, by a fine… or dismissal, depending on the severity of the case."

"I can't think this is wise."

"Samson, it is necessary." She was by the fireplace now,

looking down upon him, her emotions seemingly mastered, as she added slowly, "Or else, I do believe we shall have to leave off the reading scheme."

Instantly his breath quickened, though just as quickly he sensed her eagerness for a reaction and strained to remain impassive.

"You do see my point, Samson?" she asked, coolly. "If there's no penalty for such behaviour, we can't very well be seen to teach the children their letters only for them to go home and read to their family the kind of filth that's being passed around?"

Samson regarded her in silence. It was feverish nonsense, of course. He wasn't even sure she believed her own argument, though he understood she felt quite certain to persuade him of her object if she attacked his dearly held plans. He shook his head, intending to stand up to her, but in the overheated room he found his thoughts were in disarray. A confused assortment of images floated through his mind, like a disjointed dream: his mother reading to a hall full of children, followed by his cousin Robert, drunk and laughing at Silas, who watched in disappointment, or else a pile of new books just arrived for the children and the smiling enthusiasm of his protégé, Miss Kay.

Adelaide's fears were surely inflated by her distress. When this latest seeming terror undoubtedly came to naught, her unreasonable injunction would soon be forgotten. Yes, the most important thing was to protect the new school. And, if it meant conceding the point to fend off her attack, then so be it.

"Very well," he bowed his head resignedly, "I'll inform Henshaw to speak to the workers, though perhaps it would have more authority if we say it is at your behest?"

THREE

The evening air was warm, and Nancy's mother had propped open both doors – their own and the front door – to allow in a light breeze from the yard, though the arrangement had the disadvantage of also admitting the stink of the privy. She was sweeping the floor and evidently hot as a sweat was beading her brow, so that Nancy, sat at the table bent over the primer she'd mastered weeks before, knew better than to complain about the smell.

It was the night before the first lesson was to be delivered in Wrights' new school and Nancy could think of nothing else. She had been introduced to the schoolmaster only that afternoon; a harassed young man, who'd been at pains to make clear he was only available a few short hours a day, being already engaged to tutor the sons of a gentleman who lived in the centre of town. He'd arrived at Henshaw's office ten minutes later than the appointed time, offering a perfunctory apology. When he'd noticed Nancy, his face had turned a picture of disdain and, as Henshaw had explained her involvement, he'd proceeded to look her up and down, openly perplexed. Nancy had lowered her eyes, smarting with embarrassment, fearful her chance might be snatched away at the very last moment, until she heard with relief Henshaw firmly shut down any objection.

"I should make it clear, it's Captain Wright's express instruction Miss Kay is to assist."

To which the young man had shrugged, already indifferent, observing absently, "Well, yes, what with twenty of the rascals, no doubt I'll need all the help I can get."

Having finished with the brush, her mother shut the broom cupboard, and, at the sound of the door, Nancy heard a high-pitched giggle from the bed. Walter was still not asleep. He was finding it difficult to drop off in these lighter evenings, especially as they continued to go about their chores. Instead, he'd take to entertaining himself with a low humming sound, interrupted every now and then with a little laugh.

"Walter, get to sleep!" her mother scolded so loud and sudden, the bedsheet shot in the air from his startle underneath.

"Whist, Mam. He's not mithering."

"He should be asleep by now," her mother snapped back. She was settling by the fireplace and looked dog-tired. "Tha's too soft wi' him. Tha'll ruin him for owt if tha's not careful."

"Oh Mam!" Nancy glared at her. "Will tha leave off?" Scraping back her chair, she picked up a lantern in one hand, and the primer in the other, and walked over to the bed. "If tha can't sleep, Walt, shall we take a look at this?"

She sat down on the edge of the mattress, setting the lamp on a stool at the side and hooking her arm round the boy, who'd shuffled over, delighted by her suggestion. They both ignored her mother's heaving sigh.

"Now then, darling, take a look." She pointed at one of the pictures. "See this here. What's it of, can tha tell me?" She smiled as his little face crumpled into concentration. "Does tha know?"

"A fish?" He blinked up at her.

"Very good, son. But not quite. Much bigger than a fish. Much, much bigger." His face was blank. "Does tha remember that story I told thee? About Jonah?"

"Oh! A whale!" He clapped his hands together.

"Aye, that's right. Clever boy." She playfully flicked her

finger down his nose and he giggled. "Well, Walter, I wonder if tha can hear this. Your name and whale, they both start the same? W… alter, W… hale."

He looked at her solemnly.

"Walter begins with 'W' and so does whale." She blew out the sound, "W, w, w."

"W, w, w," he joined in.

"And this is the shape of t' letter, 'W'." She pointed at the page again and traced her finger over the lines. "See, down, up, down up."

"Down, up, down, up, down, up, down, up, down, up." Walter was grinning and couldn't stop, "Down, up, down, up…"

"Ee, look what tha's started!" her mother exclaimed with irritation.

But Nancy only smiled again and whispered, "Well done, my darling! Well done, I'll have thee reading in no time!"

* * *

The next day, bent over the mule, forcing herself to concentrate on the whirring threads, Nancy kept finding herself glancing at the clock, her nerves thrilling as each hour passed. Yates, who remained in charge of the mule room, had been informed of all the plans and was instructed to release her at the appointed time; she'd only need a nod. Yet when the hour came, her heart sank, for straightaway she realised he was determined to be difficult. The man simply wouldn't look in her direction. Try though she might to gain his attention, with a cough or a wave, he resolutely avoided her eye. She should've expected it, she thought as she dragged off her cap and bid farewell to the spinners and set off down the aisle to beg his leave.

"It's almost five o'clock, sir," she said as she came up behind him. "Mr Henshaw wants me in t' schoolroom."

"Aye, as if I didn't know tha's about to shirk off."

He'd been like this these past few months, ever since

Johnny's accident. Unsurprisingly incensed by Wright's intervention over the fine, he'd been even more enraged by her promotion, complaining whenever she left for her half-hour to read with Charlie. How damn inconvenient for those left behind! It was beyond him, he'd shake his head, that such a brazen wench as she should be singled out. He'd deliver these thoughts loudly too, to ensure the other girls heard him over the noise of the machines, stoking the jealousy he knew very well a number of them harboured.

Today, though, Nancy was too fixed on her new role to care. She was determined to reach the schoolroom before the tutor and give him no excuse to find fault on her first day.

"Well, I'll be off then," she replied and, from the corner of her eye, she caught Mary grinning. It restored her mood at once. Defeated, Yates was mumbling another complaint, but Nancy simply turned away and strode to the door to step back into her clogs. Once her laces were tied, she looked over her shoulder again to Mary, who cast a quick glance at Yates's retreat, before sticking up her thumb and mouthing, "Good luck!"

Outside, all was bright spring sunshine. Its rays warmed her skin and hit the water of the basin, so white and dazzling, she had to shade her eyes as she stepped over the cobbles, and thereby failed to notice a figure ahead of her, also rushing towards the office. It was only as she reached the bottom of the steps and was able to look up that she caught sight of a gentleman's boots as their owner entered the building. The tutor had come already! She tutted aloud at herself with irritation, taking the steps at a run, still hoping to forestall him. Yet on charging into the clerks' room, she was confounded to find only Charlie and the usual clerks.

"'Ow do," said Charlie with a smile. "Teaching today, are we?"

"Aye," she said, distractedly, her eyes still searching the room, but when it became clear there was no one else there, she swiftly made for the internal door. "Wish me luck then, won't thee?"

"Good luck, lass, good luck, though tha won't need it."

The school had been created from a disused storage room on the floor above the offices. Henshaw had arranged for it to be cleared of its forgotten contents. Boxes upon boxes of old papers and yellowing plans, Nancy had seen thrown away, together with hulking fragments of obsolete machinery, no doubt kept in case they might one day prove useful, though, as it had turned out, left to rust until fit for nothing. Once emptied, the dusty space had been swept clean and its walls and timber floorboards limewashed. A rectangular blackboard had been fixed to the far wall and, facing it, a series of three wooden forms, one behind the other, had been wedged into the limited space. Up in front of the board, there was a lectern and a stool for the schoolmaster.

As she reached the top of the stairs, she saw, with relief, she was the first to arrive after all. She glanced back down. Where on earth had the man got to? She couldn't fathom, though at least it meant she had time to catch her breath, as she waited on the threshold, taking in the smell of the lime and the neat, airy orderliness of the room. She wondered what the children would make of it and hoped they wouldn't be too weary. Over the past few days, she'd been considering how she might begin to help them. How best to convey her love of learning? How best to fill them with the same excitement? And, above all else, how best to make them see that what they learned here, in this little room, could be the means of their escape from the mill altogether?

All at once the sound of a man's voice echoed downstairs and, without thinking, she hurriedly stepped over the threshold, her head cocked, straining to listen. But there were no more footsteps and when she looked about herself, she was surprised to find she'd entered the schoolroom at last, so clean and fresh and white. After another long moment, all remained quiet on the stairs. Aye, she was quite alone. Perhaps she could permit herself to look around?

First, she crossed to the long wall of windows opposite and

looked down upon the yard. How far off the factory buildings seemed from here! Then she turned into the room again and smiled at the pile of slates in the corner. As she made her way towards them, she ran her hand dreamily along the smoothed, wooden forms. Ah, it was all so wonderful! Almost as though she herself had entered the blank pages of an open book; one of new and exciting possibilities, with the future, as yet, unwritten.

Next, the tutor's lectern caught her eye, suggesting itself to her, and she hurried towards it, her clogs ringing loud over the subdued thrum of the machines. Then, as she gripped its sides and raised her chin, she found herself, in an instant, eye to eye with Captain Wright, whose tall figure now filled the doorway, watching her.

Straightaway, she jumped back, as though the lectern had burst into flame and, like a fool, knocked over the stool behind, sending it clattering to the floor. Once she'd righted it, she glared at it a second longer, before forcing herself to look up with a face scorched red with embarrassment.

"Perhaps we needn't have hired a schoolmaster after all?"

"Oh, please don't!" she bowed her head. All thoughts momentarily blurred by the sight of him at last and the frustration of her first opportunity to thank him. Oh, and by such mortifying vanity too. "No one were meant to see such foolishness."

"Not at all. You look quite the part."

Nancy examined the floor.

"I hear from Mr Bell you've made excellent progress."

She groaned inwardly again. By remaining silent, she'd allowed him to raise the lessons first, and it was all she could do to stop herself from clicking her tongue at her own stupidity.

"I was very pleased to hear it," he said, gently, coaxingly almost, so that now she was compelled to look at him. His eyes were as soft and sad as she'd remembered them.

"Sorry, sir. It's just… I…" she paused, urging herself to be calm and clear. "Sir, tha has to understand, I'm overwhelmed

wi' what tha's done for me. I've wanted to thank thee so much.
I hope tha knows."

"Yes, I do."

For a moment they looked at one another, neither one
knowing what to say next. Then, from downstairs, there
was the bang of a door, swiftly followed by the chaos of
approaching children, shouts, coughs, laughter, the clatter of
boots ascending the stairs and, from further away, a distant
complaint, the tutor, late again, crying, "Let me through, let
me through!"

FOUR

He had almost mastered it, Samson thought, as his fingers traced the keys again, sending another cascade of notes circling round the walls of the study, his body at last beginning to inhabit the music, as his inner ear imagined the golden voice of the soprano, the woman singing as she spun. It was so wonderfully ingenious, this way the music had of forcing his hands at the piano to mimic the perpetual motion of a spinning wheel, the up and down rhythm of a treadle, whilst, at the same time, blending with the intensity of the poem in a perfect expression of longing and loss.

> "Ah, might I grasp
> And hold him!
>
> And kiss him,
> As I would wish,
> At his kisses
> I should die!"

By God it was astonishing; he had to try it again.

This time, he started out faster and more confident. His fingertips anticipating the revolving pattern of the notes, sensing and shaping the circular path of the music, which was just beginning to soar when, to his dismay, there was a knock at the door. Like a petulant child, he crashed his hands down on the keys and a discordant chord rang out.

"Yes," he heaved with an irritable sigh.

It was the maid, Ellen. She edged into the room, looking at him cautiously, clearly wary of his tone, "Beg pardon, sir, but mistress has sent me."

"Don't tell me. She has a headache?"

The girl dropped her gaze and nodded, though he thought he detected a fleeting smile break the surface of her solemnity.

"And she wishes me to desist a while?"

"Aye, sir." The girl's face relaxed a little, gratefully. "She's taken to her room wi' a vinegar tea and needs a bit o' quiet."

This had happened before, and on more than one occasion, and though he knew he was being uncharitable, he could not but observe that Adelaide only seemed to suffer such a complaint on those evenings she'd failed to organise some diversion for herself.

"Very well then," he said flatly, closing the lid of the pianoforte. "You had better go and see she has all she needs."

Ellen looked up at him now, offering a frown of sympathy. He shrugged and smiled back – it wasn't the poor girl's fault after all – and nodded towards the door to indicate she was free to go. She bobbed a curtsey and hastened away, but just as she was about to leave, she turned around. He looked at her enquiringly.

"For what it's worth, sir, I thought that last piece very fine."

"Thank you," he smiled at her again, widely this time, surprised and pleased.

When she was gone, he walked back to the piano and took up the sheet music. Dusk was falling, but there was still enough light to read by. He settled on the stool and began to make out the words, translating from the German as he went along. It was a slow and painstaking task. It took time and care to identify each word, to strain for its meaning within the piece, so that after only a short while he found he needed to sit back to rest his eyes. It occurred to him then, in this quiet moment of reflection, that the whole process, this careful construction of an idea from the letters on the page, was rather like learning to read in the first place, and the thought made him smile once again.

In truth, these days, his thoughts never strayed for long from recent events at the mill, and now he was content for them to wind once more in an inevitable direction, like a path homewards to the newly opened school. By the time it was dark enough to require a lamp, he found he was not as depressed by Adelaide's injunction as he'd expected.

* * *

When Samson had met Nancy in the schoolroom, he'd been gratified to see her studies meant as much to her as he'd hoped. Although there hadn't been the opportunity to say all he'd wanted to say, he was happy they seemed to understand one another. Now the silence between them was broken, and Nancy so often in the office, he felt he might relax his self-imposed reserve, and at last make apology for his original tactlessness.

It was for such purpose, the following week, he permitted himself another early visit to the schoolroom, though when he arrived, he found to his surprise, the class was already in progress. Not wishing to disturb the lesson, he slipped in quietly at the back, so the children were none the wiser, though the tutor himself seemed disgruntled by the scrutiny. After a short while, Samson understood why. Though the man was competent enough, it was clear he would have struggled to maintain control without Nancy's assistance. For it was she, and not the tutor, who truly held the children's attention, encouraging the little ones to look to the front and placing her finger over her lips when chatter threatened.

On that occasion, Samson had only succeeded in exchanging a smile with her before one of the clerks from downstairs had sought him out and he'd been obliged to leave, his plan frustrated. After that, he found he had to be out of town for a few days, attending to business in Liverpool, so that another week passed by before he could try again.

This time, he was determined to speak with her before the afternoon's lesson got under way, but just as he set out from his office, Henshaw emerged from his own room and waylaid him on the stairs. Had he forgotten the pressing matter of the disputed contract? Their lawyer had just arrived to discuss it. The meeting had been arranged for some time. There was no question but that Samson must join them. Irritated, he turned back down the stairs to Henshaw's office, where, much to his chagrin, the whole business turned out to be an altogether unimportant and dull affair. In the end, he didn't arrive at the schoolroom until the lesson was almost over.

Although the children were still reciting the alphabet, the tutor was already putting on his jacket and Nancy was beginning to take in the slates. From his vantage at the threshold, Samson spotted one of the older boys lean forward and pull a pigtail from under the ragged cap of the girl in front, who whipped round crossly, her eyes narrowing on the culprit as she reached over to pinch his arm. The ensuing yowls and shouts and laughter brought the proceedings finally to a close, as the noise rose into a great clamour to leave, and then receded again, just as quickly, with the children's footsteps trailing downstairs. The tutor now set off towards the door as well, seemingly anxious to make an appointment elsewhere. Samson bade him farewell, already half-watching Nancy, who had settled down at the end of the front bench.

He stepped towards her, "Good afternoon."

She was wiping off the remaining chalk from the slates and stacking them neatly at her side and stopped to look up, smiling at him in surprise, as though welcoming a friend, "Afternoon, sir."

He felt that familiar lightness in his chest again and hesitated. She had not stood up to greet him, but instead resumed her task, so that looking down at her now, he felt the awkwardness of his height while she remained so self-composed and sure of purpose. He was reminded of the resolution with which she'd first come to him in his office, her fists clenched for nerve and a brave raised chin. The memory emboldened him in his own wavering purpose. He knew he must talk to her, and he pulled out his coat-tails behind him and sat down determinedly on the bench beside her. "So, how are you finding the teaching life, Miss Kay?"

"Very well, sir, though I'm hardly a teacher!"

"Well, it seems to me you're well suited to it."

"Thank thee, sir." She moved slightly, setting herself at an angle to speak more directly, her head held a little to the side, rather like a bird he thought. "In fact, sir, I should perhaps thank thee twice over. Once for tha kind observation and once again for the opportunity in t' fust place."

"No, no, you don't need to keep thanking me," he spoke sincerely. Nevertheless, for his own sake, he was pleased she'd raised it. It meant he was at last able to say, "Miss Kay, I believe I may have grieved you that day when you came to my office."

Instantly, her cheeks flared red as her eyes fixed on the slate in her lap, and he knew for sure he had been right.

"I raised the question of reading too directly. It was badly done, and I regret it very much." There, it was said, and for a moment he was glad. Yet, as another long moment passed, and she continued to remain still as stone beside him, he eventually began to wonder if perhaps he'd somehow caused her offence again, "Miss Kay, Miss Kay... I'm sorry—"

"Please, no!" she spoke at last, turning on him so wildly, he instantly drew back along the bench, his heart thudding in certain dread he had once more done the wrong thing.

"Please don't say tha's sorry," she cried again, but now he saw, with a flood of relief, this was a different distress and her bright eyes were filled with a kindness that radiated towards him. "Tha mustn't, tha really mustn't. Don't tha know, all that's happened since is beyond measure? How can tha possibly worry about any foolish umbrage I took? And so hastily, mind. Nay, it is I should say sorry to thee for jumping to conclusions."

He shook his head, "No, no."

"I mean it, sir. Tha cannot know what tha's done. Tha may think it sounds daft, but I feel as though I've been given a whole new life!"

He smiled broadly at her, unable to speak, floored by her happiness.

"I don't know how to put it," and she bit her lip in concentration. "I suppose tha might say, I feel more fully in t' world. A part of things at last. Connected, like. Does tha know what I mean?"

"Yes," he said huskily. His mouth had turned dry and he sounded strange to himself. She must think him foolishly inarticulate.

"It's as though I could finally do summat wi' me life. For me and for other folk too," she paused to take a breath. He followed her eyes as they swept around the room. "All this. This opportunity. Tha must understand, it's wonderful to me, sir. Just wonderful. I just wish…" She stopped abruptly, seemingly overcome with self-consciousness.

"What is it?" he frowned.

She bit her lip again.

"What is it you wish?"

"I'm sorry, sir, I were forgetting mi'sel."

"No, no, you must tell me what you were going to say."

"It doesn't matter."

She averted her gaze through the window, but Samson was determined to establish what she'd so passionately wanted to convey, bending his head forward, forcing her to look at him, his eyebrows raised in pressing enquiry.

"All I were going to say…" she started reluctantly. "The thing is, I love that I'm *able* to read. I just wish I had *more*! More to read, I mean. We have a Bible at home, of course, and I get me hands on the occasional paper. But Mam says we can't spend on owt that's not necessity, so…" She shrugged and her words trailed away.

"Of course!" Samson exclaimed, at once reproaching himself for not thinking of it before. "Of course, you must want books! Why, you can borrow mine. And I'll gladly let you have my newspaper once I'm finished with it."

Her face flushed pink again. "Nay, nay, nay, sir! I don't want tha thinking I were complaining. Or that I were asking for more."

"Nonsense! It would be no trouble to me. Indeed, it would be a pleasure." His thoughts were racing now, scouring his shelves of books, recalling his favourite writers and trying to imagine what she might best enjoy. "Perhaps you'd like to read some poetry?"

Yes, perhaps some from those modern fellows, he thought. That wonderful collection – Coleridge, and the other one, Wordsworth? Yes, indeed, William Wordsworth, and some Shakespeare of course. He pictured himself presenting them to her, offerings of beauty, like shining jewels, treasures to lay at her feet. By God, he was in danger of becoming quite absurd!

"Poetry?" She blinked at him. "Does tha really think I could follow it?"

"Of course!" he said warmly. "I shall bring you some tomorrow."

FIVE

JOSEPH

Why Nancy?

I still wonder. What was it about her made her stand out like she did? It's not like she was the most beautiful girl I've ever had, though she'd a pretty face, I won't deny. It was nowt obvious, that's for sure. She certainly wasn't one of those curvy, teasing types that can get a lad going with just a way of walking; I should know, I've had enough of them.

So, what was it? Why her? Well, if truth be told, it's not the sort of thing you can put into words, not easy like, not without sounding soft. But since I've begun talking this way, I suppose I'll be done with it and say it straight out. The thing about Nancy, the thing that really hooked me: she just seemed more *alive* than other folk.

I'd noticed her again since our collision in the dark... All right, all right, I *looked out* for her. Saw her most mornings, as it goes. She'd be making her way amongst workers off to the morning shift, alongside the canal towards Wrights, whilst I was forcing my way through the crowd in the opposite direction, to the plot on the far side of the mill where we were getting started on the chimney. Even though she was short, you couldn't miss her. There was too much spirit about her not to notice, a sureness in her step, a certainty about her. Every windswept spring morning, her head was up, wild hair frizzing, and she watching the world and all that went on, not like all the others around her, them with their eyes downcast, fixed only on their clogs.

And I swear it was as though she made me see more too. I mean *really* see things, as though for the first time. One morning, I remember 'specially, I'd given myself a thick head from too much ale the night before. Yeah, it was one of them dirty, great sore heads you get when pain throbs like hammer blows. I wasn't in the best mood, you understand, and dreading the prospect of a whole day up the stack. But as I came on close to Wrights, the sun was rising, and the sky ahead red, when I suddenly caught sight of her, set apart from the rush of folk, under a wide, old tree I'd somehow never noticed before by the side of the towpath. Balancing on tiptoes, she was. That slender body of hers stretching upwards to reach the tips of her fingers to the lower branches. I thought perhaps she was trying to pick something, but as I got closer, it was clear she was just wanting to brush her hand through the new leaves. It was like something a kid would do, and it made me stop, still a little way off, mind, as she'd never yet let on to me. And I swear I forgot my headache, watching her, half-laughing, imagining the pleasure of that stretch and the feel of the leaves upon my skin.

After she'd gone, hurrying off towards the factory, I couldn't help but step under the tree myself, and looked up into its spreading body above, as morning light streamed through the gaps between the boughs, so that when I looked down again, it seemed great chunks of me had been consumed by dark holes and I but a pattern of light and shade, dappled like the dirt track beneath me.

It was a knack she had, even then, even from afar, a kind of power to stir me and heighten my every sensation. And, by God, I liked it: that force within her. 'Cos for all life's not easy round our way, it's still for living, int it? Still good to

147

be young and alive. Good to feel your muscles stretch as you shift out of bed of a morning, good to feel the sun on your skin. Even better to taste the juice of wild berries wash round your mouth, like stolen kisses, sweet.

SIX

That such words should have been woven together, that someone, somewhere, had wrought them to such beauty, that even here and now, in another time and another place, they should have the power to whisper to her soul. With a deep exhalation, Nancy placed the book reverently in her lap, her face filled with incredulous wonder as she slowly shook her head.

She was crouching on an upturned bucket for a seat, bent forward into the soft light, which trembled from the lantern she'd positioned on top of the coal shed. Still absorbing the effect of the poem, her eyes cast around the dim shadows of the deserted yard, passing over the rude houses, the broken windows, the passage from the street lost to darkness, darting in a restless motion, unable to alight on something external that might begin to meet this stirring which burned so fiercely within. Only the night sky ahead seemed to answer, a black canopy strung with celestial jewels, semi-veiled in gossamer smoke drifting from the mill, as she imagined herself plummeting from the edge of the earth into its infinite vastness, feeling altogether and at once, immense as the heavens and tiny as a star.

Wait! Was that a cry? For a second, she thought she heard something from within. She'd come outside earlier to avoid disturbing Walter and didn't know how long she'd been reading, only that it had been light then, and now night had fallen. She listened intently, a frown creeping over her face, waiting to see if she was wanted inside. But there were only murmurings from behind other people's windows and the occasional slurred call from the street beyond, dulled drunkards staggering home from The Elephant or some other grog shop, whilst closer at hand, not five feet away, there was the incessant scratch and scurry of hungry rats. She'd been mistaken, there was no crying. Surely he'd be asleep by now?

She took up the book again and leaned closer in, leafing through the pages to find another one Wright had recommended. Her eyes squinted at the text in the gloom. But just as she'd begun to labour over another first line, there was a creak from behind, and their door opened.

What now?

Frustrated, she looked round, expecting her mother's disapproval, but found, with relief, it was only Jemima from upstairs, no doubt heading towards the privy.

"'Ow do?" Nancy nodded.

Jemima mumbled something in reply and stepped out over the cobbles into the shadows.

Nancy retrieved her place and started to read again in earnest, so that by the time Jemima came back, she was making good progress through the poem, her thoughts fixed entirely on making sense of the words. Unwilling to lose her thread, she didn't bother to look up, assuming the girl would retreat as morosely as before, but, only a few lines later, she heard a small cough beside her and turned around to discover Jemima hadn't gone inside after all. There she was, hovering, just beyond the glow of the lantern, in which light Nancy now caught a flash of her eyes, watching her intently.

"What's tha want?" She couldn't keep the irritation from her voice.

"Nowt," said Jemima, a little too quickly, and looked down at her feet.

"Doesn't look like nowt." She didn't move. "*Well?*"

"Nowt, nowt, it's nowt." The girl shrugged and looked into the yard, but just as Nancy decided to take her at her word and raise the book again, she added in a low voice, "It's just I were wondering… I wondered, is it hard?"

"Eh?"

"Reading, like. Is it hard?" She was mumbling again, but Nancy recognised this defensiveness all too well. "I mean, how easy were it to learn?"

"Not too hard." Nancy spoke gently. "Not really. Not if tha's got time and someone patient to help thee."

Jemima didn't reply.

"It's wonderful too. Once tha's got the trick of it. I'm reading some poems." And she held the book aloft with a grin. "Right grand they are an' all. Who'd've thought it, eh?"

Jemima stepped a little closer into the pool of light so that Nancy could make out her face all dotted with pimples, but even though the girl's narrow eyes remained intent upon her, Nancy still wasn't sure of their expression. Lord, what had become of the happy girl who would skip down the stairs to coo at Walter? Little gifts she'd loved to bring: a bird's feather to tickle behind his ear, a scrap of velvet ribbon he'd drag across his cheek and that ball she'd woven from willow with hard peas inside to shake. Now Jemima was a young woman, almost the same age as Nancy had been when she first arrived in Manchester, though looking at her in the lamplight, Nancy doubted she'd be troubled by the likes of a Richard Smith. It was an unkind thought, she knew, or might be considered so, but that Nancy envied her the freedom from that kind of attention and the heartache it brought, though she'd also seen enough of Jemima's sideways glances at the boys who wrestled in the yard to realise she'd never understand such envy, even if Nancy were so tactless as to mention it. Nay, it was clear the girl was wary of her and of the possibility of her pity.

"I'd help thee, Mima," she offered, lightly.

Jemima swallowed, as though about to say something, but then looked down at her feet again.

"If tha wants."

The girl didn't speak.

"It's up to thee," Nancy said, shortly now, needled this time by Jemima's reluctance, and turning back to the poem before it got too late.

But Jemima still didn't go inside. Instead, she pointed one of her clogs outwards and started to shift it, tracing a line in the dirt and then retracing it. Eventually she whispered, "Aye, maybe."

Nancy looked up.

"But don't say owt." Jemima cocked her head towards the Wilsons' window, and Nancy nodded with a complicit smile.

"Si'thee then," the girl managed at last as she slipped inside the door, leaving Nancy to roll her eyes to the empty yard; she'd need to go back to the first line.

It was tricky this one, and it took some time to reach the end, but when she did, she remained strangely unsatisfied. Even though it wasn't easy, she was sure she'd understood the nub of it, and beautiful though the words were, this one touched too raw a nerve. A doting father delighting in a beloved son. A boy with a happy future, growing up in the countryside, free. She bit her lip and tapped her fingers impatiently along the edge of the book as she read it through one more time,

"...For I was reared
In the great city, pent 'mid cloisters dim,
And saw naught lovely but the sky and stars.
But *thou*, my babe! shalt wander like a breeze
By lakes and sandy shores, beneath the crags
Of ancient mountain, and beneath the clouds,
Which image in their bulk both lakes and shores
And mountain crags."

Well and congratulations to thee, she thought. Aye, good for him, and his escape to the country. Good for him, whose boy'll know a life of comfort and joy, and none of the miseries of the town. Just as she knew nothing of this man or his world, the poet who seemed so pleased with himself, only that his words had managed to plumb a guilt so deep she rarely allowed herself to admit it. She turned back to the cover. One S.T. Coleridge. A man seemingly in love with the land of her birth. How he would've approved of their quaint old farmstead, she thought, as she pictured the little framed sketch propped on the mantel inside and decided this was not a poem to share with her mother.

Oh Lord! That really was a cry this time. All at once, she could hear the unmistakeable sound of Walter wailing. Grabbing the lantern, she whirled round, setting the rats off again, and hastened inside.

Her mother's candle was out, but from her own lamp at the door, she could make out the dark bulk of her, bent over Walter's bed. "That's enough now," she was saying, her words firm but not as harsh as lately.

"What's the matter?" asked Nancy, holding the lantern high, illuminating Walter, who was tousled and tear-stained and resolutely sitting up in bed.

"An apple," he sobbed, "an apple, an apple."

"Eh?" Nancy turned to her mother for an explanation.

"Don't ask me. Lad's hungry. Like the rest of us. But he seems to have got it into his head he wants an apple. Or there's someone wi' an apple to be had. I can't fathom why."

For a second, Nancy was as mystified as her mother, but then a thought occurred to her, and she swung the lantern away and over the table covered with books and newspapers and the reading primer they'd looked at earlier, discarded with its page open at the beginning of the alphabet. "'A' is for…" There it was! A picture of the inevitable apple shining in the foreground, a tree laden with fruit behind. Nancy wondered where the serpent himself was, it all looked so tantalising.

Her mother was trudging towards her now, about to look over her shoulder, and though she knew she wouldn't be impressed, Nancy didn't manage to shut the book in time.

"By, Nancy!" she exclaimed. "I told thee no good would come of it!"

"What?" Nancy wheeled round, bristling for a fight, but Walter had been drawing in great gulps of air between his cries and now began to cough and splutter violently.

"See to tha lad," her mother said and made off, back to her own bed.

Thrusting her lantern on the table, Nancy closed the primer, set the book of poems on top of it and blew out the flame.

"Hey, Walt, come on now, come on," she spoke firmly, but her sternness only served to increase his distress. Sighing, she lifted the blanket and got in beside him, feeling in the darkness the gathered ridge of tangled sheets beneath and a pillow sodden with tears. Sensing him near, she stretched out to draw him in, pierced as always by the jutting angles of his small bones, so limp and loose within his slip of a body, as though their embrace were the only thing holding him together. And then she began to rock them both, just as she had done when he was a baby, all the while lamenting she had no more milk left to give. Gently, she shifted, back and forth, shushing and shushing, over and over, until his moans eventually quietened, his tears subsided, and he felt heavier. All the storm's wild power blown out, she thought, as he lay exhausted in her arms.

Her mother had fallen asleep too, or rather her approximation of it with its fretful mutterings, and all else was silence, until, without warning, a great, gaping groan rumbled, like thunder from a cloud, and echoed round the walls, making her start in alarm out of her own semi-slumber. It took a moment to realise the sound had come from within: a loud whine of protest from a body whose own hunger had emerged during her tussle with Walter's, goaded from its quiet lair, like a predator tempted by a chop of meat, dangled just out of reach by the circus master, raw and carnivorous.

Prodding at her stomach to quieten it, she lay back down. Staring at the ceiling, she wondered whether Mr Coleridge or his beloved son had ever felt so famished. Or Captain Wright for that matter. Irritably, she shifted in the bed, trying to find a position comfortable enough for the meagre hours of sleep left to her, but when she shut her eyes, unbidden images came which she couldn't blot out. Food. A steaming bowl of stew, great chunks of tender beef, a thick slab of buttered bread.

Or else, a scene of mountain crags soaring above a crystal stream that ran onwards into an orchard full of blossoming trees.

She tutted aloud and bitterly. How was it everything had changed and yet nothing?

SEVEN

MARY

When folk got wind of what Nancy'd been offered, learning to read and teaching little 'uns, there was that much talk about the place and none of it kind. Most of 'em were just jealous of course. I wouldn't be surprised if it wasn't Molly Kennedy spread most of it. Her and that sister of hers who always sang to her tune. All of it laughable too. Suggestions of some attachment between Nancy and sobersides Henshaw. I mean, really!

Nobody but me and Nancy knew the truth, that Wright must've come up with it himself. Nancy thought perhaps it was 'cos she'd talked so much of a child needing a mother's love, and I confess I laughed at her for that and told her not to be so unworldly. But when I offered what I thought was the real explanation, that she was a right bonny girl and happen the master had taken a shine to her, if you know what I mean, she fair flared up at me and told me I was as bad as Molly.

She said sorry of course. And so did I. We weren't ones to fall out. I told her I wasn't implying anything on *her* part. And we both laughed then at the thought. Him being such an owd dour sort of fella. Nowt like t' other one she was about to meet. I speak of Joseph Price, you understand. Joe. A handsome devil if ever there was one. Golden hair, burnished skin, muscles that ripple like troubled water, nowt like any of the other hungry beggars round here. Aye, I suppose there's not many a lass could resist his outward charms. But if you want *my* opinion, he was always a wrong 'un, and I saw it mi'sel that day we first spoke with him, down at Knott Mill.

It was Eastertide, and the mood in town was, for a few days at least, that bit more cheerful, what with spring coming and folk making most of the factories being shut. My Mick had gone away for the holiday, over to the sea air of Liverpool to visit his mam, whose apron strings he'd never quite cast off. Her and the rest of her brood. They'd come from Dublin many a year since, but they'd none of 'em got further than Vauxhall Road. None of them aside from my Mick, who followed me back to Oldham the summer I were sixteen, after I'd spent a month or two with my sister who'd married a fella out that way. She'd been right sick after her first-born and needed a lift, and that's how I first got talking to Mick, who lived on the same street; me taking the air with the new babby in my arms.

Well, you probably know, it costs more than a bob or two to take the coach out that way, so's I'd said to Mick I'd stay at home. To tell truth, I was glad of the excuse, though I daresay Mick saw through it. Right from the start, his lot didn't much care for me, what with me stealing him away as they saw it, and not even a Roman too! And it only got worse over the years; aye, since there were no babbies of our own. I remember around about that time, I'd had just about my fill of their advice and conjecture and prayers to St Ann; their barely concealed amazement that a woman so wide in the hip should struggle in that regard and the whispers I'd imagine after I was gone of "barren bitch". So even though I was sad to see my Mick go, I was in no doubt at all, I was best off out of it.

Any road, what with me being on my own for the festivities, I'd suggested to Nancy we take a walk into town on Easter Monday, to see what was afoot at Knott Mill Fair. There's always entertainment down that way on Easter, like nowhere else I can think of for music and dancing and folk just enjoying themselves, right lively it is. But Nancy wasn't keen at first. Full of her reading, she was. Spending every last minute with her head bent over a book. Said she didn't want to waste the holiday. Besides, there was the problem of Walter and all. Her mam deserved a break, she said. She didn't want to leave him, same as every other day.

Well, I remember wondering why the lad couldn't just come with us, but since she was always that touchy about him, I said nowt and agreed to go call on them instead, though, I admit, I still hoped to pick my moment and persuade her to the fair.

When I arrived, it was Nancy who opened the door, with a smile as wide as usual, though she seemed a sight lost in thought as she asked me in, and once my eyes had grown accustomed to the gloom, I saw from the books and papers set out on the table, I'd interrupted more studies.

Her mam, who I only ever saw at chapel, was at the fireplace, bent over a heap o' socks she was darning, for a few pennies no doubt. She raised her head, nodded hello. From my reckoning, she'd be getting on fifty by then, but by, she looked a good sight older, and not at all well. Her skin wasn't just pale, it had a sort of clammy sheen to it; I suppose you might even say, waxy. She made no move to stand up or speak to me and carried on without a word.

Nancy, meanwhile, was bustling at the table, and I was left feeling a bit awkward, not knowing whether to stand or sit down. I'd been hoping to see Walter, but he didn't seem to be around. Perhaps playing outside, I thought. I knew he could be difficult at times, of course, but truth was, he was always right affectionate with me. Ee and that bonny! I suppose I was fancying a little dangle of him on my knee before he got too big.

"Here it is!" Nancy cried, and waved a newspaper at me, all excited.

I thought she'd just been tidying, but it seemed she'd been all the while looking for something particular.

"I've been reading about that Hunt fella, tha knows the one? Him who speaks on t' vote?"

"Aye," I said.

Indeed, there weren't many in Manchester hadn't heard some talk of reform by then, or of Henry Hunt and his way of speaking for the working man. Don't forget, things were especially hard that year. We'd all endured a terrible cold winter, and price of bread was sky-high. There'd been turn-outs all through '18, and not just weavers neither. Aye, most factory folk like us lived in constant fear of the layings-off which were forever whispered round town. That being so, most workers at Wrights were too afeared to join the clamour for the vote, 'specially since Henshaw, still loyal to the old mistress, had made it known anyone supporting reform would be punished, whether with docked wages, or worse.

"What a to-do he caused at the theatre that time!" Nancy laughed. For, you see, Hunt had been in Manchester earlier that year and broken up a performance at the playhouse in town. "Says he's planning on coming to Manchester again in t' summer." She pointed at the page for my benefit, though all them wavy lines meant nowt to me back then. "Does tha know, Mary, I'm minded to go along."

At this, Mrs Kay looked up sharply, and I decided not to voice my own opinion. Nevertheless, Nancy rushed on, "It's time, Mary! Time for us workers to speak up for oursel'! Reformers are getting organised all over t' North. And they need our support, else things'll never change."

I smiled warily, still with half an eye on the mother.

"I've been reading all about it. About vote and Parliament and lawmaking and whatnot, and does tha know, there's not a single man in th' House of Commons to represent Manchester? Now, I ask thee, how is that fair?"

"Nay, Nancy, it's not." But before she could go on, and alarm her mother any more, I changed the subject. "Now then, tell me, where's tha Walter? What's he up to then?"

"Walt? Why he's here," Nancy replied, as though it was

obvious, and she bent down to look under the table as I realised the little tinker had been crouched on the floor all this time. "He likes hiding here when I'm at me books."

"What? On a grand day like today?" I bobbed down to be level with him and smiled. "Why's tha not out in t' sunshine, Walter? Tha could go and play in t' yard?"

His eyes – by, with their long dark lashes, they've always been beautiful – they met mine, but only a fleet moment. Then he snatched 'em away again and seemed to curl his slight, little body even deeper into himself, almost as though he was trying to fit into the hollow of a shell.

"This is what he's like," Nancy smiled wearily as I stood up again. "He can't abide noise."

She looked out of the window into the yard, where some lads were fooling around in the afternoon sun, yelling at the top of their voices and breaking into peals of coarse laughter.

"What about if he's wi' thee? Does that help?"

"Oh aye. Tha likes to be with tha mam, don't tha, son?"

She bent down to him again, but he'd begun to hum, like he always does, a sweet, tuneful melody it was too, though I got the feeling, even then, it was to block us out.

"Well, how about we both take him on a little trip? Why not see what's going on at Knott Mill?" She was doubtful and gave me a look as though to say she thought we'd settled against. But, still, I pressed on. "And if it's too busy, we can just find a spot by the canal to enjoy the sun? 'Appen it's just what the pair of thee need."

Nancy seemed struck by this and gave a small nod, which I took to mean she agreed they needed it, but not necessarily that they'd come. She folded up the newspaper and set it down, casting a wary glance at her mother, whose expression was still hard to make out.

"Tha can get a bit o' peace, Mrs Kay," I said, laying it on thick with a respectful tone, not that she seemed a jot impressed.

"Is that all right wi' thee, Mam?" Nancy asked, and I

could see she was caught somewhere between an old childish instinct to please and a new desire to assert herself. Mrs Kay looked across, stony-faced, and after a long pause said in a flat voice, "Aye. But watch the lad."

I'd no idea until then what a difficult sort she was, Nancy's mam. Although I daresay I should be more charitable. It's not like she didn't have her reasons, what with worry for Nancy, all on her own in the world, and the boy with all his quirks. And when I think on it, knowing now what came next, she must have been falling proper poorly at that point too. But whatever was going on, I know I was right glad to be gone from the place and came away wondering how someone like Nancy could be the way she was with a mam like that.

At last, we three set off, heading towards the centre of town at a leisurely pace, out of Ancoats, beyond Piccadilly, strolling past all them fine, new buildings on Mosley Street which, with their pillars and porches, seemed like palaces to us. One of the most impressive is that library they put up. The Portico, they call it. Built to resemble a Greek temple, so they say, not that I'm any judge, but right elegant it is to look at, and when we got up aside of it that afternoon, I remember I couldn't resist teasing her, "Tha'll be going in there next!"

Well, I meant it for jest and thought she'd laugh and tell me not to be so daft, but instead she stopped right in the middle of the street and looked up at it in open admiration, and I swear I saw a glint of determination in her eye.

Any road, not two yards further, and I couldn't resist another chance for sport. This time, I cocked my head down one of the side streets, observing, "Ada and tha man live near here, don't they?" I knew she wasn't as easily offended on that account anymore, and she play-bashed my arm, as we both took to laughing and lamenting poor Captain Wright's misfortune to have found himself lodging with such an aunt.

Of course, as we were heading in the direction of Knott Mill, our path took us across the expanse of St Peter's Field. The whole spot seemed quite sparse that day, what with it being cleared for the making of a new road, and the grass that was left wasn't the greenest, a bit scrubby if truth be told. But it didn't matter. It was such a beautiful day. Still chilly, mind, but early spring sun was breaking out from behind cotton clouds, and singing birds swooped above us, to nests they were building in the trees that remained here and there. Walter, having gained a bit of confidence, was skipping ahead, and we drifted happily onwards, everyone around us dressed smartly, strolling with friends, not rushing on business, each with that same floating lightness when winter's finally done and all summer's ahead.

Ee, you'll have to wait a minute… I'm sorry… Nay, nay, I'll be right. It's just I can hardly bear to think on it now, how blithe we were in *that* place, that day.

Well, and let me tell thee about the fair instead. Mood was right jolly down there, what with all the folk milling about amongst the stalls with their brightly coloured awnings. Vendors were calling, and the air smelled right good with the scent of their wares. There was all sorts to buy, though none of us had owt to spend: cones of nuts and marzipans, peppermints and liquorice sticks and them plump little Eccles cakes crammed with currants. Not to mention all kinds of smallware too: snuffboxes and trinkets and toys for little 'uns, bilbo-catchers, nine-pins, tops and buzzing whirligigs. But, much to my amazement, Walter was interested in none of it. He didn't even stop at the striped booth where old Mr Punch was having a bash at Judy, even though we wanted to! Nay, above all the gay chatter and laughter, he turned to us with a look so intense, I stopped with a pang o' fear he was getting anxious. But I needn't have worried, 'cos he smiled broadly then and said, "Music! I can hear music!"

So that's what we did next. We followed him, following notes on the air, jostling through the crowd to a spot nearer the canal, where a large group had gathered on the grass around a band o' players, a half-dozen or so, who were belting out a right lively tune. Well, what with fiddles and pipes and a banging drum, it was very noisy, and yet, strangely it didn't trouble Walter a bit, not like other loud noises can. In fact, he was positively drawn to it. And so we stopped awhile to listen, and to watch the musicians at their instruments, and the lads and lasses in the audience, a fair few who'd clearly spent too much of their afternoon in the grog shop, a-swaying and a-swaggering and all a-flirt with one another. To tell truth, though, it wasn't long afore we were infected with merriment too and began to clap our hands and tap our toes, whilst Walter, his face alive with glee, set off on a joyous jig of his own. Lord, he was that fast and frantic, the rest of the crowd ended up cheering his performance as much as that of the musicians.

This went on for song after song, until eventually Nancy nudged me and, with a nod of her head, indicated a ruddy-cheeked woman with a harassed expression forcing her way through the crowd. She was dressed in an apron that was dirty with beer stains and had evidently come from one of the taverns down that way, as she was bearing a tray laden with tankards of ale which she held aloft for the lead fiddler to see.

"We best calm Walt down," Nancy said, and she was right, for he'd gotten beyond giddy by then. As he twirled past us, she tried to grab him, "Walt, Walt, this is t' last one. Last one... Last one, mind."

But he was not for listening and paid no heed, dancing on and on, unaware of the musicians signalling a break to one another, as they speeded up to a dizzying pace for a grand finale. Meantime, in front of 'em, Walter spun and spun, faster and faster, in a whirling world of his own, until the song roared to its rousing conclusion, and the music was done with a loud wassail from them with a drink, and all the rest of us cheered.

Straightaway, the crowd started to break up, but our little Walter, bless his heart, was still prancing on like an excitable horse. As the players set their instruments on the ground and moved to claim their quarts, they called over to him, winking at one another. It was only then, as one of their shouts carried across, it finally dawned on him the music was finished, and he almost tripped over himself coming to a stop. Ee, and then didn't his bottom lip start to quiver and his eyes well up with tears as the musicians and them that were left of the crowd started to laugh, not altogether kindly.

"Come on, let's get away from here," Nancy said, glaring at the men, so they were left in no doubt what she thought of 'em. She swept her arm round Walter, a bird's wing over a fledgling, and tucked him close to her hip, where he proceeded to clutch her thigh and bury his head into the folds of her dress, so that to move anywhere involved her in a sort of lurching limp, dragging him along with the leg he was clinging to, sobbing all the while and making a right show. Eventually, when we'd managed to put some distance between us and the scene, she stopped.

"Walt, that's enough now." Her voice so firm, he came out from her skirt, his beautiful face all mottled pink with tears. Then, bending her knees to get level with him, face to face like, her arms holding each of his to keep him in place, I thought she was about to give him a right to-do. Ee, but I was that mistaken. Instead, she stuck out her own bottom lip in a cartoon of misery and bellowed at the top of her voice, a cry as loud as any newborn, "Wahh!"

Now, I wasn't sure at first whether Walter wouldn't start himself again in that manner, either from being so afeared of the noise, or else from anger that she was mocking him, just like those men had done. But, again, I was wrong. For this was clearly one of them tricks a good mam has up her sleeve with which to entertain and distract, for Walter's face did indeed crumple, but this time into a fit of giggles.

"Again!" he shouted. "Do it again, Mammy!" And she obliged. And it was that gratifying to see the poor lad restored to happiness, I joined in mi'sel, bawling as brazen as the day I was born! We got a fair few stares from passers-by, I can tell thee, but as it was clear we were in jest, most folks just laughed along with us.

After that, we were in high old spirits, and though I can't

for the life of me recall why, we took to chasing one another up and down the towpath. Well, as you can probably tell, I'm not built for that kind of thing. "Slow down, lad, slow down!" I cried, getting mi'sel right out of puff, as, half in earnest, half for Nancy's benefit, I clutched at me jiggling bubbies as though to stop 'em from bouncing. Ee, how it made her howl! What a laugh we had! Until it was clear from my gasps for air, I couldn't keep up anymore. So then Nancy suggested a more sedate activity: a game of throwing sticks in the canal. Well, I'd not done owt like that since I was a lass, and Walt and me, we got right eager, scratching round under the trees for the best sticks and then chucking them in the murky water to see who could throw them furthest, straining to see how far we could follow 'em before they floated out of view.

EIGHT

Thank God for Mary! Nancy watched her from the bank and smiled as she and Walter leaned out over the bridge, laughing together like old friends. She felt sorry now how irritated she'd been when Mary'd not left off about coming here; hadn't she been right to persuade them out? The air down this way had done them all good, she could see it already from the fresh rose in Walter's cheeks, and she hardly knew where this last half-hour had slipped, so absorbedly had she been able to muse in the low afternoon sun, whilst they entertained themselves with their game.

She couldn't get the idea of Hunt out of her head. Nor the other night and Walter's piteous cries for food. The two were somehow of a piece in her thoughts, the one leading to the other, just like the waterfall she'd watched as a girl, tumble through the scree, frothing white into the tarn in the fells above the farm. They'd endured so much already since those days in Westmoreland, she and her mother, and now poor Walter too. All these hard years in Manchester, and their daily deprivations only getting worse. Something had to change. Hunt had to be right. Justice for people like them must surely begin with a right to choose who made the laws in the first place. If them in Parliament showed even half a mind to their concerns, it stood to reason their circumstances would improve.

Of course, in one respect, life had already got better. For hadn't she spent this whole spring long reading Captain Wright's wonderful books? And hadn't they filled her with unexpected joy? She frowned. Aye, she'd been inspired and, aye indeed, she was grateful, but there was something troubling in her good fortune too. She wasn't sure why, perhaps it was Yates's taunts that niggled, but there was also something uncomfortable in being the lucky one. For why shouldn't everyone enjoy the same? Not just the children in the schoolroom either, but Mary and Jemima, and countless others at Wrights and beyond, who she couldn't possibly hope to teach herself.

She picked a blade of grass, absently twirling it in her fingers. It had bothered her, this seeming injustice, especially these last few days since that terrible night with Walter, though she'd never let on to anyone, not even Mary. Yet now she'd had this afternoon to reflect, she began to see perhaps she could begin to make redress. Her eyes wandered over the scene, evening light on the water, primroses along the bank, new life bursting forth everywhere, even here amongst the warehouses and chimneys. Aye, she realised with a sudden restlessness which made her stand up and stride along the towpath, perhaps this growing movement for reform could enable her to do something really useful. Something for other folk too. Never mind Yates and what they said at the mill about reform; she'd be careful. If she could only find out more, if only put her hand to the right books, and papers, and pamphlets, well, and then, could she not do her part? Aye, and spread the word far and wide to those who couldn't read for themselves.

Smiling to herself, she moved back towards the others on the bridge, just as a chill wind swept across the canal. She grabbed at her shawl. *Walter needs home*, she thought; his jacket was far too thin to be staying out much longer. Besides, it was getting late, and she pictured her mother, alone in the room in Ancoats.

"Come on, you two!" she called. "It's time we were off!" But Walter's face crumpled in disappointment and, behind him, Mary put on a plaintive look. "Oh go on then!" she laughed. "Five more minutes, Walt. Five more minutes and then home."

Eventually, when Walter was persuaded, they began to retrace their steps, away from the canal and back towards town, but as they approached the spot where the band had performed, a sound of fresh cheering carried on the air and, straining to look ahead, Nancy made out another crowd forming. This time, there were silken banners of every colour flapping in the wind and each of the poles topped with a flash of bright scarlet. With a catch of her breath, she realised these must be the caps of liberty she'd read about.

"'Ow do!" A girl's voice addressed them, and Nancy reluctantly turned her attention back to the path, where Molly Kennedy was walking arm-in-arm with her sister, Peg. She couldn't help but smile to herself at the sight of them, since they'd both over-curled their hair, and their best bonnets were perched precariously, unwittingly comic.

"Did tha see what's going on?" she asked eagerly, nodding towards the crowd.

"Oh, it's them reform lot starting up," said Molly, absently plucking an almond from the paper cone she kept clutched to her breast. For a half-second, Nancy wondered if she'd thieved it.

"Aye, there'll be speeches before long, I expect," said Peg, looking back.

"What and tha doesn't want to listen?" cried Nancy.

"Bor-ing!" retorted Molly, still crunching on the nut. "Why would we ever want to listen to *them*?"

"Aye," said Peg, less convincingly. "What good would it do us?"

"Well none if tha takes that attitude."

"What's tha mean?" Peg replied, as Molly glared.

"We should be supporting them of course! Don't tha

see? If they manage to win the vote for workers, we'd have someone speaking up for us at last. We'd have some say in t' way factories are run. And t' level of wages, not to mention taxes." Her voice was low and strong with rising passion and, to her own amazement, the words kept coming, as though she were some kind of practised orator. "Think about it. Doesn't tha want more than a couple o' saved pennies in tha pocket to spend on a day like today? Enough so's not to walk past them currant buns every time. Enough, at the least, to make sure tha *never* goes to bed hungry? I know I'd do owt to make sure Walter never wants for a good meal."

Peg had been listening closely, and now she dropped her sister's arm to turn back towards the meeting. Mary raised her eyebrows at Nancy, in acknowledgement of the girl's conversion.

"But what if someone spots us?" the girl asked, and, for a second, Nancy caught the same anxiety flit across Mary's face. "We can't lose our jobs."

"Don't be daft! They can't do owt about us being at a fair! What harm can there be in listening?"

Peg seemed persuaded by this, though Molly remained unimpressed. Her mouth had fallen slack, her eyes dulled with disdain. It was clear she was annoyed by Peg's interest, though she'd no notion what to say to reassert herself and proceeded to do the only thing she could think of; reaching out her free hand, she pinched the bare skin of her sister's arm. For a moment, no one said a word, and they all stared at the mark that flared red against Peg's pasty skin.

"Come on," Molly snapped at last, without a trace of shame, "tha's not going to stop here dreamin' all day. If they want to risk it, that's their lookout," and she gripped Peg's elbow and roughly dragged her away.

Nancy watched them and shook her head. "Can tha believe that?"

"Nay, she's no better than a spoiled child," replied Mary.

"It's a shame, mind, I think tha'd persuaded the sister. Pity she'll never stand up to *her*."

"Aye, well, I tried," Nancy replied, adopting a breezy tone, unwilling to waste any more time. She'd taken hold of Walter's hand and was swinging it back and forth to keep him entertained. "*We're* going to take a look, whatever they say, aren't we, Walt?"

He laughed up at her, and Mary joined them, inspired by Nancy's confidence, taking his other hand. Then, heading off to the assembly together, they whooshed him up off the ground on the regular count of three.

By the time they reached the edge of the crowd, there was already an impressive number of people gathered round a smaller, inner party of reformers who were carrying the banners.

"Look!" Nancy breathed with surprise, "They're all women!"

Well-presented ladies, they were too, thought Nancy, as she and Mary nudged forwards to settle on a spot from which to watch. Before long, a slight woman of forty or so, wearing a white dress beneath a smart pelisse, stepped forward. Upright and dignified, she proceeded to hand a scroll bound in red ribbon to a short, stocky man at the centre. He made quite the show of thanking her for it, bowing ceremoniously, before raising himself up and greeting the crowd.

"Ladies and gentlemen, we, the members of the Patriotic Union, are honoured to be joined by these gracious ladies," he gestured at the line behind, "who've so generously given up their holiday to travel from Blackburn."

He turned with another dip of his head towards the woman who'd handed over the scroll, which she acknowledged with a courteous smile.

"These ladies, I'm delighted to inform you, are supporters of our noble cause for Parliamentary reform. Indeed, it is their belief there's a great deal that women can do to help in the struggle. Accordingly, they've requested I read aloud this message to the womenfolk of Manchester."

Nancy could hardly believe her ears. "Let's get nearer," she said to Mary with a cock of her head, and they pushed forward a little further, still holding Walter's hand.

Around them, there was polite murmuring, as the man unrolled the letter and held it aloft, loudly clearing his throat before he began to read. "'Dear Sisters, we've come today to beseech you, the gentle ladies of Manchester, you mothers, sisters and daughters of hard-working families, to call upon your menfolk to join, with sturdy hearts, the campaign for Parliamentary reform.'"

Nancy widened her eyes and grinned at Mary.

"'Consider, if you will,'" the letter went on, "'how many of you have passed a hungry night filled with fear of the morning and of discovering your famished children taken to the Lord?'"

From the gathering, there was a universal cry of "Shame!"

"'Is it not time to call for an end to such poverty and wretchedness?'"

"Aye!" Nancy shouted with the others.

"'Is it not time to emancipate our suffering nation from tyranny and borough-mongering?'"

"Aye!" again.

These words, these cries, the clapping and the cheering, together somehow set the crowd alight. It was just as though flint had struck a spark, thought Nancy, and all hearts burning with the same idea of change. Excited, stirred up, she felt the same heat rising within, impatient thoughts racing, so that when the speaker once again urged them to persuade their husbands to the cause, she suddenly felt emboldened to settle the one remaining question that still troubled her. Heart beating, listening intent, she waited for the next pause, and then, raising her chin, shouted out loud, "But what of those of us with no menfolk?" Ignoring the gasps from behind, she added, "Do we not get a vote?"

At this, the speaker's eyes darted nervously round the spectators to locate the person who'd spoken. Nancy held her arm aloft, proud to be identified. Flustered, the man inclined his head towards her vaguely and then turned to the same woman who'd handed him the letter. There followed a brief, uneasy exchange before he pointed out Nancy.

Then an extraordinary thing happened. The woman herself stepped forward and at once fixed Nancy with a penetrating stare. Puzzled, she returned her gaze, as the woman began to speak in a voice that was loud and confident, her words enunciated with deliberate care, "We believe *progress* is best served by *universal suffrage*." By which, of course, she meant votes for men only, though Nancy found herself strangely undismayed. For there was something in the woman's intense look, something in her consciously, stiff demeanour, that suggested otherwise. Aye, she meant something more, so that when she'd finished speaking and stepped back into line, Nancy mirrored the woman's short nod of satisfaction. Aye, she'd understood the something unspoken.

Meanwhile, Mary, disgruntled, whispered in her ear, "But she didn't answer tha question."

"Aye, she did," Nancy smiled. "She did. One step at a time, Mary, one step at a time."

NINE

JOSEPH

Easter Monday. That's the day we first met. Or so *she* thought.
Easter Monday down at Knott Mill Fair. There was still a chill
in the air, I remember, and the sky was white and big with low
clouds, but along the Bridgewater that didn't stop the party.
Folk may have it rough round here, but they know how to
make the best of things, and that day there were hundreds of
'em milling about. Party people, doing just that, making the
most of a rare holiday.

I'd gone down with some of the lads from work, looking
for a good time. Same as year before, when I'd woken up next
morning to find myself in a hovel in Little Ireland, straddled by
a dark colleen with knotted hair. And, yeah, I won't lie, fella I
was then, I was up for another such adventure if I could find
it. Wasn't too disappointed with the choice neither. There was
a band playing, drink flowing and all the town's lasses, mill
girls and maid-servants parading by, casting sideways glances
at us from under their flowered bonnets, as we laughed and
joked and egged 'em on.

I've no idea why, not anymore, but for some reason, after
a while, I found myself separated from the rest of the gang.
Suppose I must've been chasing some pretty face who'd got

away. But, as it goes, I wasn't on my own for long, not before I ran into another workmate, Archie Thompson. Nice fella, decent like, older than me, we were often up the stack together back then. He's a sober sort too, old Archie, and he certainly was that afternoon, what with having his missus and his vast number of offspring in tow.

"Hey, 'ow do, Archie, how's it going?" I greeted him more warmly than was polite, what with all the ale I'd swilled. But I can't have been too far gone, 'cos I recall noticing a wariness in his smile and one of his little 'uns gawp at me as though I was one of them turns at a freak show. It brought me up short, good and proper, as I didn't want to embarrass the man, not in front of his family.

Forcing myself not to slur, I enquired respectfully where they were heading, and he pointed to an open spot of land nearby, where folk were starting to gather to listen to some speakers for reform. I should explain; in the past, Archie'd often spoken to me of the need for the vote, and though I'd always granted he had a point, I'd never managed to get too agitated about it. Maybe 'cos, unlike like him, I'd not burdened myself with a wife and a houseful of brats to feed. No, as far as I was concerned, what money I earned was my own.

I can't lie, Archie's missus had clearly got the measure of my inebriated state and didn't bother waiting on us; instead, she walked off with the children, towards the gathering. Archie, anxious not to lose them in the crowd, but ever-courteous, cocked his head in their direction and asked, "Will tha join us?" And so that's how I found myself falling in with him and the general flow of the crowd.

I don't know what I expected from the meeting, but it certainly wasn't what happened next, 'cos when we got up close, it seemed the whole thing had been devised by a group of women! There was maybe a dozen or so of 'em, perhaps even more, facing the crowd, and none of 'em fair of face, it has to be said. No, they were an altogether more grizzled set of ladies than any I'd hoped to come across that afternoon, though some of 'em were carrying banners on flagpoles with a bright red cap atop, all of which I'd have thought a sight too heavy for their refined little wrists. From where we stood, I could only make out a couple of the inscriptions. *Repeal the Corn Laws,* said one, in bold white letters, and on the other, in gold thread, *Liberty*.

It turned out the speaker was to be a man after all, though it was the womens' words he delivered, written on a letter for him to read out. I've probably no need to tell you, I wasn't the object of their address. No, their message was for *other women*, all the mams and grans and lasses of Manchester. For it seems, according to their reckoning, it's they who have the most important work to do! To entreat their menfolk to agitate for the vote. Ha! "Entreat", my arse! Nag and pester, more like! But, judging from the cheers and whoops around me, it was clear the crowd agreed with them. Though there were other responses too. On the fringe, a bunch of drunken lads, not unlike the mates I'd lost earlier, were laughing and jeering, passing bawdy comment on the old maids, I've no doubt. Whilst, behind me, there was another group of more mature ladies, shall we say, tutting loudly in disapproval at them of their own sex. And, all around, there was a general uneasiness, as we each of us eyed one another, trying to guess the next person's opinion, none of us quite sure if constables weren't on their way.

As I remember, it was at a point near the end of the speech when another voice came from within the crowd. It was a woman's voice, low and measured, but brimming with feeling, as she shouted out loud, "What about those of us with no menfolk?"

Not surprisingly, this met with a degree of laughter, and more distaste from the harridans behind me, but, even so, the voice continued, undaunted. "Do we not count? Me mother and me?"

Like most folk, I shifted about then, to try and see who it was speaking and following the direction of all eyes, in a heart-stopping moment, I recognised her at once. Straight off. That girl with the book who'd taken my breath away.

I'll be honest with you, I don't recall what was said next. Hard to explain what I was feeling. Only that it was like I'd been transported someplace else or stepped out of the usual march of time. The thrill of seeing her there, and the revelation she had no man in her life.

Ha! What a fool!

Well, whether on account of the atmosphere or simply down to the ale I'd consumed, I found myself suddenly bold. I know it sounds ridiculous now, but it seemed too strange then, to see her there like that, and for it not to mean owt, and so I determined to seize my chance and speak to her at last.

I had to be quick about it, mind. Even though she was cheering the end of proceedings along with the rest, large numbers of the crowd were already breaking away, I daresay conscious of the threat of the authorities. I needed to hurry. So's, straightaway, I turned to Archie and said I thought I'd spotted an old friend over on the other side and begged his pardon to excuse me. He tried to contain his relief as he shook my hand, but I know I wasn't the only one glad to part company.

When at last I got up close to her, I was disappointed to find she wasn't alone. Yeah, she had that buxom friend of hers with her. Always with her, she was. Mary's her name. Mary McDermott. Yeah, and I can tell you now, even after all this time, you don't want to listen to what that one has to say.

There was also the boy between them too. Little fair lad, I now know to be Walter, though I swear that day I thought it was Mary he belonged to. He was pawing at the skirts of their dresses, seeking leave to move on, pointing towards a ragged old man on the side of the path just beyond. Old fella was a right sorry sight, all bent over with rheumatism he was, but, even so, he was still managing to whistle out a tune on his pipe with his swollen fingers, his hat upturned on the ground, inviting pennies none could spare.

"Go on then, lad, we'll follow thee," I heard them say, and as he skipped past me, I knew I had to make my move.

Archie was far behind now, so I was free to play whatever part I liked, and right on the spur, it seemed my best chance would be to work on her interest in reform. And so I opened smartly, "Good day, ladies. I hope you don't mind my observing your interest in t' talk this afternoon." Confident and pleasant, I told myself, but earnest as well.

Well, not surprisingly, big lass weighed me cautiously, but Nancy was friendly enough. I like to think when our eyes met, hers lingered a while.

"Aye. We weren't the only ones." This from Mary.

"Yes, indeed, madam. But not all's prepared to do owt about it," I indicated the diminishing crowd and shook my head. "Sadly." I produced my most solemn face. They didn't say owt, but nor did they move on.

"It's just that if you're interested in assisting the cause, and helping your'sel of course, then there's plenty can be done for reform here in Manchester."

I don't know what was I thinking, but there was still no reply, so that's when I grinned at Nancy, broad and direct, the kind of smile that never fails me, and, at last, I thought I saw a glimmer of response, perhaps even amusement in her eye, almost as though she'd seen through me and guessed my business. It gave me hope.

"Where is it you work, if you don't mind me asking?"

Mary was tight-lipped. But I shot another of my looks at Nancy, and she relented.

"Over at Wrights. In Ancoats. We're in t' mule room."

"Oh aye!" Such surprise I mustered. "I'm working on t' new mill next door! What a coincidence!"

"Tha's a builder?"

"Aye, well I'm on t' stack."

"Oh! A steeplejack? Tha's a brave lad then!"

"That's me!"

She unfolded her arms, which I knew was a good sign,

and allowed herself a short laugh. We looked a full moment at one another then, and I noticed for the first time her eyes were the colour of acorns just before they're ripe, somewhere between green and brown, but the thought tripped me up in my performance, and to my dismay, all at once, little 'un was back and pulling at her sleeve.

Mary butted in, taking the lad by the hand, "We should get him back."

"Aye, I'm coming."

Anxious to secure a second meeting, I blurted, "What's your name?"

"Nancy."

"Nancy?"

"Nancy… Kay."

"Well, pleased to meet you, Nancy Kay. I'm Joseph Price. But everyone calls me Joe."

The lad was fussing something rotten now, like one much younger than his years, I thought, with his quivering lip and thrashing arms. It was odd. He was odd. And I wondered why Mary couldn't just take him off home. But Nancy looked anxious and called gently, "I'm coming."

"Right nice to meet you," I said again, beginning to despair, as she gave me an apologetic smile and started to back away. "'Appen I'll stop by Wrights one evening and let you know about…" I had no idea what I was gonna say, but it didn't matter 'cos she'd already turned, and I watched her walk away.

For a moment, it was like a weight settling in the pit of my stomach. I didn't know what I was feeling, whether it was dejection, or anger, or another swill of that first hurt pride, and I'll not lie, my first instinct was to leg it away and find the nearest alehouse. But then, once they both had the boy's hands held secure, all of a sudden, I was happy again, 'cos she looked back over her shoulder at me – I swear it was almost coquettish, the way she did it – and called out across the distance between us, "That'd be grand, Joe."

TEN

Nancy frequently sat on the back bench of the schoolroom, a child on each side; those who weren't keeping up as well, Samson supposed, since the rest of the class would be busy with an assignment, and the tutor circling the room. He noticed she was always animated with these little ones, patiently explaining the lesson or else offering gentle encouragement, so that their faces would either be tilted up at her, rapt with attention, or else creased in concentration in an effort to please.

She preferred to take off her cap whilst she taught, and Samson liked the look of her hair as it frizzed round the heart-shape of her face. It was an unusual colour, he thought, somewhere between honey and the soft, liquid orange of amber. She appeared in better health these days too, he was pleased to see, and early freckles had come up on the bridge of her nose.

He tried to visit upstairs as often as he could, keeping an eye on things, he'd tell Henshaw, though he usually only arrived after the lesson had finished and Nancy was left to tidy up. He liked to bring her his newspapers, just as he had promised; he still took a selection from London, finding the local *Mercury*, Adelaide's paper of choice, not to his taste. He continued to bring books as well, together with other items he thought might interest her: pamphlets he'd studied on education and the cuttings about the factories legislation he'd made whilst still at the cottage.

One afternoon at the beginning of May, he arrived at the schoolroom to find the children and their teacher already gone and Nancy wiping clean the board at the front. Sun dazzled through the windows the full length of the room, lighting up the motes of chalk dust she'd disturbed in the air, so that she appeared almost lost in cloud and glowing. He could hardly look and dropped his gaze, only to spot, with a pang of disappointment, a small pile of books he'd lent her stacked in the corner of the room.

"Hello," he said, a little too brightly.

"Oh, 'ello, I was hoping tha'd come today," and she moved towards the books. "I've brought these back for thee."

"So, I see," he frowned. "You do realise I'm happy for you to keep them as long as you like."

"Aye, that's very kind of thee."

"I mean it," he said, but as he spoke, he thought he saw a trace of uneasiness settle on her face. Perhaps, after all, they were unwelcome, these literary offerings of his, forced upon her so fervently, she couldn't refuse, forced upon her out of his own desire for… what exactly? He wasn't sure, only that he was making a fool of himself and this was her polite way of asking him to desist. Quickly, he reached down and seized the books from the floor and, without looking at her, mumbled. "Perhaps they're not to your taste."

"Nay! Nay, it's not that!" she cried vehemently and reached over to place a hand on top of the pile for emphasis. Her wrist brushed his hand. "I've loved 'em."

"You can't have read them all yet, surely?"

"Oh, but I have, sir! I have!"

From her good-humoured outrage, he could see she was telling the truth. He laughed in relief.

"And if I didn't love 'em…" she carried on, holding her head to the side in thought, "even if they didn't all suit, I still found 'em interesting."

"Well then, keep them!" he said, holding them back out to her with a smile.

"Nay, nay," she said, awkwardly. "Thing is, it's not that I wouldn't *love* to deprive thee of them for longer, it's just me mam's put her foot down. Says it's bad enough to live in t' just the one room as it is, never mind turning t' place into a library. Perhaps I could take just one or two at a time?"

"Ah. Of course," and at once, he felt a selfish fool again, ashamed of his failure to appreciate her circumstances.

"It's hard for her," Nancy carried on. "Our place. For me mam, I mean. Even though we've been there many a year, it's not what she's been used to most her life." Samson's expression must have formed a question because she added, "Did I never tell thee? We used to live on a farm before we came to Manchester."

"Really?"

"Aye, up north. A little spot in Westmoreland. Me grandfather were tenant there, and then me dad; he took it on when he married me mam. Right nice, cosy house came wi' land. Well, tha can hardly blame her, I suppose, for always harking back."

"But you must miss it too. The country, I mean. How old were you when you left?"

"Fifteen. I were fifteen, and both me dad and me brother dead and gone. And for all the country were grand, I weren't keen to stay in a place filled wi' so many ghosts. Nay, nay, I'm not like me mam that way. I'm not one for longing for t' past. I think tha should always be looking forward."

Samson smiled, but too many thoughts had crowded his mind to know what to say.

"She's like a lot of folk, me mam. Afeared of change, she is. Not that she's happy wi' way things are now neither!" she laughed a moment. "But the way I see it, clinging to the past, resisting change, well, for me, that's more frightening than owt else."

She'd moved over to the front bench and took up one of

the small slates and a cloth. "Would tha mind if I do these now, sir?"

"Not at all," he said. "Indeed, I'll join you," and he sat down, taking the first of the cleaned slates from her and setting it on the bench beside him to form the start of a pile.

In the companionable silence that followed, he found himself wondering at her words. Was he clinging to the past? He hardly knew. Certainly, until recently, he'd not liked to think of the future. Yet now, he realised, he'd hardly thought of Isabel at all since he'd come to Manchester. Indeed, although his memories remained fond, it occurred to him he'd stopped pretending their marriage had been some kind of grand love affair. The truth, he now acknowledged, was a little more ordinary.

His young wife had been the daughter of Sir Edwin Sutton, the wealthy landowner of the Elton Hall estate in his father's parish. A beautiful girl, striking even, with a pale complexion and a shock of dark hair. As a young soldier, home on leave, he'd thought it happiness itself to simply look on her. With his fine prospects in a share of the Wright family fortune, not to mention his own glittering military career, her parents had readily approved the match, and they were married quickly, long before they discovered how little they shared in terms of interests or disposition.

She had been a kind-hearted soul, cheerful and loyal to him. But she had enjoyed company and parties and was overly preoccupied with her clothes, and she'd never been able to understand his need for solitariness; she'd found it puzzling at first, at times even hurtful.

As for Samson, what pained him most peculiarly about those years, for reasons he could never quite fathom, was how endearingly eager she had been to indulge his interest in the piano, which she herself had played a little. Whenever she managed to persuade him to perform for a party of guests, she would always declare the superiority of his talent, so that he'd find himself feeling strangely dishonourable, detestable even, as she laughed lightly, enjoying the joke at her own expense.

Yet sweet and good-natured though Isabel had been, reflected Samson, it wasn't his feelings for *her* which had kept him from looking to the future these past few years. Rather, it was another loss that haunted him. The loss of a baby, their only child, dead within an hour of his mother. Yes, even now, here in Manchester, it was this father's grief that still had him in its grip, exerting its power in dark and lonely moments, usually late at night, when, without warning, melancholy would descend like rain, and he'd rediscover the presence of a boy still curled up for shelter in the deepest, hollow core of him.

They'd considered themselves fortunate, he and Isabel, when his leave had coincided with the commencement of her lying in. She'd chosen to return to her parents at Elton Hall, and during the first few days after his homecoming, all had been eager anticipation as they soaked up late summer sunshine in the newly landscaped gardens. Yet, despite all the luxuries of the place, the suite of rooms given over to her, and the attendance of the best physicians and midwives, her pains had come upon her violently.

Samson had paced the grounds, waiting in a state of nervous suspense, until the sudden urgency with which he was summoned to the chamber filled him with dread. He arrived in haste, too soon for the maid, who was still rolling up the bloodied sheets. She met his eye in a blink of panic and bowed her head. Isabel appeared already laid out. Her black hair swept into a dark plait against the white of the pillow, and her closed face so perfect, she could have been a doll put to bed by a child.

Tearing his eyes away from her, he remembered frantically searching the room and lighting upon the bundle being bathed in a bowl by the fireplace. All was silent.

"A boy," the midwife, who held him, had mouthed.

Samson had drawn closer, his gaze fixed on his son's body,

which seemed to glow, strangely pale, almost celestial, within a bath turned pink by blood. He had sunk to his knees beside him and prayed – just as he'd done so many times on the field for other fathers' sons – as all the while the midwife had coaxed the little mite to life with a vigorous rub, up and down the bumps of his tiny, pronounced spine. He didn't know how long she tried, how long he watched and waited, only that no war cry came. His son's battle was already lost. Samson had risen slowly and retreated silently from the room. He had not knelt another moment in prayer ever since.

"Your boy, he was born in September 1812?"

"Yes," Nancy looked up startled.

"I remember because that's when my son was born too." He saw her look of confusion and added, "He died the same day. His mother too."

"Oh, sir, I had no idea."

She stopped her work in shock and, after a moment, began to shake her head sorrowfully. "I'm so very sorry."

Her face had shrouded in pity, and they sat together quietly awhile until eventually she spoke again, tentatively, "Tha were thinking of them that day, weren't thee? When I came to th' office and were such a tartar."

Samson nodded and breathed in deeply as Nancy tutted under her breath, clearly angry with herself. He sensed she was about to apologise and shook his head with a look that said it wasn't necessary, so that her face dissolved instead into a weak smile.

It wasn't fair to pain her, he thought, as he returned her smile; she had sorrows enough of her own to endure, without listening to his. Thus, with a sudden slap of his thighs, he briskly adopted a new tone, "But that's the past. And, as you say, it's the future we should look to. Now, tell me about your boy. Walter, isn't he?"

"Aye, Walter, sir."

He liked that she smiled fondly at the speaking of his name.

"And are you teaching Walter to read too, or will you wait until he's in the mill?"

Nancy hesitated at this, her hand stayed, holding the last of the slates suspended in the air.

"I beg your pardon, that's none of my concern."

"Nay, nay, sir, that's not it at all." She put down the slate and dropped her hands in her lap. "How can I say?" She looked round the room as though for guidance. "It's just that our Walter, well, he's a bit *different* to other lads. Delicate, tha might say."

Samson thought he understood.

"He's wonderful and clever of course, and most lovin' boy in England, but, truth is, he's still a babby in many respects and I tremble at the thought of him here." The words were rushing from her, like liquid from an unstopped bottle. "It's loud noise, tha see. He hates it. So, what wi' t' machines and t' other lads and lasses, and all the teasing he'll get, I cannot say how he'll go on."

"No, I see that," Samson replied warmly, "I do see that." He fell silent, once again wondering at the burden she bore, and hoping she'd feel a return of the sympathy he'd felt from her. After a little while, however, he ventured on, "You know, Nancy... If I may call you that?"

She nodded, smiling.

"I've been thinking, Nancy. In spite of your fears for him, which I understand of course, Walter *is* fortunate in one important respect."

"How so?" she frowned again.

"He has you."

185

ELEVEN

JOSEPH

Archie didn't know what to make of me the next day after the fair, so sudden was my conversion to the cause, I suppose, and I daresay there's many thinks I've no right to be put out by the suspicions he voiced later, not after the way things turned out.

Ha! All that talk of treachery. Me, a spy?

(Oh why did I not tell her? Why did I just not tell her? I was no seasoned radical. I wasn't converted to the cause until then. Right there and then, in that moment at Knott Mill. Not 'cos of hunger, nor anger, nor even the grand idea of democracy, fine though I suppose it is, but all and only 'cos it meant I could get closer to her.)

It was another dry day, with the sun promising the start of summer. Up atop of the chimney, already gone thirty feet, inside the column wide enough for the two of us, Archie and me, we set to work. Soon as I got chance, once the bricks were winched up and we were into the flow of mortar and lay, I started to quiz him about reform. Well, he had a good laugh at me at first, and I had to endure a whole lot of ribbing that perhaps I'd taken a fancy to them fine ladies with their banners. Ha! Like they'd be so lucky, I said, until eventually I'd persuaded him, and he laid off with the jokes and began to tell me about the meetings he'd been to a couple of year back. How they'd been calling for the vote. How representation in London could help us up here.

As he spoke, I looked out over the top line of bricks. Below and beyond spread the sprawling buildings of Manchester, its thoroughfares and waterways stretching into the far green distance. Unlike so many folk, I didn't mind all this change. To me, the factories, the chimneys, all them warehouses and terraces, they were all a guarantee of work. This was where the future lay! And I was the one building it! It was no fairy-tale kingdom, I was certain of that, but as I drank it all in, part of me imagined myself a soldier at a castle parapet, not yet a victor perhaps, but stirred and ready for battle.

That's when I realised I wanted my fair share of it. Manchester was a success, so where was mine? Why should I risk my neck at such a height for the owner of the land I'd break it on? Or sweat in my shirtsleeves to line the pocket of his tailcoat? What was I labouring for, if it wasn't for me? Nancy and them agitators were right to fight. It was time the few were stopped from getting rich off the back of the many.

"So, tell me then, Archie, why did you stop with going to them meetings?"

"Eh?" he said, standing up straight from the pail. "Does tha not remember how they stopped young Bagguley and them weavers wi' their blankets from marching to petition t' Prince Regent?"

"Aye," I said, though truthfully much of it had passed me by.

"Well, a neighbour of mine back then were one of 'em. A hand-loomer, he were." He trowelled another tongue of mortar. "It were him that got me interested in fust place, what with t' weavers having such a hard time. Any road, he got himsel' deep involved in t' protest and, sorry to say, he wound up in t' clink." Archie shook his head sorrowfully. "Tha can imagine how I felt. It were just too close to home, and I've been wary o' that kind of trouble ever since. Got my family to think of, after all."

"Yeah, I see that," I replied, "but, what with taxes and prices both being so high, is it not time to make another stand? 'Specially with so many calling for change. Surely they'll be hard-pressed to resist this time, if all t' workers join together?"

He looked over his shoulder at me then, with an admiration I don't care to think of now, and said thoughtfully, "'Appen tha's right, Joe. 'Appen tha's right."

So's after that he promised to ask round for me, and before long he got wind of a meeting of the union for reform, down in a tavern at the far end of Deansgate. Upshot was, he decided on coming too, daft old fella! I think it was me being so keen, me without any ties to think on, had pricked his conscience. Any road, that meeting in the alehouse with Archie, one rainy night at the beginning of May, that's where I first heard of Hunt.

A storm had been brewing all day. First of many that summer. Winds were that high at the top of the chimney, and we like the last pair of a set of nine-pins, ready to be knocked down. Away over the tops of the Pennines, we could see it, the sky seething with clouds as black as night. Course, we didn't mind a bit, 'cos it meant we could come down early, and after we'd stalled the horse, we were able to set off in good time for the meeting, walking along the canal, out of Ancoats and down through town.

We must've been a hundred yards or more off the alehouse when the rain finally came. Manchester rain, lashings of it, bouncing off roofs and sills and thoroughfares. It was that heavy, we had to dash, laughing and cursing, as puddles from the street splashed up our legs with every stride. We ended up under the porch, out of breath, boots and breeches sodden, and the peaks of our caps plopping dirty great drops like blocked guttering.

Even though we were early, there was already that many crammed in, we had to shove the door for folk to shift enough to let us in. Speeches hadn't started yet, and the tiny room was loud with shouts and laughter and tankards clinking, as I craned my neck to look over the crush and locate the bar, where lamps were already lit and steaming up from the damp lifting off all the wet clothes in the place.

We elbowed our way as best we could through the press o' people, most of 'em men, mainly mill workers or labourers like Archie and me, though there were a fair few girls too. Course, I kept my eye out for Nancy, though I didn't hold out much hope, not with being so far from Ancoats. It had been over a fortnight since we'd met, and I was desperate to talk to her again, but I'd reckoned the best thing was to come along to the meeting first, so's I'd sound that much more convincing.

After a good long wait at the bar, we'd just got served our ale when there was a general shout and a man of about twenty appeared, seemingly hovering several inches above the assembly at the back of the room, his head near to skimming the low ceiling. I stretched up again over the crowd and saw he was balanced on a barrel, a table being too high for his purpose.

As the noise in the room began to quieten, Archie whispered to me, "That's them from the *Observer*," and he nodded towards the two newspapermen I later knew for John Knight and James Wroe. They were near the front and urging the man to speak up.

"Go on, Jack!" cried another voice from the crowd.

Well, this Jack wasn't anything like I'd expected from a so-called "Jacobin". There was no wild hair or fiery looks. In fact, if anything, he seemed a clean-living sort, fresh-faced, almost soft I'd say, with neatly cropped hair. His voice was quite high too, and more educated than most, and when he spoke, it was with an earnest seriousness.

He started by thanking everyone for coming, to a round of cheers and cries of support, but then he made a mistake. "We're all good men here," he said, to a murmur of approval, which was suddenly pierced by a loud screech, "And *women*!" This was from one of the big lasses near the bar, much to the laughter of the crowd.

Plainly not one for the ladies, Jack's cheeks burned red. "Begging your pardon, and *women*, of course!" At which his critic winked, bringing her hand to her lips and blowing him a kiss. Well, a gang of youngsters behind me whistled, as bawdy as you like, whilst laughter started up again and poor, green Jack could only smile, blushing 'til his eyes watered, waiting for the noise to quell.

Eventually, some big bearded fella up front came to his aid and shouted, "Whist will thee! Let's hear the man!" And at last the room fell quiet, and Jack got properly started.

"All we men *and women* seek is fairness for the good working people of Manchester."

Understandably, this was to hearty cheers.

"No say in the taxes imposed on us! Is this fair?"

This to loud boos and nays.

"No say in t' price of our food. Is this fair?"

More nays and angry cries.

"No member in London to represent a single one of us. How is this fair?"

Again, a loud chorus of disapproval. By now, young Jack had hit his stride and was looking far more sure of himself.

"My friends, enough! No more to 'no say'. Enough to hunger and wretchedness. Enough to no representation. Let's demand what's right and just. A repeal of the pernicious Corn Laws that deprive us of fair prices. Representation for this great town in Parliament. And a vote for every last working man."

I'll hand it to him, the whole assembly was astir now, stung by the injustice of it all. And, I'll admit, even I got carried away in the moment, cheering and whistling, buoyed up on the same swell of hope and pride this unlikely little man had somehow managed to conjure in all of us, just as though he were some kind of magician.

But as I walked home later, after yet more speeches and a bellyful of ale, it wasn't reform I was thinking on. No, it was Nancy. I pictured her again, heading in the same direction as on that first winter night, leading me on. And I remember nodding to myself, even as I paced the dirt-black streets, thinking it was going to be the best summer ever.

SUMMER

ONE

The farmhouse nestled comfortably in the valley of a gentle incline, with smooth fields sloping from the front door, downhill towards the village, whilst behind were the grey, drystone stables, and the upper enclosure where the sheep grazed in the lee of the fells beyond. Over to the far side, was Ann's favourite spot. A generous orchard, where she'd spent half her childhood racing through the trees, under the shelter of their branches, jumping up to heave down laden boughs and sniff at the ripening fruit.

Edward's picture of the farm, a miniature, less than seven inches across, was bound in a modest, wooden frame and propped on the mantel. It had been there since the first night in this place and in every other room they'd had to lodge previously, ever since their eviction from the farm itself. It was always there, though Ann didn't have to look at it, to see it, to feel it. The farm lived within her. It visited her in her dreams, as though she were the place herself, fixed and certain, and the farm something unearthed and ephemeral.

She never spoke of it, told no one about such foolish yearnings, and yet still her soul cleaved to those dreams. Those dying moments of sleep, suspended between night and day, when, still slumbering, the landscape of her former life was laid out before her, glistening at the edge of sensation; sunbeams bursting through the new leaves of an awakening tree, dappling the spread of counterpane with bouncing light and illuminating the Moses basket beside her where a baby slept, as all but one of her babies did now.

Such dreams did not come often anymore. Sleep itself seemed wary of her, as she lay in the darkness, afraid to abandon herself. She used to blame it on the foreign sounds of a life which, even all these years later, was still strange to her. The night-long rattle of Walter's chest close at hand, the early tap of the knocker-up at the window, followed by Nancy's dark, fumbling haste for the shift, then outside clogs on cobbles and the constant thump of the mill.

Now it seemed Sleep was as afraid as she was; too cowardly to risk the searing shock of agony which some nights could prod her awake like a poker set to embers. So, instead, she and Sleep would settle on a guarded half-slumber and each morning she'd stir in her single pallet to the deepening consciousness of a private pain, which was as hard and round as it was cruel in its mimicry of those earlier times. Whenever she placed her hand to it, through the clammy cloth of her nightgown, her breath would catch as she touched the solid substance of memory itself. But this was no quickening, she understood, no quivering of life within. It was, she silently conceded, in rare, brave moments, the dark, exacting opposite.

Yet on this hot summer morning, Ann awoke to other worries too. Nancy had been back late these last three nights, and when she asked her where she'd been, she didn't know whether to believe her reply. Only at George Leigh Street, she'd say, spending time listening to speakers. Politics, philosophy, democracy; fine, fancy words she'd scatter like fool's gold. God in Heaven, she was even for joining a Society. But as much as Ann was impatient with this excited chatter about liberty and suffrage, whatever such words could ever mean for them, she couldn't help hoping this was the only reason for Nancy's behaviour.

The truth was, she couldn't be sure there wasn't something

else, some*one* even, working upon her daughter. For in the brief intervals Nancy was at home these days, there was such a lightness to her, that same restlessness Ann always feared. She'd watch her, unable to stick to a task for more than five minutes at a time, before she was up and flitting round the room or finding some reason to slip out to the yard. Or else she wouldn't leave off Walter, petting him and indulging his moods, despite all Ann had said not to treat him like a baby any more.

She looked over at him now, still lying in bed, already wide awake, his thin arms raised in the space above him, hands in perpetual motion, making shapes, squares and triangles which he lengthened into steeples and studied intently through squinting eyes, all the while to a repetitive, low hum. He wasn't like any of them, she sighed. Not Nancy, nor Nathaniel, nor even her late, beloved Eddie. Not like that useless rogue of a father of his either, wherever he was these days. That, at least, was a blessing.

She could never fathom it, she still couldn't: why Walter was so nervous, so solitary, wary of other boys and overly fond of his mammy's coat-tails. Such looks he had too, fine features to match his delicacy of temperament, which only served to make him stand out the more. With dark, long-lashed eyes and his mouth, a sweet bow, he'd never look like any of the lads round here, and would no doubt remain prettier than most of the girls too. She feared for him in Manchester, this loud and ever-changing town, turning seven next birthday, in the shadow of the mill, which would surely claim him.

If only she could take him back to the farm. She pictured him there often, imagining him gambol through the fields, spinning and turning and falling with a cry of joy into hay as bright and golden as his hair. Racing up the hills and throwing sticks for Beauty, the eager terrier of her girlhood, whose tongue would hang open in shared excitement. She wished above anything he could have all this. To be safe, to be free, to breathe the fresh air of her homeland, where there'd be no one to notice him, no one to be different from and impossible to be strange at all.

It must be time to get up, she thought wearily, shifting herself slowly, inching upwards, careful of the pain, wincing all the while, until eventually she was sitting upright, her back against the wall, a fresh sweat trickling down the vale of her cleavage and its already sticky skin. Now she'd found a spot that was bearable, she paused and looked over at Walter again. She had a better view from this angle and, without warning, the sight of him, soft and messy from sleep, suddenly roused the fierce tenderness she'd been trying so hard to tame these past months. She felt her purpose weaken.

"Come here, lad," she called over to him. But he didn't look up. "Walter, lad. Come on and give your grandma a cuddle."

With a pang, she noticed the wariness in his eyes and knew that she was confusing him; he was already bewildered enough by her of late. She'd dropped the bedtime lullabies. Made him take himself to bed. She couldn't even remember the last time she'd kissed him. Yet, somehow, something about this morning was different, as though a balance had been tipped, and all at once her own need of him was greater than any desire to toughen him up. She smiled and patted the narrow space beside her. "*Come on!*"

At last convinced, he trundled over in surprised delight, and hopped on to the mattress, but the careless movement disturbed her position and sent a shot of fresh pain through her abdomen. She shut her eyes and took a noisy breath up through her nose, holding it a few seconds before exhaling slowly.

"Sorry." He knew better than to laugh these days.

"Nay, nay, tha's all right, son." She gathered herself, still breathing heavily. "Come on here." And she stretched her shrivelled arm round his slender frame, drawing him towards her with what strength she could muster to plant a kiss on top of his head. "Now, what were that song tha were singing just now?"

They sat together like that for a long while, humming

and whistling and Ann admiring his compositions, until the sun was high in the sky and cutting through the grime of the window. From the noises outside – a ball being thrown against a far wall and the chatter of wives undoubtedly hanging washing the length of the yard – it was clear the day had begun, and the rest of the court was already busy.

When they finally got out of bed, she turned Walter away and peeled off her sweaty nightdress. Bunching it up, she dried herself down with it, and then threw on another single, cotton layer, the only thing she could bear to wear in the heat. But even then, as she proceeded to cut the last of a three-day old loaf for breakfast, she already felt a fresh sweat forming.

"Be a good lad, Walter, and open the door."

He crossed over obediently and began to jiggle at the handle, which was always stiff, his face turning red with the effort. Ann watched him but didn't go to help. For all their cuddles, he still needed to stand on his own two feet. Eventually, he gave a stronger tug, and the door flew wide at last. Outside, the door to the yard was already propped open, and a welcome draught swept in, stirring across her, blissfully cold for a second on her wet skin.

"Well done, lad."

After they'd finished the bread, she began to sweep the floor – only the dust left last night from Nancy's clogs, as Walter had already scavenged for any crumbs they'd let slip – when something hit the wall outside with a loud thwack. She looked up, startled.

"Hey! Give it back!" came a voice from the far side of the yard.

The ball they'd heard earlier had clearly rolled astray and been clouted by some unseen newcomer.

There was laughter then, quite deep, and a man's voice, amused. "All right, all right. Don't fuss. I'm only having a laugh!" This was followed by the sound of a boot scraping, the smack of a return kick and another shouted exchange.

Walter rushed back to his unmade bed, escaping the noise,

and Ann tutted, turning to resume her task just as there was a firm knock on the still-open door. She looked round again, and this time there was a young man almost in the room already. She realised he must be the rogue from outside.

"Mrs Kay, I presume."

Ann folded her arms around the broom handle. He had good looks, this one, heightened by youth and health. His face was rounded and open, with more colour than most of the lads in Ancoats, who, even in summer, wore an ashen pallor. Indeed, there was something about him reminded her of the gypsies who sometimes came in their painted caravans and set up camp, for a month at a time, back in the valleys of Westmoreland, though, in truth, he was too fair to be one of that sort.

Then she spotted something strange. His hands, so big and strong-looking, were deeply stained, a colour somewhere between orange and brown, as though they'd been dipped in a bowl of blood, and under each of his nails, there was a semi-circular crust of red.

A brickie, she thought.

His blue eyes were twinkling at her inspection of him, and he seemed to be suppressing an amused smile.

"Tha presume correct," she replied at last, pointedly looking at his cap, which he'd not removed. "Who wants to know?"

He took the hint and doffed the cap with an exaggerated gesture, smiling broadly. "Delighted to meet you, Mrs Kay. I'm Joseph Price. A friend of Nancy's."

So here he was then, the expression of her fears and the very last thing Nancy needed right now. Nay, none of them needed another Smithy, not least since Nancy was still married to the original. Aye, for all she *hoped* that scoundrel had found his way to the bottom of the canal, for all they *knew*, Nancy was still a wife and not free to entertain the "friendship" – whatever *that* entailed – of which this new man spoke.

"I told her I'd try to get hold of this." The man reached into a canvas bag slung across his chest and brought out a rolled-up newspaper. Ann said nothing and kept her arms folded, so that he had to reach past her to set the paper on the table, leaving the smell of his sweat in the air between them.

Then, in the awkward silence, Walter jumped up from the bed, making the man startle, so that Ann couldn't help but smile. He'd clearly thought they were alone. She watched his face puzzle into a frown.

"'Ello little 'un!" he attempted with grating brightness, but Walter walked past without acknowledging him, humming a new tune. At this, the man pulled a bewildered face, shrugging his shoulders at Ann. The gesture enraged her. She gave the smallest nod of her head and hoped he'd realise it was his dismissal.

"Well, good day to you then, Mrs Kay," he said quickly and, with another doff of his cap, swiftly backed himself out the door.

TWO

JOSEPH

I'd not waited long after that first meeting in the tavern to persuade Archie and a few other of the lads from work to see if we could go brew up a bit of interest at Wrights. Thought a band of us would lend me an authentic air. So's that's what we did, one evening at the end of the shift, waiting just outside them great iron gates for all the factory workers.

I saw her straight off amongst the crowd, no cap, nor shawl, just her curls blowing free in the wind, and by the time she was out from under the arch and met my eye, there was already a couple of dots of pink in her cheeks. Perhaps they were brought on by the breeze that was getting up, but back then I liked to think it was 'cos she was pleased to see me.

"'Ow do," I said, taking off my own cap and walking towards her. "'Appen you'll not remember me..."

"Course I do," she smiled. "It's Joe int it?"

Well that was a good start, I told myself, drawing back my shoulders and offering my best smile. But next didn't she go and say, "Not fallen then?" which took me aback, I'll be honest, as I tried to fathom how it was she'd found me out, until she added, with a laugh, "Off tha chimney, I mean!"

I laughed along with her then, and heartily, pleased she'd

remembered as much about me. After that, we fell into talk quite easily, and I wasn't surprised to find she was all for joining the Female Reform Society which was rumoured to be setting up.

"You've heard of t' Union rooms on George Leigh Street, I take it?" I asked, only 'cos Archie had taken me there the night before.

"Oh!" she said, impressed. "Has tha been? What are they like?"

"Same as a school, I'd say. Rooms for classes, and there's a small library. 'Appen you should come down your'sel and take a look? There'll soon be talks for women too, I believe."

"That'll be Mrs Fildes organising them."

"Yeah, that's her," I said, though, in truth, I didn't have a clue.

"A library tha says?" she asked next, and I could tell from the eager look on her face, her mind was racing through the possibilities. "I were just thinking that's what I need. Pamphlets and whatnot. A chance to get me hands on some proper reading."

"Well, it may be I can help you there," I said. You see Archie had just lent me a book by that fella, Paine, said he thought I might find it interesting. So's now I tried the title out on her. "Perhaps you might like to borrow my *Rights of Man*?"

"Oh!" she cried, her eyes big with excitement. "Thomas Paine? I've read about him. Aye, if tha doesn't mind, I'd love to!"

"Grand," I smiled. "'Appen I'll pass by same time tomorrow then?"

"Aye, do. I'll look out for thee."

So's that's how we got started, and course, once I'd established myself as a true believer, if I were going to get anywhere with her, I had to carry on with it.

Ha!

Sometimes, looking back, I can scarcely credit the lengths I went to, wandering all over town to procure books and newspapers – some of 'em risky to get hold of and all – or else pamphlets on this question, or handbills on that, essays by Cartwright and Cobbett and even Hunt himself. All of 'em from all over the place, and from all different kinds of fella, all just so's I could pass them on to her.

I'd walk out of an evening to the Union rooms too, where there were talks most nights through the summer, and I'd be sure to see her. All sorts ended up in there, some from the factories round about – though there were a great many more too frightened of the consequences to come along – growing numbers of hand-loomers and even tradesfolk, all led by the the Patriotic Union Society, men who Archie would point out to me. We'd often listen to them, earnest speakers all, 'specially the likes of Wroe from the *Observer* and Saxton whose missus used to address the women.

Some nights we'd even go further afield, to reform meetings in the towns up north, men and women together, on a cart Archie was able to borrow. Me, Nancy and Archie and a whole load of others. Mary, inevitably, and her fella, Mick McDermott, some of Archie's old crowd, though never his missus, who'd stay at home with the kids, a handful of spinners from Wrights, and some younger lasses, including Nancy's neighbour, Jemima Wilson. All of us crouched together, me half-listening to the talk of reform, yet all the time driven to distraction by the warmth of her sat up close, as we swayed over the track out of town, beneath skies clear of smoke and bright with stars.

THREE

Trade was slow. That's what they all said, the masters of Manchester's mills who speculated over the complexities of the market, scratching their heads over pricing and contracts and the fine balance of supply and demand. Meanwhile, for Nancy and her fellow workers, the reality of the downturn was stark: less pay, more hunger and the threat of laying-off.

Amidst this increased hardship, a particularly sombre mood had shrouded Wrights one week in early June, when Lizzie Flannagan, a popular woman from the carding room, the sort who always had a good word for anyone, met with the kind of tragedy every mother feared. When her husband had been laid low with brown lung more than twelve months before, Lizzie had become the sole breadwinner for their young family of six, but since trade had slowed, her wages had been stretched to snap, and, with food so scarce, her two youngest, their bodies already wasted to skin and bone, had succumbed to an infection they'd no strength left to fight, dying in the same bed, on the same night.

As soon as word got out, Nancy and Mary had gone over to the Flannagans' rooms straight after their shift, to offer sympathy and to see what they could do, but they hadn't been able to get so much as near the front door for the number of people crammed in the yard, white-faced with shock, to pay their respects.

After that, anger was in the air like a contagion, and Nancy found it easier than she'd ever imagined to persuade more workers to the cause. She had to whisper round the factory though, arrangements for meetings at the Union rooms, or in the alehouses round about, careful to avoid the likes of Yates or Molly Kennedy, who'd like no better than to stir up trouble for her, since the old mistress's injunction against reformers was still emphatically in place.

Despite all this unrest, Nancy was grateful that at least her hours in the schoolroom remained unchanged. Most of the children were progressing well and so was she, as she practised the formation of her chalk letters alongside them, her hand improving all the time, and the curves and loops gradually becoming smaller and more sure.

She continued to stay on to clean up after the class as well, and ordinarily this would be the time Captain Wright would come to visit her. She had grown fond of their discussions, debating the merits of the poems he lent to her. (They were both agreed on the new style of the *Lyrical Ballads*, albeit with a few exceptions, and Lord Byron, as well as Milton and Shakespeare of course, though half of it, she admitted, she couldn't yet follow.) Or else they would expand shared ideas for the school. She wondered if he might set up a small library at the back of the classroom; he suggested talks and lectures on all manner of topics, to be open to all of the workers. However, as spring had drifted into summer and he'd become more embroiled in the business, their plans had foundered.

It was then, as the crisis deepened, and Nancy's enthusiasm for reform grew, she began to privately wonder at Wright, that such a man should go along with his aunt's prohibition. Indeed, she found it difficult at times not to challenge him about it, so certain was she of persuading him of the justice of their demands. Yet on the occasions they met, which were less frequent these days, she found she simply couldn't raise it. Time and again she'd urge herself to be brave and speak out, but at every opportunity she'd hold back and remain silent. Of course, some of her reluctance was, in part, a fear of consequence – whilst she trusted him enough to treat her fairly, she still couldn't be certain whether loyalty to his aunt might not ultimately prevail – though, in truth, her reticence had more to do with how troubled the man seemed, harassed as he was by the demands of dealing with the decline in trade and all that meant for everyone in the mill. He may be the master, she thought, but he was also kind, and she didn't want to add to his evident burden.

Nevertheless, the unspoken question of reform had become, in her eyes, a growing impediment to their unlikely friendship. It saddened her not to talk to him about it and made her feel dishonest, so that on evenings like this, when she'd concluded he was too busy to join her, it was increasingly with a strange and cheerless sense of relief.

In any case, she reasoned, she couldn't have lingered long tonight even if he had come. There was another meeting she wanted to go to, out at Middleton this time. Archie Thompson, Joe Price's friend, had told her all about a fella there with a great gift for words; Bamford his name was. They were arranging a wagon to take a few over that way to listen to him, right grand it sounded. She couldn't remember the last time she'd been so far from town and had spent the whole day looking forward to it.

With her schoolroom chores almost complete, she rushed through the last of them while bolting down a small crust of bread she'd kept in her apron pocket, knowing she wouldn't get another chance to eat all evening. Not that there was any more food even if she were to go home. Walter should have her share of the soup, she'd told her mother in the morning.

"Aye, and he needs his mammy home too," she'd replied. Nancy bit her lip at the memory. Why could her mam never see she was doing all this for him?

She closed up the schoolroom, fixed her cap, and was just about to head downstairs, when all at once Wright stepped out from a door below and appeared at the bottom, his head almost hidden behind a sheaf of papers.

"Oh!" they both exclaimed and then laughed at one another's hesitation, she still at the top, and he, waiting at the bottom.

"I'm just on me way," Nancy said, though she only moved when he beckoned her down. As she came lower, she noticed he looked tired. The thin skin beneath his eyes was tinged a dark, purplish brown and his pale face drawn with anxiety.

"I'm sorry I must be running late," he said.

"Nay, it's me, I'm off early. Off out tonight."

She saw his face drop and, not for the first time, understood her power to disappoint him. Almost without thinking, she tried to cheer him, adopting a bright, new tone, nodding playfully at the papers in his arms, "Are them for me?"

"What? Oh no. This is some music. Well, wait, yes. Actually, this one *is* for you," and he awkwardly extracted a newspaper from the rest of his bundle. She took it politely, even though these days she preferred the *Observer* which Joe supplied, or better still, the *Black Dwarf*.

"Thank you," she smiled and then added, "Music tha says?"

"Yes, some pieces I ordered from London just arrived."

"What kind of pieces?" she asked. They were walking beside one another now, out through the clerks' office and into the yard.

"For the pianoforte."

"Oh!" she exclaimed. "Tha plays?"

"Yes, I do."

"And tha likes to, doesn't tha? I can tell by tha face."

"Oh indeed! In fact, I'd say I enjoy it above anything. Well, almost."

"Really? And tha never told me 'til now!" she exclaimed.

He shrugged, grinning at her, like a little boy she thought, surprised to see how animated he'd become. She pictured him at the instrument, alone and intense, and straightaway it seemed to make sense of everything she knew about him. "How wonderful!"

They walked on a little further, before she began again, "Does tha know, I've only ever heard one the once. A proper piano, I mean. Not a church organ, that doesn't count, does it? Aye, it were back when I were a little girl in Westmoreland. Squire from the neighbouring parish acquired one and there were that much excitement. Such a to-do. Invited half t' county to come and listen he did!" She thought for a moment and frowned, "Or maybe that were his wife did that. Any road, I'm no expert, but I don't think he were any good!"

At this unexpected verdict, Wright laughed loudly. "Well, I've been playing a long while now, so I hope you'd judge me competent!"

"Oh, our Walt'd love it!" she beamed back, clutching her hands together and looking up at the sky. They'd already reached the far side of the yard and had stopped just before the wide brick arch. "Somehow music brings out the best in him."

He smiled warmly at her.

"He used to love me mam singing to him of an evening, lullabies and such. She'd such a beautiful voice."

"Does she not sing anymore?"

"Ah," Nancy said, avoiding his eye, "she's not so well just now, sir."

At this, she sensed Wright look down at her anxiously. She wished he wouldn't. "I'm very sorry to hear it," he persisted, but she looked away again. "If there's anything…"

"Aye, thank thee," she replied with a dip of her head. "Well, me friends'll be wondering where I am, so I best say goodnight sir," and she stepped away from him, waving the paper in the air with a forced jollity. "And thank thee once again."

Wright simply nodded, but even before she'd escaped, she saw his eyes fill with the same sadness she'd noticed before. However, this time she was shocked to find herself unaccountably irritated by it. By him. His concern. His melancholy. Infuriated even, so that she hastened her steps through the shade of the tunnel, panting for air, and turned out on to the street at last with a great gasp of relief.

She wouldn't let him ruin things. Not tonight. Not with such an adventure in store. Nay, nay, life was hard enough without brooding and being so solemn all the time.

Desperate to be gone, she looked up and down the thoroughfare, but there was no cart yet, nor any sign of Joe who'd promised to meet her. Where were they? She frowned and chewed her lip again and began to pace the section of road beyond the mill entrance, but just as she'd reached the next corner, ready to turn back, she absently glanced down the side street, and, to her surprise, there he was, though he hadn't seen her: Joe Price, the handsome radical, whose attention was so flattering, teetering on tiptoes to get a good look at himself in the plate glass of one of the mill's high windows.

FOUR

JOSEPH

I was right and all. It did turn out to be a grand, fine summer. At least at first.

Every morning, before it got too hot, I'd climb up our growing tower of red, into wide skies of blue. Smoke from Wrights' chimney was already drifting away at that height, so that up top there were light breezes and birds winging past us. I know it sounds daft, but it was just as though my thick head was finally being cleared of foolishness and my mind awakened at last. Full of new ideas I was, and full of Nancy, and I swear it felt just then as though I could reach out from our little platform and touch the very heavens.

Ha!

Well, all this time, whenever we met, I could tell by the flash of her eye, she was pleased to see me. Course, I knew she was fired up by the talks and the gatherings and the prospect of change, but it wasn't just that; there was something more. Something in the way she spoke, the way she moved, something about her look; it was obvious she liked me.

Even so, there remained something distant about her too. Something cool and remote that only served to intrigue me all the more. I mean she never told me a thing about herself.

It was always reform she wanted to talk about, that and the latest reports in the paper I'd get a hold of for her. Or else, if I really pressed her, so's she'd have to reveal something, it was only ever a fragment of her childhood she'd give away: the farm she'd grown up on, or the brother who got taught to read when she didn't. And she'd keep up this reserve even as our little group larked about, taking a drink in the Prince Regent or singing on the back of the cart on the way home from t' north, so that somehow it always felt we were sort-of-together and sort-of-not, all at the same time.

In truth, the thing she most liked to talk about, apart from reform, was that class of hers at the factory. She was always that pleased when young Peter finally mastered his alphabet or young Paul, his grammar. Yeah, she was that fond of them little tinkers, I'll be honest, I'd find myself getting almost jealous. But, at the same time, I'd tell myself not to. Not to mess up. Not with this one. You see, it was becoming clear to me she was a special girl and that perhaps the time had come at last to change my ways.

And then, just like that, talk of Hunt was suddenly all over the place.

I remember going to the Union rooms one warm night round the start of July. We'd made good progress on the chimney that day and been late coming down off the stack, so that by the time Archie and I arrived in the room, there was already a big crowd. Lucky ones who'd got there early were settled on forms, but as many again were jostling at the sides and back. It was stifling warm, and all the windows had been opened wide to let in a bit o' breeze.

Some of the Female Reformers were there too, and when I searched the room for her, I spotted Nancy squeezed up with Mary on the end of a row. As I recall, Mary was looking red in the face and overheated, and I laughed to myself to see Nancy hand her a pamphlet with which to fan herself.

Eventually, Joseph Johnson, an eager reform fella and secretary of the Union, weaved his way through the crowd, bounding up to the lectern to announce the grand plan. "It's numbers Hunt's after. He says that's what'll do it: big numbers; masses of us; just the sheer pressure of scale."

Well, I hardly need tell you this was the beginning of talk of a great public meeting and the plan to invite Henry Hunt, the famous champion of suffrage to Manchester. The idea was to bring together the whole county of Lancashire, all us reform societies from the town, and them from surrounding areas too, from Bury in the north to Stockport in the south, all to assemble as one body, right in the centre, on St Peter's Field, to call for the vote and a reform of Parliament at last. Largest assembly ever seen, that's what they were after, and, in a new strategem, we were all to commence exercises at once, like an army of sorts, drilling on the moors beyond town to ready ourselves and practise proper comportment.

As we all spilled onto the street afterwards, the air was still balmy, the sky not yet dark. Amidst all the chatter and leave-taking, I looked across at Nancy and straightaway sensed a new excitement about her. She had a spring in her step, and her face was bright and lively, and when she talked on what we'd heard, she got almost breathless trying to keep her words up with her thoughts.

"I'll go!" she cried. "Just try and stop me! And to the moors fust. We all need to know what we're doing."

And as for me? Well, I nodded earnestly enough, as though in innocent agreement, even as I was thinking such a trip to the moor might finally be my chance to get her on her own at last.

Well, shortly after that night, the summer turned fierce, and I mean baking hot. Every morning, shirtsleeves rolled, lugging bricks, the sun blistering every inch of my bared skin, and cloth plastered to my spine with sweat, so's I'd've gladly ripped it off, if it weren't that my back would only get sore with blisters too. And after such a day's toil, came uncomfortable evenings, muggy and stale, when the sun hung heavy and stubborn above the half-built chimney, like an angry, red boil in the sky.

It was such a relief then to make our escape from the oppression of town. Walking with the others beyond the road, onto the dusty track north, swigging warm water from flasks we'd not been able to keep out of the sun. Up towards the moorland, where open space and the scent of flowers awaited. Nancy'd name them as we passed, swathes of pale willowherb which she plucked at and twirled, lily of the valley, chicory, purple heather and, on the clearing, endless yellow buttercups. And we, with our own colours too, she'd say, banners of every shade and the red caps of liberty.

The drills themselves were designed to resemble the great assembly itself, like some sort of grand rehearsal. Up front, a lady from the Female Reformers would hand over a letter and one of the liberty caps to the main speaker, who set the cap on the end of a pole from which one of the many banners waved. Next, all the aims of reform were restated: a commitment to universal suffrage, annual parliaments and free trade. Fine words designed to stir our resolve, all delivered in a near-shouted address, so the many scores of us spread across the green plain could make 'em out, as they echoed around the dun-coloured hills.

That first night, something else was impressed on us too, same as it was every night after, and whatever folk think of me, I swear I respected it, same as the next man. So, here's the thing they stressed: the importance of *peaceableness*. It was vital we walked the streets in an orderly manner. Essential we dressed as smartly as possible too, best Sunday trim preferred, so's no one could deride us for raggedness or dirt. And, above all, on no account was there to be any resistance to the authorities by violent means.

No sticks. No stones. No brickbats.

For the most part, this was met with murmurs of approval, and many of them near me nodded sagely as though to demonstrate how sensible they could be. But there were other voices too, them that asked was it wise to go into such an encounter without means of defence? Didn't the Union men know what that big bastard Nadin – him that was deputy chief constable – was capable of? Or that half the county's militia was already mustered in readiness? And, I confess, I wondered the same myself, and how any red-blooded man could ever stop himself if he was under attack.

But the Union lot were having none of it. Speaker's words went something like this: "The moment one of us lifts a fist in anger, we've lost the argument; the moment another throws a stone, we've gifted them the excuse they need to shut down our protests. We must not be what they expect of us. We must be what we know ourselves to be. The finest of men and women, good and true!"

Well, this last was to zealous cheers which drowned out any dissent and got everyone eager to move on to the next stage, which was to practise our manner of arrival into town. A number of Union men, striding round the edge of the crowd, shouted directions to file into lines, from which we were required to form row upon row of half a dozen men at a time, whilst the ladies and them with flags were directed where to stand and how to hold them aloft. Once everyone was in place, we were set off marching and soon learned how to maintain a steady pace, with cries of "Slow it down!" or "Shift tha'sen!", so that no row went too far ahead, nor any other caught up in the row in front.

As we marched on, music played and a merry jollity spread through the crowd, as laughter mixed with outbursts of song. Meantime, amidst all this activity, *my* greatest enjoyment remained a glimpse of Nancy a couple of rows ahead, her hair aflame in the last of the sun. I remember she'd just cast me a smile over her shoulder, and I was basking in the pleasure of it when, to my annoyance, the young lad next to me disturbed my thoughts, elbowing me in the ribs and pointing to a nearby thicket, all dotted with fruit it was, "I'll be back for some of them when we're done."

It was gone nine by the time the marching was over and most folk were weary by then. Mindful of their shift in the morning, they set off straightaway, back to the already sleeping town. Yet there was a good number of us who lingered too, making the most of the cooling evening, and being out in the open with trees and flowers and grass to walk our bare feet through.

It was just as these stragglers, our own little band amongst them, finally started to break up when I saw Nancy, who'd been talking to some folk I didn't know from Wrights, walk over to Jemima and take her arm, to follow Mary and Mick towards the track which led down to the road. Well, I can't tell you why, perhaps it was the Devil's work, but there was something about the gesture, that casual taking of the girl's arm, that fired a sudden rage within me. There was such an ease and intimacy to it she seemed determined to deny me, despite her smiles and her friendship and the attraction I could feel between us. I daresay some might call me conceited, but it just didn't seem right that she could walk away into the night like that, with only the most fleeting goodbye to me, and so that's when I decided, I had to waylay her.

"Hey!" I called out, and my voice sounded loud and echoed in the valley. A few folk, including Nancy, turned around. "Nancy! Do you like raspberries?" It was a bit lame, I admit, but I wasn't far off the bush the lad had pointed out.

"I love 'em!" she cried. "Why?"

"There's hundreds of 'em, on t' yon incline." I pointed my thumb behind me and gave her one of my broad smiles.

Call it luck or fate, or whatever else, but Mary hadn't heard me. She and Mick were already a way ahead, so for once Nancy had no wary looks to put her off. Only problem was she'd taken responsibility for the young lass, Jemima, and with a sinking heart, I saw her ask her to join us. Still, it was better than nothing, I thought, and so it was the three of us who headed out, back over the moor.

"Is it not a bit early for them?" Nancy asked as we approached.

"Take a look for yourself."

She and Jemima reached the bushes and stopped, their eyes widening in astonishment at the thicket that spread atop a long ridge and spilled over an incline beyond view.

"Oh, my Lord above, Joe! There's enough here for an army!"

On closer inspection, however, it was clear a few of our comrades – no doubt the young 'un who'd put me on to it in the first place amongst 'em – had taken the choicest fruit from the higher ground and that a better spot was going to be in the little valley of sorts downhill.

There was already a rough route through where some of the bush had been trampled in the past, so I scrambled down it first, kicking out the way the worst of any trailing roots. To tell truth though, it was a bit steeper than I'd credited, and when I got to the bottom, the girls were still at the top, humming and hawing over the best way to descend. I took a few strides halfway back up and held out my hand, "Come on, I'll grab you if you slip."

Course, it was Nancy who came first, taking the path slowly, holding her arms out wide either side to keep her balance, her face fixed with concentration. As for me, my heart was pounding in my ears as I watched every step of her progress. Then, when she'd almost made the bottom, I decided I'd not waste my chance and offered her my hand anyway. It was darker down there in the shadow of the hill, but the last rays of the sun just glinted in her eyes as she reached for me, letting me guide her the rest of the way. Instant her hand touched mine, the feel of it felt so right, not soft nor smooth, but small and firm, like her body, which passed so close, I could smell the very sweetness of her.

"Is tha coming?" she shouted. She'd dropped my hand as soon as she was down and was half-laughing up at Jemima, who was still fussing with her petticoats and pulling an anxious face. In the end, she caused that much to-do, Nancy suggested I climb back up to her, to which I agreed, though only to oblige Nancy, as the stupid girl giggled and grasped at me the whole way.

By the time Jemima and I were back level, Nancy'd already begun to pluck at the bush. "These ones are t' ripest," she pulled off a fruit and turned to me, her eyes full of challenge. "Over here." And she popped it in her mouth with a gleeful laugh.

I didn't move, or pick any berries myself, not at first any road; I just wanted to watch her. Above us, the sky had turned to twilight, stars full out and a faint sliver of moon. In the half-light, her body leant into the tangle, stretching to reach the fruit, and in an instant, her fingers were at her mouth again, licking off the juice.

I think she knew I was watching her, and I think she enjoyed it too, being admired. Like as if the whole thing was a bit of play-acting of the sort you find in the Theatre Royal, the scene a kind of enchantment and she some sort of spirit with power over mortal men like me. But then, looking round at the gathering dusk, just like that, she broke the spell, "We'd best be gone soon, afore it gets too dark."

"Aye, Mam'll be wondering where I am," piped up Jemima, who I'd forgotten all about.

"Mine too," agreed Nancy. "Quick, though, afore we go, let's pick some to take back!"

"But how will we carry 'em?"

Nancy thought a moment, "I know!" And she took out her cloth cap which she'd folded in her pocket and turned it out as a makeshift bowl, swiftly filling it to the top with the plumpest, reddest raspberries she could find.

"Our Walter'll love these!"

FIVE

Adelaide had spent all day out of town on a visit to Hugh Osborne's sister, whose husband's landed estate lay beyond the north of town and whose coach and liveried driver had been sent to collect her in the morning. It was in the same coach she was now making her return journey, setting out as the sun was falling slowly through the sky, and the sweet scent of high summer was on the air.

Being the only passenger, she sat in the middle of the front-facing seat, so sumptuously upholstered she might have been on a throne, carefully spreading the silk skirt of her pelisse around her. Naturally, the track out of the estate was smooth, and the carriage steady, so that she was able to settle back comfortably into the soft velvet and reflect on her visit.

They had enjoyed a pleasant afternoon, she and her hostess, Lady Louisa, conversing in the shade of a rose arbour, the latest innovation of the estate's talented gardener, who had disciplined the lovely pinks and whites to spread artfully over their little shelter. Afterwards, they'd been joined by Sir William and sat down to an early dinner of roasted lamb and claret, the three of them together around the head of the table, their intimate party dwarfed by the proportions of the vast dining room.

Throughout, Louisa had treated her with an attentiveness which Adelaide could not but find gratifying, remembering as she always did, the early years of their acquaintance, when Louisa had been barely able to disguise her distaste for the company of an innkeeper's daughter. It had been hard-won, this acceptance, or at least the show of it, Adelaide thought, as she often did on these occasions. She'd applied herself diligently over the years, cultivating her voice, her manners, and her taste, spending Silas's money to best effect, so that now, even after the shame of Robert's intemperance, not a single one of her carefully selected set could say she wasn't one of them. She nodded grimly to herself, striving to feel the same satisfaction she'd ordinarily derive from such observations, though today, for reasons she couldn't quite determine, she felt strangely flat.

It was another uncomfortably warm evening, and the carriage was small and stuffy. Having been out since morning, and now with a heavy dinner inside her threatening to bring on her biliousness, Adelaide was weary. She fanned herself a short while, but it wasn't long before her eyelids started to grow heavy, and though she tried to stay awake, stretching her eyes wide every time they startled open, they would keep on drooping closed again, as the measure of the horse's tread and the sway of the coach steadily lulled her into a light sleep.

After a half-hour or so, however, the surface of the path changed. Rocks and stones and rutted seams of dry dirt caused the wheels to stick and then to drag, and the ride became bumpier and bumpier, until, at last, Adelaide was jolted full awake, the feathers on her bonnet bobbing up and down furiously. With every lurching movement now, she found herself sliding one way and then the other, until eventually, clawing her way from the middle to the left side of the carriage, she held tight on to the window frame. Chancing to look out, she saw the most extraordinary sight.

A bank of purple, tufted heather stretched from the edge of the track up towards a higher, flat level of moorland, which itself gave way to brown hills that rose up against the horizon, and in their shadow, on a sizeable clearing, were assembled hundreds of workers. No, indeed there were thousands of them! All of them dressed as if they'd just come from the mills round and about, though none of them from Wrights, she hoped; hadn't she been right to make certain of that? They had divided into groups, and were marching in formation, row upon arm-linked row, like the movement of a vast army. Upon their banners were emblazoned words she couldn't make out, no doubt the mottoes of reform, and atop their poles, carried for the purpose, were red and white bonnets, which she recognised as Phrygian caps, like those worn by Marianne.

She leaned closer towards the window, unable to believe her eyes. Yet just as she was looking upon this, the very embodiment of her fears, there was a sudden, sharp hit to the window on the other side, and she shrieked. Oh, dear Lord, they were being set upon! Pressing her body deep into the corner of the coach, she nevertheless craned to get a view out of the window that had been struck, though all she could make out was a pair of ragged children racing in an adjacent field.

Just then, the carriage gave a violent jolt, almost sending her out of her seat again, as it came to a standing stop. Adelaide froze with fear, her heart beating; they had been seized!

A moment later, the coachman's head appeared at the door.

"Why have you stopped?" she cried. Then, seeing he was alone and untroubled, she added, "You fool, we'll be ambushed!"

"Madam, forgive me. I heard thee cry and thought that something was the matter?"

"Something the matter? Of course there's something the matter! Did you not hear that noise? A brick was thrown at that window not two minutes ago!"

The coachman frowned doubtfully and took a step back to assess the side of the coach.

"Begging tha pardon, madam, but I think tha's mistaken. I can't see any damage. A brick'd have smashed up t' window."

"There was a brick, I say! Or a stone perhaps." Clutching at her stomach, which was cramping painfully now, she looked nervously out towards the moor. "It's the Jacobins! Can you not see them?" and she flung her arm towards the assembly. "Make haste! Make haste!" She was shooing him away now. "We need to be gone from here at once. At once! Before we're set upon!"

* * *

From her velveted enclosure, Adelaide couldn't see the coachman climb back into his seat, shaking his head at the sight of the gathering five hundred feet away or more, nor spot the children closer at hand, a boy and a girl, squealing with merriment through the high grass, and though she heard the man gee up the horse, she gave no thought to his laughter and the cry of, "Little tinkers!"

SIX

It was breakfast time and another day of hot sunshine poured through the tall windows of the dining room, making the silverware glint. Adelaide, who'd eaten no more than a slice of pear, was pacing the room's length, up and down, working the ring on her left finger. Now and again, Samson could sense the flick of her eyes towards him, as he sat at the end of the table, sheltering behind an open newspaper. It wasn't long, however, before she realised he was ignoring her, whereupon she heaved a sigh so immense it demanded a response.

Without looking up, he relented so far as to say, "Aunt Adelaide, you must try to calm yourself."

"Calm myself? Calm myself? Clearly, Samson, you cannot imagine what it's like to be ambushed in such a manner!"

At this, he finally lowered the paper, raising his eyebrows. She would do this from time to time, he'd noticed, momentarily forget his military career as it suited her, though it wouldn't be long before she'd invoke it again.

"If they can throw a brick at a defenceless woman, what else might they be capable of? A trained mob!"

Samson was acutely aware the increased hardship of the last few months had won more and more workers over to the idea of reform, and of the plan to welcome the famous "Orator" Hunt to a great meeting, just down the road, on St Peter's Field. It was this proposed assembly, above anything, which was causing Liverpool's government and the local authorities so much consternation. As for Adelaide, it seemed she could think of nothing else.

Yet Samson had read enough about this Hunt fellow to recognise the man's approach was not one of aggression. As he understood it, Hunt's idea was to harness the power of numbers in a show of workers' respectability and thereby confound the authorities' expectations. There would be no violence and no riotous mob but rather a vast, peaceable assembly of reasonable men. This, he was certain, was the message that was so exciting the workers in town and no doubt at Wrights too, though, unsurprisingly, none of them, not even Nancy, dared talk to him about it. He'd frequently endeavoured to explain the idea to Adelaide as well, though each time he did so, it seemed precisely Hunt's reasoned and intelligent approach that affronted her the most.

"I've told you, Adelaide, be assured, the protest will pass off peaceably. That's what their main man advocates."

"Whist, Samson! For a military man, you're astonishingly credulous! But even granted as you say, and most of them don't want trouble, it only takes a few louts to break ranks and you've a riot on your hands."

"Well then, you arrest the troublemakers."

"Samson, you don't seem to appreciate the gravity of this."

"I think there's a danger of overreaction."

"The town needs to be prepared. The Yeomanry must be on their mettle."

Here it was! He'd been waiting for it. The question of whether he should offer his military experience to the local militia hadn't gone away. Adelaide had continued to wheedle it into conversation these past months, or else, when the mood had taken her, she'd simply come straight out with it, demanding he write a letter to the Major. However, Samson had found himself even more opposed to the idea than when it had first been suggested by Hugh Osborne at that dreadful dinner party. Indeed, after these last months at the mill and his friendship with Nancy, his natural sympathies were now further removed from Adelaide's than he could ever have imagined, though he knew better than to declare so openly. Instead, he said wearily, "You know my feelings on the matter."

"But, Samson, please. For your poor dear aunt."

He wasn't sure whether there was a flash of irony in her eye, but she was smiling sweetly at him, her fingers working the mourning brooch she still kept pinned to her breast. He returned a courteous nod, straining for a residue of the pity he'd discovered towards her soon after his arrival in Manchester. Yet the truth was he'd become heartily sick of the game-playing she maintained between them. She was so often like a small child, he thought, always after her own way, never knowing when to stop.

"Will you not at least seek some assurances the town is ready?"

It was Samson who sighed now. What on earth did she intend him to do? That he should simply turn up and extol his own military record in exchange for information? No, he could never bring himself to be so high-handed. Besides, what the devil use were these men in any event? Surely they'd simply bungle along until the authorities discovered they weren't worth the money wasted on them.

"Go and see the Major. Or Captain Birley," she importuned again.

"On what basis? I'm not a soldier anymore."

"Yes, but you've *real* experience, Samson. Half of *them* are shopkeepers!"

He made no reply, but stood up and folded his newspaper, struck by something new in what she'd said. He wiped his mouth with a napkin and placed his teacup on the tray for the maid, all the while conscious of a creeping unease. Danger. Yes, indeed, there was a danger he'd not fully appreciated before, though it was not the one his aunt feared. Rather, it was the threat posed to the reformers by the Yeomanry's inexperience, especially considering the size of the anticipated crowd.

Perhaps, after all, he ought to ascertain more information about their plans. At the very least it would mean he could silence Adelaide by thinking she'd won a surprise victory.

"Very well, Aunt, very well, as you wish, I shall see what I can discover. But you must promise me one thing in return."

"What is it?"

"To put such concerns out of your mind."

* * *

That afternoon Samson left the mill early. The sky had been cloudless all day, and for hours a fat boll of smoke had squatted immobile above the roof of the factory. When he'd gone to inspect them, the heat inside the machine rooms had been brutal. His shirt was wet in seconds, and his face so damp, wisps of cotton had stuck to it, ageing him in an instant with a beard of white bristles. Immediately, he'd ordered an extra break for the workers to cool off in the shadow of the mill. Yet even now, towards the end of the day, the sun continued to beat down, so that the breeze that was picking up across the canal still wasn't enough to shift the stifling air. As he set off from Ancoats, holding his jacket over his shoulder, he pondered what else might be done to alleviate the workers' discomfort in this heat.

The atmosphere in town was equally oppressive, though altogether more sluggish. There were fewer pedestrians and the carriage traffic was slow, clogging the thoroughfare. The horses, irritable with heat, their rear haunches glistening with sweat, pawed at the ground, sending up choking clouds of dust, as their passengers coughed and spluttered and bad-temperedly cried to their equally indisposed coachmen to move on. Even the children who customarily gathered at the corner of Charlotte Street were lethargic, their youthful energy drained, as they perched on the edge of the pavement, or splayed on a grassed verge like the feral cats of the continent, too lazy to spin their tops or bowl their hoops.

Samson himself, dishevelled from the day, was also tempted to succumb to the heat. Here was the house and its high-ceilinged coolness; he could simply retreat to wash and to change and to rest. However, he'd been thinking all day about what he'd decided at breakfast and was determined to carry on to Portland Street, which was only round the next corner after all. This, he understood, was where the Yeomanry had mustered these past weeks. It was also where the men liked to drink.

Turning into the road, he was instantly hit by a powerful, earthy smell, a blend of hops and horse-shit, heavy on the air, though when he looked both ways, up and down the street, there was no sign of the Yeomen or their horses. He'd noticed on previous occasions the soldiers sometimes stationed themselves in a yard a little way south, though that wasn't where he was bound. Instead, he set off, craning at the buildings, seeking out their preferred tavern.

He was surprised to find it was a tiny building, so small he almost missed it, hemmed in on both sides by taller neighbours, and with a door so low, Samson had to duck his head to get through. Once inside, his eyes took a moment to adjust to the brownish light before he could make out that, besides the bar itself, there was little more than a narrow corridor to house the patrons.

Despite the early hour and the infernal heat, this small space was crammed with young men in military uniform, the blue coatee and white breeches of the Manchester and Salford Yeomanry, though a great number were in rolled-up shirtsleeves, having discarded their jackets in an untidy pile at the far end of the bar. There was an overwhelming smell of sweat and flatulence and stale, boozy breath. The whole scene put him in mind of countless similar dens he'd visited during his army days, and he felt suddenly weary.

The men were occupied in an arm-wrestling competition taking place between two of their number at the bar. An older, balding man with a short, stocky frame had just dispatched a taller man who was clearly the worse for wear for drink and laughing at his own defeat. Meanwhile, the company's attention had shifted to finding a new opponent for the victor, and Samson saw the men turn on another youngster he couldn't quite make out but who was evidently reluctant, given the crowding and cajoling that had started up.

Nearer to Samson, a hollow-cheeked officer with protruding eyes and greasy hair slicked off his forehead had been taking wagers. One of his pockets bulged, like his eyes, and he held a piece of paper and a pencil close to his chest. When the previous man had lost, several of the group, undoubtedly the gamblers, had jostled around him and he'd opened his arms wide, appealing for more space. Now the same men pressed him again, but he was decisively shaking his head, clearly unwilling to take a chance on the new man.

As Samson moved closer, the shouts and cheers were mounting, and he saw the extent of the bald man's advantage in both weight and experience over the challenger, who, with long, dark, glossy hair, looked more like a woman and not yet one and twenty.

Samson had just managed to summon the innkeeper when the bald man, in a single lunge, pinned the young man's arm down, to an almighty cheer and thunderous drum roll of hands along the length of the bar. Straightaway, the winner was handed a tankard of ale, and he threw his head back, with a shout of, "For King and Country!" before draining it in a single draught.

Meanwhile, a number of men were piling in on the defeated lad, prodding him in the back and messing his hair. When he flinched to avoid another shove, it was in Samson's direction. Although he was wearing a fixed, nervous grin, Samson could see from the boy's large, brown cow-eyes, he was frightened.

"Young lad's a bit green," he observed to the innkeeper, who was also watching the sport.

"He's new. Only signed up last week."

"Really? Do they get many?"

"Oh aye. They've been appealing for weeks. What wi' all this talk of t' meeting."

"The Hunt assembly?"

"Aye. Big 'un planned on t' Field."

Samson was just beginning to think he might learn something after all, when there was a loud cry for service from the other end of the bar, and giving a brief nod of leave-taking, the man stepped away.

The contest appeared to be over, and a few of the Yeomen, having received their winnings, were retrieving their jackets and heading for the door. The noise began to drop, and Samson was about to give up and go home when he noticed the young, defeated boy was now on his own, perched on a stool.

"Here, have this," Samson offered him the tankard of ale he'd purchased but not touched.

"Who are you?" the boy asked warily, taking the drink just the same.

"I'm Samson Wright. How do you do?" He proffered his hand with a friendly smile, but the lad didn't move and looked at him coldly.

"Are you of Wrights' mill?"

"Yes, indeed. Silas Wright was my uncle."

"Ah, *my* uncle knew him."

"Oh, and who's he?"

"My name's Baldwin," the lad said in a dull tone. "George Baldwin."

Samson nodded, "Ah."

"You've met my Uncle Harry, then?"

"Yes. He's a friend of my aunt's."

"Well, he's *my* guardian, and all this is *his* idea." He waved his arm around the bar in a vague and hopeless gesture.

"I see, and how do you find the Yeomen?" Samson gestured to the men who remained.

George laughed contemptuously, "Most of the time, in here!"

"But are they not in earnest, preparing for this Hunt fellow?"

"Oh indeed! The cutler's already sharpening their blades!" The boy's voice was flat, his face impassive, so that Samson couldn't be sure whether or not he spoke in jest.

"And what about you?"

"I shouldn't be here at all. I should be at my studies, preparing for my matriculation," he stared dejectedly at the glass. "I go up to university in a few weeks, but Uncle Harry doesn't much approve. Says I must make myself useful until then."

"I see." Samson felt a pang of pity, remembering the uncle's brutish manner. He could easily imagine him capable of bullying his young ward. "Actually, you misapprehend me; I wondered, in fact, if you believe there will be trouble?"

Two more of the soldiers, red-faced and sweaty, staggered past them and sniggered. George frowned, and Samson could see the boy was discomfited, so he didn't press his point and looked away, affecting a casual air. This nonchalance worked an effect, however, because after a moment, George spoke again. "The way I see it, I don't think we'll be called upon. I've heard the protesters aren't looking for trouble, and even if they are, the magistrates will surely order the Hussars in before us. Besides, the magistrates are seeing to it there'll be no loose stones or bricks on the field, so unless the crowd come armed, they'll have no chance at violence."

Samson digested this information. He couldn't determine precisely why, but something about the magistrates' plan troubled him. At least it would be information to offer Adelaide.

"I think you're right, George. About the reformers. Let's hope so." Samson held out his hand again, "Good luck, son."

This time, George shook it.

SEVEN

JOSEPH

Now we're getting to the nub, and since I've got started, I suppose I'll have to go on. Those summer nights up on the moors, there was a good few of 'em as it turned out, as more workers joined the cause. From middle of July right into August. Don't forget, the assembly was first called for the ninth, it being decided folk could take a Saint Monday to attend, but that meeting was banned for being unlawful 'cos of its declared intent to elect a member for Parliament. Sent some folk into a panic that did, but for most, like Nancy, it simply hardened their intent, and it just meant everything was nudged on a week, with a meeting to be on the following Monday, sixteenth of August.

Not all them nights stayed so warm and clear; there were a good few thunderstorms too, brought on by the strength of the sun. They were quite something to watch as well, when all the frustrated heat of the day, trapped between the buildings and the smog of town, rose up at last in a mighty temper tantrum across the sky, and all you could do was find shelter from the pelting rain and stop in wonder at the display.

Night I'm coming to was one such night. It was still hot and dry as we made our way up to the customary spot on the moor and explained to those new to the company what the plans were for the march, the formation we'd walk in and such. All the while though, black clouds were looming over the tops, and, above us, the sky turned a dirty yellow, same colour as a poor beggar with jaundice.

With the threat of deluge in such an exposed spot, it was decided the meeting should finish up early, and most folk made a hasty retreat, though I found myself waylaid. In the breeze that was blowing up, an elderly fella I'd been marching aside was struggling to roll up his banner. It was vast, this one, and I couldn't avoid seeing him scrabbling at its corners as they flapped in the wind, making a proper mess of it, he was, trying to wrap it round the pole. I admit I thought about sloping off, anxious to stay with the others, but he caught my eye and there was nothing for it but to offer my help.

Turns out he was a jovial old soul, 'cos once we were done, he kept me back even longer, thanking me fulsomely, and saying what a good lad I was 'til I could've punched him to shut up and let me go, as the rest of the moor was already near deserted. I searched for Nancy then, with my eyes, but I couldn't see her anywhere. Far off was a group heading towards Ancoats and I thought I could make out Mary and Mick, arms linked as usual. I wasn't sure, but it looked as though young Jemima might be with them too, but there was no sign of Nancy and I assumed she'd gone on ahead.

Right dejected, I took my leave of the old fella, who was heading in a different direction, cursing him under my breath that he'd made me miss my chance to walk with her as I set off alone. But I shouldn't have been so harsh, 'cos I was only a few yards down the dirt track, when I heard another voice call out to me from behind. A voice that made my blood thrill.

"Hey! Joe Price!" the voice said, "Is tha heading off wi'out me?"

And there she was, a dark figure outlined against an even darker sky, floating towards me like a shade. I remember hearing my breath catch. I could hardly believe my eyes. God, I was so excited and terrified, all mixed up together.

It was only when she got up close, I realised where she'd been. Laughing, she showed me her teeth, dirty with juice, and then she tiptoed to hold a raspberry just above my mouth, which fell open obediently. The taste was so delicious, I moaned out loud. She waited until I'd finished and then held another aloft before dropping it in again.

"That's tha lot, mister!" she said firmly. "The rest are for Walter and me mam."

We fell into a kind of rhythm then, walking beside one another, she holding out her cap full of fruit in front. Even though it was much earlier than we'd ever walked back, with the clouds menacing above us, it felt more like the dead of night. It gave me a sort of cover and made me bold, and I shifted over to walk closer to her. I noticed she didn't try to move away. I tell you, my mind was spinning, wondering what I should do next, whether I should declare myself at last, when, into all that confusion, she said quietly, "I won't be able to come up on t' moor again."

I think I must've stopped in my tracks, 'cos what I remember of what came next, we were stood still, facing one another.

"I mean I'm still going to th'assembly. Of course. Nowt'd stop me. But it's just I can't be away at night, not anymore. It's me mam, she's not well."

My thoughts were reeling, like thread off a bobbin, and I couldn't make out whether what I'd taken to be the start of something was really the end.

"I'm sorry to hear that," I said, though I daresay I sounded quite mechanical. After all, it wasn't her mam I was most sorry about, but she seemed to understand something of my disappointment.

"I'm sorry too. It's been a grand summer."

Well, this really was beginning to sound like goodbye and, all of a sudden, in my despair, I blurted out the truth, plain and simple. "Nancy," I cried, and my voice sounded strange, even to me, "I really like thee."

And what did she do? Ha! She looked away, back towards town and said, "I know tha does." Just like that. Lightly, as though it was nothing. Nothing. Well, I don't know what I'd expected, but I suppose I'd flattered myself the attraction wasn't one-sided. And I'll not lie, in that moment, as the silence stretched on, I felt my pride begin to bruise like a rotten apple, and I just wanted to be gone, off to an alehouse somewhere to drink myself stupid. So's that's how I ended up saying, quite cold like, "Forgive me. It seems I've got myself the wrong end of t' stick."

But at this, she turned back to me, her face dark and frowning. "Nay, nay, Joe."

Well, I admit I was confused, and I wasn't sure whether it was some kind of tease, but without thinking, I reached out and slipped my arms round her body, fastening my fingers together at the small of her back. She neither struggled nor said a word, and I stared at her profile, trying my best in the dim light to read her feelings proper. Around us, the track was quiet, and the only noise came from the swirl of the wind bringing on the storm.

"Can I kiss thee?" I whispered.

And that's when she turned back again, quite quickly this time, with a new strangeness in her look, as though she was seeing me for the first time. I moved closer. Above the sound of the breeze and the growing rustle of the trees, I heard her breath quicken with mine. She looked down, but in my arms, I felt the smallest lift of her middle towards me, and from that tiny shift, I was certain she was yearning just as much as me. I couldn't wait any longer, and I bent down to kiss her mouth, which opened as soft and delicious as the fruit she'd fed me.

After a few moments though, she pulled away gently, and we tried to make one another out in the dark, both with silly nervous laughs. Me, I thought it might just be a suspension, a moment of wonder before we found somewhere to go, but then she said, "There's summat tha needs to know."

She wanted to walk on a little, so I took her arm, and we

wandered along the road to town as she told me all about Richard Smith.

I won't lie, it was a blow. I had no idea she'd been married. Was married. It hadn't crossed my mind she might not be free. And I don't think I said anything, not for a long while. I couldn't arrange my thoughts. On the one hand, I felt enflamed with jealousy and anger at how that rotten bastard had treated her, staggering off, stupid with drink after landing her a black eye. But on the other, and mind I'm not proud to admit it, it was like the Devil himself was whispering in my ear, saying perhaps I could have her more easy.

We were nearer home now, and the sound of thunder rolled in on the air, like a drummer boy heralding the start of an advance, when she stopped and turned towards me again with a deep breath. "There's summat else too."

But I shook my head and placed my finger over her lips, "Shush."

I don't know what made me do it. God knows now, how I wished I hadn't. But at that moment, with the storm gathering round us, with the taste of her kiss still in my mouth, I just didn't want to hear any more. I was done with disappointment, though I'm not sure, even now, what I thought I was asking for. All I know is I wanted her.

"I don't care about Richard Smith," I declared. "It doesn't matter."

Then I kissed her again and it was perfect. Like nothing else mattered before, nor ever would again.

We clung together, only a stone's throw away from the factories and chimneys, promising to meet for the assembly, as the rain came with great, grey clouds against black, writhing and clashing and firing out searing white forks of lightning. We were drenched within a minute and screaming and laughing and running hand in hand back towards our lives that would never be the same again.

EIGHT

"Tha's not going," Ann said.

Despite the heat, Nancy was bent over the stove, waiting for the kettle to boil. From her bed, Ann could see she was deliberately fixed on it and choosing to ignore her. When she'd got home earlier, Nancy had looked pleased with herself, announcing she'd managed to procure some tea. Ann couldn't remember the last time they'd had any. She'd smiled gratefully, even as she fretted to herself; surely Nancy didn't still believe she could make her better?

She rested her head back on the pillow, tired from the effort of looking up. She hadn't been able to get out of bed for the past week. The pain was so deep in her belly now, she felt it might work itself out the other side. She knew she looked a fright too. It hurt to plait her hair, so it fell wild and unkempt around her, and when she tried to shift it out of the way, the dry skin of her wasted arm hung so limply, she thought it might slide loose from the bone. Walter could barely dare to look at her.

The days were slipping by, as though she was watching their past life in some fast-flowing watery reflection: dim light in the morning, Nancy away to the mill, blurred images of the yard, Susan Wilson bustling, afternoon light pricking motes of dust swimming on the air, and Walter now more afraid inside the house than out, waiting until the sinking of the sun.

"Mam."

She opened her eyes, and Nancy was above her, a steaming cup in her hand, her face shiny with heat and laden with concern.

"Let me help thee." Placing the cup on the floor, Nancy reached over to gently lift her into a sitting position, tilting her forward slightly as she gave the pillow a vigorous plump. The movement brought on the pain, knifing sharp, and she shut her eyes tight to whirling patterns of red and white, as the worst passed. She lay back and sensed Nancy watching, though she kept her eyes shut.

"Tha can play at nursemaid all tha wants, but I still won't have thee go off to that protest."

"Mam. Shush now."

"I mean it." She opened her eyes to glare fiercely.

"We'll only be gone a few hours. Any road, Susan'll look in on thee, just as normal."

"It's not me I'm fess about."

"Well, tha needn't worry about us."

"That fella's going, I suppose?"

Nancy's eyes darted away. She'd never yet managed to draw her on him.

"There's thousands going, Mam. It's a grand thing to do."

"How does tha make that out, when fust one's just been outlawed? How does tha know there won't be trouble?"

"'Cos that's the point, Mam. It's a peaceable assembly. *Peaceable*." She smiled to show her emphasis was in good humour. "It's to get the point across we're decent folk who deserve a hearing and deserve a vote."

"But what about wuk?"

"Most folk'll just change their shift. I'll get a swap and be back in time for t' class."

"Aye, well, let's hope so. But tha can't take Walter."

"Why not?"

"I don't know how tha can ask me 'why not'!"

Nancy sighed. "Come on, have some o' this tea afore its cowd."

Nancy passed the cup to her, but her bony hands shook as she lifted it up, splashing the tea against the side of her mouth, making her cry out before she could stop herself. Nancy rushed to help, but she batted her off. They looked away from one another.

It was early evening, and the room was quiet. There was no one clattering upstairs, all the Wilsons were out making the most of the weather and Walter was alone in the yard, happy enough. Last time she'd been able to make him out through the window, he was busy forming lines in the dirt with a stick he'd been playing with these past few weeks.

"I'm telling thee, tha can't take Walter to a thing like that. He cowers at t' smallest sound. Like a frightened rabbit, he is. How'd tha think he'd fare in a crowd the size tha says there'll be?"

Nancy took back the cup and sat down on the edge of the bed. There was, Ann thought, a trace of doubt on her face, but then she replied, "Mam, he has to come wi' me. I want him to see it. It's important. I'm doing it for our future. For his."

"Whist, Nancy. Does tha know tha son?"

"Yes, Mam, I do," she sighed. "I do. But I have to go, and I can't leave him here. Tha's too poorly. Any road, he's more afeared of them Wilson boys on his own, than of a crowd if he's got me wi' him." Ann had the feeling she was trying to convince herself. "Besides, Mam, tha didn't see how well he did at Knott Mill. There were plenty o' folk there and lots o' noise and he had a right good time."

"What about Susan? Can she not come down here?"

"Susan's planning to look in on thee, like I said, so don't fess about that."

"Well then she can watch over Walter too."

"I don't want to ask her again. She already does enough.

Besides, she's coming to meet Jemima and fetch her home afterwards."

Ann shook her head. "I don't know why tha had to get that one involved in all o' this." She sank back into the pillow again and shut her eyes, resolutely this time, so that Nancy didn't bother to answer. The disagreement had been too much for her, and she drifted into an uneasy slumber.

Later, when she opened her eyes again, the sun was still up, but the light trickling from the window was low and mellow, and she sensed the evening had shifted towards night. Nancy had brought Walter inside. He was looking hot and dishevelled, with tousled hair and knees that were dirty from spending half his day out in the yard. They had dragged a chair beside her bed and he was sat in Nancy's lap; she was reading to him. They hadn't seen her wake up, and she watched them for a few moments, listening.

"So, Walt, does tha want another one? Let me see. This one's called *The Hares and the Lions*." And Nancy snatched out her hand like a great claw and gave a quiet growl.

"Oooh yes!" he clapped.

"It goes like this: 'The hares harangued the assembly and argued that all should be equal. The lions made this reply "Your words O hares are good; but they lack both claws and teeth such as we have."'"

Nancy stopped abruptly, and Ann knew she'd felt her eye upon her. They looked at one another uneasily, but neither of them spoke. At last, a vast yawn overcame Walter, and Nancy seemed glad to put aside the book.

"I think it's time for bed, young man."

"Will tha sing to me, Mammy?"

"Eh? Me?" Nancy replied with a light laugh, though Ann knew she was trying to soften the blow; he was too afraid to ask her. Nancy looked over in apology and she gave a small nod of consent.

"Mammy?"

Nancy cleared her throat and started falteringly,

"A North Country maid up to London had strayed
Although with her nature it did not agree,
Which made her repent, and so bitterly lament,
Oh, I wish again for the..."

But her voice began to catch, and her eyes fill with tears,
so that when the song reached the chorus, Ann tried to help
her and joined in. She sounded dry and weak, but she still
held the tune,

"Oh, the oak and the ash and the bonnie ivy tree,
They flourish at home in my own country."

Even so, Walter shot her a wounded look and turned away,
twisting inwards on Nancy's lap, placing his arms tightly
round her neck so that the song died. Nancy stood up, holding
him like a baby, and smiled sadly over his head at Ann, who
closed her eyes again.

NINE

It was still light enough to read without a candle when Nancy returned to sit beside her mother, and yet she found she didn't have the heart to pick up a book. She was agitated and anxious and knew there was no prospect of concentrating whilst all these troubled thoughts continued to unravel like so many fraying threads.

Tenderly, she peered over her mother, careful not to make a sound, though every time she looked at her like this, she'd register the same shock. It was like a blow to the chest, how shrunken she'd become, how thin the grey skin pulled tight over the ridges of her skull. "Oh Mam," she whispered to the silent room and shook her head.

For now though, her mother's breathing was calm and regular, and she was sleeping peacefully for the first time in days. But even as Nancy wished with all her heart this respite might signal recovery, she knew very well the necessity of steeling herself. For a week or more, she'd been suggesting she call on the apothecary, who might be able to ease the pain, but until now her mother had mustered her limited strength to object. She didn't want any money wasting on her, she insisted, and though Nancy hated to see her suffer, this vehement, selfless protest was so like her mother, it gave her a morsel of hope and made her reluctant to persist.

Then there was Walter to worry about too. He was even

quieter these days and always hungry. She couldn't keep ignoring the growing expanse of bony limbs poking from his clothes. If her fears were realised, and her mam soon gone, what would become of him all day? She couldn't depend on Susan Wilson forever. So what would she do? Were all her plans to save him from the mill to come to naught after all?

Of course, there was always the hope that the Hunt assembly might indeed bring about change. If the Government could at last be prevailed upon to think of people like them, then food prices would surely come down. She'd earn more money. Life would be easier.

On the other hand, what a dreadful risk it was to attend the meeting. Though she'd made light of it to her mother, she knew very well if Yates got wind of her involvement, she could easily find herself without a job or any money at all.

Sitting up straight, she suddenly realised she'd taken to wringing her hands, and promptly sat on them to stop herself. At the same time, she cast another wary look at her mother. Was she right about the assembly? And about Walter too?

Yet to give up now would be a terrible thing. Nay, the very worst. She may as well take a knife blade to hope. She couldn't do it. Nay, nothing could persuade her to abandon this chance for change. Not after all that had happened this year and how far she'd come. No matter the cost, she knew she must never do that.

Besides, surely she could rely upon Captain Wright not to see her thrown from the mill?

Captain Wright, she sighed, there was another train of thought.

And Joseph Price. Oh Lord, quite another.

The man was a flirt. Of that she'd been certain. She'd seen it for herself from the first and never doubted it. At least, that is, until the other night. For all that he was smart and droll, not to mention good-looking, so far as she'd been concerned, he couldn't possibly be in earnest. He wasn't serious. He was the sort who never could be. And, not being anxious for his feelings, she'd permitted herself to be flattered, basking without seeming consequence in the compliment of his attention, bound up as it was, with all the excitement for reform.

Now, all that had changed, for had she not been mistaken in his feelings? Aye, the man was sincere; he must be. Her breath quickened just thinking about it, as though she'd run all the way home in the rain again. The howl of the storm gathering round them, the writhing clouds above and something astonishing in his tone, making her turn to a flash from his wide, grey eyes of such terrifying intensity, it lit her up, and in that instant, the world had seemed to tip, as her body unexpectedly responded to his.

In the quiet of the sleeping room, she breathed out a low whistle and dropped her eyes to her clogs. It wasn't seemly, thinking such thoughts with her mother so ill and not four feet away. She shook her head.

Had she misled him all this summer long? She thought she'd been careful not to, but even if she had, did it matter now? For if it were true, if he really did care for her, well then, what then? Could she, *did* she love him in return? She'd heard of plenty of folk who lived as man and wife without being married. So why should they not see where things could lead? Perhaps, after all, he might be everything she and Walter needed.

Yet even as she rehearsed these arguments, and the memory of desire continued to pulse through her, another more closely guarded part of her remained strangely untouched, desolate even, as a lone walker upon the moors. It was as though, even as she reasoned it out, even as she surrendered to this new possibility, something else still snagged, something deeper and altogether more painful. Perhaps it was simply grief-in-waiting, she thought, looking at her mother again, though she wasn't sure. The only thing of which she was certain was to examine the feeling no more.

Casting round the room for a diversion, she once again

alighted upon a book. She contemplated it a moment, reading the words on the spine and stroking the smooth skin of its surface. Then, without thinking, she brought it up to her nose and inhaled the tang of its leather, finding herself utterly unable either to read it or to set it aside.

Another half-hour or so passed in this strange suspension before her mother woke again, groaning and clammy with sweat. Nancy hurriedly went to fetch a pitcher of water. She poured some of it onto a cloth and gently wiped the hollows of her face, which glowed white in the darkened room, like the marble angels that guarded the graves down at the Collegiate Church. Then she poured the remainder into a fresh cup and, raising her mother gently, helped her to drink a few small sips.

"Tha's a grand lass," her mother breathed, sinking back, but Nancy found she couldn't summon any of her usual banter in reply, and simply shushed her, like a sleepy child.

A little while later, she realised she must have drifted off herself as she awoke with a start to find her mother twisted awkwardly in the bed, the sheets trailing on the floor. She was straining to the side, looking towards the hearth behind her and grimacing in pain.

"What is it, Mam?" Nancy asked in alarm, but her mother was too filled with her object and its frustration. Nancy followed her desperate eyes, trying to fathom what was bothering her. There was the fireplace and the stove, the tinderbox and the rag rug beneath. What was it she was after? Her own eyes wandered over it all and then stopped.

"Ah. Is it t' picture tha wants, Mam?"

She got up and collected the sketch of the farm from the mantelpiece and carried it over. Pulling up the sheets and perching on the edge of the bed, she held it up for them both to admire.

"It were so beautiful."

Her mother's wasted arm emerged from under the bedclothes, clawing at Nancy's sleeve, struggling to find the strength to give her a squeeze.

"Look, Mam, I can prop it here on t' shelf." She leant over the bed and set it up carefully. "There now, we'll leave it here and tha can see it all the time, whenever tha wants to. Just until tha's better."

At this, her mother's eyes met hers with a look so piercing Nancy fell to her knees, flinging her arms around her, a body as bony and broken as the fledgling she'd once picked up below a swallow's nest in a tree just beyond the farmhouse in the picture.

TEN

Despite all the difficulties of the decline in trade and the tumult in town, or perhaps in part as an escape from these things, Samson still tried to make his visits to Nancy at the end of the school day. He had stopped pretending to himself it was to hand her his newspaper. He knew he was being foolish, but he found he needed to see her more and more. He didn't flatter himself to think the feeling was in any way mutual. In fact, he rarely wondered about that at all. It was enough she didn't seem to mind him.

One afternoon, just a few days before the Hunt meeting, he was excited to come to her with a proposal. He'd been thinking a lot about her worries for Walter and the boy's love of music and had decided to ask if she might like to bring him to Charlotte Street to try the piano. He was nervous and unsure of what she'd say, but on balance he guessed she would overcome any objections, unwilling to deny Walter the opportunity.

However, as soon as he entered the schoolroom, he realised his scheme was unlikely to go to plan. She was visibly distracted, and though she gave him a brief smile, she didn't meet his eye. It was ridiculous, he knew, but he couldn't help feeling wounded.

She had already begun to clean the slates, but for some reason, she was rushing, setting them aside carelessly. In her haste, she managed to knock over the pile. Most of them spilled, like a set of dominoes, on the bench beside her, but the top one skidded and fell off, cracking in two, sending a shower of tiny splinters all over the floor.

"Oh Lord!" she cried impatiently as she knelt down to pick up the pieces, holding them aloft. He saw they'd broken with matching edges in a jagged lightning bolt. For a brief, futile moment, she tried to marry them together again, before setting them down with a sigh. "I'm sorry."

"Nonsense. It was an accident," he said calmly, settling down on the bench himself. He was sure her despondence must have something to do with her mother, and he said gently, "Nancy, wait a minute. Come and sit here by me. There's no rush."

From where she knelt on the floor, she lifted her head to look at him. It was the first time their eyes had met, and to his horror, he saw hers were filled with a terrible, fearful confusion he couldn't understand. He was shocked. "Nancy..." he started, but he didn't know what else to say.

Still kneeling, she leant back, balancing on her heels and, in so doing, exposed a paper tucked into the pocket of her apron. She saw him look at it and met his eye again. This time, inexplicably, her expression changed from pain to defiance. That raised chin, that fixed stare; it reminded him of that astonishing moment they'd first met, when she proffered that poor boy's finger in her open fist.

"What is it?" he asked, referring to the bewildering oscillation of her mood.

"Why? Does tha want to see?" she spat out the words and scrabbled in her pocket, determined to misinterpret him.

"No, no," he said, leaning away from her, almost cowering as she got to her feet.

"Here! Go on, take a look," and she thrust into his lap the printed handbill, which he saw at a glance was signed off *Henry Hunt*.

"Disappointed in me reading?" she asked, sarcastically, her lip curling into a sneer.

Samson was dumbstruck, barely able to recognise her, though he was not in the least surprised by the paper. She'd always chosen her words carefully with him, but it was clear she supported reform. And why should she not? Why indeed would she imagine he would blame her for doing so? No, what he didn't understand was this sudden, cruel hostility. This seeming disdain. He was amazed at it, and afraid, and though he sat impassively enough, his sickening heart beat in his chest like the flapping wings of a trapped bird.

"So, will thee away to tell Aunt Ada?"

Samson was stricken again. Dear God, Adelaide, and her damned edict! Why had he not put a stop to it? Why had he not seen it would prevent Nancy from being honest with him?

"Or perhaps tha'll be having words with the magistrates?"

His face was blank with disbelief now. She didn't mean it; she couldn't. She surely thought enough of him to know that was something he would never do. Nevertheless, that she could keep taunting him like this, careless of the consequences, and of his feelings, at last awoke the anger he knew she was trying to goad. Was this the true extent of her feeling? Did she really consider him only a means to an end? A devoted fool to be taken for granted?

He remained on the bench, still as stone, without looking at her. Meanwhile, she went to the back of the room to retrieve a dustpan and set to sweeping up the mess she'd made with short, brisk strokes across the floor, all the way up to his boots. He knew he should move out of the way, but knocked sick with shock, he found he couldn't, so that she had to scurry around him like a beggar before a throne. He hadn't thought it possible to feel so bitterly towards her, and he wished with all his heart he could simply erase the whole episode and start again.

At last she was finished cleaning, and from behind, he heard her put away the brush and walk towards the door. She was leaving, and as certain as the slate was irreparable, he knew it would never again be the same between them. His heart was racing and his mouth almost too dry to speak, but he needed to say something, "Nancy!"

She was already halfway out the room, the back of her small figure framed by the door. She hesitated at his voice, and he saw her shoulders sag.

"Nancy," he repeated.

Slowly, she turned around and with a fresh wave of confusion, he saw her face was as pained as his own.

He wanted to go to her then, to comfort her, but she was already backing away. All he could think to do was lift up the handbill which he'd been holding all this time, half-crumpled now, and, looking first at the paper and then back at her, he said gravely, "Take care, Nancy, take good care."

THE SIXTEENTH OF
AUGUST

ONE

MARY

I could hardly believe it when I woke up that Monday morning: the dirty yellow of the last few stormy days was gone. Above the chimney smoke, there was a blue sky again, and the view towards the centre of town was clear. Stepping into the yard, the air still felt warm but not so oppressive as the past few weeks. Ee, it seems another lifetime ago now, and I can hardly bring mi'sel to say it, not after all that's gone since, but I do remember thinking to mi'sel, nowt but good could happen on such a day.

I went to see Nancy first thing, long afore we were meant to assemble at New Cross, just to check on how things were, what with her mam worsening over the weekend. I'd come from George Leigh Street, where I'd stopped to collect some boughs of laurel, donated by one of the more well-spoken Union men from his garden out of town. Quite a spectacle I was too, I can tell thee, what with my arms full, lost in wreathes of leaves, all glossy and green.

Nancy must've spotted me from the window, 'cos she stepped into the yard to meet me, so as not to disturb her mam.

"Susan says she'll stop wi' Mam all t' time, though I'll

still bring Walter wi' me," she announced firmly. "He's scared here, poor thing. It'll do him good to get away."

She was already dressed in her best, white linen, which shone so bright in the morning light it seemed to glow. It showed up the colour of her skin too, which was a little darker than usual on account of all the sun; it made her look healthy. Right gradely she was. Aye, even with her face all etched with worry for her mam, and for Walter, and for whatever else was on her mind she wasn't letting on to me. 'Cos there *was* something else, I could tell. She had such a grim determination about her, different to the common excitement I'd say, something not far off defiance.

"Here, give us a hand, will thee?" I said, all puffed out and tired of carrying the foliage, so that when she held out her arms to help, I dropped the whole load on her with a relieved sigh, which made her exclaim, "*Mary!*"

We both laughed then, and I was glad to have lightened her mood, as I brushed my hands and picked off the stray leaves and tendrils which had clung to my dress and reached out to pluck off a small spray.

"Laurel," I declared.

"Like the Romans!" she replied.

I took off my bonnet and attached the stalk with a small pin I'd left there for the purpose. "I'm taking rest for t' others. All t' lasses are wanting some."

Nancy placed the boughs on the ground and bent down to break off a sprig for herself.

"Can I take some for Walter?"

"Course, course," I said, and then added cautiously, "Is tha sure about bringin' him?"

"Aye," she said, quick with irritation. "Honestly, Mary! Tha doesn't know what it's like, the worry of a child. How could thee?"

Well, that hurt, I'll not lie, and if she'd not been in such a state herself, I'd have told her so. Mind, I wouldn't have needed to, 'cos she realised straightaway she'd touched a wound, and was widening big, sorry eyes at me, and trying her best to mollify. "He'll be grand, just wait and see. There'll be music and singing, and he'll be wi' me and thee… He loves being with thee, Mary," and, ee, she gave me such a solemn look then as I'll never forget. "Aye, it'll be grand."

She'd begun to spin a stem of leaves in her fingers as she looked up at the morning sky. It was shot through with stripes of gold, bold and strong, like the colour of victory. It must've helped lift her mood 'cos I watched the same sense of optimism I'd woken with begin to dawn on her. She took a deep breath, and expanded her chest, as her face widened into a smile, and she proceeded to address me as fine as any of them leading ladies of the Reform Society.

"It's going to be wonderful, Mary! We'll make history! Just think on it, people'll look back in t' years to come, and say it were us, here in Manchester, that won t' vote for ordinary folk."

I smiled then and reached to embrace her, just so she'd know I was done with taking any offence. I can still recall the feel of her against me, so small she was, it was just as though I was cradling a little bird. But after a moment it was me who broke away, mindful of the time and anxious to help the others to the laurel. I picked up the boughs again, pretending to keel under their weight, rolling my eyes to the heavens, all of it to make her laugh.

"Tha daft apeth!" she cried at me, "I'll si'thee in half an hour."

TWO

"Ellen, Ellen!"

Adelaide strode the length of the hall, opening the door to the study without knocking, knowing Samson to be out. She glanced at the window and tutted. Turning on her heel, she swept out and on into the drawing room, next the dining room, and then through the door to the servants' quarters, stopping only at the top of the stairs down to the kitchen. Having scoured each room, there was no sign of any of the maids, but she'd established every window on the ground floor was open, either to its full extent or at least significantly ajar.

"Ellen!"

This time she heard a sudden flurry of activity and Ellen's voice from afar off, calling as politely as she could from a distance, "Yes, ma'am, I'm on me way!"

While she waited, Adelaide extracted a silk handkerchief from a hidden pocket in her gown and dabbed the soft, wet down of her upper lip. Such infernal heat, she thought, it was almost as though the Jacobins themselves had summoned it from the depths for their business.

Ellen now emerged at the bottom of the stairs. Adelaide swiftly stowed the handkerchief and, even before the girl had got level on the landing, began, "Did I not give orders for the windows of this house to be kept shut?"

"Begging tha pardon, ma'am, but I thought what wi' it being so warm—"

"Never mind the weather! Get them shut! And kindly ensure that everyone downstairs is clear: no one is to leave this house today. Do you hear?"

"Yes, ma'am."

"And once you've attended to the windows, I want the silverware removing from the dining room."

Ellen's brow formed a question.

"All the candlesticks and the platters and the epergne, of course. I suppose you might take the cutlery as well whilst you're at it. All of it to be taken upstairs. You can put it in Robert's room, and mind you cover it with a blanket and lock the door."

Ellen still looked bewildered, but the girl knew better than to ask.

"Go on, run along."

Earlier that morning, Adelaide had taken similar measures upstairs. Just before dawn, in the grey light that had seeped beneath the curtains, she'd risen from a broken sleep, troubled as it always was by dreams of Robert, and crept across her bedroom to turn the key in the lock. Then she crept back again to the large chinoiserie cabinet set against the wall opposite her bed. Very slowly, so as not to make a noise, she opened its rickety top drawer and carefully extracted a small marquetry box, shiny with varnish, which contained the smaller items of her jewellery. Without opening it, she set it down on the unmade bed and returned to the cabinet to extract those pieces that didn't fit into the box. Necklace after necklace, and lengths of creamy pearls, which she ran, cold and heavy, through her fingers, the beads of jet she'd been wearing all these long months, her glittering diamond drops and umpteen gold and silver bracelets. All of them laid out on the bed to fine effect, so that by the time she was finished, she imagined it not unlike a display in that new arcade in London she'd read about.

Next, she crossed the room to the wardrobe, where she took

down her best Indian silk shawl. For a moment, she stopped to stroke its softness, holding it up to inhale its lingering, exotic smell, all at once remembering, for the first time in years, how Silas had admired her the first night she'd worn it.

Eventually, she set it down on the edge of the bed, searching for its top corners, before throwing it out with a whipping sound, like an old washerwoman with a bedsheet, spreading it on the floor before her.

She was still wearing nothing more than her cotton nightgown, and as she bent to kneel between the bed and the laid-out shawl, she winced at the chill from the hard floor. Undaunted, however, she reached for the first set of pearls, snaking them into the silk's golds and greens and peacock blue, then folding the cloth over the top. She did the same with each item, piece after piece, until they were all safely enveloped, and she was able to draw in the remaining fabric, tucking it into place to create a peculiar sort of knapsack.

When it was done, she shuffled even lower and reached her arms beneath the bed to drag out a black wooden chest, which she placed before her. She lifted the lid. Besides a number of parchments, it was empty, and her parcel, together with the varnished jewellery box, fitted comfortably inside.

Once again, she went over to the wardrobe and plunged her hand into the swathes of clothes, reaching for the back and scrabbling along the bottom until her fingers snagged on a heavy, iron key. She brought it out and locked the chest with it immediately. Then she slid the chest back under the bed, though she didn't return the key. Instead, she left it on top of the cabinet, and, when she'd dressed, she took it up again and placed it in her pocket, to be kept on her person at all times. She patted it now as she returned to the hall, intending to supervise Ellen in the tasks she'd given her.

THREE

Samson had sat bolt upright when he woke that morning, his nightshirt clinging damp with sweat. Ever since his last encounter with Nancy, his sleep had been disturbed. It had brought back old nightmares from the war: the sounds of cannon and musket fire, and smoke clearing to reveal a field strewn with fallen comrades. In this last dream, seven sleek and silky stallions had trotted through the bodies, their riders gone, as he crawled on hands and knees back to his tent. He sensed he was wounded but didn't yet know the nature of his injury. Groaning in pain, he'd opened the flap to discover Nancy, lying white-faced on his couch. One of her arms was hanging unnaturally at her side, and as he got closer, he stared in horror at her bloodied hand, which was clutching at her own severed finger.

In the days leading up to the assembly, Samson had stayed away from the mill, preferring to work in the study at Charlotte Street. It was the only way he could think to prevent himself from returning to the schoolroom. He had recurring visions, both during the day and at night in his fitful dreams, of charging into a lesson and laying himself prostrate before her, begging forgiveness for the terrible, mysterious offence he had given.

Day after day, he would try to work at the papers spread across his desk, his fingertips at his temples or else joined together in a steeple at his mouth in an effort to concentrate.

Sometimes he would manage half an hour at a time, but mostly he sat, gazing into mid-air, returning to that last meeting and to the same questions. What had caused such terrible feelings in her? Why had she been so suddenly hostile? Those gestures of disparagement, the viciousness of her tone; where had they come from? Time and again, he went back over every one of their conversations, trying to identify any possible injury he might have caused, but in each case, he was certain that – aside from the wretched question of reform – they'd spoken openly to one another and resolved any matters between them. Indeed, he was sure they had been friends.

Was that then the reason? Did she truly imagine he'd punish her for her involvement in reform? The possibility tormented him. Bitterly, he would replay that unedifying scene with Adelaide: her dogged insistence on the prohibition, her calculated threat to the school, and he would feel his jaw clench, at once hating both his aunt for her manoeuvring, and himself for giving way to her so easily.

Often, his work abandoned, he would rise from the desk and take up his place at the piano. Now, the only music he chose reflected his despair. One afternoon, he picked out the opening bars of the Beethoven sonata Boosey had sent. The notes were rich and resonant, rippling like the moon's reflection on black, glassy water. It was unbearably mournful, and his sorrow grew deeper with the advancement of the theme, until, struck with the certain knowledge Nancy would appreciate its beauty too, he floundered and stopped, unable to play its final, dark chords.

He had spent much of the last week like this, until the previous afternoon, when the sun had shone so brightly into the study, it bounced off the polish of Silas's dark furniture and momentarily dazzled him, drawing him to look out of the window. The trees that lined the street were in full summer leaf, and in the light breeze that was getting up, they nodded to him in polite invitation, so that he'd at last decided it might do him good to go for a walk after all.

Outside, there had been a sleepy Sunday calm which, combined with the warm air and the deserted street, put him in mind of a Spanish town shut up for afternoon siesta. It seemed hard to believe that in just a few hours the centre would be thronged with people.

All the building works near Mosley Street had fallen quiet for the day, and he set off down its length, in the direction of the clock tower of St Peter's. On reaching the church's porch, he noticed a number of gentlemen taking shade from the sun. It was clear they were in serious conversation and, as he passed by, he caught a fragment.

"Six hundred of them, I believe. Mustered and ready."

"Indeed, and thank God for it."

"Yes, Hulton just needs to hold his nerve now."

William Hulton, Samson knew, was chairman of the magistrates who would be observing the proceedings, ready, no doubt, to read the Riot Act at the slightest provocation. He frowned. If this Hulton was anything like Adelaide's friends, it didn't bode well the day's best hope depended on his restraint. He shook his head and turned away from the men, walking out from the shadow of the church, wandering onto the clearing of scrub beyond.

Here, plans were visibly advanced for the land's development. It was evident St Peter's Field would soon be cut through and a section used to form an extension of the road to Deansgate. With the buildings of the town bristling on all sides, it occurred to him that the moment for the meeting was now or never; a demonstration on the scale planned would be impossible in Manchester once this last open land was gone. The reformers had to take their chance.

Eventually, as he turned in the direction of home, something afar off, over to his right, caught his eye. Squinting ahead, he took a few curious steps towards his object, then stopped dead in his tracks. It was a group of a half-dozen horses or so, their glossy flanks shining in the sun, each of them mounted by soldiers. Even from this distance, he recognised their colours, the blue jackets threaded with gold, the red-striped grey trousers and that unmistakeable black arc of plumage on the top of their helmets: the Royal Horse Artillery. *Dear God*, Samson stared, *they've brought in the guns*.

He hastened away, wondering at himself that he'd failed to appreciate the extent of the town's fear until now. *Oh God*, he thought, *Nancy*. Picturing her and her handbill and that last grief-stricken look. Did she know? Was she aware? So much of the talk of trouble and plots and insurrection, he'd dismissed as mere reactionary chatter amongst Adelaide and her Tory friends. Yet now, with sickening clarity, he realised their views reflected those of the authorities more than he could ever have imagined.

He picked up pace along Portland Street. Here, the glare of the sun was gone, blocked by the shadows cast by the buildings. As he passed by, he noticed the door of the tavern was closed, though he discerned from the steamed-up window that even on a Sunday, it was still trading and just as packed as the day he'd spoken with George Baldwin. He didn't care to inspect more closely this time and had walked on a stride or two when he heard the door bang open, followed by a low thud and bellows of laughter. He looked back over his shoulder and saw a young Yeoman was splayed on the pavement. He was moaning, and his mouth was covered in vomit. Surrounding the man was an assorted group: a sour-faced woman with hands on her hips, several other soldiers jeering at their drunken comrade and two others, older men dressed in civilian clothes, as red in the face and raucous as the rest. One he recognised as Yates, the manager from the mill.

It was these impressions from the previous afternoon which returned to alarm him just as soon as he woke, and he determined at once to take an early walk along the same route.

This time when he reached the field, there were more people about, though not yet a large body of reformers. At the far end, there was a small group of young men, shouting instructions to one another, engaged in putting up an erection of sorts, comprising a couple of old carts. He puzzled at it a moment, before he realised it would no doubt form the platform from which the speakers would address the crowd.

What struck him more forcibly, however, were the half-dozen or so men dotted at intervals across the expanse of grass, each bent forward, almost at right angles to the land, scouring the scene like birds after worms, occasionally stooping to retrieve something from the ground, which items they then placed in one of a number of barrows scattered about the field. As he drew closer, he saw these barrows contained stones and pebbles and pieces of brick. The sight of them, stacked like that, made him uneasy and at once settled his intention for the day.

Returning hurriedly to Charlotte Street, he opened the door into a flurry of activity in the hall. Ellen and the two younger maids were parading from the dining room to the staircase, laden with candelabra and silver platters. Meanwhile, Adelaide was standing at the bottom of the stairs, overseeing the whole affair. She caught him frown.

"It's simply a precaution."

"What *do* you imagine the reformers are about?"

Adelaide shot a look up the stairs to check the maids had advanced beyond earshot. "Whist, Samson! I can't imagine why a man of your experience can be so sanguine." Her eyes darted along the corridor and back up to the landing again. He was shaking his head now, his expression somewhere between frustration and anger. "I mean it, Samson. If things get rough, and by all accounts that's most likely…"

Samson held up his hands. "Aunt Adelaide, stop. You must stop this. You must not concern yourself. All will be well." He hesitated a moment, thinking of his decision on the field. "Tell me, what do you know of the magistrates' plans for today?"

"Why, that they read the Riot Act as soon as possible and disperse the rabble!"

Samson sighed in exasperation but pressed on, "Does not Osborne know where they'll be? He must have been told."

"Yes indeed, he was consulted!"

"Well?"

"As I understand it, they've been meeting for days, deciding their position. I believe it's now agreed to let matters proceed, albeit under close observation."

"Yes, yes. But from what vantage?"

"Well, Hugh says the best views are from the upper windows of the row on Mount Street. It'll be Edmund Buxton's house they use. But why? Why do you wish to know?"

"Because, Aunt," he began firmly, "I've decided to go along and watch for myself."

Adelaide could only stare, astonished. He'd wondered at first whether she might object and insist he stay respectably at home, just as she'd instructed the rest of the household. But now it occurred to him, perhaps the prospect of a first-hand account might prove too enticing for her to press the point.

"You needn't look like that," he smiled as she made a show of concern, fanning herself with her handkerchief, and muttering an uncharacteristic, "oh dear, oh dear". "I shall not be in danger, and I'll do whatever I can to help maintain the peace."

At last, she left off her flutterings, demurring with only a half-hearted solicitation as to his safety. He had been right; her curiosity was too intense. Despite herself, it was clear she was stirred by an appalling excitement and barely able to conceal a mood of ecstatic defiance.

FOUR

Nancy went back inside with the green laurel bunched inside her bonnet to find Walter sat on their bed, resolutely turned away from her mother. When he saw the leaves, he skipped over towards her with a cry of excitement.

"Can I have some?"

"Aye, aye, there's some for thee. But keep tha voice down."

Her mother was very weak now and had only woken briefly when Nancy got up and made some tea. After a short while, she'd drifted off again.

With Walter watching impatiently, Nancy extracted some of the laurel from her bonnet, breaking it into sprays. "Look, Walt," she whispered, smiling at him. "They're that shiny, they could've been polished!"

Next, she proceeded to pin them, one small stem on either side of the cap he'd dug out from his coat pocket. When they were secure, she planted the cap on his head and stood back to appraise him, "Oh my goodness, Walt! Tha's like a little emperor!"

Walter loved this and set off dancing round the table in high excitement, his arms flailing in front of him, but just as he turned the corner by the fireplace, one of his elbows caught a cup which had been left on the table and it fell to the stone floor with a resounding clang.

"Walter!" Nancy hissed in a low voice. Anxiously, she

righted the cup and tiptoed over to her mother, who nevertheless remained still and undisturbed. During the brief interval she'd been awake, Nancy had managed to comb her hair, gently teasing out some of the knots massing at the back of her head. It was greying at the roots and thinning, but brushed back from her forehead, it formed a neat, dark halo around her shrunken face, where the shadows were deepening beneath the bones.

Walter, abashed, had fallen quiet and waited beside the door as Nancy bent to listen to the slow ebb and flow of her mother's breathing. Looking down the length of the bed, she gingerly adjusted the covers, tucking them more tightly to be sure all was comfortable, and then checking the shelf for the picture of the farm.

Bending even lower, so close she could smell a strange new earthiness rising from her mother's body, she whispered, "Susan'll be in shortly."

A pause. Was it really only a few days since she'd raised so many objections?

"We'll be back before teatime."

Her mother was silent. She waited a heartbeat longer. Then she kissed her forehead gently and stepped away.

Outside, the light of the sun was glaring and everything before her turned momentarily white. Calling to Walter over her shoulder, she put on her bonnet to shield her eyes and headed towards the ginnel. It was only as she reached the street, she realised he hadn't followed her.

"Walt!" she called, but there was no reply. "Walt!" Lord, they'd be late. Joe'd be waiting already. What was that lad doing now? "Walter, come on!"

Retracing her steps back into the yard, she discovered him still close by the door, stooping to lean on something.

"Come on, Walter," she said sharply. "What's tha doing?"

He looked up and skipped alongside her happily enough, a long, stripped stick in his hand.

"What's tha got there?" she pulled a face.

"It's me stick!" he said, raising it high above his head.

"Lord, Walter. Put it down. Tha can't take that!"

Walter stopped, but his bottom lip had begun to protrude, and his eyes were welling up. Nancy sighed. Bobbing down to his level, she made him meet her eye, "I'm sorry, Walter, tha just can't take it. No sticks." Then more to herself, "Tha'll get us arrested, tha little tinker."

She made a silly face to try and make him laugh and reached out her hand. Still pouting, Walter nevertheless surrendered the offending item, and Nancy placed it back by the door.

"Good lad! Now come on, we'll have to hurry. There's going to be lovely music!"

FIVE

MARY

Mick and I stood by the cross with our boughs o' laurel and watched in amazement as the crowd grew, from a couple o' dozen or so at first to hundreds and hundreds. Not one of us not hungry, mind, have no doubt, but all of us filled and nourished by something else that day: a hope of change.

Ee, all them folk! And it weren't just them that had been up on the moors neither, but others too, who were newly curious, or just looking for a bit of fun. There were all sorts: mams and dads, older fellas and young 'uns, weavers and labourers and tradesfolk. I'm sure you can picture it: us lasses, floating around in white, looking one another up and down and comparing our finery. And plenty of fellas I recognised from round and about, now looking as smart as gentlemen. Some bunting had been set up between the windows of the buildings facing the cross, and the flags, red, white and blue fluttered in the breeze. Ee, I could hardly believe my eyes, and to think we were only one of many a contingent to come.

There were plenty of children too, I noticed, and thought Nancy would be pleased. Though it's fair to say none of these ruffians were like Walter, not with the noise they were making. Chasing one another round the legs of the grown-ups, they were, yelling and shouting, with faces flushed, caught up in the same fever as everyone else.

I don't know exactly when Nancy and Walter arrived. I was busy, you see, still helping ladies to leaves for their bonnets. From early on, I'd had quite a crowd gathered round me, and I'd had to raise my voice to get them into an orderly queue. Then, once they were sorted, I had to shout at 'em again to move on, instead of standing around, admiring each other and holding up the whole line!

It was only when all the leaves were gone and people were starting to fall into formation for the march that I saw 'em, though Nancy didn't see me, even with me calling and waving and generally jigging about to get her attention. I remember it made me laugh at first, the way she was looking hither and thither, round and about. I think I supposed she was taking in the atmosphere just as I'd done. Walter didn't notice me either, though that was no surprise. Nancy had a tight grip on his hand, of course, and he was looking happy enough, giggling every now and again at the parp of trumpets warming up.

Eventually, as I set off towards them, she looked in my direction, and I gave her a little nod to indicate I was coming over. It was only then I realised. Ee, what a terrible state she was in. Her face was white, though her cheeks were burning, and she looked altogether more agitated than I'd ever seen her afore, so that it crossed my mind perhaps the old lass had passed away.

"What's the matter?" I asked, giving Walter a little pat.

"Has tha seen Joe?"

Aye, that's what she said! Joe!

Well, you could've knocked me down with a feather, I was that surprised. I hadn't given that beggar a thought all morning. Course, I knew she'd made a friend of him, talking reform and the like. Aye indeed, there'd been no escaping him at times, him and his pamphlets. But I'd been certain no more than friendship had come of it. In fact, though he'd displayed himself like a fine cock-hen all summer long, it seemed to me she'd not given him a shred of encouragement, which is why I couldn't understand her being so bothered.

"Nay, I've not!" I said, and I must've come over short 'cos she frowned at me, so that I added in a softer voice, "But there's that many folk here, it's hard to tell."

She was not comforted by this though and couldn't look me in the eye for turning this way and that, her face a picture of bewilderment. "I can't understand it," she was saying, and her expression seemed proper disappointed. "He wanted to march wi' me. He said he'd be here."

I realised then she was truly upset, and I can't explain it, but I felt a stab o' fear go right through me. All this time, Walter was getting rattled too. No longer distracted by the musicians, he was looking up at his mam with wide, worried eyes.

"Ee, don't bother about him, lass." I put on a show of jollity. "Just look at the turnout! Hey, Walter does tha want to get in line wi' me?"

But Nancy wasn't for moving. Keeping a firm hold of Walter, she wouldn't leave off searching the crowd.

The banners ahead of us were being unfurled, and one of the trumpets started the band off in earnest with a loud tune. Everyone was taking up position, six abreast to a row.

"Come on, Nancy! Tha'll see him later, down at t' field."

"Nay, nay," she said, pretending a lightness I knew she didn't feel. "We'll just wait a bit longer. I'm sure he'll be here."

"Nancy, come on wi' us," I pleaded, battling with my own anger now, both with Joe and, if I'm honest, with Nancy herself for being so bothered about such a one as he. "Tha's waited so long for this."

"Aye, Mary, and we won't miss it, don't fret. Go on, get gone. I'll only wait on a few more minutes. We'll catch thee up!" She summoned a smile and shooed me away.

So I did as she said and went off to join Mick, who were already in line with some of his pals. But, ee, you cannot know how bitterly I reproach mi'sel for it. To have left them there like that, two lonely souls in the shadow of the cross, and Nancy's words carrying on the air, "We won't be long!"

And that's when I noticed t' other one. In the row in front of me, over to the right, staring back over her shoulder at Nancy, even as the crowd moved forward. I speak of Jemima Wilson. Now, she always was one to look out of temper, a proper little sour-face at the best of times, but I could see there was something particular consuming her that day, and as we began to fall into the rhythm of the march, she turned her head again, this time towards me, and asked outright, "What's up wi' Nancy?"

There was something in the tone of it turned me cold.

SIX

After Samson left to seek out the magistrates, Adelaide took up residence in the drawing room. Alone, unable to pay visits and without any prospect of guests of her own, she sat for a long while, conscious of the ticking of the clock. She looked over at some needlework bundled in a basket beside the fireplace, an unfinished sampler she'd started months ago in the short days of winter when she was newly a widow, now abandoned on a footstool. She couldn't bring herself to take it up. Today of all days, she knew she'd never have the patience.

She decided, instead, upon a volume she'd been lent by Esther Baldwin. A novel she'd started a few days ago, full of nonsense of course, it was so light and frivolous, she thought it might divert her. Never the most attentive of readers, however, before long she found herself re-reading paragraph after paragraph. She was just wondering whether to tackle a new chapter when a noise from outside at last interrupted her. She put the book aside without keeping the page.

There were voices, indistinct at first, but by the time she reached the window, she could make out cheers and cries of merriment. She strained to look down the street, the tip of her nose almost touching the pane, even though there was nothing to see. The road was still empty and, over on the other side, her neighbours' windows were shuttered, their houses as closed-up as her own.

Strangely dissatisfied, she was just settling back on the couch when the noise grew suddenly louder, and she hurried back to peer down the road again. Aha, here they were! A great rabble of them turning the corner into the street. Not walking but marching, several of them abreast, not keeping to the pavements but taking up the whole of the thoroughfare with casual effrontery. Leading them were several rough sorts, holding flags like standard-bearers going into battle, though their banners were too lively in the breeze and from the motion of the crowd to make out their words.

Still they came on, row upon row of them, just like she'd seen them on the moor, as she stood and watched, holding back from the window at first but gradually drawing closer and closer, until she was right up against it, her breath clouding the glass, aghast not simply at the vast number but at the presence of so many women amongst them. Women! And bringing their children too!

A pair of ruffians, not much more than nine years old, caught her eye. They'd broken ranks from the others and were racing alongside the marchers down the pavement, laughing at the crowd and play-fighting with one another. It was disgraceful, she thought, tutting aloud and drawing herself up, when all at once she felt the eyes of one of the crowd upon her.

Searching the throng, it only took a second before she met his gaze. It was an old man, older than she, dressed in a clean shirt and wearing a wool jacket despite the weather, much like the rest of the men. On his head, he wore a fine top hat that was overly big for him and cast a shadow over his eyes, which nevertheless remained fixed on her. She stepped back a little from the glass. There was something familiar about him, she had to admit, though so many old faces in town often were. Not that she'd ever allow she recognised them from her days at the Red Lion.

When the man realised she'd spotted him, he freed his arm from the neighbour he'd linked and doffed his hat to her solemnly and without any trace of impertinence, so that before she could stop herself, she'd gasped aloud, even as she carried on watching and waiting for an impudent wink, ready to be offended. But the man simply inclined his head in a neat and respectful bow and proceeded with his fellows past the window. Still astonished, she turned to follow his progress, straining to watch the back of his head recede with the rest of the crowd, as her blood rushed, and a hot flush rose from the depths of her throat, up through her face, until even the roots of her hairline began to tingle. She retreated from the window in unaccountable confusion, her hand clutched to her breast.

After that, she remained perched on the edge of the sofa, occasionally making out other noises, the jaunty tunes of a travelling band and more cheering and shouting, though all of it remained muffled beyond the closed window. Her fingers, sticky with heat and free of rings, save for her gold wedding band, twitched in her lap. Again and again, she consulted the clock on the mantelpiece, agitated and unsure of exactly what she was waiting for.

SEVEN

JOSEPH

I was already five mile or more out of Manchester by the time I was meant to meet her, and no, I'm not proud of it, but I said I'd give an honest account, and that's just the plain truth of it. I can't change what happened. Just like I can't change the way I am. We none of us can.

Let me tell you about when I was a lad. You'd never think it, but I went to one of the first of them Sunday schools in town. Yeah, and as it turned out, I was top of the class. Good at reading I was, you see, even though I was never the most attentive. Don't get me wrong, I'm not bragging. It was just the way it was. Used to make my old mam proud.

Thing is, I'd often find myself waiting for the others to catch up, with nothing to do but daydream or leaf through the Bible. Well, I remember, I used to like thinking on the twelve apostles. I know, who'd've thought it? But I had nowt else to do, and they always seemed such a motley gang to me, so's that I'd wonder which of 'em I'd most resemble when I grew up. I liked to imagine I could be a fisherman, like Andrew or James or John. I loved the idea of sailing a boat in a storm and hauling in a mountain of fish against the odds, like some kind of hero. But Manchester's a long way from the sea, and you'd never catch me moving to Liverpool. So's maybe I'd be Luke instead, a physician healing others, though in reality a brickie's son from Ardwick has about as much chance of becoming King of England. Course, perhaps it might be I'd be singled out for greatness, like Simon Peter and his keys to the Kingdom. Though, to tell the truth, he always struck me as a bit of a ditherer.

I suppose from all this, you might guess what I'm getting at. Or who, I should say. See, thing is, I'm no different to anyone else and we none of us start out thinking we'll do something bad. It's true, in all my childhood visions, I never once pictured myself a bad man. *The* bad man. The man who'd betray with a kiss. Yeah, Judas Iscariot, that's the one. Very name used to make my eight-year-old self shiver. I couldn't stop myself from picturing him, in my mind's eye, tormented in the dappled light of the tree, his legs kicking and then swinging over spilt coins.

When we'd parted that last night, me and Nancy, all soaked by the rain and away to get ourselves dry, we'd agreed between the last, snatched kisses that we'd go on the march together. I'd meet her at New Cross with the rest of the Union lot. What would happen after that, well, I didn't know. I didn't know what she was thinking neither. What she would've done, how it could've worked. All I did know is I wanted her that bad, I let her think we'd work something out; maybe move somewhere, to the factory towns up north, where we could pretend to be wed. There's them that get away with it. Who knows? Perhaps she would've done and all, if I'd only given her the chance.

Well, them few days between that night and the Monday of the assembly, I was in a kind of haze. I think it's clear by now, I'd already had plenty of girls, but I'd never felt quite like this before. She'd changed me. Or so I thought.

Truth is, I was pining for her that bad by the Sunday, I had to get out of my lodgings and go for a walk, and before long I found myself aside the canal down by Wrights. It was almost as though just thinking on that first time I'd seen her had somehow drawn me there.

It was evening-time, and the light was soft on the water as I wandered the towpath, and I swear as I looked upon it, a vision of her sweetheart face came to me, bathed in smiles, floating on the surface, as clear as though she were coming towards me, and I knew there and then, I couldn't stand to wait any longer to see her in the flesh.

So's, straightaway, I hurried from the canal over towards her place. I knew I couldn't call, of course, not with her mam so bad. But I hoped somehow I'd manage to see her. Either I'd bump into her, running an errand, or someone else who knew her could get a message to her to meet me outside.

I thought I was in luck when, just a couple of streets on, I spotted a group of girls talking on the far corner. None of 'em older than fifteen and all of 'em laughing loudly in that flaunting way of girls that age. I thought one of 'em looked familiar, and, as I got closer, I saw it was indeed the lass, Jemima, who'd been raspberry picking with us. From the quick snatch of her eye at me, and the way in which she tossed her head back, I knew she'd recognised me too.

"'Ow do, Jemima?" I said, and at that – just that! – her skin mottled pink from her neck upwards over her entire face, until her eyes seemed to water, and the girls she was with began to titter. She didn't say anything, but she nodded her head in acknowledgement.

Well, I knew what I was about and moved in closer, turning on my low voice, as though she was the only person in the world I wanted to talk to, and asked, "Will you be going tomorrow then, Mima?" I flashed her one of my smiles for good measure too, and it worked, 'cos this time she cast a triumphant look at her friends.

"Aye, course!" she cried, and the little minx even tried a touch of swagger, "Tha couldn't stop me!"

There was a choking noise then from one of the others,

and it was clear they were trying to suppress a fit of giggles. Jemima glared at them.

"Quite right too," I said, as though insensible to their laughter, and Jemima smiled, the victor again. "I was wondering, by the way, how's Mrs Kay doing? Does tha know Nancy's mam?"

At this, her satisfied smile vanished, and she replied in a voice turned flat, "I should say. We live atop of 'em. It's me mam as looks after her and Walter when Nancy's out at t' mill."

"Oh yeah," I said, "I remember now," and I paused, as though allowing this to sink in. "It's just I've not seen Nancy these past days, and I was wondering how things were?"

"Not good, me mam says. Just skin and bone now. Don't reckon it'll be long."

Well, it wasn't a surprise to me, not from the way Nancy had been talking, and I was sorry for her of course. But for me, the problem was how to get from this sad news to appointing Jemima my messenger.

"Poor Nancy," I said with a sorrowful face, and though I'll never know what possessed me, I carried on, "Poor lad, too. It's no age to lose a mam."

Straightaway, Jemima gave me a queer look. "What's tha mean?" The glint in her eye as sharp as her tongue. "Ann's not his mam."

"I don't understand…" I started, but I did, even before I'd finished.

"Oh, she never told thee? Soft lad's Nancy's boy."

Course, soon as it was said, it seemed so obvious. I mean, it's not as though she'd concealed it, nor ever made a secret of her fondness for the lad. It was just she'd never told me direct. Or, I suppose, remembering that night in the rain, I never gave her the chance. Thinking back on it now, what with the lad being such a strange sort of creature, maybe I just didn't *want* to see.

I honestly can't remember what I said next. All I know is I

had to get away as fast as I could. She was smirking, of course, with the other ones, last look I had of her, before I turned my back on 'em all.

After that, I wandered for hours, staggering like one wounded through the long summer night until dawn came with red streaks in the sky. I was weary by then, and perched myself on the edge of the canal, my sore feet dangling down. I'd been right round town, from the dark fortresses of the mills in Ancoats, quiet for the only time in the week, past the looming shadow of the Collegiate Church, tramping the full length of Deansgate, onwards to Knott Mill where I'd first spoken to her, and then all the way back again, to the bank of the Rochdale Canal, where even at the dead of Sunday night, there were barges on the move and boatmen calling.

Sky above me had changed all colours, from jewel-blue to coal-black, before slowly sliding into sludge-brown just before dawn. And there I was, tiny beneath it, disappointed all over again that things weren't as they seemed, or as I wanted 'em to be. She wasn't free to run away into the life I'd dreamed up. Even with her mam as good as dead, she was still tied. Yeah, and to such a child as Walter. Perhaps you'll think I exaggerate, but I swear it made me nothing short of sick to think on him, those girlish looks, those owlish eyes and the way he'd clung so fearfully to her that day at the fair. That peculiar way of humming he had too, as he looked right through you, just as though you weren't there at all.

Strangely enough, as I sat pondering it all, another Bible character came to mind. This time, it was my namesake, Joseph. As a growing lad, with all my new manly pride, I'd never understood how he'd been able to accept Mary's child as his own, and that morning, as I pictured Walter, I knew for certain I could never accept him. No, not even if he'd been my own, I thought, I could never bring myself to love such an oddity.

Dear God, what a bitter tasting cup I drank that night, raging all the while against the lad and his dad and even

Nancy herself, who'd not been straight with me. And yet, at the same time as an angry thought rose up against her, like vomit after too much ale, there was always another to cheat me of my anger and turn it on myself. How could I blame her for not telling me something that was staring me in the face? And when all the time I'd been spinning *her* a story? Ha! To think she'd taken me for some well-read radical.

As the sun came up, slowly spreading a glow over the town, the streets began to fill with the first workers heading to the factories, just as though it was any other Monday morning. Vast numbers of 'em, it seemed, tramping in their clogs, too hungry and too afraid to defy their masters and fight for freedom on the field. Did I imagine a greater weariness in their tread? Did their skinny bodies seem that bit more drooped? I don't know. Perhaps some were shamefaced. Or perhaps not. 'Cos maybe, after all, these were the wise ones? Them's that know nowt ever changes.

Still hunched by the water, wound up tight, veering from fury to grief and back again, I pictured the words blazoned on them banners they'd be waving later: *Liberty*, *Fraternity*, *Love*. And in my mind, I rose up, like a vengeful soldier, his sword raised, and I tore every last one of 'em down, ripping 'em to shreds. 'Cos all them hopes and plans I'd spent so much of the last months listening to, working towards even, all of 'em were bound up with the break of that particular day. And yet here it was, and no different to any other morning. In an instant, I saw it all for the dreaming it was: impossible, foolish and green, the stuff of child's play.

So's, of course, that decided it. I wasn't for going on the march. I just wouldn't show. I'd shut Nancy right out of my heart and take the road out of town.

Picking myself up from the bank of the canal, I swear I intended to go right there and then without looking back. But call it the Devil in me if you like, I was that shaken up, I suddenly felt an urge to do something more. And so, my eye chancing upon a loose stone on the towpath, I stooped down to pick it up and promptly hurled it with all my might towards the canal. Well, it wasn't what I intended, but I managed to hit the cargo of the next boat which was coming on, and before I knew it, there were a couple of boatmen, Paddies they were, snarling and waving their fists and hurling all kinds of abuse at me, "Ye feckin' eejit!"

Well, it got me blood pumping, didn't it? Caught me up in a mist of anger, as I shouted back worse profanities over my shoulder and legged it away, almost without knowing it, towards the new mill.

It was quiet when I got there, it still being early, and the half-built buildings, black against the dim light of dawn, looked more like a ruin than the beginning of something. Swiftly, I hastened over to a tower of brick pallets which stood in the shadow of my chimney, and I grabbed at 'em, cramming one, yes even a second, into each of my jacket pockets and taking another in my fist. Then I strode away, and I can't lie, this time, I knew exactly where I was heading.

EIGHT

Even as the sounds of merriment still whirled on the warm air, the roar of the crowd and bugle blast, all Nancy could hear was a small, cold voice within, hissing to her silent self, "Fool!" She'd done it again. The stupid, stupid fool!

Had all those people been looking at her and thinking it too? Jemima, who'd been so tetchy with her of late, gossiping with a gang of girls from down the street, stealing glances at her and smirking. First smile she'd seen her crack in weeks. Oh well, she'd thought, *they* could think what they liked. But dependable, old Archie Thompson, proud and dignified in his fustian suit, he had been a different matter. He'd looked bewildered and shrugged sadly when she'd asked where Joe was, and she still couldn't shake off the strange sense of responsibility she'd felt for his disappointment. As for poor Mary, appealing to her to come, her kind face, full of an indignance on her behalf she didn't deserve, even after she'd been so hurtful as well; oh, she'd hardly been able to meet her eye.

The minutes crept on as the people moved out of sight, and she, twitching from one false hope to another, as all the while, sickening dread burrowed deeper, like the onset of disease, the voice in her head relentless, telling her it was always going to end like this. And it was right. She was right. For even before the sound of the march receded, she knew he would not come; she had always known.

Joe wasn't all he seemed. She hadn't needed Mary to point it out; she'd sensed it for herself, a vague feeling at first, nothing she could put her finger to, not until that night when she'd surprised him, waiting for her on the quiet street which ran the north side of the mill. Clearly believing himself alone, she'd caught him straining to get a good look at his reflection in one of the high-set windows and been unable to stop herself from laughing and crying out in good humour. "Hey, Mr Price, is tha done preening?"

She'd expected him to brush it off in the same spirit, and of course he had done, but not before she'd clocked his face freeze and his eye gleam cold. It was the work of a second. Just as quickly, he was recovered again and flashing one of his wide smiles. Yet there and then, in that moment, she'd known she'd never love him. Not truly. But wasn't that exactly the worst of it? That her heart wasn't broken, that all this hurt and anger, it wasn't about *him*. Nay, nay, it was about *her*. It was about her making the same old mistake. She shook her head and clenched her fists, feeling the palms hot and clammy beneath her curled fingers.

Of course, he'd interested her from the start, with his talk of reform. Truthfully, she'd been as excited by that, and the books and papers he brought for her, as she'd been by his good looks. Though, before long, there'd been no denying the attraction between them too. That much was clear from the way she'd behaved the other night. Dear God, would that she could stop that stormy scene playing over in her mind's eye! That handsome face of his and the confidence he had in his own body, and she, after all those weeks of holding back, succumbing to his first touch, like some kind of strumpet! And for what? For what? A fumble in the dark! And the same mistake. The *same* mistake! It was she and Smithy all over again. Except that this was worse, far, far worse, for the fact of Smithy himself, and their pitiful marriage, hadn't gone away.

So much for reading! So much for change! Stupid, stupid girl, she'd learned nothing.

And all this, even as her mother lay dying. Lord, just thinking it, made her hot with shame and her breath catch in a strange choking sound. "Oh, Mam!"

That she'd wasted these last precious evenings with her, confused and distracted, ruminating over a man she knew she didn't really trust. Oh, she could hardly bear it.

Her poor mother, consumed by love, hollowed out by grief, exhausted by always thinking the worst and always being right. Oh, if Walter weren't here, she'd race back to her in a heartbeat, to fling herself beside her bed and beg forgiveness for every last petty argument, every tut of irritation, every stupid, wrong-headed decision that had brought her here, alone with her boy, in this deserted street.

It was too much. Grief drenched her, like a black cloud, pouring guilt and misery, so that she had to turn from Walter, to shield him from her tears. In doing so, she was reminded of something else too. Someone. Another person she'd turned from, crying. The other person she'd let down. For just as terrible as her other mistakes, amidst all her selfish turmoil, hadn't she cruelly attacked the man who'd been her greatest champion?

Oh, Captain Wright, she wept to herself. Samson. Her… friend? What was it he was to her? She hardly knew. Except it was all over now, and he'd probably never speak to her again.

"Oh, Walter, what have I done?" she wailed, turning back, bending down, wrapping her arms round him, feeling the comfort of his body close. But just as soon as they embraced, she felt his own bony shoulders begin to rise and fall, as he spluttered, choking into her dress. Instantly, she broke free, holding him away to examine him. His cough, it seemed, had been the sound of his own stifled tears, which burst forth now in unrestrained sobbing and Nancy felt a fresh, new stab of remorse. What on earth was she putting him through?

She squatted down to face him, "Oh, shush, Walt. Please, darling, shush. What is it?"

"I liked the band, Mammy."

"Oh, Walt!"

She wiped his eyes with her hands, and then her own, and, standing up again, drew him into her skirts and blew out a heavy sigh. First, she looked down the road where the parade had gone; it was a long way ahead of them now. Then she looked back the other way, towards Ancoats, and pictured her mother again, lying under the sheets in the quiet room. She stood, uncertain.

Then, across the empty street, a small gust picked up and the little flags of bunting strung on the buildings opposite caught her eye, waving enthusiastically, reminding her of the day's noble cause. Were they really to miss out? Would she really allow Joseph Price – nay, her own folly – to prevent her from showing Walter what she knew to be right? After all, she thought, she still had him, and they both had the future.

"Please, Mammy," he asked again. "Music?"

"Yes, my darling, yes!" She took up his hand and started to run. "Hurry now!" she cried, Walter tottering and laughing at her side.

NINE

Samson walked past St Peter's Church and turning the corner of a high-walled garden, found himself on Mount Street. It wasn't difficult to identify which of the houses was Mr Buxton's, since several men were just arriving. Amongst them, he spotted the white hair of Hugh Osborne, and when he drew closer, the older man stiffly raised his hat to him, as the party passed by and into the house. Thereafter, a great deal of other people continued to come and go, so that Samson was satisfied he wouldn't arouse undue attention by loitering on the steps.

Looking towards the field, he understood at once why the house had been chosen: the windows of the upper level must look directly upon the makeshift hustings and, at the same time, afford a clear view of the entrance to the croft from Peter Street. Although Samson didn't have the benefit of such a room, he found if he remained on the step and strained upwards, he achieved sufficient elevation to take in a general view of sorts. And what an impressive sight it was! The broad sweep of open land was steadily filling with thousands of people, all of them remarkably well-trained, marching in, one regimented section at a time.

He had no idea where the Ancoats people might be, though he squinted to read the legends on every banner to try and find them. Nevertheless, he saw only those from Bury or Oldham or Stockport, or else slogans like, *No Corn Laws*, *Liberty* or *Unite and be Free*, and wondered, with a frown, what the men upstairs would make of the black cloth claiming, *Equal Representation or Death*.

There was nothing, however, in that vast sea of bodies and banners that bore the name Ancoats. Even so, he kept on looking, even as he acknowledged it was futile, searching the growing mass of people in the vain hope of spotting her.

TEN

MARY

As we marched down Oldham Street, arm in arm in our rows, the sun shining on and music keeping us in time, most folk on the pavement stopped to wave and cheer. Some of 'em even joined in, walking at the side, or following us from behind. As for the toffs, I suppose they'd arranged to be out of town for the day, or else were peeping at us from behind their shutters. Course, I was still for worrying about Nancy. I was that sorry she wasn't with us and missing out on this marvellous feeling, but even as I fretted, I couldn't help but get swept up in it all.

When at last we reached the point where we were to file onto the field, we came alongside some of the other contingents who'd had a sight further to come, them from Middleton and Rochdale as I remember, and all over the show. And it was just as if a giant mirror had been held up, 'cos they looked the same as us, and we, like them, dressed tidy and respectable in the best of clothes, with our laurel leaves shining. Ee, the atmosphere was right grand. There were trumpet calls and bugle blasts, and all of us bursting into cheers and applause for one another!

From the clock on the church tower, it was just coming up to midday by the time we processed onto the field to more cheers from them that were there already, and we made our way towards the wagons fashioned like a stage at the far end, surrounded by flags and banners and red liberty caps, each one bobbing on its own pole. Ee, it was a sight! And there were that many people, I can't tell thee. Thousands upon thousands of us, and plain as day to me that whatever Nancy decided to do, she'd never be able to find us, not now, not within a crowd so great.

Even as I was thinking this, more and more folk were coming up behind, and we found ourselves pushed closer and closer to the front, so that I remember saying to Mick, "We're going to get a right good view."

Well, we can't have been there more than twenty minutes, and the crowd already doubled in size, when, all at once, we found ourselves pushed by an almighty heave of bodies, not from behind as you'd expect, but in the opposite direction, coming from the front-side. I staggered a moment at the swell, and almost lost my footing, my heart beating fast at the sudden thought of being trapped under so many legs. Then, as I righted mi'sel, I must've trodden on somebody's foot, though I never made 'em out. All I know is I heard a tetchy voice cursing me and crying out, "Great clumsy lump!" Ee, I can't lie, it fair made me flush with anger, though it seems daft now to think on it, that I were bothered by such a thing.

All this while, Mick was busy looking over the heads of the others, talking to David Wilson, who'd come along with Jemima, and wondering why there'd been such a push. It seems the crowd on the left of the field had been parted by a number of special constables. Mick pointed 'em out to me, and if I stretched up I could just see 'em, in their dark suits and tall hats. They'd come from the direction of one of the houses on Mount Street, and once they'd forced their way through, they'd separated themselves out into two rows, facing one another, thereby clearing a pathway of sorts all the way from the house to the hustings.

"It's to make it easier for to arrest 'em!" we heard say.

Mind, not once, nor twice, but again and again, as the same rumour or something like it swept round the crowd, so that it wasn't long before there was a whole load of pushing and shoving going on around the makeshift stage, as them that were closest linked together to form a chain of bodies round it, trying their best to block the access the constables had made.

"Ee, dear," I said to Mick, "I hope no one forgets themsel'."

"Don't be worrying, Mary," he replied, surveying the field. "Look about ye. Everyone's in good humour."

He was right and all. It was remarkable. That vast, open area of St Peter's Field seemed already near full with men, women and children, good-tempered all of 'em, and still more piling in. I looked at the clock. It was nearly one, and the meeting wouldn't long be getting started. As the anticipation grew, I cast my eyes about, standing on tiptoe now and again and shifting my head from side to side to see past gentlemen's hats or kiddies balanced on the shoulders of their daddies. Where were Nancy and little Walter? Had they come? And if they had, how were they faring?

Well, at last the speakers came! Hunt's open carriage swept in from Deansgate side, with a great whoop of welcome I'll never forget. Nay, he couldn't have had a more tremendous reception if he'd flown in on a winged chariot! In fact, it was a barouche he was in, all decked out with flags and followed by some lasses I recognised from the Manchester Reform committee. Course, it took 'em all a fair while to make towards the hustings, what with everyone on the field straining towards 'em to get a good look, but the music and clapping and cheering kept up all the way.

As for me, I was that excited, my hands were in the air waving, and my throat near hoarse with all the shouting, and when the carriage eventually passed us, I was that pleased to get a right good look at him. Hunt, I mean. Ee, he was handsome. Very tall and broad he was, with a fine crop of silver hair just showing under his grand white hat, and such an agreeable mouth, which kept breaking out into immense smiles. Hardly surprising, mind, given the size of the crowd and the warmth of the welcome.

Next, he and the other speakers climbed up onto the platform, and I think it was Hunt himself who helped the lady from the box seat of the carriage. Mary Fildes, it was, president of us Female Reformers, who we'd listened to on more than one occasion at the Union rooms. Ee, how I longed to turn to Nancy then in my excitement. To see Mrs Fildes up there, looking so refined in her white linen and regarding us all with such a pleasant and satisfied demeanour.

ELEVEN

They were surely only twenty minutes behind the others, or perhaps just a little more, but even after hurrying a distance, their clogs ringing out on the empty streets, it was clear to Nancy that the north of town was deserted. The marchers had already passed through, and most tradesfolk hadn't opened for the day. All the stalls, shops and yards, which would normally be bustling, were shut up, graveyard quiet: cartwrights and blacksmiths, milliners and bootmakers, butchers and grocers, all of them taking an extraordinary Saint Monday. By, wouldn't some of them at that very moment be congregating on the field? A thrill darted through her just to think of it and, without realising, she picked up her pace.

A few strides more, however, and Walter began to drag heavy on her arm. She looked down at him, slowing behind her. He was already out of breath and panting, and in the quietness of the abandoned street, she could make out the rattle of phlegm on his bony chest. She stopped to let him rest, and he sank against her legs, his arms hanging loosely around her waist.

"Come on, Walt. Tha's me little emperor. Tha can do this, can't thee?"

"Not yet, Mammy," he said hoarsely and began to cough. Nancy frowned, looking back towards Ancoats, wondering again whether they shouldn't just be done with it and go home, when, from the south, a fragment of cheering reached them.

"Listen!" she breathed excitedly. "We're not far off now!"

Walter tilted his head up, his chin still lost in her skirts, his round eyes pleading for more time.

"I tell thee what," she smiled at him, "what if Mammy gives thee a lift?"

At this, still serious Walter nodded solemnly and stretched his arms towards her.

"Only for part of t' way, mind!" She bent her knees and gathered him up. Although he was nearly seven, he was still short, and so thin after these last few hungry months, she was certain she'd be able to manage his weight and make up some time. "Aye, tha's as light as a bird's feather!" she laughed and flicked her finger the length of his little nose.

Even so, they were inevitably slow, stopping from time to time as a coughing fit took him, or when she needed to stretch out an arm for relief, so that when they eventually reached Piccadilly, it had also fallen quiet. There were none of the crowds and banners and players she'd expected, just a few people left milling about or taking shade in the shadow of the closed-up shops whilst on the corner, a collection of stray cats mewed plaintively from thirst. Oh Lord, it would be impossible to find the others now.

"Never mind," she said out loud, as much for herself as for Walter.

She was hot, out of breath and tired, deflated with disappointment and ready to fall again into wretched self-reproach. Without thinking, she set Walter down on the pavement and breathed out a loud sigh, though straightway he began to whimper as before, tugging at the folds of her dress.

"Nay, lad, don't start, now," she snapped. But the irritation in her voice only made things worse, and he started to cry in earnest.

"Oh, Walt!" she groaned wearily, though she scooped him up again, stroking his wet cheek and absently setting little popping kisses across his forehead. They stood there for a moment, in the middle of the road, Walter nestling into her neck, and Nancy not knowing whether to go on or to retreat, until she was forced to stand out of the way by two oncoming horses which had just turned into the street.

The horses, one a bay and the other grey-white, were being walked at a leisurely pace by their riders, who despite their cavalry colours were slouched quite casually in their saddles, laughing and joking with one another. When they passed her, the soldier on the bay glanced over and, without meaning to, she met his eye. Immediately, he pulled on his bridle, and the horse stopped with a loud neigh and a roll of its head, the yellow-white of its near eye flashing, the man all the while appraising her slowly, until lowering his head closer, he smirked, "Well, good day to you, pretty miss!"

Nancy didn't smile back but rather gripped Walter tighter and raised her chin defiantly, at which the soldier broke into cheerless laughter and, kicking his heels into the horse's sides, trotted on.

Meanwhile, Walter still nuzzled at her neck, weeping quietly, the leaves pinned to his cap tickling her chin, his tears running the length of her exposed skin to wet the collar of her dress.

"Come on, Walt. What's the matter?"

"The band!" he sobbed. "I wanted to hear the band again."

She prised him away from her and leaned back to get a good look at his blotched face. More tears were balanced on the rims of his big eyes, poised to drop from his long lashes. Her poor boy.

"Yes, my darling," she bit her lip and looked towards town. "Yes. I already told thee tha shall, so tha shall."

It was decided. The sun was still shining, and the crowd was within earshot. The soldiers hadn't been called upon, it seemed, and unsavoury though that last encounter had been, even they seemed in a good humour of sorts.

"Come on then!" she cried, taking in a deep breath through her nose. "What we waiting for?" And she rejigged him in her arms and began to hum the notes of a tune she knew he liked as she set off at a brisk march, bouncing him in time, and he now squealing with laughter, all the way to St Peter's Field.

TWELVE

JOSEPH

Yeah, I was mad with fury and, yeah, I had a brick in my hand. But I wasn't there. I swear. No matter what you hear. I never went near St Peter's Field. It was always meant to be a peaceable meeting, and even with my blood boiling, I wasn't for spoiling that. From all I've heard since, none of the reformers were. No, no, it was nothing like that, no matter what folk say. I was away out of Manchester long before all that started.

No. Where I was going was a lot closer. Head down, cap low over my face, I turned left down the next side street, just before you get to them gates. Then I was up at those high windows where she'd met me that time. I jumped to check there was no one about. All was still quiet. Weighing it in my hand, hard and coarse, like all the others that had made that wretched place, I lifted the brick and chucked it through the glass. Over the smash it made, I heard it land inside with a clang of metal off one of the machines and, afterwards, nothing. So's then I sent another through the next window, and the next, until at last there came a shout, and I ditched the other bricks at my feet and ran, my cap falling behind me and wind whistling in my hair.

By the time I stopped, I was already halfway to the moor. Panting for breath, I bent over and sank my hands on my thighs. When I looked down at 'em, I saw they were dirty and red.

THIRTEEN

They arrived at the north end just as a great cheer went up. It was so loud, Nancy feared for Walter, but safe in her arms, he didn't seem to mind. From this distance, there was little detail of the hustings to make out, just the flapping of the banners and the cheerful red liberty caps set out in front, and that vast circle of bodies joined together as one around them. But just the sight of them – all those people, all of them brought together in the same hope she cherished – it was enough to make her half-laugh, half-cry aloud in exhilarated disbelief.

"Just look, Walt!"

Oh, thank God they'd come! How could they ever have missed this? It seemed nothing short of a miracle, the meeting, so long planned, was at last spread before her, the breadth of the field, as colourful as the wild meadow flowers on those nearby hills.

FOURTEEN

It wasn't possible for him to make out the words of the speaker from the house on Mount Street. Samson thought it might be Hunt himself who was talking, but he was at too great a distance to be sure, and in any case, there was all kinds of noise carrying on the air. A collective murmur rippled from the crowd, interrupted now and then by shouts or applause, and, from afar off, occasional flourishes of music. There was plenty of bustle closer at hand too, in front of the houses, with onlookers exchanging observations on the crowd.

"Wonder what the devil Hulton makes to it."

"Nervous, no doubt. There's more here than anyone credited."

All at once, through these bystanders, a large, dark, surly-looking fellow barged past him and bounded up the steps to the house, hammering on the door for admittance. Not a few moments later, and the door burst open again. This time, another younger man with a harassed expression emerged, clutching a raft of papers so tightly his knuckles had turned white. In his haste down the steps, he almost knocked Samson over.

"Watch out!" Samson said, righting himself and brushing down his sleeves. He looked the boy over, trying to make out his purpose, adding coolly, "What's the hurry?"

The boy merely glanced at him and waved the papers, blurting as he sprinted off, "These must away!"

Samson watched him deliver them to the horsemen who had evidently been stationed outside the house in readiness. They turned tail now, and Samson saw one of them ride in the direction of Portland Street. He swallowed. Dear God, the Yeomanry!

His heart racing now, he stepped down to the pavement and took a few paces towards the periphery, joining the closest group, who were still blithely attending the address. He had no plan. He didn't know what he could do. He simply hoped he might be able to help.

Then, over Hunt's shouted oratory, came the noise he was dreading: a low, gathering sound at first, building, louder and louder, until with the thunder of hooves, suddenly they were there, scores of Yeomen, their faces red and wild-looking, rowdily taking the corner into Mount Street.

They came to an untidy halt outside the walled garden and parallel to the crowd. The horses, which had been spurred to a furious pace, now restlessly pawing the street, sending up great clouds of brown dust, into which one of the constables walked. Amidst a great deal of coughing, this constable consulted with one of the Yeomen, who in turn shouted to the men behind. Samson understood it was a command. Sure enough, after a moment, several of the party followed the first Yeoman, trotting their horses towards the opening of the passage created by the constables.

From the hustings, Hunt had spotted them. Civilised to the last, he appeared to hail them with an ironic wave of his white hat and invited the crowd to give them a cheer.

FIFTEEN

Walter was still pinned to her hip, his legs tucked up either side of her thigh, arms clutching round her neck, his whole body tensed like stretched thread on the mule. Only his head moved, turning this way and that, wary of the crowd ahead, but nevertheless still listening for a dance of notes on the air.

There was no prospect of hearing the address from this far back, she realised, but she didn't dare risk more tears by asking him to walk again, so instead she readjusted him in her aching arms and set out across the scrub.

Bearing towards the left, she wove them in and out of the fringes of the crowd. Dipping her head and apologising as she nudged past row upon row. Stopping every now and then to shift Walter's weight and to judge if she could hear well enough, and each time deciding, nay, the volume could be improved upon, so that moving forward, step by step, they were drawn deeper into the throng.

By the time she discovered she was too closely hemmed in to let Walter down, it was too late. Surrounded by a press of bodies, she suddenly felt a low, deep rolling beneath her. Lord what was it? Sensing it in her feet first, rather than hearing it, the very earth of the field had started to shake, nay, to reverberate, on and on, just like the floorboards of the mill in full pelt. Then all at once a loud huzzah blared around them and she raised herself on tiptoe to follow the crowd's eye. What? Had they really cheered the arrival of the Yeomen? She frowned, confused, looking about her, trying to catch someone's eye to ask what was happening, but everyone was consumed by the presence of the soldiers. Their whipped horses were snorting violently now, and at one great shuddering exhalation of distress, Nancy felt Walter freeze in terror.

"Tha's grand, Walt. Tha's grand."

But the cries around them were turning to hoots and hisses, hot breath hurling past her cheek, voices shouting, close and shrill. Walter pressed his hands tight to his ears, writhing in her arms, so that she had to exert all her strength to fix him firm against her.

"Stay still! Tha's grand!"

All around her were bodies, men and women taller than she. It was impossible to see what was happening or hear anything properly, but she knew well enough the proceedings had taken a decisive turn. In rising panic, she decided they must push their way out. Out, back, back, towards the edge of the crowd, when, without warning, there was a sudden heave, and a weight of bodies pressed upon them so heavily, they were slammed sideways, pinned up so close against the people behind, she could feel the thread of their clothes against her skin, smell the warm breath knocked out of them.

She righted herself and clutched Walter closer still, but any direction she turned now, there were bodies hard up against them, all gripped by alarm, as cries rose ahead, urgent shouts of, "Break, Break!" and nearer at hand, great rasping gulps for air.

Walter was beside himself. Screaming and scrambling up her sweat-soaked body as though trying to scale a brick wall, his arms flailing above them, gasping in panic for air.

"Shush, baby, shush!" she cried, dragging him downwards, but there was no respite. It was as though they'd been launched in a tiny boat, on a surging sea, and each roll of the crowd set them crashing and tumbling this way and that, all the time

Walter clutching at the sky like one being drowned, as people swam at them in terrified retreat from the front.

Then, in the sinking of a wave, suddenly there was only absence in her arms. Walter was gone.

SIXTEEN

MARY

"What is it, Mick?" I cried, grabbing a hold of him.

"Look!" he shouted, and I followed his alarmed eyes.

Dear God, I don't know how to tell thee of the horror.

Afore me, all I could see were horses' hooves. Up in the air, high above me it seemed, rearing. And then the wild flash of their terrified eyes. I could make no sense of it at first, what I was seeing. And the noise! Dear God, the shrieking and wailing of the folk around me, drowned out by the frantic snorting and whinnying of them creatures. I know now it was the Yeomanry, come to accompany the fella with the arrest warrant, but for us on the ground, desperately scrambling away, hurling ourselves back against the solid mass of people behind, it was like fiends of Hell had broken loose and come to Manchester on horseback, glinting sabres raised.

SEVENTEEN

"Nay!" she screamed, darting her head around, to the left, to the right, down, down, down amongst all those legs.

"Walter! Walter!"

But her voice was just one of many, as all about her was shouting, howling, agonised groping for breath. She was being dragged backwards, away from the spot she'd lost him, urged by the people pressing up against her to get away.

"Run! Run for tha life, their blades are out!"

A young man's face sprang up close, covered in blood running from the top of his head, fixing her with eyes that glared white out of the red, before he dazedly staggered past her. After him, between the dark shapes of those surging towards her, she now made out other figures, men on horseback. With swords! With swords first whipped high above their heads, and then plunging low, hacking.

Amidst the blasted, sweating heat, Nancy turned cold with terror.

"Walter! Oh, dear God, please no. Walter!"

She knew she must not move on. She could not leave the spot where he'd fallen. And so she struggled against the streaming tide, shoulders and arms bashing into her, sending her this way and that, heart racing, breath catching, dirt-grit in her mouth. Most of those crashing past her were splattered with blood, their arms above their heads to fend off more blows from behind. But still she pushed forward, determined to get back to the spot, her foot kicking against something soft, almost tripping. A body lying prostrate and trampled on the floor. Searching in dread, even as more bodies trod over it, her eyes spotted a leg. It was protruding from a bloodied skirt. A fleeting second's gladness. It wasn't Walter.

Then she looked up again, into brown cloud. A thud. Heat at her shoulder. Red behind her eyes.

EIGHTEEN

It was the work of a moment from the cry of, "Here's the warrant!" and the crowd's jeers, to the bugle blast of the Yeomanry's advance. From where he remained on the fringe, Samson watched some of those closest to the rows of constables begin to push forward to narrow the avenue to the hustings. However, the Yeomen, whose blood was up, merely kicked their spurs deeper in frustration, thrusting onwards to force their passage through, all the while their horses becoming more and more terrified, startling at the press of people, rearing this way and that in alarm, their inexpert riders unable to control them, and lurching out into the crowd.

There was noise and panic everywhere. Samson didn't know which way to look. Straining first towards the hustings, he saw the constables with the warrant gain the platform and, within seconds, the speakers rounded up. Hunt and a couple of the other gentlemen leaped down but not by way of escape. Samson could tell from the booing that started up, they'd been seized.

Meanwhile, the Yeomen, clinging to their flailing animals, had dispersed pell-mell into the crowd. Samson followed the progress of one, charging away from the hustings into the heart of the assembly, and in a starburst flash, hot sun on cold steel, he understood the rider had brandished his sabre.

"No, no!" he roared, running deeper into the rush of people, his hat falling behind him, just as a spurt of red, bright as a berry in the sunlight, formed an arc in the air towards him. He felt it land, warm and wet, soaking his shirt. In front of him, he saw an elderly man, bent almost double, clutching at the side of his head, his wrinkled face contorted in pain. His ear was off. Samson's mouth fell open in horror, but before he could offer help, the man was already lost in the crush.

In front and behind, and everywhere he looked, the Yeomen were out of control, wading through the mass of people, unable to direct their horses, slicing down their blades, first on one side and then another, careless of whomsoever they struck. From the sweat-glisten of his bald head, Samson recognised one of them as the victorious arm-wrestler from the tavern, his eyes now aflame with demonic delight, his muscled arm swinging down to hack into the shoulder of a young man who was trying to escape, so that the blow came from behind. Samson saw the man's eyes pop with shock as his body bucked and his face dissolved into pain.

"Desist!" Samson cried, but he could barely hear his own voice over the din. All around were shouts and screams and horrible gasps for air, as, choking and exhausted, body after body fell, trampled in the chaos. It was as though the terrified crowd itself was become a turbulent ocean, seething with great angry ripples produced by a goaded sea monster beneath, ready at any moment to consume the next unfortunate Jonah, as Samson, trying to hold firm to the spot, time and again, reached into the darkness between torsos, arms, heads, to grab at them falling, to pull them back from the depths, but all in vain.

Looking towards Mount Street from where he'd watched for so long, he tried to assess how far he was from the outer edge, and whether his rescue efforts might prove more effective there, but on turning again, he had to jump out of the path of another horse, whinnying loudly. Instinctively covering his head, he nevertheless caught a glimpse of the rider. It was George Baldwin, his cheeks blood-spotted and eyes bulging in terror. Raised in the air, his sabre was clogged with gore.

"Away! Leave the field," Samson commanded. "Let the people go."

George looked as though he would escape in a second, but the horse reared again with a terrible sound, its hooves kicking high enough to glint in the sun. He simply couldn't control it, and now it spun around the other way, knocking over a man and charging back into the middle of the field.

Samson wiped a slick of sweat from his forehead and began to work his way sideways, closer to the periphery of the crowd. Eventually, when he was near enough the edge, he turned back to look into the heaving mass. There were more horsemen now, he realised: the Hussars ordered in to sweep the field. He shook his head in disbelief.

Then, close at hand, he heard a scream and saw a young woman collapse, overwhelmed by the weight of the crowd coming up behind her. He rushed forward and reached in, fending off the charge as best he could with one arm, at the same time heaving her out with the other. As she scrambled up, grabbing at him, too shocked to offer thanks, her foot caught on the hem of her dirtied dress, which ripped apart so that she ran off half-exposed in retreat.

Straightaway, a couple of children were about to be trapped in the same manner, and again he launched into the oncoming crowd to save them, a little girl with loosened plaits, whose bloodied nose appeared to be broken, and a small fair-haired boy, who seemed remarkably unhurt and looked up at him mutely. Once they were clear of the worst, there being no parent to deliver them to, he walked with them hand in hand over to the pavement close to Mr Buxton's house.

"Stay here. Don't go anywhere. Do you understand? I'll be back soon to help you."

The girl nodded solemnly, with eyes purpling with bruises, but the boy's gaze remained fixed on the ground. Samson hesitated. Then, all at once, another great groan came from the field, and he ran back to see if there was anyone else he could get out.

NINETEEN

Adelaide had just taken up the novel again when she heard a howl, loud and close. This time it wasn't muffled by the closed window but had come from inside the house. She burst out of the drawing room to investigate, only to find Mrs Halliwell and the maids already hastening down the stairs, their faces wide-eyed, mouths hanging open in speechless horror.

"Goodness, what on earth…"

"Oh, ma'am, has tha not seen?" said Ellen.

They had clearly been assembled at an upstairs window.

"Take a look outside. There's been trouble summat awful. We just saw a poor, owd fella stagger down here with his arm half-hanging off! Oh, the blood on his shirt, it were like a butcher's apron. And there's more of 'em coming. Oh, ma'am, dost tha think we should open up and help 'em out?"

"Stay away from the door!" Adelaide ordered, sweeping back into the drawing room and at once seeing scores of the mob rushing past, many of them weeping, their smart clothes in disarray, running and looking over their shoulders in terror.

There was crying within as well, and Adelaide could scarcely believe Mrs Halliwell had sunk into a chair by the fireplace. She was shaking her head and twisting her hands in her lap. Ellen was kneeling before her, trying to offer comfort, but caught Adelaide's look from across the room.

"Her lad were for going. Him and his sweetheart."

Adelaide tutted and turned back to the scene outside. The two younger maids had followed her up to the window, and now they all watched fresh wave upon wave of people, a great number of them clearly injured, their clothes torn and splattered with blood.

"What does tha thinks happened?" she heard one of them whisper.

"Clearly they've started a riot!" Adelaide declared. "I knew it."

"But surely they wouldn't have hurt so many of their own?"

She frowned, uncertain.

The numbers were beginning to dissipate, but her attention was caught by the figure of a small girl at the top of the street, walking alone towards them. She can't have been more than four, the same age Adelaide had been when her mother died. The girl's dark hair was knotted about her head, so thickly it encircled her face like an enormous bonnet, whilst the hem of her dress hung undone, and when she came closer, its front showed soiled with dust and dark blotches of blood. Now she was right by the house, Adelaide could see her pretty little features were scratched and bruised, and she was sobbing with abandon, not knowing where she was heading. Despite the heat of the day, Adelaide shuddered cold.

"The poor little mite!" cried the young maid, moving towards the door. "Surely, ma'am, we should bring her inside?"

Adelaide, still strangely fixed on the child, held up her hand. There was a pause, and then she cried, "Wait!"

A man, who appeared uninjured, had turned into the street at speed. When he spotted the girl, he rushed towards her and bent down.

"Keep that door shut!"

The man picked up the girl and ran on.

"Shameless!"

TWENTY

MARY

Me and Mick, we managed to stay together, though God knows we were crushed on all sides. Behind us were the horses going wild and the sickening sound of them butchers. Jabbing and chopping they were, as though we reformers were nothing but cuts o' meat. Everywhere terror, folk fleeing, and all the breath of us squeezed upwards into a universal croak, hoarse and desperate. And as for underfoot, ee, it turns my stomach just to think on it, a carpet of injured bodies there was, which we tripped over the length of the field.

I don't know where it was we ended up, through a storm of truncheon blows, but we had to stop a moment. I was panting that hard, and my chest a-heaving that much, I thought my heart would bust, though I couldn't tell thee now whether it was with exertion or fear or sorrow.

"Mary, come on, we're not safe yet," Mick urged, his arm round me, racing us onwards, heading for the north of town and home. It was only once we were beyond Piccadilly that he allowed us to pause again, and I cannot tell thee how sweet it was to stop right there, in the middle of the street, with half the town streaming past us, embracing one another with the pure relief of still being alive.

He's not a big man, my Mick, but he's always been strong, and at first it was so good to be held safe. Yet even as he hugged me, I could feel he was not himself, and rather than standing firm and sturdy, he was shaky, so shaky, almost as though he'd been hollowed out somehow, so that it was more that he clung to me to stop himself from falling over than I was able to lean on him, and then when we pulled away from one another, I saw his face haggard with exhaustion, and all the weight of the crowd, and the effort of escape, and the first tears I'd ever seen him cry.

"Mick, oh Mick," was all I could say, over and over, patting his back like he was a boy rather than a man. I still don't know how it was that we found ourselves that way round, with me doing all the consoling, but eventually he looked up and, with his tears still rolling, smiled weakly at me and whispered, "Away, let's get ourselves off home."

Well, what a to-do I had with mi'sel then. The state he was in. He was fit for nothing, and I was that worried about him. Believe me, I wanted nothing more than to hasten home as fast as we could, to rush inside and fling the door shut, and hide ourselves under the sheets from the rest of the world. But thing was, ever since we'd got beyond the field, I'd not stopped looking for them, and even as Mick wept on, all I could think was, at least we have each other!

"Mary, come on away home. There's soldiers and constables and all sorts abroad."

"But, Mick, how can I?" I cried. "What about Nancy? And little Walter?"

TWENTY-ONE

Before long a great number had managed to escape, but under the glare of the mid-afternoon sun what was left behind was more devastating than any battle he'd ever fought. Some of the Hussars, still on horseback, were circling the field, which was strewn about with groaning bodies, the ground around them flecked here and there with pools of blood, like ink on a blotter. At the front, other soldiers were collecting up what remained of the reformers' banners, tattered remnants fluttering against the harsh sky. Samson watched them tear them down, the last colours, red and green and gold and white, the letters ripped apart, the words lost forever.

The scene had fallen quiet too, the great clamour over, so that he was able to hear quite distinctly, a choking sound close at hand and he turned to find a dishevelled figure scrambling towards him, ripped strips like ribbons floating from her white, soiled dress, her eyes blazing, intent on the large bulk of a man who lay in the distance between them. From this side, Samson could see the man's scalp was half off, his brains spilling to the ground, and he hastened forward, shouting to her to stop, hoping to protect her from the worst. But she'd found who she was looking for, and, sinking to the ground in a single desperate movement, she stretched her arms around him to see into his face. When she did, her cry roared into the silent sky, "Da!"

Samson could only watch as she cradled the corpse, rocking it back and forth like a baby, careless of the blood from its wounds, which swiftly crept over the cloth of her ruined dress.

There was nothing left to be done for them, but from the moans that rose into the air nearer the hustings – now almost entirely dismantled by the cavalry – a great number of the injured were still alive and needed help. He raced onwards towards them, and as he got closer, one detail drew his eye: a flash of amber.

No!

A body on the floor. Curls tumbling around the head.

He was running now, through the waste of lost clogs and trodden hats and dirty scraps of garment, straight over to the woman who was lying on her back, face up to the sky.

"Nancy!"

He fell at her side. She was wraith-pale, with grey circles round her eyes, and her lips, thin and dry. There was a wound, in the hollow between her shoulder and chest, oozing blood.

"Nancy!" he repeated and seized her hand to feel for a pulse. At his touch, her eyelids fluttered and then flicked open, but the whites of her eyes were shot through with red and her gaze was swimming, unable to alight. He leaned in, blocking her from the dazzle of the sun, and at last she was looking at him. She smiled fleetingly, to show she was glad he was there, but then her face dropped again, her mouth setting in a tight, grim line.

"Oh God, Nancy!" he cried, unsuppressed, in a warm gasp close to laughter, a strange mix of relief and anguish. Thank God she was alive, but there was no time to lose. He sat up quickly, tearing off his jacket and ripping at his shirtsleeve for cloth to staunch the blood. He shuffled on his knees and gently slipped his arm beneath her. At once, he felt the shock of her body, so light and hard, he had to shake off the disconcerting sense of handling a skeleton. As soon as he'd created a gap between her arm and the ground, he deftly threaded the makeshift bandage beneath her, and back round, knotting the ends together tightly on top of her shoulder. As he carefully laid her flat again, he saw she was trying to speak.

"Everything will be well," he said, looking around the field. It was all eerie desolation and the low moans becoming quieter. Outside the houses on Mount Street, he noticed with dismay, the two children were gone, but there were people there, and activity, and a couple of carts had arrived. He was hopeful someone had taken care of them.

"Nancy," he said gently, "I'll look after you. Everything will be well." He tried to smile and tentatively brushed his fingers along her cheek, but she was weeping and straining to move, forming words that would not come.

"You must try not to," he said, touching her cheek again, more certain this time, stroking her over and over, then searching to understand what it was she was still determined to say, as her face filled with mounting horror and she pleaded with her eyes.

"What is it? What is it?" He bent his head lower towards her. At first, he couldn't hear, but as he turned to set his ear just above her mouth, a terrible chill ran through him as he made out the word, "Walter."

"He was with you?"

From the way she strained upwards, fierce as a wounded lion, he needed no answer. Straightaway, he half-rose himself, up on his haunches, searching all around them, but the only casualties he could make out were of grown men and women, and he tried to reassure her, "There are no children here. He must've escaped. He'll be found. Have no fear."

But her eyes were flashing terror now, and two red spots had appeared high on her cheeks, vivid against the ghostly pale. "What have I done? What have I done?"

"Shush, shush," he murmured, bending nearer, smoothing her brow. "Try not to, try not to. He'll be found. I shall make sure of it. But, first, we must tend to you. You must be well for him."

He leaned back on his ankles and looked over to where

the carts were being loaded with the wounded. Shouting to a nearby soldier, he pointed at them and asked, "What's happening? Where will they go?"

"Off to the Infirmary. There's already a wagonload ahead of 'em."

Samson nodded and then leaned in close to Nancy once more. The grey around her eyes and lips had deepened, and tears were rolling down the curve of her face, dropping to darken the dried earth below. Her limited strength was drained, and she was quiet again. It was evident she needed a doctor as soon as possible, but with the Infirmary overwhelmed, she could wait for hours.

There was no question but that he must take her to Charlotte Street and send for Mr Slater straightaway.

"Nancy," Samson whispered again gently. "Listen, let me tell you what I'm going to do."

She turned her eyes to meet his gaze, which was grave and soft.

"I'm going to take you to my house. Once the doctor's seen you, I shall go and find Walter myself."

Nancy, finally exhausted by grief, gave a tiny nod of consent, closing her eyes in surrender, as he hooked his arms beneath her and slowly lifted her up.

TWENTY-TWO

MARY

I think I knew already from the quiet of the ginnel that they hadn't come home. As we came into the yard, Susan Wilson, who was standing in the doorway, started towards us, her face white with worry. Behind her was Jemima, already changed back into a grey dress, her shoulders rounded in a deep droop as she chewed at her nails. When she lifted her head to mind who'd come, her face showed streaked with tears. On seeing her again, something niggled, though just then, with all that was on my mind, I didn't bother trying to put my finger to the cause.

"Oh Lord, please tell me they're wi' thee?" the mother said, shifting her head from the side of me to the side of Mick to see if Nancy and Walter were walking behind.

I shook my head and thought I was going to be sick.

"Aye. Well, my Davy's off out again, looking for 'em. Risking cavalry an' all sorts. Lord, I dread to think…" She shook her head. "And owd fella, too, Charlie Bell, who were calling on Ann. He's gone looking for 'em an' all." Then, stony-faced, she added, "I don't know what she were thinking of, taking t' lad wi' her."

Well, course, I was glad to hear there were some folk

already on the lookout, but I'm sorry to say she put me into a right temper, taking that tone. I know she's a good woman, and she'd done her bit, what with helping with Mrs Kay and all, but to start calling Nancy, even as we didn't know whether she and the boy were alive or dead, well, it sent me into a passion.

"Now listen 'ere," I started. "Nancy thought long and hard what were best to do wi' Walter." Mrs Wilson's eyes shot to heaven as I levelled up to her. "Tha can sighs all tha like, but there's none to compare to that girl—"

"Aye, tha's not wrong there," she interrupted. But her tone was proper nasty now. "She's one of a kind, and that's a fact. Filling my lass's head wi' all this reform business. Look at state it's brought her to?"

Jemima had slumped down now, her back against the wall, quietly weeping, whilst her limbs trembled, startling jerkily every now and then.

Well, perhaps it was the mood her mother had put me in, but when I saw her snivelling to herself like that, I suddenly recalled the look she'd stolen at Nancy down at New Cross. And as soon as I did, I was certain as my name's Mary McDermott, that she'd had a hand in Joe not turning up. Ee, how it lit a flame inside me then, roaring up, as I felt my fury rise.

"Aye," I said archly, fixing my eye on the girl. "But at least tha weren't alone today, were thee, Jemima? Not like Nancy and Walter. Didn't come wi' us, *did they*?" I paused, and watched her sink lower to the ground, gnawing at her nails again. "Waiting for Joe Price, weren't they?"

At this, a scarlet blush rose up the young lass's throat and burst over her face as though she were in the grip of a high fever. She couldn't look me in the eye. And I knew I was right. But her mother noticed none of this, as she seized on the mention of Joe and began another line of attack. "Well, I've heard it all now!" Her voice full of self-righteousness. "Is tha telling me, this has all been about a spot of gallivanting wi' some fella? For shame, the lass is still married, int she?"

Well, you can imagine my reaction, and I was just about to shout her down, when Mick stepped forward, with a touch on my arm as though to say, "calm down".

"Now come on, ladies! It's a terrible thing we've all been through today, so it is. Y' all of ye's upset. Don't ye think it'd be best to hold your tongue 'til we know what we're about?" It wasn't clear which of us, me or Susan, this was meant for, but we both of us were cowed, and as though she'd only just remembered the patient inside, she excused herself to go and check on Mrs Kay.

Jemima moved pretty sharpish too, upstairs at a pace, throwing one last, frightened look over her shoulder at me.

TWENTY-THREE

"In the kitchen, now!" Adelaide bore down upon the maids. "You too, Mrs Halliwell. You'll be best off in there. It will take your mind off things." She stood at the threshold of the drawing room and waited for them all to file out, following them towards the back of the house, waving them ahead to the servants' quarters, "I'll have no more talk of opening doors, do you understand? We are in the utmost danger. We must not admit entrance to anyone, do you hear?"

Yet just as she was trying to give these orders calmly, fixing them with a stern eye, a heavy bang landed on the front door and she couldn't conceal her startle. From this distance down the corridor, it was impossible to make out anything through the slim windows on either side of the door, though the maids behind her teetered and tiptoed, eyes popping, to try. Briskly, she shooed them back and shut the door.

Alone in the hall, the banging was getting louder, and Adelaide felt a flare of fear. For a moment she stood rigid, fixed to the spot, not sure of what to do or where best to hide. Besides the hammering of a fist, she could now make out a secondary sound, a kind of scraping, and then a deep-voiced shout so urgent, it made her jump.

"Open up!"

She inched further down the corridor and then flinched again at the ferocious voice repeating itself, "Open up!"

Behind her, the maids were screaming. Adelaide's heart pounded.

"Open up for Christ's sake. It's me!"

Samson!

She scurried up the remaining length of corridor, but once she was at the door, she hesitated again, suddenly afraid he might not be alone. What if in this unguarded moment, blindly following his command, she opened the floodgates to a sea of rioters? Moving quietly, she pressed herself up against the door and gingerly edged her head towards the window, craning her neck to squint out onto the porch. A woman's skirt! That's all she saw, before his voice, thunderous with anger, made her jump again.

"Adelaide. I can see you're there. Let me in!"

Too frightened now to resist, Adelaide fumbled at the bolt in her haste.

"Quick!"

As soon as the lock was released, there was a flash of Samson's boot, and she had to leap out of the way as he kicked the door wide open. He stepped over the threshold, a young woman in his arms, like a groom with his bride, save that the girl's body hung limp and pale, Samson's elbow propping her drooping head, in which her eyes were closed shut. Her white dress was brown with dust and mud and, at the top, there was a rough ligature already stained black with blood. Until she gave a small cough, Adelaide was certain the girl was dead. Samson himself was in disarray. He wasn't wearing his hat or jacket, and his shirt, half-ripped, was hanging out of his breeches.

"Good gracious!"

Adelaide rushed to close and bolt the door and then turned to see him heading towards his study.

"What on earth…?"

"Send out for Mr Slater."

Adelaide didn't move.

"And fetch some sheets and a pillow."

"Samson, I'm sorry, but what are you thinking of?"

He glared at her.

"Fetch some sheets and a pillow. Now."

At this, she hurried out of the room and up the stairs to the linen cupboard to fetch him what he wanted. As she came back down, she could hear the servants muttering behind the door at the end of the corridor. She must get this woman out of here as soon as possible. Taking a deep breath, she re-entered the study, and in a low, conciliatory tone began again, "Samson, is not the Infirmary a better place for her?"

"Ha! There's scores of them been taken there."

"Why, what's happened?"

Samson ignored the question. He was still carrying the woman in his arms and indicated the chaise longue with a firm nod of his head.

"Adelaide!"

Sighing, she spread out one of the cotton sheets, pulling it taut over the cushioned seat.

"She'll be seen quicker here," he said, speaking softly, as he settled the woman down and knelt on the floor beside her. "You've sent word for the doctor?" he asked, without looking behind, confident this was in hand. Adelaide started to spin the remaining ring on her finger and was about to object again when she stopped, suddenly arrested by what she saw. Samson had placed his arm on the pillow above the girl's head and was searching her face in an agony of tenderness.

For a moment, all remained still and silent in the room, but had anyone entered, they might have noticed a strange, lost expression haunt Adelaide's face, as the sag of her skin and its deepening lines were laid bare by the high sun which streamed in at the window.

Eventually, she mastered herself, "Are you going to tell me who this woman is?"

"Her name's Nancy Kay. She's one of our own. She teaches in the schoolroom."

"Ha! What did I tell you?" she spat, her face contorting. "I knew no good would come of it!"

Samson, still kneeling by the couch, remained silent, though she thought she saw his mouth tighten.

"Why? Why has she not been discovered as a reformer before now?" Judging from the state of him, however, Adelaide was in no doubt as to the reason, though she knew enough to hold back from voicing her suspicion, which might only serve to define a feeling he'd not yet fully acknowledged to himself. Instead, with simmering rage, she began to pace the room, moving back and forth between the window and the desk, shaking her head at the piano and eventually standing over him, "She can't stay here, Samson, you must see that."

He looked up at her, incredulous, "Can you not see the peril she's in?"

"Well then, get her to the Infirmary! Heaven knows who'll be here next, breaking the door down to claim her."

"She has no one. Only a young son, who's lost. Indeed, as soon as she's tended to, I must seek him out myself."

"A child with her!" Adelaide exclaimed, but Samson did not see her look of disgust. Nancy had become fretful at the sound of their voices and his attention was taken with soothing her back to sleep.

"Let's just see what the doctor says, shall we?" he whispered, when she'd settled again.

At this, Adelaide stopped still. Samson looked over at her. She didn't meet his eye.

"Adelaide?" he pressed. "The doctor *is* on his way?"

Her silence was answer enough, and, with a cry of anguish, he raised himself from the floor. Too angry to speak, he shot her a look of contempt and raced from the room shouting for Ellen.

TWENTY-FOUR

MARY

From the emptiness of the yard, we could hear all sorts of cries and shouts from the streets beyond, like echoes from the field. It was almost as though a mighty great brick had been chucked in the canal down one end of town and its ripple was just being felt up here in Ancoats, as constables and cavalry chased after any poor souls as were still left on the thoroughfare. Hard to believe it was only mid-afternoon and the indifferent sun was still shining directly overhead.

I couldn't sit still. I paced the cobbles, back and forth, just like Yates or one of them other bastard overseers at the mill, until it pierced my heart to think on how Nancy'd laugh at me taking 'em off. Instead, from time to time, I'd head down that stinking ginnel and peep round the corner to see if I could make out anyone coming up the street. Many a time I did see stragglers from the meeting, every one of 'em dirty and dazed-looking, some bruised and bloodied, but none whom I longed for.

"Nothing!" I'd burst out in frustration as I returned to Mick, who was perched on a stack of coal sacks and would shake his head in weariness. And though my heart was sore for him, and for Nancy and for Walter, and for all them sorry assorted casualties limping home, it was becoming clear to me, my overwhelming feeling was one of crimson anger, such as I'd never felt afore. That the authorities could've ordered such a thing. To set upon a crowd, all of us plainly peaceable, with respectable intentions. Just and fair ones too. For them to set upon us, women and children mind, with not a single stone thrown, to set upon us with horses and blades, well, you can see even now… it still makes me shake with rage. Aye, and I'll say forever and a day, it was beyond the very Devil himself.

TWENTY-FIVE

Fair. Small. Big eyes. Beautiful eyes. A boy in a cap, an old brown cap with leaves pinned to it. This was who he was searching for.

"Find him, find him! Please, just find him! Tell me he's safe." Her ragged breath had caught in a cough, and she'd crumpled in pain. "Please God! Please God!"

It had been terrible to watch her, flailing under the sheet, straining to get up, her hand clutching at Mr Slater's sleeve, as the old man used an unexpected strength to keep her pinned down.

"It's all right, Captain. I'll stay with her. She needs some brandy. It'll help her sleep."

"Go!" she'd howled. "Just go!"

And he had fled, out the door and down the steps, running over the pavements which were littered with soiled clothes, searching to the right, to the left, down passages and alleyways, all the way back to the field.

"Fair-haired. Small. Big eyes. Beautiful eyes, he has," she'd sobbed. "Sad eyes. Scared eyes." And she'd wailed so mournfully then, he thought his heart might break. "Wearing his uncle's old cap. An old, brown cap wi' leaves pinned to it," she'd paused and frowned. "Ohhh, but it'll be lost now, won't it?"

A little fair-haired boy. This was who he must find. A beautiful, beloved boy. A boy he'd never known.

He reached the field. It was almost empty now, so that the sky seemed enormous over the half-dozen or so remaining casualties, some still groaning, a few quiet, and the dazed figures searching amongst them, floating as though shades risen from the bodies themselves.

He ran its breadth, from Mount Street to Peter Street and back again, his tattered shirt flapping in the wind, desperately searching for the little fair-haired boy, and all the while seeing only a curl of tiny pink baby, silent like still water.

TWENTY-SIX

MARY

I don't know how long we were there. An hour, maybe more.
By then, I was all for retracing our steps. I couldn't stand
to be so helpless. But Mick held me back, too afeared that
constables or militia were still abroad and might even then
be on the way. Everyone was the same. No one stirred from
the houses backing onto the yard, and the streets beyond were
empty with an uneasy silence, broken only by the thrum of the
mill, which had carried on regardless.

Then a lass turned into the yard. She was a slight thing,
short like Nancy, and for a second when I first laid eyes on her,
my insides turned over, thinking it was her, but just as quick,
I saw she was a plain little Jane and evidently a stranger to
the place. Her body was bent in a shy nervousness, her eyes
darting from under her cap, as she was clearly trying to make
out the numbers on the doors.

"Who's tha looking for?" I rushed towards her. "What
number does tha want?"

Susan Wilson, who must've been watching at the window,
had already joined us by the time the lass started to speak.

"I'm looking for Nancy Kay's house."

"Aye, well, this is it," Susan said, casting me a look as though to say, keep out of it.

"Are you her mother?"

"Nay, Mrs Kay's inside. She's very poorly. I'm watching over her."

The young girl frowned a little, uncertain of how to go on.

"Does tha know summat about Nancy?" I burst out.

Well, the girl was more unsure than ever, glancing between me and Susan, trying to work out who she should be addressing or whether she wasn't meant to speak in front of one of us.

"I'm her friend, tha see. Her best friend. I wuk wi' her at Wrights."

At last, her face relaxed a little, and she looked directly at me. "Ah, well, I wuk for t' master, Captain Wright. That's where I've come from. She's there."

"What? Nancy? At t' master's house?"

"Aye. At Charlotte Street. I'm sorry to inform thee, she's injured, though t' doctor's wi' her now, and she's been made comfortable." She stopped, as we moved closer in, her forehead creasing, as once again she looked uncertainly from me to Susan and back again. "Look, 'appen I should speak to her mam. That's what me orders were. Fust, to let her mam know, and second to see if her lad got home."

Well, I don't know which of Susan or I gasped loudest at this, as we both realised Walter was still lost and alone.

"Oh Lord! Walter's not wi' her?" cried Susan.

As for me, I couldn't say owt for the ache in my heart.

"Look, can I not speak wi' her mam? It don't seem right to come all this way and not tell her t' news direct."

"Nay," Susan said firmly. "She's sleeping now. But she's right bad. It'll not be long now. She's past this kind o' shock, and that's a fact."

She was a good girl, this maid, and looked right sorrowful to hear this, and at last unburdened herself, explaining everything. "It's as the master feared," she said quietly. "He were already on his way back to t' field to look for him when

I left. And he's sent another to th' Infirmary to make enquiries after the lad there."

"Oh, dear God, what's happened to him?" Susan said again, wringing her hands. "I dread to think on it, I really do…" Then, for the girl's benefit, she added, "Soft in th' head, he is, tha see."

Ee, I could've swung for her then, talking so plain, 'specially knowing how Nancy would've felt. Except, of course, the unkindness of the words aside, there was a truth of sorts in what she said. Susan Wilson knew it, and so did I. Beautiful, awkward little Walter, so much more vulnerable than most his age, and now alone and adrift on a turbulent sea.

TWENTY-SEVEN

"A boy. Have you seen a boy?" Samson appealed to whomever he came across. A pair of greybeards holding one another up as they limped towards the church. They shook their heads mournfully. A clergyman, walking in the opposite direction, prayer book in hand, apologetic in his haste to the Infirmary. Whilst a Hussar on horseback, patrolling the edge of the field, shamefacedly pretended not to hear.

A number of constables also remained, tensely pacing the pavement in front of the houses on Mount Street. As Samson approached them, dishevelled and desperate, their hands were straightaway at their truncheons, until he confused them entirely with his refined voice, "Have you seen a young boy? Fair. Small. He's wearing a cap." Most of them turned away. "A brown cap, with leaves pinned to it. He's been parted from his mother."

"Well, what she expect bringin' him 'ere?" said the last of them, as he cleared his throat with a guttural sound and landed a glob of spit on the ground. "Shameless hussy!" It was just as well the bastard had stepped away quickly, Samson thought, as he stopped himself lunging after him.

Dear God, there was nothing to be discovered here, and he turned towards the expanse of field again. He was floundering, unsure of where to try next, and angry at his own uncertainty. Then, just as he was about to set off over the scrub once more, another wagon, empty to collect more casualties, skirted the corner of the street, kicking up a fresh cloud of dust. Shielding his eyes from the sting, Samson shouted up to the driver, "Have you seen a boy? A little fair-haired boy? He's been separated from his mother."

"Sorry, sir, there's that many at th' Infirmary and on all t' streets between, I couldn't tell thee." The carter shook his head sadly. "By God, what a terrible business."

Samson nodded distractedly, about to move on, when the man added as an afterthought, "I suppose tha's already checked the cellars down yonder in Windmill Street?" He pointed to the row of houses that fronted the edge of the field where the hustings had been. "I've heard a crowd of 'em got stuck down there."

"Oh thank you," cried Samson, instant hope flaring, already running, shouting over his shoulder once more, "good man, thank you."

There seemed to be no one left on the street when he reached it, though he could see through the windows of the houses, huge numbers of wary onlookers still shut up inside for safety.

Starting from the end of the row, he intended to inspect each and every stairwell, but even before he'd looked down into the first, he now noticed, a few yards ahead, a man he thought he recognised. He had grey hair and a stooped frame and was leaning over the cellar railings of a house not two doors away, seemingly addressing someone below.

"Mr Bell, Mr Bell!" Samson cried. "Is that you?"

The man turned at his name and replied in surprise, "Aye, sir! What's tha doing here?"

Samson reached the house and warmly took Charlie Bell's hand, at the same time looking over the railings into the small yard. There, sitting amongst flattened weeds, in the corner of the walls, was a small boy, cowering like a caged animal.

"Is this Walter?" Samson whispered to Charlie Bell.

"Aye," said the older man, astonished.

"I found Nancy on the field," Samson explained. "A doctor's tending her at my house."

"Thank Lord!" Charlie breathed, lost for words, and fumbling in his pocket for a handkerchief which he brought to his face. Samson, grateful for the old man's concern, patted him on the arm.

Eventually, when he was composed enough to speak again, Charlie nodded his head towards Walter, "Don't ask me how poor lad's ended up here. I've just come a-searching mi'sel. I've been down there trying to coax him up an' all, but he's that afeared, he's not for moving. I'd only just come back up to look out for Nancy's neighbour who's searching too."

Samson was gazing down at the boy, whose head rested on his scuffed knees, so that he couldn't yet make out his face. The relief at finding him was already draining away into concern for how afraid he was. He whispered to Charlie again. "Tell him who I am."

"Look, lad. Here's Captain Wright. Tha knows, from t' mill."

Walter curled deeper into himself.

"Listen, he's found your mammy. She's safe. She's at Captain Wright's house."

Walter didn't move. Charlie shrugged, "I don't know what to do. It's looking like we'll have to drag him up."

"Wait," said Samson, putting out his arm, gently barring the old man from the top step. "Wait a moment."

Softening his voice and moving closer to the rail, he called down, "Hello, Walter." He waited. "I'm a friend of your mother's. She's been very worried about you." He waited again. "She asked me to come and find you."

Walter tightened his grip on his knees. Samson frowned. There had to be a way. All around them was eerie, unnatural silence. The whole town, it seemed, had fallen quiet. He stopped and listened for something, anything, he knew not what, only that after a long moment, he thought he had heard it, above them, away up in the distance, beyond the clouds that were forming overhead: a far-off whistle, the song of a bird on the wing. And all at once, he knew what he had to do.

Quietly, and ever so slowly, from the top of the stone stairs, he began to hum. It was only a simple melody, a gentle fragment of a half-forgotten lullaby, but it was enough. After a few notes, he saw Walter's arms begin to relax. And so he kept on singing as he took a step down, and then another. By the time he reached the bottom of the staircase, Walter looked up at last.

They blinked at one another in strange recognition.

TWENTY-EIGHT

MARY

I closed my eyes a moment and pictured him. Those golden curls atop that milky-white face, shaped like a heart it is, just like his mam, his long lashes blinking, casting shadows, and his skinny arms flapping in a dance to a tune only he could hear. I can't tell thee how clear it was, that image in my mind's eye, how vivid. And that's why what came next was so strange, as though I'd had a vision of sorts. Or a premonition. 'Cos when I opened my eyes, he was back, standing for real in the yard, and I swear, something deep inside of me knew, right there and then, the way things would come to pass.

Charlie Bell was gently steering him by the shoulder, with David Wilson following behind. Right knocked about he looked and all, poor mite. He'd lost his cap, and his hair was all knotted and dark with dust. Aye, and the pocket of his jacket was ripped and hanging loose, and all his clothes as dirty as though he'd waded through a river of mud.

Well, Susan rushed forward first, arms wide, to fall upon "her Davy", letting out a great yelp of relief, so that straightaway, Walter's hands shot to his ears. Then the yard filled up with young Wilsons – save for Jemima – who charged downstairs to greet their father and discover what had happened. Course, all this noise and bustle was too much for Walter, and all at once, he took heel and raced inside.

"Oh Lord! He'll wake Ann!" Susan exclaimed, chasing after him, though she needn't have bothered. Even before she'd got to the door, he was out again, his face wild with fear. Poor lad had swapped the terrors of the field for the quiet horror of his grandma's deathbed. Again, he looked round the assembled group. Susan was gentle now, her arms open, smiling and gesturing him to go to her. But her lads, big and loud, were stood right behind her, and Walter wasn't for going anywhere near them. For one awful moment, he looked trapped, like a cornered animal with nowhere to run. And then, before I knew owt else, I felt him fly at me, his arms stretched round my waist, and his head burying in my belly.

"Ee, lad!" was all I could say. I was fair knocked breathless, and not just with the speed of his movement neither. Nay, though I'm still bashful to admit it, him choosing me like that, needing *me*, silly old, big lump Mary, well, amidst all that sadness, it was like I'd suddenly gulped a golden ray of happiness.

I bent down and hooked my hands under his arms and hoicked him up, light as air. Then, once he was settled on my hip, I reached to dry his tears. He stared wide-eyed back at me, on the brink of starting again, so I tried giving a small pout mi'sel. It was just enough to make him smile a moment.

I looked at all the folk then, a little coy of them watching us together. "'Appen, I should take him? For tonight, any road?" I ventured. Then, looking at Mick, "We *must* take him." Well, maybe if Mick hadn't been so exhausted he might have raised an objection. Or if he'd known what it would mean. But he's fond of the lad too, so maybe not. Either way, he nodded.

Susan looked relieved at first and bustled inside to sort packing a change of clothes for him, and when she came out again, she ruffled his hair.

"Be a good lad now. Think on tha mam and tha grandma," and she painted on a cheerful smile.

But when she turned to me, I saw there were tears in her eyes, and all at once, all the awkwardness between us dissolved, and I reached out to pull her into an embrace.

TWENTY-NINE

Even through closed eyes, Ann sensed it was still day. Behind her lids glowed red, like dying embers, but every time they opened, there was only white glare, too painful to be celestial. Light and heat streamed in at the window and from the open door. She could make no sense of it, the length of the day, the people who had come and gone and come again, always white and bright.

There was no one here now, and she was satisfied. It was good, this solitude. She could make this place somewhere else. She screwed up her eyes to make out the picture on the shelf. She followed its familiar lines, the sweep of the walls enclosing the sweetness of the hills to home. Somewhere, upon the gentle incline, the sheep were bleating their contentment, and nearer, in the orchard, amidst the birdsong, came the bark of Beauty and the laughter of children.

When the sun finally begins to sink, she thought, she'd take an evening walk in the dappling shadows of those trees. She'd breathe in the scents of twilight: closest, the perfume of sweet grass and lavender and, further on, the heavy promise of ripening apples. Underfoot, there would be soft earth and bracken and the first fallen leaves, and above, hidden within the lace of branches, black against the pink sky, a nightingale would sing a song of home, and she would be back where she could love them all.

For now though, there was no music. Not yet, not in this place. All she could hear was the sound of her own breathing, fast and ragged. Who would've thought it could be so tiring? She rolled her head on the pillow and closed her eyes, returning not to darkness but back to that tormenting burn of red.

They were not shut for long. Suddenly, they snapped open again, alert as a new mother. There was a cry. A child's sob. She turned her head. She thought, "There's a boy." His outline wavered against the white, cropped hair standing on end and his shirt out, dirty from play all day in the fields. "Edward!"

Ah, but she was mistaken. There was no one here. Her babies were in that other place, and she must wait. This long day couldn't last forever. The sun would soon tire. Then, it would drop its way through the sky, and she would feel that shift within, that movement through the glade.

THIRTY

The shadows were lengthening and the lamps in the hall all lit
by the time Samson returned to the study. When he'd arrived
home earlier with news of Walter, he'd found Mr Slater still
sitting with her. She'd just fallen into a fretful sleep, and the
doctor had urged him not to disturb her but to go and wash and
change his clothes. Now, he discovered the room remained
in semi-darkness, its familiar shapes obscured, the desk, the
wingback chair, the piano all shrouded by the day's draining
light at the window. From the depths of the gloom, Ellen
raised her finger to her lips and got up from beside the couch
to come to him.

"She's settled properly now, sir," she whispered, coming
up so close she forced him to step back into the hall where she
could speak up. Whilst he'd been upstairs, Nancy had roused
a while, she explained, and she'd been able to inform her the
lad was safe. "Once she knew that, sir, she sank back with
such relief. She's that exhausted, she were out like a light."

"Thank you, Ellen. Will you go back to her?"

"Not yet," she hesitated and looked down at her feet. "I
need to attend to the mistress. Don't worry though, one of t'
others can sit wi' her."

"No, that won't be necessary," he replied, adding forcefully,
"*I* will sit with her myself."

Ellen looked up in surprise but recovered herself enough

to ask, "Does tha want some supper now, sir?" She nodded towards the study door, which Samson understood to mean she'd bring something for him there, though straightaway she cast her eye warily over to the drawing room where he supposed Adelaide was spending the evening. It was clear the girl was unnerved. When he'd come home with Nancy in his arms, shouting for assistance, it was the first time he'd asserted authority in the house, and with orders evidently distasteful to the mistress. It must have alarmed them all, no matter their natural sympathies – which he'd no doubt were with the stranger in the study – he understood they were nevertheless afraid to obey him because of his aunt.

He watched the girl, jumpy with nerves and divided loyalty, and at once heartily wished himself rid of Adelaide at last, and the whole household with her, so he alone could nurse Nancy in peace.

"Is there some soup? Some bread? Anything. Just prepare a tray and leave it at the door. After that, you and the rest of the servants are not to concern yourselves with me."

Ellen's face filled with confusion.

"Let me be clear. Go tend to Adelaide if you must. All I ask is you leave the study undisturbed. I shall come and ask for help when I need it."

Ellen nodded earnestly and dipped in an awkward curtsey, before turning to hasten down the corridor.

When he finally re-entered the darkened room, Samson shut the door behind him softly. It was getting late, but there were no candles burning, and for a moment his eyes needed to adjust to the meagre light still filtering through a narrow gap in the curtains before he stepped quietly towards the couch.

There she was, beneath a white sheet, so still and lifeless, he was straightaway filled with a terror she'd stopped breathing. Quickly, he moved closer, hovering to watch keenly, like an anxious mother over a newborn. Yet something in his movement, or the touch of his breath upon her face disturbed her, and she moved her head with a gentle moan. He started back again, just as quick, his heart thudding in renewed panic that he might waken her, yet at the same time drenched with relief.

He walked over to his chair, which was set at the fireplace as usual, but before he sat down, he sank his weight upon its wingback, and slowly eased it round, until it was sufficiently angled towards the makeshift bed. The rest of the room could be rearranged in the morning.

For a long while, he sat upright on the chair's edge, an anxious knot tight in his stomach, as he gazed at her, listening, alert to any change, ready to come to her aid. He needn't have worried the size of the couch might not do, he thought, smiling sadly; the little bump formed by her feet was some distance from the end. All of her looked small and frail, and her sleeping face so tiny, surrounded by its mane of curls, which even now he wondered at as they spread exuberantly, the full extent of the pillow.

As the chink of sky between the curtains deepened from blue to jet, Samson's thoughts began to crowd with images from the afternoon, horror upon horror he tried to dislodge with a shake of his head. But still they paraded across his mind, all those people with their flags, every colourful banner stitched with hope. Not one left that wasn't ripped or trodden by those brutes.

How many people had been struck? He hardly dared guess. Scores of them injured and abandoned on the field, and scores more, no doubt, laid up in their homes like Nancy. That they could have charged on innocents like that, and brandished their blades in a heartbeat, and not a stone left on the ground with which the people could defend themselves. Dear God, it was beyond humanity. He only had to shut his eyes and frightened faces, battered and bleeding, stared back at him. Or else, he saw again that image of Nancy afar off, fallen and trampled, recognisable only by the colour of her hair.

Outside in the hall, the clock struck twelve, and as he moved in the chair, he noticed his neck and arms and legs had all tightened and begun to ache, whilst the old injury in his shoulder throbbed as painful as a tooth gone bad. A nausea, low in his stomach, had been rising up all the while too, into his throat and collecting in his mouth, the sickening flavour of bile, like nothing he'd tasted before, not even after the bloodiest of battles.

Meanwhile, the room had lost all the day's heat, and a chill crept in through the window and under the door. For a moment, he wondered whether it would be best to go to bed. Perhaps she wouldn't want him there all night. Perhaps he should summon a maid to sit with her for a few hours. But even as he thought these things, he knew he could not bring himself to leave her. Instead, he stretched round and lifted a footstool from the fireplace, setting it in front to straighten his legs upon, and then he reached down again, this time to the side of the chair, to retrieve the jacket he'd taken off earlier and left on the floor. Spreading it over himself, he sank into the depth of the seat and felt the slow return of warmth.

He lay awake like that for a long time, all the sounds of the house silenced. Curled up in the dark, like an infant in the womb, absorbing only the soft rhythm of her breathing, calm and regular.

TO AUTUMN

ONE

MARY

The hours that followed are mostly a fog to me now, though I do recall that first evening, the master proved right thoughtful. Afore we went to sleep that night, he sent a lad to tell me I needn't go to the mill in the morning. My job was safe, but I was to stay at home with Walter. Right glad of it and all I was, and not just for Walter's sake neither, though Lord knows he needed someone with him, but for my own too. Ee, the aches you get off the mule at the end of a shift are as nothing to the pain I was in. My shoulders were as stiff as a corpse and my back throbbed with bruises that bloomed like great blue flowers, larger by the passing hour.

Poor Mick was even worse. When he'd first stripped off his shirt, I couldn't believe my eyes. In fact, it knocked me that sick, I had to turn away a second. Only way I can describe it, was as if he'd been down a coal mine. His neck, his back, top of his arms, all of 'em were like a great, black pudding, dense with livid blood trapped just under the surface. Well, I tried to soothe him best I could, dabbing at his skin with a cloth dipped in lavender water, but he winced at every touch and my heart ached to think he was suffering so much, all for protecting me and taking the worst of the blows.

Meanwhile, Walter sat on a low stool by the hearth, clutching his knees to his chest and rocking to and fro. We could get nowt out of him, not even after all manner of coaxing, so we had no idea why his injuries weren't so bad, though of course we thanked the Lord for it. Just some bruising on his shoulders and a scratch on the lower part of his right arm, he had. Course, he wasn't able to tell us what had happened to Nancy neither. All we could suppose was she must've done a good job of shielding him before she was cut down herself, and that afterwards he'd been able to find a way of crawling out, what with him being so small.

I'd first noticed the scratch I mentioned over at Nancy's place. It hadn't looked so bad then, but later that night as I was seeing to some stew for the three of us, I caught sight of it again and noticed that it'd begun to look a deal worse. The wound itself seemed deeper and darker than before, whilst the skin that bordered it had flushed up reddish-pink, the colour of shyness. I remember puzzling over for why, but thought it best not to alarm him by making a fuss, so I decided I'd take a closer look when he needed changing for bed and turned my attention back to the pan. It was only when I glanced back up that I caught him at it. Picking it he was.

Well, I didn't stop to think and shouted aloud, "Walter! Nay!" But, of course, the suddenness of it, not to mention my tone, frightened him good and proper. All aquiver he was, his beautiful eyes blinking large at me with fear, and before I knew it, he was over at the door and trying to escape.

"Ee, lad, I'm sorry," I said, in my gentlest voice, though I was far from calm inside, wondering if I could manage him in such a state. "I didn't mean to scare thee. But that scratch on th' arm, it's going to get a sight wuss if tha doesn't leave it alone."

At this, he looked down in surprise to inspect the arm I'd pointed to, staring at the slash of red he'd only just left off, fascinated you might say; I swear it was just as though he'd never seen it afore in his life.

"Come on, lad, shall we fix up a bandage for it?" I said cheerfully, and don't ask me why, but this seemed to work. He let me take his arm, which was weeping now and all clarty, and allowed me to bathe it and wind some cotton gauze round it, and afterwards he even seemed to take a sort of pleasure in fiddling with the flap of cloth which poked out of the knot I tied.

It was just as well Walter and I stayed at home quietly like this 'cos as we'd feared, there was all kinds of trouble abroad. Ee, Mick brought that much news home on Tuesday night, I could scarcely take it all in, like as if the very earth of Manchester had been given a great shaking and the foundations were crumbling all around us. Scores arrested all over town, he said, and more trouble at New Cross on the night after the meeting, a fella shot dead they said.

As for what had started the trouble in the first place, the authorities were talking about brickbats and stones and blaming the crowd for setting on the Yeomen. Well, that much I could credit; not that the crowd set upon them, of course, but that the bastard magistrates would put out that they did. But then, when Mick said he'd also heard word of a people's army forming in t' North, thousands of 'em heading with pistols and pikes and vengeful intent upon Manchester to torch the Royal Exchange, well then, I felt sick to my stomach with fear and disappointment. To think all our peaceable intent should come to such a pass. Though, of course, as it turned out, none of that outlandish story ever came to owt, and I don't know who it was started it in the first place, whether the militia or the Government, or else the town's own grief and anger, breeding rumours as poisonous as a plague of vermin to run riot through the streets.

However, there was one particular rumour I had no trouble believing, nay, none whatsoever. For it seems early on the morning of the meeting, there'd been some windows smashed up with a brickbat at the side of Wrights, and one of the spinners who Nancy'd persuaded to the Union had caught sight of the culprit. Swore blind it was the steeplejack, Joseph Price. Well then, some folks suggested perhaps it wasn't just windows he'd been at, perhaps he'd been causing trouble down at the field too. Maybe he was one of them spies the Government had set on to see what the reformers were about and taken money to make it look like we were out for trouble.

It seems that nice fella, Archie Thompson, got wind of all this too and was that cut up with disappointment. He'd had his suspicions about Joe at first, he said, what with him being so suddenly converted to the cause – well, that was the first I'd heard of it, but it rang true all right – and yet before long, the lad had seemed so earnest. Any road, even though no one knew where he'd got to, Archie declared Joe wasn't to come anywhere near him or their chimney ever again. What a pity, I remember thinking, as I'd have gladly seen him throw himself off the top with the shame I'd make him feel if ever I got the chance to give him what for, the two-faced, lying bastard.

There was other news that day too. Early in the afternoon, I was sat watching Walter, still hunched into himself, toying with his bandage, and me all the while wondering how I might make him feel a little safer, when I heard a light tap at the window, so quiet I thought I must've imagined it, until I looked up and saw the solemn face of Susan Wilson peering in behind Walter. When she saw she'd got my attention, she put a finger to her lips and beckoned me outside. I told Walter I wouldn't be long and headed to the door, knowing full well what she'd come for and my face must have shown it.

"Aye. It's Ann," she said. "Late last night. God rest her soul."

Well, though I shook my head with sorrow, somehow I couldn't find words enough to meet with the enormity of it all, what with Nancy so badly injured and the poor confused lad inside.

I was grateful Susan seemed to understand, and she put her arm around my shoulder, "Ee, lass, I know, I know. It's a terrible do." And we both shed a fair few tears then, I can tell thee, skriking together like sisters, and not just for the Kays neither, but for all the terror and pain and grief in Manchester.

Eventually, when I was able to speak again, I told her Captain Wright was sending word every few hours from Charlotte Street and that the latest was Nancy was steady if not yet fully recovered. She was glad to hear it, and we both expressed our hope she might be home soon.

"Perhaps I'll leave off telling Walter about his grandma until I've had chance to see her. What does tha think?" I asked.

"Aye, that sounds for t' best." Then, cocking her head towards the door, she whispered, "'Ow is he?"

I shrugged at this, and again she seemed to understand, "I can imagine. It can't be easy, and that's a fact." But just as I'd started to shake my head mournfully again, she added with a tut, "Not wi' him being such an oddity."

Now, I know she meant nowt nasty by it, and it's only a way of speaking, but it didn't half raise my hackles, her calling him that. So you'll understand that when she next suggested perhaps he'd better stay a while longer with me and Mick, I replied as quick as you like, "Aye, he's going nowhere. Not 'til Nancy's right."

TWO

"'Peter-Loo'?" Adelaide thrust the open newspaper onto her lap. Such whipped-up nonsense! To take the name of Waterloo in vain. It wasn't right. She'd seen the numbers with her own eyes after all; it stood to reason the mob had been out for trouble. The Yeomen must have been provoked. The magistrates had seen fit to arrest the ringleaders, hadn't they? Thank heavens they'd got that scoundrel Hunt languishing in gaol now and not so self-righteous. Why then this remorseless hullabaloo? The papers wouldn't leave it alone. And nor would Samson, though he'd barely spoken to her since he'd come home with that woman.

In an angry rustle, she set the newspaper to one side. She should've known better than to read one left behind by him. Her eyes wandered over the drawing room, searching out something else to do. There was, of course, no prospect of receiving any visitors, not whilst her home remained this makeshift infirmary. It really was too much; she ought to put her foot down and insist upon the woman's removal. Though, in truth, it was becoming increasingly difficult to raise the possibility. The optimism of the first night appeared to have given way to anxious watching, and the fiery look Samson had reserved for her in those first few days was gone, replaced this morning by a watery-eyed distractedness. Really, the whole distasteful affair was making her feel quite queasy.

She didn't even like to leave the drawing room these days and risk running into the servants, most of whom had assumed a new aloofness towards her, eyeing her more warily, if not with open reproach. It was most provoking. Wasn't it enough she'd acquiesced in Samson's scheme? Yet even if the maids weren't quite bold enough to speak out loud, they were certainly whispering amongst themselves about the casualties of so-called "Peter-Loo", and the kindness their master had extended to the mill girl.

It wasn't the only thing they were saying about her either, Adelaide was sure. It only took one look at Samson to understand he had more motive than charity. His face had always worn a battered look, but now it was positively consumed with pain, though when he spoke of the patient, it would soften guilelessly, awash with tenderness. Good grief, she'd even caught him yesterday morning, letting himself in at the front door, come home from an early trip to the market, like a conscientious housekeeper, clutching a basket full of fruit; full to the brim, it had been, spilling over with early apples, cherries and various berries. What a fool he was making of himself!

She took to the floor, treading the Persian carpet as she'd done for hour upon hour these last few days, like a prisoner in confinement measuring the length of his cell. Absently, she made her way to the window, though she didn't linger for long. Only a few days ago, she'd found herself face to face with the girl's friend, a stout woman she recognised from the mill, and a small boy whom she assumed was the child, waiting for admittance. Presenting themselves at the front door! The effrontery! On catching her eye, the woman had bowed, seemingly polite, though Adelaide sensed she was not entirely sincere, and something of the moment triggered a memory: a group of mill girls, this one amongst them, whispering closely in the factory yard, looking up to nod at her respectfully, then cackling like a coven as soon as her back was turned.

Now they were in her house again, these people, and she

powerless to ask them to leave. What might they be doing? Where might they wander? Samson may be trusting, but she wasn't taken in. All at once, another thought struck her, and she stopped in her tracks, her frown deepening. Then she swept from the drawing room and headed downstairs.

In the dim light of the lower hall, amidst the usual clatter from the kitchen, she could hear a low hum of urgent chatter. She listened a brief moment, straining to make it out, though she had a good idea already it concerned the visitors upstairs. Then she hastened to the door and burst in on them without warning, to watch their faces flame red, as all voices ceased and all heads bowed to their individual tasks, pan scrubbing, potato peeling and the measuring out of flour.

The room was oven-warm already and filled with the homely smell of a fresh bake. She raised her eyebrows, but didn't ask Mrs Halliwell or any of the others what they'd been making; something for the boy again, no doubt. Instead, she avoided them altogether and strode over to the small cupboard fixed high on the far wall. The house keys were kept inside, and she helped herself to the one hanging alone from a leather strap on the hook at the end.

She recrossed the room, still without looking at them, though she knew they were watching her, and left without a word, to linger again a short while at the bottom of the stairs. This time, all remained quiet and she smiled grimly; they knew better than to start up with their gossip.

Robert's bedroom was on the second floor of the house, at the back, down a narrow, windowless corridor, unadorned by portraits or paintings. It was a long time since she'd ventured up here, and she was dismayed to find the air smelling stale and unpleasant. Under her feet, the floorboards creaked beneath a threadbare runner as she walked to the last, low door. Here, she hesitated a second, and looked back towards the stairs. Then, steeling herself, she bent down to insert the key. Straightaway, she found she had to apply a firm pressure which she only now remembered it had always needed, working the lock a moment, until, at last, the door fell open to reveal a room full of dust and shadows.

From the threshold, she recognised, with a small jolt, the familiar striped paper, saw the bed, the chair, and the chest of drawers where they'd always been, albeit shrouded now in great swathes of dust-cloth. At the same time, she heard a sharp intake of breath, though it was a second before she realised it was her own. Yet it was really no more than that: a quick gasp at the slice of the blade, almost painless if she kept her hands fisted, before she was able to recover herself and blot out the image of the last time.

Instead, looking round the door, she found what she'd come for: a great lumpy pile collected on the floor by the fireplace, covered carefully by two spread blankets. She bent down and lifted up the corner of the first, counting the silver pieces beneath, one by one, nodding, seemingly satisfied.

THREE

MARY

We set out in the sunshine on the Wednesday after the "massacre" as folk had started calling it. Captain Wright had invited me to take Walter to see Nancy, who was still laid up in Charlotte Street. It didn't seem right after all that had happened that the long summer should keep drifting on, as carefree as the clouds floating in the blue above.

As we made our way, Walter's small hand clutching mine, I could tell he was thinking of his last trip into town. He kept walking that close, he got tangled in my skirt every few paces, and when a large horse rounded a corner right in front of us, we both of us jumped out of our skin. The size of it, noise it made, it brought it all rushing back, and I had to stop a minute to bide for my own beating heart to leave off racing, never mind poor Walter.

Captain Wright had directed us to come to the front entrance, and taking a leaf from Nancy, who always said anyone was anyone's equal, I took him at his word and walked Walter upstairs from the street with my head held high. Now, it's a strange thing, but somehow we always know when a pair of eyes is looking on us, almost as though we can feel 'em land. Well, as we stood in the fine porch at Charlotte

Street awaiting admittance, I felt just such a sensation and, almost without thinking, turned my head to find mi'sel looking straight at her, that owd cow, Adelaide Wright, standing by the great drapes at her window, gaping at us.

I know that sounds disrespectful, ungrateful even, given Nancy was being so well looked after in her home – not that any of it was Adelaide's doing, I soon found out – but in fact, in that moment, when we stood eye to eye, with all that had passed over the last few days, and in acknowledgement of her service to my friend, I bowed politely. I couldn't pretend much warmth to it, but nevertheless I was proper courteous. Well, and do you know what she did? She raised her nose like she'd smelt something rotten and slipped away from the window without a trace of civility. Ha, and wasn't I right about her all along?

As for Wright, as soon as I saw him, that was another thing I knew I'd been right about. Lord, he looked terrible. He had the stubbled beginnings of a grey beard and his eyes, which were always hooded, seemed even heavier, with matching dark circles beneath.

The maid who'd come to the Kays' house on that first afternoon let us in at the door with a welcome smile, but Wright himself came into the hall to send her away. I'd never been up so close to him afore and hadn't realised how tall he was. He fair loomed over the pair of us standing a little coyly, taking in the grandeur of the place. A great length of hall it had that smelled clean with polish, and a grand, sweeping staircase and, over to my right, a gold-framed mirror in which I spied mi'sel looking right plain and dowdy in midst of it all.

Straightaway, Wright stooped down to kneel in front of Walter, and his tired face lit up, "Hello again!"

Walter, for his part, was not so keen to renew acquaintance and took to hiding behind me. I laughed, nervous like, as Wright stood tall again and said, "Thank you for coming. She's longing to see you. Come along inside."

We followed him through the nearest door into a brightly

lit front room. It was clear to me its usual purpose was as a study 'cos its walls were lined with leather-bound books, and a large desk was pushed against the wall so as to be out of the way. In fact, for such a grand room, with its high ceilings and fine furniture, it had quite a cramped feel. In the window stood a large, wooden structure, which was neither a table nor another desk, and which I soon realised must be the pianoforte Nancy had told me he'd spoken about. There was a sturdy wingback chair and an occasional table with a jug o' water and some tumblers, and a couple of other upright chairs which had been brought in, no doubt for our benefit. They each faced a couch, which ran alongside the wall from the door we'd entered. As we turned around, I saw it was made up as a bed, from which, propped on thick pillows, Nancy greeted us with her arms held as wide as she could manage.

I waited a moment to allow Walter over first, but he hung back, his shoulders rounded, and his head drooped low as he found himself a footstool to sit and rock upon, just the same as at home. Well, it was upsetting, but I thought it best not to press him, and so I went to her mi'sel.

Tucked under them crisp sheets, she looked so tiny, and her skin, which had been so ruddy the last time I'd seen her, was gone greyish and sallow. I reached down, gingerly mind, as I was so afeared of hurting her, and kissed her forehead. As I moved back, still hovering over her, we smiled at one another, and I was that filled with emotion, all I could say was, "Ee, lass!"

Well, I don't know what it was, relief perhaps, but somehow the pair of us found this comical, and at the same moment started to laugh, so that Wright, who all this while was waiting at the door, must've wondered at us like a pair of madwomen. But when I looked over, he was smiling kindly enough, if a sight awkwardly, as he excused himself to go and find us some refreshment.

By then Nancy was straining to get a look at Walter and,

with some effort, addressed him, "Hey, Walt! Is tha not going to come and see me?"

His eyes darted over at this, but he was obviously distressed, and he straightway resumed his swaying action to the sound of a low hum. I can't tell thee how sorry I felt for them both then; each of them longing to embrace the other and yet so thoroughly cast apart.

After a moment, I went back to him and opened my arms, inviting a hug of my own. I thought maybe I'd be able to coax him closer if I was holding him. But he refused me and glanced at her again. I think the poor mite was too guilty to take any comfort from me.

"Never mind. Tha'll come and see me later won't thee, son?"

She beckoned me back, but just as I was taking a chair, she frowned and patted the couch beside her. Something about her expression made me realise she didn't want to be overheard, even by Walter, so I perched where she directed.

"Oh, Mary! How is he? I cannot tell thee. I thought…"

She wasn't looking at me as she spoke, but all the while studying Walter intently, and her eyes, which had always been so lovely, seemed changed, dull somehow, and filled with tears she wouldn't allow herself to cry.

"Aye, I know, lass," I replied. "But he were found. That's what tha needs to think on." I patted the sheet over her legs gently to make my point, "And getting tha'sel better."

"But to have put him in such danger," she went on, as though I hadn't spoken, whispering more to herself than to me.

"Nancy, tha mustn't think like that. None of us could've known what them bastards would do. I still can't believe it."

But she was shaking her head and with a terrible sigh, declared, "Mam were right."

She looked back at me now, questioningly, her mouth open to speak again, and I realised word hadn't yet reached her about Mrs Kay. Well, I dropped my eyes, and she stopped herself from going on. I hadn't known if she'd heard, and I'd been fretting whether it was right to tell her, what with her still being so frail. It seemed Wright must've concluded the same. Course, for all my worrying, I should've realised she'd guess it for herself, as silence filled the room like a ghostly presence. When I looked back at her, she'd turned her head towards the wall, her body rigid under the taut sheet.

Meanwhile, Walter was distracting himself with a poker at the empty fireplace, though it was too long and heavy for him to handle properly, and he'd already displaced a number of old coals onto the fancy rug. Even so, I was glad of his play, and that he wasn't looking over at his mam in such distress.

I'd just knelt down to start clearing the mess, when the master returned, opening the door with a polite cough, and ushering in the maid who was carrying a tray laden with a teapot and a plate full o' warm scones.

"I'm sorry," I said, still at the coals, "I took me eyes off him a moment."

Samson – and I may as well call him that now, since I did afterwards – just shrugged at the smuts on the rug.

"Leave them," he said, turning to Walter and offering him a plate. Well, the poor lad was frozen to the spot, his face clouded with confusion. It was clear he was frightened of the big, fine-spoken man and of going any closer to the sickbed, but at the same time, his eyes were like saucers at the treats on the tray, as the aroma of a fresh bake coiled temptingly through the room.

"I'll choose for you, shall I?" Samson smiled as he filled a plate and parted two scones down the middle, serving 'em dripping with melted butter and a dollop o' dark jam spooned on top. "There you go, young man. Get stuck in!"

Without looking at him, Walter walked over and reached for the plate and took it back to the stool, where he sat down and balanced it on his lap. But before he could take a bite, Nancy cut in, as loud as she was able, "Walt, what does tha say?"

His head jerked up, and he met her eye for the first time.

"Thank you, sir."

Nancy gave a slow smile of satisfaction and sank back on the pillow, too weak to take more than a spot o' tea.

I suppose I ought to be ashamed to admit that even as she lay so poorly afore us, Walter and I spent the next few minutes enjoying this unexpected treat, savouring the flavour of creamy butter and the tang o' berries in that jam. Ee, but it were a feast to us! And the little lad ate every morsel – as did I – and then licked every one of his greasy fingers clean!

As I recall, Samson had moved towards the window and settled on the seat at the piano, though seemingly not to play, as he faced out at us, watching Walter with an indulgent smile.

The room fell quiet then, and I admit I began to feel a sight uncomfortable and unsure what to say next, so I began to bustle about a bit, collecting plates and stacking 'em up, the sort o' thing us women do to cover over any awkwardness.

It was just as I was searching round for yet more discarded crockery that I happened to catch a look pass between 'em, Nancy and Samson I mean. Well, it had such a quality to it – full of unspoken meaning – so that, once again, I revisited my old suspicions about his feelings, and, let's say, I began to wonder upon them even more.

Any road, it seems the raise of his eyebrow and her nod of consent was agreement to invite Walter over to the piano. Samson spun round on the stool, and Nancy tried to raise herself a little higher on the pillow in anticipation.

"Now, Walter, do you know what this is?" he asked over his shoulder in a matter-of-fact sort of tone. Walter, still timid, didn't reply.

Undaunted, Samson half-stood and lifted what was a hinged lid on the instrument, fixing it upright and exposing an expanse of black and white, Then he sat back down, as though as quiet as before, and without warning showered the room with a quick spray o' sparkling notes. Walter was amazed, his little neck instantly craning to see what it was had made all the noise. Well, Samson knew what he was about, or perhaps Nancy had tutored him, but either way he understood to secure the lad's attention by allowing the room to sink back into silence. Then, all of a sudden, he attacked the piano again, this time with a thunderous flourish. It was such a shock that I gave out a cry, swiftly followed by Nancy and Walter laughing at me.

Samson looked over his shoulder now, "How about a go, Walter?" And he shuffled to the edge of the stool, making room for the lad, patting the leather beside him in invitation. Walter, his face still lit up with laughter, finally looked over at his mam, his brow creasing into a question. Her eyes sparkled back at him, just like they used to, as she nodded her head towards Samson, "Go on, my darling."

And so that was that. Walter took up his place beside Samson, his short, little legs swinging from the stool as Nancy and I exchanged a smile at his first note, cautious and quiet, followed by a faltering series of one after the other. Course, it wasn't long before he was crashing down on what Samson called the "keys" and making a right old din, so that I started to wonder what owd Froggatt would be making to it on t'other side of the door.

"Right now, how would you like it if I taught you a tune?" Samson skilfully brought the noise to a close. Walter nodded his head solemnly.

As they picked out the notes together, I took the opportunity to move my chair nearer to Nancy, 'til I was so close I could smell the scent of lavender coming off them clean, white sheets.

"What have I done, Mary?" she started again with her self-reproach.

"Nancy, tha were standing up for what tha knows is right. Tha were taking a stand for *his* future, for goodness sake. Nay, nay, it's not for the likes of thee to go examining tha conscience." It seemed strange to me, this reversal between us, and me the one doing all the fiery talk.

She seemed to recognise this too, raising her eyebrows, "Hark at thee! A true Jacobin tha's turned out."

Well, I laughed this off, eager to keep on talking and to find out what had really gone on and why she'd got herself in such a tangle over Joseph Price. "If only we'd been together Nancy," I started, "'appen we'd've been able to help thee."

She didn't reply, so I went further, all the time whispering so as not to be heard by the others. "I tell thee, I'll swing for that Joseph Price if I ever set me eyes on him again. He's the reason. He's the reason tha were alone and friendless."

But didn't she go and surprise me all over again as her face turned the picture of remorse and her eyes widened, "Oh, nay, nay, nay, Mary!" she said. "Tha mustn't. Tha mustn't say that. Tha mustn't think that."

"But it's true! Didn't tha leave off coming wi' us to wait for him? I can't tell thee how it pained me to walk away, leaving thee all alone." But she was shaking her head in protest, as though to defend him, and I found mi'sel getting right agitated. Aye, and not just wi' Joe neither. Ee, it's a dreadful thing to doubt a friend, and worst thing in the world to think ill of someone tha loves, but just at that moment, I couldn't stop mi'sel from wondering what on earth she'd been thinking.

"Well, and is tha going to tell me he showed up then? 'Cos a fine job he made of looking after thee if he did." On and on I went, so much it makes me ashamed to think of it now, what a lather I worked mi'sel to, and her so poorly as she was. "Well?" I asked as she'd given me no answer.

"It's true," she sighed, "tha's right. Course he didn't show."

"I knew it."

"But tha mustn't blame *him*. It's all me own fault. I should never've been meeting him in fust place."

"Oh, come off it, Nancy. Tha's never letting him wriggle off th' hook like that?"

"I mean it, I've only mi'sel to blame."

"He breaks tha trust and tha's the one to blame?"

She sighed again and bit her lip. "If I'd been in proper earnest, Mary, I'd agree wi' thee." She stole a look at me then, all guilty-like, apology in her eyes, though Lord knows she had no need to say sorry to me.

"What? Tha means…" My face must've shown my confusion.

"Joe's handsome, anyone can see that, and for all he didn't show on Monday, I still don't believe he's a bad lad. But surely tha knows, Mary, he were never really the sort o' fella for me."

Well, I was amazed. And even more so as I watched her gaze fall fondly upon Samson. *Ah*, I thought as I began to understand. I realised then I'd never get to the bottom of it all, but I suppose, amidst my astonishment, I was just glad to know she'd not had her heart broken as well as all else.

The music had stopped a moment, and in the quiet I could hear her breathing was getting shallow. It was clear I'd tired her out.

"Can I get owt for thee, Nancy, luv?"

She turned her head slowly to me and reached for my hand with a sad smile. "Oh, Mary, tha's already done so much."

We watched Walter again, his head bent intently over the piano. He had picked up the phrase by then, a sweet run of notes and was playing it repeatedly; a sound so lovely and pure and simple, I can recall it even now. Nancy and me, we were still holding hands, listening to the tune, and I don't know why I said what I said next, but 'til the day I die, I'll never be sorry I did. "I love him."

She took in a short breath and then exhaled deeply. "I know tha does," she began, but her voice was weaker now, and I had to bend my head to the pillow to hear her. "I know tha does, Mary. And I thank thee wi' all me heart."

Eventually, when they were finished, Samson asked Walter if he'd like to visit again to play the piano, and Walter agreed eagerly, turning back into the room with a little skip. In his excitement, he forgot his fear and for the first time approached the makeshift bed, from which Nancy was able to reach out and hug him.

After that, we visited Charlotte Street every afternoon. And being used to the way she was now, Walter was happy to go to her, though Lord knows, she was paler each time. Ee, how she beamed with joy to hold him, and so I'd say, "I think maybe I'll take a walk and leave thee to it for a bit," and they'd smile agreement. "Shall we say an hour?"

On the last occasion, as I closed the door behind me, they sounded so happy together, the three of 'em, I often like to think on it. Samson was at the piano, picking out a light tune, and, from her bed, Nancy was saying, "Hey, Walt, look at this fruit! Shall we try some of these berries?"

FOUR

On the morning after the massacre, dim light trickled into the study through the gap in the curtains he hadn't thought to fix. He was still half-asleep. In a troubled dream which had not yet dissolved in the watery light, he was trapped under a dark weight, though his body was too stiff and sore to try and work his way out. Then, a small sound, muffled yet close by, reached him and at once chased the dream away. His eyes blinked open, and his blurry vision cleared, adjusting to the light, to discover Nancy watching him.

Her face was still as pale as the moon, floating in the honeyed sky of her hair, but her eyes seemed brighter and her lips had some colour again. She spoke in a voice almost restored to strength, "Ah, I'm sorry, I woke thee."

Hope flared within him then, so strongly he couldn't contain an eager smile, before a sudden awkwardness overwhelmed him. "You're… I'm, I…" A self-conscious heat spread from his throat up to the roots of his hair. He flung off the jacket which had served as his blanket and sat forward.

"Do you need something? Let me get you a drink." He stood up quickly, ignoring the pain shooting through his body, and made to pour her some water with a desperate attentiveness when, just as abruptly, he stopped, amazed. She had laughed. He turned, to discover her amused eyes were pointedly directed at his legs. Looking down, he realised he was still wearing his boots.

"Tha could've taken them off tha knows," she grinned. "It's not as though I've not seen thee wi'out 'em afore!"

He felt his face redden as his thoughts raced to the memory, but his heart lightened; she wasn't embarrassed by their situation.

Indeed, she tapped a space beside her on the couch. He put down the pitcher and sat a little further off than she'd suggested. He joined his hands together, placed them in his lap and took to examining them. Beyond the closed door, the house was still and quiet, and outside the only sound was birdsong. Just as he'd drifted to sleep listening to the sound of her breathing, now he was conscious of his own, light and rapid.

"How can I ever thank thee?"

Samson shook his head in earnest at this and met her eye, her expression flitting between smiling gratitude and sorrow. He couldn't think what to say.

"And after I behaved so awful too." Her voice was filled with remorse, "I was... I... I don't know..."

"Put it from your mind. It's not important now."

"Aye, tha's right," she replied decisively. "It's not."

Then, after another moment, her brow creased. "I've been lying here trying to fathom it. I mean, I know the cavalry charged, of course. But why? Why would they do that?"

Samson sighed heavily.

"I mean, were there folk causing trouble? Were there summat going on nearer t' front? Summat I don't know about."

"No," Samson said firmly. "Not that I saw, and I had the same view as the magistrates who set the devils on."

"Well then, why? It were a peaceable meeting." She was getting agitated, "It were always going to be peaceable."

"I know. I know. You don't have to persuade me, Nancy."

"Then tha understands what we were about?"

"Of course."

"That we were only asking for what's fair."

"And why should you not make such demands?"

"Then, tha's for reform?" she asked, a bright note of wonder entering her voice.

"Nancy, have you forgotten? I knew nothing of Manchester and its deprivations before this year. I had no notion of what life was like for the workers here. But over these past months, you have shown me." He smiled gently at her, but she looked down with a meekness he had never seen in her before. "It's true. *You* have educated *me*. Now I see how things are. How hard life is." Looking at her bowed head, he added quietly, "How hard things are for *you*."

Suddenly there was a short choking sound, and he moved forward anxiously. His words had touched something within her, and her emotions, already disturbed and volatile, at once gushed forth in an anguish he could hardly bear to watch. Her head twisted from side to side and tears rolled unchecked towards the pillow.

"Things *will* change, Nancy." His voice was deep with conviction, but she dismissed his words with an impatient sigh and shook her head more fiercely. "They will, I swear," he continued, "because they must. I didn't fight for such an England as this."

"But how? Look where all this lot has got us!" she cried hopelessly, lifting her uninjured arm and letting it drop again at her side with a heavy thud. "Doesn't tha know, there'll be all hell to pay? Nadin and his constables'll be out even now, as we speak. Rounding 'em all up!"

"Yes, perhaps you're right. There will be reaction, certainly." His jaw set for a moment as he thought of Adelaide and Baldwin and those thugs in the Portland Street tavern. Of the magistrates and their excuses and Lord Sidmouth sending his orders from London. "But, you know, there were so many witnesses. Word will get out. They'll not be able to stop it. And when it does, when people learn what happened here yesterday, then there will be outrage and things will change."

Her tiny frame was heaving all the while with the effort

of crying, as she gulped in air with jagged, panting breaths until, eventually exhausted, she surrendered to his argument, "I hope tha's right."

"Come, have a drink," he said, standing up and retrieving the pitcher. "You must try to rest. That's what the doctor says."

After she'd sipped some water and leaned back on the pillow, she looked up at him weakly. "I'm sorry."

"No. Don't say that."

"It's Walter. It's all been for Walter. I just want him to have a better life."

"I know," he said and once more sat beside her.

"Tell me again. He's wi' Mary, they said?" He nodded, and she seemed satisfied. "That's good."

"Perhaps she could bring him here to see you?"

Her eyes, still wet with the last of her tears, looked up at him for a second before her face crumpled again, "Ah, but he'll be frightened," and she gestured at herself, the tight binding at her shoulder and the shape of her limp body beneath the sheet. "He'll be too frightened of all this."

"Not if I distract him."

She looked at him quizzically. "But how would tha do that?"

He raised his eyebrows to pique her interest further, and for a long moment relished the pleasure of her curiosity, congratulating himself on the change in her mood.

"Go on, *how?*"

He chuckled, and she shook her head, amused, yet still confounded, as he stood up and walked towards the window.

"Ohhh!" she exclaimed. "The pianoforte!"

When he was ready at the stool, he raised his hands theatrically and, grinning over his shoulder, waited another long moment until at last she laughed from the couch, "Get on wi' it!"

He looked out at the sky then, which was brightening as the sun climbed higher, and he felt his heart might explode with happiness. He knew it must be a joyful tune, and he picked it out with light, careful notes which danced through the air between them. Over the sound of the melody, he could hear her gasps of appreciation, and he played on and on, lost in the pleasure of the moment, until, with a shock, they both heard another voice above him: Adelaide, shrill and imperious, calling for the maid. He stopped playing and turned around, his eyes raised to the ceiling, and, without thinking, he grimaced. Nancy's momentary look of alarm dissolved at his expression, and they both laughed again like naughty children.

Later that day, after the doctor had been to check on her and she had spent some more time sleeping, they had again fallen into comfortable conversation. He, attentive on a chair brought up right next to the bed, and she propped higher on some thicker pillows he'd asked Ellen to bring in.

"Tha knows, I've always wanted to ask thee summat," she began, a mischievous grin curving her lips.

"Go ahead," he said, half-laughing, with a pretence at nervousness.

"Why did tha not listen to me that day?"

"When?" he asked, although he knew what she would say.

"That time in t' mill. Fust time we lay eyes on one another."

"Ah, I thought so."

"Well, *why?*" she continued. "Why would tha not let me help poor Johnny?"

"Well," he began and then shrugged. "I suppose I was... afraid."

"Afraid, tha says."

"Yes."

"Afraid!" she laughed now. "What of?"

He smiled at her but looked away. He could tell she was enjoying this and waited for more.

"Afraid of change? Of tha new life, of taking over at t' mill?"

"Perhaps."

"I see."

"Well, not entirely." He turned, open and guileless, towards her, and saw her dear features, so animated as usual, even as she lay against the pillows. "Actually, in fact, no. I'm not afraid of change. Not anymore."

"Well. What then?"

He breathed in, "I was frightened of you."

At this, she threw her head back and laughed. "I knew it!"

"By God, Nancy, you were like a demon!"

Suddenly she stopped laughing, and for a second he was gripped with alarm he had offended her, but before he could say any more, she was straining out of the covers, leaning over to reach for his hand with her own. In an instant, he grabbed it and brought it to his lips.

* * *

All that week, Samson consulted Mr Slater twice a day and carefully followed his instructions. Nancy remained in bed, taking plenty of rest. Having staunched and bound the wound to her shoulder on the first night, the doctor had re-examined it two days later and declared it to be healing satisfactorily, though he remained concerned at the lack of a return of colour to her face. Each time he left, he continued to warn of overexertion.

"She must stay where she is. But then Adelaide's so good, I'm sure she wouldn't dream of hurrying her away."

One morning, towards the end of the week, after he'd packed up his bag, Samson noticed him exchange a look with Nancy as he squeezed her hand kindly. Following him out through the hall, Samson observed, determinedly cheerful, "She's doing well, don't you think?"

The doctor stopped at the front door and turned around, poking his spectacles further up his nose to peer at him. Suddenly, Samson was conscious of the ticking of the clock as the doctor weighed his words. Eventually, in a subdued tone, the old man replied, "Outwardly, yes. But you must understand, she's been seriously hurt. There's always a danger of infection. And, of course, it's still impossible to know the extent of her internal injury."

At these words, a bolt of fear shut so tight round Samson's heart, he winced. The aged doctor, discerning his distress, held out his liver-spotted hand and gently tapped Samson's elbow, "Keep heart, though, man! There's every reason to hope."

Samson breathed in deeply; there was to be no question of losing hope. As every day passed, he rejoiced at any sign of recovery. Look how she was able to sit up for a full half-hour, and how much more food she was taking: this morning, a bowl of porridge with a swirl of amber honey and, just earlier, more pickings from the basket of fruit he'd brought from the market the other day. She was still nibbling at the thin slices of apple and pear he'd cut for her himself with his penknife and sucking at the shiny cherries whose pits she collected carefully in her fingers.

It was Sunday evening and they had spent another afternoon with Walter. Nancy now lay quietly. Outside, the first rain for almost a fortnight fell in a grey sheet, and the room descended into gloomy shadow. A damp, rotten tang of the vegetable market rose on the air, and Samson realised the plate piled high with apple cores and seeds needed to be taken away. First though, he lit the lamps and, feeling a chill creep through the window, set about kindling the fire. When he finally stood up and looked round at her, he saw she had become ashen white. She looked back at him pensively.

A terrible dread awakened within him. He set himself at her side, kneeling by the couch, his eyes searching her face for colour, trying to erase the change that had come over her.

She reached out her hands. Their touch was cold as she ran her fingers into the grey hair at his temples, holding his head as he let out a moan of anguish.

"I'm frightened," she whispered.

"No," he said. "Shush."

"Not for me. Not for me. I'm frightened *for him*."

Samson nodded, understanding, but unable to speak.

"How can I leave him?"

"No, no, no." He moved closer and seized one of her hands, once again bringing it to his lips.

"Or thee," she said gently. "How can I leave thee, my dearest." She sighed, trying to master herself, swallowing down her tears. "Tha'll be a friend to him, will tha not?"

"I'll love him like a son."

"But he must stay wi' Mary."

"Of course."

She nodded, satisfied, and settled back against the pillow as he rested his head in her lap.

They lay like that until the last of the daylight had drained from the sky, and the large globe of an almost full moon appeared, suspended in the middle of their rectangle of window. The rain had stopped, and in the clear night, shot through with red from the late sun, it glowed an unearthly orange. She stirred a little beneath him, and he lifted his head, following her gaze to look out at it.

"Is that a harvest moon?" he asked, picturing her as a girl coming home from the field.

"Aye," she said. Then, "Nay. It's very like, but it's too soon, int it?"

* * *

In the morning, Samson, who'd watched all night, bent to kiss her forehead. He went to part the curtains. Outside, the street was shrouded by early mist, whilst above, where a white autumnal sky was clearing, a group of swallows had gathered, swooping in formation and then flying out of view. He sat down heavily at the piano, and shutting his eyes, as a succumbing to pain, he played the sonata which he'd always known she'd love. He wondered if she could still hear it in the place to which her soul had soared.

EPILOGUE

My darling Walter,
I hardly know how to begin to tell you how much I love you
and how sorry I am to leave you. Please forgive me.

I am sorry this letter is not in my hand. I never did master
a quill so well and now that my strength is failing, our friend
Samson is writing my words for me. I have asked him to read
this to you when he thinks you are ready. One day soon, my
darling, I hope you will read it for yourself.

I know that you have many fears, especially after what has
happened to us, and I wish with all my heart I could stay and
help you to see how much that is still good and wonderful in
the world. Remember, things are not always what they seem,
and you will find joy when you least expect it. So always be
ready for new experiences, Walter, and try not to be afraid,
especially of change, for without change, you cannot grow
into the fine man I know you can be.

Imagine, you're going to learn the piano! Samson will
teach you. He has been a great friend to me and he will be to
you as well. He believes you have a talent, so tend it like a
candle and you will shine. Be sure that somewhere, where I
am waiting for you, I will be listening proudly.

Make sure you work hard and learn your letters too. I
hope you will remember how much I loved learning to read.
You cannot know how dear these last months have been to me

when I was able to read to you. I hope that you will love your studies too, and that one day you will see, as I have seen, the power of the written word. Imagine, Walter, even after I am gone, I can still speak to you like this!

So, my darling boy, master the pen, as I did not and use its power for good. For truth and for justice, and never let anyone forget what you and I and all those others sacrificed for liberty on St Peter's Field.

Above all, whatever happens next, wherever you go, whatever you do, my son, always remember you are loved, by me and by your grandma too, and let this knowledge help you to be brave.

God bless and protect thee always, the most precious blessing of my life.

Your loving mother

ACKNOWLEDGEMENTS

It has been an honour to write and to publish this memorial to the brave reformers of 1819. As a proud descendant of Lancashire cotton-workers, it means a great deal to me to keep the memory of their sacrifice for social justice alive, especially in our own divided and turbulent times. I'm also grateful for this opportunity to thank the people and institutions who have helped me along the way.

First, a nod to the superb libraries and museums of my great home city of Manchester, including the Peoples' History Museum, Central Library and the Portico Library, as well as the National Trust's Quarry Bank Mill at Styal, whose working spinning mules inspired the opening scene of the story.

I would especially like to thank one of the leading figures of the Peterloo Memorial Campaign, Martin Gittins, for kindly reading an early draft of the novel and offering such helpful feedback. Also to Karen Shannon and her team at Manchester Histories, for their excellent planning of the Peterloo bicentenary commemorations. Through their vibrant networking sessions, I was able to connect with Martin and others, and receive support and encouragement for the project, as well as the exciting opportunity to be involved in the commemorations themselves. In this regard, big heartfelt thanks also go to my superbly talented musical collaborators, Claire O'Brien, Shane Cullinan and Brigitte Schwarting.

Thanks, of course, to all of my lovely friends and colleagues for their interest and enthusiasm, and especially to my early readers for helping me to believe in the story and in myself as a writer: my dearest friend for a lifetime, Marianne Sheppard, my fabulous mentor, Rhoda Anderton, my literary touchstone, Briony Martin, and, not least, my NaNoWriMo best "buddy", Clare Barton, without whom the story might never have been written at all. Clare, thank you so much, I will never forget November 2016!

A number of other people have helped shape the novel through its many drafts, in particular the author Alison May. I'm so grateful for her inspiring workshops, positive critique and unwavering cheerfulness throughout the submission process. A huge thank you as well to Robert Peett, whose editorial advice was as generous as it was astute, and whose ongoing encouragement has been so kind. And Emma Darwin, whose enthusiasm for the extract she read at Jericho Writers' Festival of Writing gave me fresh impetus to find a publisher in time for the bicentenary.

I am so happy the book eventually found its home with the dynamic team at Legend Press. Special thanks go to my excellent editor, Lauren Parsons, for her belief in the story and all her hard work in getting it ready to go out into the world, in short time to coincide with the bicentenary.

At its heart, the story offers a portrait of familial love, and I'm every day thankful for my own fantastic family whom I love so much.

To my amazing sister, Stephanie, thanks for being both the best sister and creative advisor anyone could wish for.

To Pat and Tom, my truly wonderful Mum and Dad, thank you for your immeasurable support in all things, always, and especially for loving me – and the story – so much, you read and discussed draft after draft!

To my brilliant husband, William, Renaissance man and greatest champion, thank you for recognising the importance of following a dream, and for all you've done to help me realise this one.

And to our darling girls, Annie and Carmel; this book is for you – the most precious blessings of my life.

If you enjoyed what you read, don't keep it a secret.

Review the book online and tell anyone who will listen.

Thanks for your support spreading the word about Legend Press!

Follow us on Twitter
@legend_press

Follow us on Instagram
@legendpress